MISTAKE

IN

TIME

Anna Faversham

©

Copyright Anna Faversham

First published 2022

All Rights Reserved. This book is copyright material and must not be copied, reproduced, transferred, distributed, leased, licensed or publicly performed or used in any way except as specifically permitted in writing by the author as allowed under the terms and conditions under which it was purchased or as strictly permitted by applicable copyright law. Unauthorized distribution or use of this text may be a direct infringement of the author's rights and those responsible may be liable in law accordingly.

This book is a work of fiction and, except in the case of historical fact or clearly in the public domain or written permission granted, any resemblance to persons, living or dead, is coincidental.

TO

MY FATHER

Table of Contents

Chapter One
   A white sports car
Chapter Two
   The old, musty case
Chapter Three
   They will have no tomorrows
Chapter Four
   Injection of joy
Chapter Five
   No future with him
Chapter Six
   Audacity was her ally
Chapter Seven
   An adventure together
Chapter Eight
   Liberty smelt a rat
Chapter Nine
   Surprise
Chapter Ten
   Semi-house-trained big puppy
Chapter Eleven
   Pink nylon sheets

Chapter Twelve
    The chattering surrendered
Chapter Thirteen
    The line went dead
Chapter Fourteen
    Toddling like a penguin
Chapter Fifteen
    The fate of six people
Chapter Sixteen
    Hungry for more
Chapter Seventeen
    Food for thought
Chapter Eighteen
    Sneaky things, thoughts
Chapter Nineteen
    Preferably forever
Chapter Twenty
    Groovy, baby, real groovy
Chapter Twenty-One
    We adopted them
Chapter Twenty-Two
    Pilgrim's Progress
Chapter Twenty-Three
    You are not a ghost

Chapter Twenty-Four
   Damned by a rampaging virus
Chapter Twenty-Five
   Wet feet
Chapter Twenty-Six
   Auction of Promises
Chapter Twenty-Seven
   The exquisitely English art
Chapter Twenty-Eight
   Trouble makers or potty
Chapter Twenty-Nine
   Locked away from inquisitive eyes
Chapter Thirty
   Marks out of ten
Chapter Thirty-One
   Bleakheath Bozos
Chapter Thirty-Two
   Clay-brained fleshmonger
Chapter Thirty-Three
   Spurting like Vesuvius
Chapter Thirty-Four
   Don't scream
Chapter Thirty-Five
   Against all the odds

Chapter Thirty-Six
   Rampallian rat
Chapter Thirty-Seven
   If only
Chapter Thirty-Eight
   I will
Chapter Thirty-Nine
   A magical soundtrack
Chapter Forty
   Full of traps and pitfalls
Chapter Forty-One
   Ooh, sneaky
Chapter Forty-Two
   The route to deep joy

Seventeen Questions for Book Clubs

Chapter One
A white sports car

Liberty had never been in the presence of approaching death before and an overwhelming, almost tangible trepidation filled her body. She wanted to say something, but what? She picked up a photograph from his bedside table. Her five-year old self smiled back at her, hand in hand with her father on a sunny beach. Maybe she could remind him of happier times. "Do you remember this, Dad?" Her fear weakened, overpowered. Her efforts were interrupted when he raised his shaking hand. It held an ornate key; the sort which would open a box not a door.

"Take this Libby." He struggled to speak. "Take it. With this you'll never be forced to..." he gasped, "get married." The merest smile played on his pale lips. "Freedom. You'll have freedom. Make the world a better place."

Liberty took the key. "Dad, what does it open?" She stroked his empty hand and held it as his spirit slipped away.

~

The key clearly meant a lot to her father but what was it supposed to open? Afraid that she would lose it, she hung it around her neck on a silver chain. There must be a box with a keyhole somewhere. None came to mind. No doubt she'd find it when sorting through his possessions. First though she must attend to contacting friends and relations and advising them of the funeral details. All this had to be packed into the evenings after work; she must now finish that essential report, then she could take time off without worrying.

"Coffee? Tea?"

Liberty glanced up from the neat piles of papers on her desk. Whenever she saw him, she felt a tightening of her muscles making it difficult to appear nonchalant or even think straight. "Thank you, Nick. You don't have to..."

"I'd like to." He raised an eyebrow. "Shall I choose for you?"

"Oh, sorry. Tea please, a strong cup of tea."

She felt her colour rising. A doctor did not usually ask a junior manager if he could bring her a drink. Furthermore, he was engaged to be married to a radiographer. Should she curb this tendency to be suspicious of men? Or not?

Dr Nylander returned with two mugs of tea and placed them both on her desk. Had he brought her two?

He read her mind. "One is for me. I only heard your sad news yesterday. I'm sorry I haven't said anything before." He sat down on the upright chair opposite her desk.

A reluctant smile helped her regain her fragile courage. "My brother was supposed to be coming from Australia to attend the funeral and help with other necessary arrangements, however, he's having, or rather his wife is having their baby three weeks earlier than expected, there are difficulties, and he can't come." She bit her lip. Here she was, talking with the most magnetic man she was ever likely to meet, and she was moaning. She never moaned. Why did she moan now?

"How is your mother?"

"My mother died over two years ago. I loved them both so much and suddenly I have no-one. They are gone, forever dust." Please God, don't let me cry.

Dr Nylander politely buried his nose in his mug.

"I've booked time off to see me through the next couple of weeks."

"Sensible thing to do." He spoke like an Englishman: he looked like a cool Italian. "If you need any help with..." his right hand waved around a little, "anything, anything at all, you know where I am." He smiled, his eyes sparkling as he handed her a card. "My mobile number's on there; you can ring anytime if I can help." He looked into her eyes, "Or if you just want someone to chat to."

His eyes were offering her much more than she could bear. She stared at the card. "Thank you." All other words deserted her.

He picked up his empty mug and went towards the door. "Don't forget, I'm all yours whenever you need me, even if I'm playing cricket."

It was unreal. Doctors were not known for casually fraternizing with the administrative staff, and as he was engaged, he probably should not be flirting with her. Flirting? Was he a flirt?

Poor Jaelyn, how could he? She picked up her mug and drank the last dregs of tea. She must concentrate on dealing with the most urgent and important items in the In Tray and the dozens of emails awaiting her attention. Furthermore, there was that blasted report to finish.

The door burst open and Jaelyn, frowning, said, "Was Nick in here?"

"Yes, just for a moment." A very precious moment.

"Where's he gone?"

"I've no idea." Liberty felt the urge to continue mimicking Jaelyn's sharp style but ignored her instead.

Jaelyn wouldn't be ignored and marched up to Liberty's desk. "What did he say?"

"Not a lot, something about cricket and he'd heard about my father dying, that's all."

Jaelyn appeared surprised. "Sorry to hear that. Won't you be taking time off?" This was said as if she were trying to rid herself of an overstaying in-law.

Liberty would like to get rid of Jaelyn. Perhaps she could take a long walk off a short pier. Her mouth attempted a smile, her eyes couldn't manage it as she said, "After tomorrow. A couple of weeks."

"Oh good." She slammed the door on her way out.

Jaelyn was a radiographer. "Nurses, doctors, radiographers, they all respond to a calling," Liberty's father once suggested expectantly, but his daughter became an administrator. She supposed Jaelyn was within her rights to keep tabs on her first-class male but there were gentler ways of doing it.

~

Four months later, Liberty had walked away from her frustrating situation at the hospital, sold the family home, sent her brother in Australia half the proceeds and bought a thriving business. All she needed to do was find a suitable little house or flat and that's what turned out to be difficult. Fortunately, the office she leased in Middleston also included an unused little attic room which she'd kitted out as a make-shift bedroom. "Needs must," she'd said, echoing one of her mother's favourite phrases. There was also a kitchen with a kettle, a microwave, a sink and a separate loo but no bathroom. She'd just have to manage until a suitable place became available. It was still January and the housing market usually picked up in the spring so she'd hang on until then.

Her work could hardly be called work. She loved arranging the events for single people. The tag line for the company was 'Events for single people with traditional values in life'. She'd been fortunate too because the man she'd bought it from sold it for less than its real value, or so he said, as he was in a hurry to move to Wales with his new wife.

Sitting at her desk, she smiled. She'd not bought the agency to meet a man, especially not the man who was currently ringing the intercom several times. She let him in.

Gregor Hode strolled into the office with a toothy smile and a hearty "Hi Liberty, how you doing?"

"Good morning, Gregor, did you get on well?"

He ran his fingers through his hair. "Nah. I knew I wouldn't. Not my type. She didn't like trains."

Liberty's eyebrows rose. "Trains?"

"Yes, trains. Fancy coming on the Orient Express with me?"

Mistake in Time

Taken by surprise, Liberty smiled broadly though hastily turned the conversation around. "You chose her, Gregor." He was cute – until he spoke. He delivered his acerbic opinions forcefully in a high pitched, nasal tone. What a shame he didn't have the gift of an appealing voice. She'd try to keep the interview short. "Let's sit down here." She pointed to the table near the window and sat in one of the chairs. He sat opposite, staring at her. She must find something to say. All she managed was "I have many more ladies in my files, let me–"

He interrupted and flashed her a smile. "I know what I like."

He really could be cute and was very much a strong-minded man despite not being as tall as most. He was also the owner of a successful night club. There'd be many a woman prepared to take him on. His eyes bored into hers; total concentration on the other person, a little bit overdone perhaps.

He assumed command. "Tall, with long dark hair, slim, with a graceful way of moving. Someone courteous, with a beguiling voice." He continued to stare as a smile crept across his face. "Someone exactly like you."

This raised more red flags with her than there'd ever been in Moscow's Red Square. She tried to look amused as she turned the pages of the file on the table. Triumphantly, she announced, "I have the perfect lady for you."

"Would you come out with me? For dinner tonight perhaps and you can bring your file, if you must."

"I'm sorry, Gregor, that's against my rules." Imagine having to cope with him for a whole evening.

"Well they are *your* rules so you can change them."

"It really wouldn't be fair to the ladies who would love to meet someone like you. Look at this profile. She's lovely. Dark, curly hair, absolutely charming and interesting too." She turned the file around so he was able to see.

He ignored the file. "We can go anywhere you'd like, local or into London, whatever suits you. I'd drive."

Oh yes, he had a white sports car. "I'm not looking to meet anyone, Gregor. I'm sorry but you'll need to give up the idea and focus on someone who'd love to meet a successful man like you." She said it firmly, softening it with a smile. "Have a look through the file and let me know who you'd like to meet." She stood and went behind her desk pretending to have plenty to do whereas, in reality, she'd not be able to concentrate until he left her office. She was relieved to watch him browsing the file carefully; surely he'd find someone in there. His brown wool jacket, toning trousers and sturdy brown shoes marked him out as a country boy at heart, and his gingery, floppy hair gave his eyes a place to hide when they needed it. It all seemed at odds with owning a night club. "There's a young lady in there, towards the back of the file, who loves the countryside and also enjoys dancing. Would you like to meet her?"

He flicked the pages over, glanced at a picture and said, "Sarah?"

"Yes, that's the one. Twenty-six; lives out towards Canterbury. Would you like me to arrange a meeting?"

"No. I'll come back tomorrow. It's you I'd like to go out with. You know that don't you?"

She'd be formal and hope it would put him off. "That's impossible, Mr Hode. If you come to some of our events, which is a particularly effective way of meeting new people, perhaps you'd meet someone there?"

Gregor gave her an appreciative smile. "You're very thoughtful."

She softened; she'd try to find him someone who would appreciate his direct manner who'd maybe even moderate it. "I'm sure I can find you someone special." He wasn't the first client to make inappropriate advances. They'd come through the door, see a smiling face and think 'she'll do nicely'. She'd just have to be firm with this one too.

"I'm looking at that someone special now. It would be to your advantage to agree. You'd enjoy yourself." He lowered his head slightly yet his eyes never left hers.

A quotation she sometimes used jumped to mind. "Love does not dominate, it cultivates." His voice grated on her and she was able to say very firmly, "I'm sorry. The answer will always be no."

He shot her a look that would have burnt through granite. "Are you gay then?"

"It's nothing to do with you if I am or if I am not." She stood and walked towards the door and held it wide. "I am not sure this agency can help you find who you are looking for. I will refund your money in full. Good morning, Mr Hode."

He was no longer cute-looking.

Chapter Two
The old, musty case

Insofar as he did not come to the office, Gregor accepted his expulsion. However, very few days went by without Liberty noticing him passing her in the street, or glancing up at her office window. She checked his address. He had a reasonable excuse: he lived quite close. Then one morning she saw him walking down Archangel Hill with his arm casually placed around the shoulders of a pretty girl. It was time to stop worrying: he'd found himself another potential partner. Phew!

She twisted the silver chain around her neck and rubbed the brass key. She must visit the storage facility where her father's furniture and belongings were stored and look for something with the right-sized keyhole; she'd put it off for far too long. It was probably best to go today as there were no appointments in her diary. Procrastinating, she made a cup of tea, turned over her desk calendar and considered the day's famous quotation.

"I long to accomplish a great and noble task, but it is my chief duty to accomplish small tasks as if they were great and noble."

Who was this Helen Keller who'd described her life? She looked her up on the Internet. A full half an hour went by as she read about the deaf and blind lady who'd accomplished so much despite her disabilities. Guilt finally shifted her from her seat but only took her as far as the window. "Hmm. It's raining. Perhaps I should leave it until tomorrow." She checked her diary. "Rats!" A full day lay ahead.

With a loud sigh, she put on her coat, checked she had the necessary documents, grabbed her umbrella and ran to the car park.

At the vast storage facility, an attendant showed her to the container labelled with her number. It was chock-full. She'd forgotten just how much she'd stashed away here. Deciding what to do with it all was yet another job.

Almost an hour later, frozen and about to give up, she noticed a battered, rectangular, possibly oak box, perhaps eight inches high and at least two feet long. It lay inside a huge, musty-smelling suitcase containing her mother's small collection of old coins and a dozen or so postcards. Could this chest be what the key opened? She leant forward to pick it up but it proved to be curiously heavy. She moved some of the things cluttering her access and tried again.

"Let me know if you need any help," called out an employee. "I can give you a hand to shift anything big, if you like."

"That's very kind, thank you. I think I can manage."

The key fitted. She turned it, lifted the lid, and shut it again promptly. After putting it back in the suitcase and closing the catches, she called the man back.

"I'm so sorry, but I think I do need help."

"No problem. What do you want shifted?"

"That old suitcase near the back." She pointed it out. "It has a lot of old postcards and other heavy stuff in it. I'm going to take it home and sort it out."

Liberty watched the well-built man lift the case.

"Blimey lady, you're dead right. You sure it ain't a dead body?"

She thought it best to enter into the spirit of his joke and laughed. "Post cards and my mother's coin collection." It was true but not the whole truth – no wonder witnesses in court had to declare they'd tell the *whole* truth. "I'm so sorry..." Why did the English always apologize for things not their fault?

"No problem." He plonked the suitcase outside the container, set the alarm and closed the door. "It'll save me lifting the weights in the gym tonight."

An hour later, in the car park near her office, she realized she was unable to escape the problem of hauling the suitcase up to her office. If only it had wheels. She'd take the items out bit by bit. First, she surreptitiously put the box into her sturdy canvas shopping bag which she always kept in the boot. Naturally, most of it stuck out. Then, after slamming the boot and locking the car, she did her best to walk nonchalantly to her office, clutching the bag to her chest. Though longing to check the contents properly, she forced herself to return to the car and bring all the contents of the suitcase back. The old, musty case could be left in the car. Shopping bags didn't attract so much attention.

She made tea, microwaved some soup and took it on a tray to her desk. One more task before she would allow herself to examine the contents of the box. Her glimpse of the contents when she was at the storage facility had alarmed her. While pulling the window blinds down, the sparkle on the pavements caught her eye; it was only rain yet somehow she felt it was an omen. Was it a good omen? Or a bad one? And what was the omen? Sparkles or rain? She chastised herself – how very silly. She must stop this nonsense. Her mother used to believe in such premonitions, giving them the respectable name of insight. Taking the key from around her neck, she sat at her desk. Ignoring the tea and the delicious aroma of the soup, she turned the key in the lock and lifted the lid. Several sheets of blue notepaper lay on top of a cotton cloth covering the contents. She'd read the letter first; it would help her confront the contents. It appeared she had never really known who her father truly was and perhaps the message would relieve her anxiety.

The telephone rang and scuppered her intentions.

Chapter Three
They will have no tomorrows

Liberty excused herself immediately from the untimely telephone caller and returned to her all-important letter.
"Dear Libby,
"If you are reading this, I will be in Heaven if God is forgiving, or Hell if He is not, or maybe simply rotting in my grave."

Liberty's eyes widened and her heart raced. How could he start a letter like that? She read her father's scrawl again. What had he done? "You will by now have seen the contents of the wooden chest."

She had not. She pulled the cotton cloth away – her eyes widened. "The jewellery was your mother's. You might recognize one or two pieces which I bought her but you will not have seen the rest. In her later years I'm afraid your mother became light-fingered. She could not help it. When I found what she was doing, I tried to return two of the items to their rightful owners. However, it was fraught with difficulties. They were private individuals and had already claimed for the items from their insurance companies and preferred to have the money. Some had price tags and were clearly taken from shops. At the time, I had no idea of the extent of her hoard; she'd hidden most of it. I didn't want to report her to the police or anyone else as she clearly wasn't well. If I'd known which companies had paid out, I would have returned the jewellery to them. I became more and more concerned, confused even; she had been such a good woman, and I didn't want to sully her name. Then, after your mother died, I found another hoard and shortly after, as you know, I suffered a stroke and so I just swept everything into this chest and tried to forget about it. Under no circumstances must you attempt to sell or wear anything except her engagement and wedding rings and the long pearl necklace. They are natural pearls, not freshwater pearls, inherited, and will be worth a considerable amount. There's a brooch, I bought her with matching necklace, you'll recognize them. I don't know what you can do with the other jewellery. My apologies for leaving you with such a dilemma. Be sure not to tell your brother."

Liberty sat back in her office chair, swivelling from side to side, giving herself time to think. She picked out the long string of exquisite pearls and hung them round her neck. She put the diamond cluster engagement ring on her right hand ring finger; it fitted very well. He had kept many secrets and must have loved her mother immensely. One by one, she laid the other pieces out on the desk. It appeared her mother liked sapphires and diamonds for, apart from the string of pearls, there were no other gems amongst the seventy-two items comprising rings, necklaces, bracelets, brooches and earrings, some clearly in sets. She read on.

"Underneath the jewellery you will see a cotton bag containing one ounce cast gold bars. I bought several each year in the early 1960s and paid about £12 for each. I've lost all interest in following the gold price. It has rocketed, that I do know, so do not sell them for under £500 each, but do your homework first in case you can get more for them. All are branded with their registered serial numbers."

Liberty peeked inside the drawstring cotton bag then carefully removed and counted them. There were forty, all twenty-four-carat gold. She stared at the ceiling. "Oh Dad, you've already left me half a house and quite a lot of money in the bank too. I didn't expect..." She could say no more and reached for some tissues to mop up her tears.

The letter finished with:
"I leave you with my love and I expect you to be as good and kind as I meant to be."

What a load to lay on her shoulders. The soup and the tea were almost cold. Nevertheless, she drank the tea, surrounded by the letter, the jewels and the gold. Out of the blue, she remembered the telephone call. It was close to three o'clock and on this cloudy, wet February day, dark clouds reigned. She switched the light on, took a deep breath and returned her client's call.

"I'm so sorry I couldn't take your call. Is it all right for us to talk now?"

Scarlett seemed eager to talk. The GP surgery she worked in suggested she might be extra busy in the coming months. "His grandfather has just died, you see."

Puzzled, Liberty asked, "Whose grandfather?"

"I'm sorry. I should have said that one of the doctors is Chinese and, naturally, he keeps in touch with his grandparents."

"I see." She didn't really.

Her client continued in a whisper, "I overheard the words 'pandemic in China'." Then, returning to her normal voice, she asked, "So can I put my membership on hold for the moment, please?"

"Pandemic? It's not that bad, is it, Scarlett?"

"Nine cases have been confirmed here in the UK."

Only her professional focus saved her from scoffing and citing 'flu as being much worse. "Of course I'll put your membership on hold. No problem at all. When would you like it to resume?"

"I'll let you know. I'm very worried. My friend says it's like the plagues of the middle ages."

Liberty managed to stifle a splutter and the call ended amicably. "Be careful, Scarlett, and I'll keep you in touch with forthcoming events."

The intercom rang. Rats! This day is becoming as chaotic as a hurricane in hell. She raced across to answer and then wished she hadn't.

"Hello Nick. What a surprise. What can I do for you?" Oh no, what a stupid thing to say.

"You could let me in. It's cold out here."

"So sorry, Nick, I... er." She pressed the button to let him in. Aagh! The jewellery. The gold bars. She stuffed the bars into their bag and put them back in the box on her desk. The only thing she found to cover the sapphires and diamonds was her jacket which she hurriedly took off and slung over the top of the collection.

Flustered, she announced, "Come in," when he knocked on the office door.

Nick, ever the professional in a calf length, navy blue coat and shiny black Oxford shoes, tilted his head in his customary salutation to all females, and Liberty's stomach took flight.

"You left something behind."

"I did?" She anxiously watched as his teasing smile grew. "I haven't noticed anything missing." Why hadn't he phoned, or at least texted?

"My apologies for not calling ahead."

Yet again, he'd read her mind. "I can't think what I left. Something important?"

"Yes very." He looked adorably solemn. "You've left behind a lot of people who are not at all happy about your resignation."

Liberty became aware they were standing very close together. "Forgive me, Nick, please sit down." She indicated the chair facing away from her jacket concealing the pile of diamonds and sapphires.

"Thank you. Do you mind if I take this wet coat off first?"

She really must stop shaking. Please God, don't let it be visible. She took his coat and hung it near the radiator. "Tea? Coffee?" A few moments in the kitchen alone would give her a chance to calm her frazzled nerves, take the expensive pearls off and return with a friendlier persona. After all, he was not a prospective client, just a connection to her past.

"Coffee please, with milk."

When she brought the warming drinks, she sat opposite and asked him what he meant.

"Would you like to return?"

"Surely everyone knows I've invested in a business? I've kept in touch with a couple of colleagues, haven't they said something?"

"Not to senior management, no. However, I have them to thank for telling me where you are now. There have been many complaints about your replacement. 'Greasy dunderhead' is one name he's been called."

She looked shocked. "Who called him that?"

"I did."

Ah, yes, he was well known for his insults and put-downs. If he wasn't so damned good-looking with oodles of Italian charm, he might not get away with it. "Of course; it had to be you." She started laughing and the anxiety slipped away. "He can't be that bad."

"He can and he is. He is an abomination, an eyesore and a prig."

"Nick! H.R. would not have taken him on if he was so bad."

"Human Resources: what a terrible name for a department which should view people as treasures. No wonder they don't find any. Though to give them their due, they found you."

Liberty fell in. "You are teasing me. Stop it." He was such a flirt. "What did I really leave behind?"

"Me. You left me behind."

"Stop it, Nick."

"Actually, I'm perfectly serious about you returning to work. I cannot be certain how this will pan out but, as you know, Coronavirus arrived in Britain last month. Since then several more cases have tested positive. It's mostly rumour at the moment but let me ask you a question before I say any more. How is your company doing? Thriving, I hope."

A huge smile settled on Liberty's face – she was able to answer. "Definitely thriving. I receive several enquiries a day and I have plenty of bookings for the next event in March."

Nick frowned. "I have an uneasy feeling, and I am not the only doctor who's saying they feel the same. Sources in Asia are concerned that this might go world-wide. If you're wondering how this will affect you and your events company, it is this: on 23rd January, the Chinese city of Wuhan went into lockdown."

"Lockdown?"

"It's a word we'll all be using shortly. People are not allowed to leave the city. They are restricted in who they can meet. Wuhan remains the epicentre but the virus is spreading here – increasingly."

"Is it like 'flu?"

"Worse, I'm afraid. Over two hundred people have died in China so far. And many more will find their tomorrows are murdered."

"Tomorrows murdered? What do you mean?"

"They will have no tomorrows."

"Are you saying they will be dead?" Oh drat, her astonishment had made her sound ignorant but he always spoke as if he were from another century.

"I am. He took a few sips of coffee before continuing. "I think you are not going to be able to hold events where a large crowd of people mix. They might even ban them."

"What! In England?"

"I can't be sure, but a few of my colleagues are becoming convinced this might be the start of a pandemic. We daren't express our opinions, not yet."

Liberty noticed his eyes narrowing, something he did when he was assessing the other person. Her heart thumped.

"If we are right, your business, *which involves introducing strangers to each other*, may have to close. That is why I am here. I am alerting you to the probability of your not having any income for many months. Make plans *now*, Libby, and my suggestion is that you prepare to return to the hospital which will be in dire need of your organizational capabilities. We have a job description for a new position and, if it becomes necessary, you are the right person to fill it."

Liberty cupped her hand around her mouth. Her eyes stared hard into his. This was not some kind of ruse, he was serious. And she had already received her first cancellation.

Chapter Four
Injection of joy

Sparkles or rain? The good omen had come true. There were sparkles galore, now hidden in the bottom drawer of the filing cabinet which she kept locked. A more secure place was needed. Maybe she should get a bank deposit box? The jewellery should be valued first but her father had warned her of such difficulties. As for the gold bars – her father had grossly undervalued it. She wilfully ignored the second part of the omen – in the weeks that had passed since her first cancellation, it was all too apparent.

Liberty had installed a small television which hung on the wall in order to keep up with the rapidly changing news of the rampant Coronavirus damaging her business. The one o'clock news was scary. No wonder twenty-five people had already cancelled for the booking of forty covers she'd made three months ago. A decision must be made: to cancel completely or hope things would get better. Reluctantly, she cancelled.

Watching the news on the TV, she learnt that people were panic-buying food. She owned up to being guilty of doing the same. She possessed neither fridge nor freezer so perishables were put in a large bread bin and put outside on the fire escape at the back of her kitchen. At this time of year, it was as cold as any fridge. Her stock of canned soups and meats from the nearby Marks and Spencer was stored in every nook and cranny of the little kitchen. As there were no events to organize, and with all her members having been granted extended membership, she had very little to do. It was a perfect time to give the office a thorough clean.

The landline rang.

"Hello Liberty, it's Nick. Just calling to see if you are up-to-date with the repercussions coming down the line."

What a nice man. Jaelyn doesn't deserve him. "Hi Nick. I've begun to realize how right you were. I now don't have a job." She laughed even though she felt more like howling.

"You can put your job on ice and come back to it when we know more about this vile virus."

"You make it sound as though it has evil intentions."

"It has evolved to destroy."

Liberty's varying emotions were running rings around her. Joy, fear, confusion – all were fighting for her attention.

"Will you have dinner with me tonight?"

His question allowed joy to win although confusion was not far behind. What about the nasty Jaelyn? Or is this about hospital matters again? She shut down all feelings except joy. "That would be wonderful."

"Give me your address and I'll call for you at seven-thirty, if it's okay with you?"

"The time is perfect and you can collect me from the office. I'll explain when I see you." She said "goodbye" to his "arrivederci", put the phone down and took a deep breath. Her insides were spinning. She'd work like blazes until five-thirty and then she'd get ready.

Filled with new-found energy she decided the first job was to sort the filing cabinet because it was in a terrible state. Her predecessor had clearly not liked filing, and bringing out dusty files would spread the dust so she'd deal with that later. Reluctantly she picked up the file from her desk with the 'cancelled' sticker. It could be rearranged for later in the year so was filed in the section marked 'Future/Possible Events'. She continued filing the pile of papers sitting in the tray on top of the cabinet. "Aha! What's this?" She pulled out a file from the cabinet marked 'Caves' in huge red writing and took it to her desk. Three leaflets on different caves lay on top of a slim, red leather book. She opened it, frowned and sat down at her desk to read what seemed to be personal notes. The handwritten heading caught her eye: 'Diary and rules for going back and forth'. Whose handwriting was this? Perhaps it belonged to the woman who founded the agency, Laura somebody or other. How very odd. Back and forth to where?

Annoyingly, there wasn't time to read it all, not if she wanted to tidy and clean the office before Nick visited. Finishing the filing would have to wait. Again.

~

Liberty was ready and eager to go at ten past seven. Nick collected her at exactly seven-thirty. In between, she'd read the notebook.

"I thought we'd try 'The Restaurant on the Green'. Do you know it?"

"I do, I'm planning to have an event there later in the year."

"I'm surprised to find you're working late; I hope it's for good reasons."

"It is," said Liberty wondering if she needed to tell him she was practically homeless. She decided to explain over dinner so she gave him an enigmatic smile.

They walked out of pedestrianized Archangel Hill, down towards the car park. Liberty tried to guess what sort of car he owned. BMW? No, it would be British. Jaguar? Yes, that's the one.

Wrong. It was a muddy Land Rover and he suggested she should be careful as he held the door while she climbed aboard. The interior was spotless.

On arrival, they were shown to their reserved table in a corner by the window with a view of the garden and the fountain. It felt slightly spooky that so few people were eating out this Friday evening.

After choosing their starters, main courses and a wine, they faced each other with smiles. His was confident: hers diffident.

"So tell me," began Nick as he raised his glass, "what are your plans?"

To stave off the inquisition, Liberty raised her glass too.

Nick was not a man to give up. "What shall we drink to?"

A successful businesswoman should not allow her mind to go blank, but it did, except for "I've decided to visit some caves." There, that should keep him occupied on something other than the hospital.

"It is a cold, March evening, there is a looming pandemic, and you want us to drink to your visit to freezing caves?"

Her smile helped her anxiety slip away and she began to giggle taking her from bewildering apprehension to silly schoolgirl in a matter of seconds. What was it about this unavailable man apart from his sheer irresistible presence? Liberty finally broke the silence. "I think it might be called 'displacement'." Now she was underway. "I am aware that my new business is threatened when I've only just got started. I am going to contact all my clients and tell them there will be no more events until it is safe to resume. I shall direct them to our website, where they can keep up-to-date with my plans." She paused as she thought of the warnings she'd been given and the omen, that damned omen: sparkles or rain. The jewellery represented the sparkles and now the rain clouds hung low, promising a downpour. "I know that if at all possible, I don't want to return to the hospital." Not if she must suffer seeing him and Jaelyn exchanging glances. "I do know I need to find a suitable place to live. I've been staying in the office for the last couple of months." Liberty didn't dare look at him. "And I am becoming increasingly concerned about people beginning to stockpile food." She took a deep breath. "And I have no fridge nor freezer in the office." She raised her eyes to glance into his and looked away quickly. "My displacement therapy is this." She opened the little red book and showed him the notes on the caves. Before he had a chance to read, she said, "I shall purchase a small fridge-freezer, install it, stock it, and then I am going to visit those caves. Maybe you'll understand why when you've read about them."

Their first course arrived.

Nick cupped his hand around his chin as he concentrated on the book rather than the crab starter which gave Liberty an opportunity to surreptitiously admire her dinner companion in his aqua T-shirt, blue jacket and gold wristwatch; being Nick's, it would be real gold.

"Whose book is this?"

"I'm not sure, but the founder of the agency's name was Laura and some of the restaurant owners previously indicated to me that she was a most unusual person. One even said she appeared to have been dropped here from another planet." Hurriedly she added, "Figuratively speaking, of course."

Nick raised an eyebrow in response then read aloud. "The Caves. Essential to follow the rules." Puzzled, he frowned. "Rules for what?" He began to taste the crab starter.

"Read on and, I can't say it will become clear, but it certainly gets interesting."

"Hmm. So I see. I think I'll whisper, I don't want them," he indicated the only other diners, "to think we're nuts."

He leaned closer to the flickering candle; Liberty's breathing rate increased, he was using his gentle, bedside manner voice.

"Arriving on the beach, I begin to forget who I am so it is essential to make notes and take them with me."

Liberty was entranced; never before had she been so mesmerized by the voice of a man, she hadn't heard a word he'd said, captivated by his soothing tone. He had not only the look of a stylish, cool Italian but also the charm.

"This beach, that will be after...?" Not wishing to be overheard, Nick sat back in his chair while the waiter removed their plates. "Smells delicious," he murmured, smiling with gratitude when the duck legs in cherry sauce were placed in front of Liberty and himself. Only in between courses did he study the red book with interest.

While the chocolate puddings were being served, Nick declared he'd come with her to the caves. He gave her a smile that would melt Antarctica in its entirety, but Liberty reined in her feelings and responded with, "And how is Jaelyn?"

He looked uncomfortable. "As pestiferous as ever. She's visiting her parents in Newcastle 'while she can' she says." He shrugged his shoulders and whispered, "I'd meant to talk to you about the virus – all I will say is that if we want to see these caves, we ought to go tomorrow. Premier League football fixtures have all been cancelled which should tell you what we're in for." He raised his eyebrows and added, "And the Prime Minister has suggested we don't visit restaurants and pubs anymore and he's urging those who can to work from home. And the word 'unprecedented' is being used a lot." He toyed with his fork, took a mouthful, then lifted his eyes from his plate and smiled. "It's Saturday tomorrow, and I'm not working." He reached across the table and covered her hand with his. "And you won't be either."

He managed to look delighted and sound masterful at the same time. She must stop this nonsense. Masterful, who uses such a term today? Who wants to! However, she responded enthusiastically as she withdrew her hand.

"Would you like me to call at your office, say nine o'clock, whisk you off to choose a fridge-freezer, or do you want to order one online?"

Liberty shook her head. "Not online." She rather liked the idea of spending more time with him, even if she had a nagging guilt about Jaelyn. He'd called her 'pestiferous'. It didn't sound like a compliment. Anyway, Nick clearly wasn't afflicted with loyalty and an apt saying popped into her mind – when the cat's away, the mice will play.

"So we can look at some, order one if you like, then I'll drive us down to the caves."

He called for the bill, settled up and swiftly drove her back to her office, waited until she had the key in the lock, then touched her cheek with a kiss. "Thanks for a very interesting evening. See you tomorrow morning, nine o'clock." He visibly enjoyed her wavering smile then turned and disappeared fast.

She closed her door slowly, telling herself she only had to wait until tomorrow for another injection of joy.

On the other side of the road, a hooded figure emerged from the shadows before slouching down the hill, head down and hunched, like a question mark.

Chapter Five
No future with him

Dark clouds covered the sun causing the surging sea to look sinister, slyly luring the brave to a watery oblivion.

"I wouldn't want to be one of those paddle boarders, would you, Nick?"

"I used to enjoy surfing. Haven't had much time recently," he said wistfully.

Liberty glanced at his profile as he drove the last mile or so to the caves' entrance. Not one lone glance, several. With the fridge-freezer ordered earlier, she had nothing mundane to hold back her excitement.

Once parked, Nick was about to get out when Liberty said she wanted to take a quick refresher look at the red book. "I want to find out which particular cave this person went along. The website says it's a real labyrinth." She pored over the book. "I'm becoming more sure it's Laura who's written this. I found some event planning papers definitely written by her and the handwriting is the same." She hesitated before saying, "Laura talks about keeping to the right as that takes you to 1814."

"I assume you don't mean the year 1814?" Nick leaned across to peer at what Liberty was pointing to."

"Um... I think she was researching a glitch in the tunnels as it alludes to something supernatural. I'd like to find out what happened to Xandra Radcliffe, one of her clients. Laura kept paper record cards before she computerized the profiles and on Xandra Radcliffe's profile she's written 'At Foxhills 2009/1814' and then she's put a line through the rest of the card."

Nick frowned. "What are you saying exactly?"

"Laura mentions going to see various people and when I checked them out on the Internet, they all lived in Regency times."

"What!"

"And when I looked up Laura, I discovered she's married to Matthew Redfern who is a..."

"Psychologist in Harley Street."

"Do you know him, Nick?"

"I've read some of his papers in medical journals. Long time ago though."

"Perhaps the caves gave her inspiration for a historical novel but I haven't found any books written by her, although it's possible she used a pen name, I suppose." Liberty shrugged her shoulders and continued, "I can't think it can be what it looks like. She can't actually have gone back in time, can she?"

"If she did, she's returned to 2020 and is sensibly keeping quiet about it." He paused before bouncing into life. "Come on, let's go. Tell me, would you like to live in 1814?"

"I'd adore it. I can lose myself in Regency novels, I'm there, in a manor house, in beautiful clothes, and I have servants."

"A few, or many?"

Liberty laughed. "As many as necessary to run a traditional, comfortable household." There, she didn't sound too greedy.

He took her hand to guide her across the busy road and insisted on paying the entrance fee.

A man dressed as a nineteenth century smuggler acted as the small group's guide leading them underground through a narrow tunnel which opened out after about fifty yards into a huge cavern. His voice echoed as he told them about chalk mining in the eighteenth century and smuggling gangs using the caves to bring their booty up from the beaches.

Nick whispered, "Life in a manor house might be enticing but what if you were born into a smugglers' household?"

"How exciting!"

He raised his eyebrows to enquire, "Have you imagined being a washerwoman?"

The guide coughed loudly. "It's most important that you," he raised his voice, "do not wander off and investigate on your own. There are people who have done that and, to this day, they have never been found."

A man behind Liberty scoffed quietly. "Rubbish. That's just marketing nonsense, trying to give us the shivers."

Unfortunately, not quiet enough. "I'm afraid it's true. A homeless chap was seen forcing open the door when the caves were closed and boarded up. He'd sat under the shelter outside for years," he waved his arms towards the entrance, "ex-soldier, he was, Billy Beggar, we called him. About 2009, and he's never been seen since. The caves were searched," he shrugged, "but nothing. No body even. Nothing. So don't go wandering off, please."

Nick and Liberty exchanged discreet, wary looks.

Whereas most followed obediently and in hushed awe, the bearded man asked many questions including wondering why one of the caves leading off to the right had waist-high iron bars across it.

"Some of the tunnels are yet to be made completely safe and some have chalk falls blocking their way."

Liberty's heart thumped. Laura had written about a rock fall. Keeping your hand on the right wall would guide you past it. And there was something about squeezing through a slit. Liberty turned to Nick. "Look out for a slit in the chalk walls."

Nick frowned. "In the notes?"

"Yes."

The guide was expounding on the caves' history in the later years and how the community saved them from collapse when Liberty noticed at head height a slit behind the bars just big enough for a bulky person to pass through. The little red book was accurate, though there was no mention of bars; they were obviously a recent addition.

After the tour, Nick and Liberty ordered coffee and cake in the Caves' Café and compared their tour to the notes in the book.

"Some of this is illegible, unfortunately," Liberty said thinking out loud, "which is strange because much of what she has written is in admirable calligraphy. I think she is attempting to disguise what she's saying." She then emphasized, "The key thing to remember is, despite his tales of people never being seen again, Laura has explored those caves and Laura has returned to a normal life." Or so it seemed.

In a mock ominous voice, Nick responded, "As far as we know." He scraped his chair back and stood. "It's certainly taken my mind off work. I have a feeling I'm going to be very much in demand in the coming weeks."

"You sound worried, Nick."

"I wish I weren't." He slowed his walk to hold her hand and look directly in her eyes.

Liberty felt a blush rising and wished she knew how to stop it. She tried thinking about her work in the hospital but the times she had come across Dr Nicolo Nylander blocked all else. She blushed even deeper. Now here she was, following him to his Land Rover for an hour's journey alone with him. She could ask all sorts of questions and she did, starting with, "Is your Italian grandmother still alive?" It wasn't such a silly question; elderly people's health was always a hot topic in hospitals, however, she wished she could rephrase it – it was one step away from asking if she'd died yet.

"She's in her nineties and lives with my parents. The house is big enough and they all get along well. My brothers live close by too, so she has plenty of attention." He laughed as if he were enjoying happy memories.

Liberty wanted to ask if they liked Jaelyn, realizing just in time that any mention of revolting Jaelyn would spoil the day; so much better to let him drive wallowing in happier times. And they did; exchanging amusing stories from childhood.

They were pulling into the car park in Middleston town centre when the warmth of a beautiful evening turned icy. Nick's mobile phone vibrated. He checked the caller and ignored it. Even in vibration only mode, it stole his attention.

"Someone wants me to do something," he offered by way of explanation.

Liberty felt her muscles tighten. "Jaelyn?"

"Unfortunately, yes."

"Shouldn't you answer it?" He was her fiancé even if she was a confounded nuisance.

"Maybe you're right. I wanted a whole day without endless interruptions; clearly too much to ask."

Liberty tensed. He seemed perturbed yet appeared to shake off his annoyance and said, "'For every minute you are worried or angry you lose sixty seconds of happiness.' A quotation I have personalized and try to remember when necessary. And I adapt it for all sorts of negative thinking, as I hope you can tell." He chuckled. "My apologies."

They walked in silence to her door, he pecked her on the cheek, and thanked her for a wonderful day together. "Perhaps we can squeeze in another one next week if I haven't been chained to..." he sighed.

"Jaelyn?" she offered.

Nick frowned and appeared to want to say more, shook his head slightly and gave her a hint of a smile.

Liberty let herself in and said as brightly as she could manage, "Thanks, Nick." In her heart she knew there could be no future with him. He was chained.

On Sunday, she slept until nearly midday. After lunch, she pored over the little red book and packed a rucksack. Then she researched online the approximate value of each item of jewellery she owned before hiding most of it in her bedroom between the floorboards and the loft insulation.

On Monday morning, 23rd March 2020, the fridge-freezer she'd chosen with Nick was delivered and manoeuvred into a space in the kitchen. On Monday afternoon, she drove to the supermarket, filled a trolley with food and her car with petrol. On Monday evening, she studied the little red book again, wrote out her plan until, very tired, she set her alarm and went to bed early, as contented as a cat curled in front of a glowing fire.

At 8.30 p.m. the Prime Minister announced a lockdown in an attempt to contain the rampaging Covid-19 virus. No-one should leave home.

Chapter Six
Audacity was her ally

The following morning, Liberty announced, "If Laura can do it, I can do it." She checked she was dressed for the occasion. "Best I can do."

She thanked her father, his being dead did not prevent her chatting to him. He knew his beloved daughter needed freedom and he'd made it possible. She didn't need a man and certainly not one who was shackled to another woman. She told the fridge she'd be back to consume all its goodies in a couple of days, locked the door, heaved her backpack over one shoulder and her heavy black leather handbag over the other. Not yet eight o'clock and she felt as happy as a big sunflower. She was off, like Alice in Wonderland, to disappear down a hole and find a magical world. There was no point in trying to organize events for her business, so setting off for a once in a lifetime adventure was a good way of using this downtime.

Having gone to bed early, Liberty had not heard the Prime Minister's announcement that all should stay at home. Central Middleston, eerily quiet, caused her to drive apprehensively but she put her foot down a little more as she headed towards the empty motorway then rocketed away as if she were in pole position in the Formula One World Championship. "Damn that man," she shouted as she hit the ton.

A vehicle chasing her flashed its light in vain; she never once looked in the rear view mirror, her eyes were on what lay ahead.

Clutching her handbag and slipping on her backpack with its vital kit, including the little red book, she left her car parked as securely as she thought possible and strode off to the caves.

Mistake in Time

A man whistled a tune as he appeared to be shutting up the café, odd at this time of the morning, while another inspected inside the caves. She'd decided it would be better if she didn't pay an entrance fee because then they'd be making sure she returned. If only the man inspecting the caves would pop across to the café. This was the one thing she could not control. She needn't have worried. Men do like to start the day with a cup of coffee and that was his downfall. Liberty sneaked in unnoticed. Audacity was her ally.

The passage descended to the vast cavern she'd been in with *him*. She vowed she'd never say his name again. Her torch wasn't needed as all the lights had been switched on. The air smelt dank, and the rivulets of water running down the walls formed little streams on the chalky paths, adding to her rising anticipation. "There it is." Her whisper did not echo but the voice from the caves' entrance did. What did he say? She slipped out of her backpack, climbed over the bars meant to deter wandering visitors and easily slid through the slit on the other side. It was unlikely the man even knew of her existence as he'd be getting ready for the tours. However, best to disappear quickly.

To ease her apprehension, she repeated, "If Laura can do it, I can do it." Hurrying along the wet, sandy path, she recited what she remembered of the little red book's rules, all the time feeling the cold, damp walls. A man's voice again. Was someone else in *this* tunnel? Fear replaced apprehension. Perhaps it wasn't such a good idea. Through clenched teeth, she whispered, "If Laura can do it, I can do it." She remembered she had to turn a corner and maybe then she'd look for her torch and check the book. The voice grew louder and Liberty began to panic. She recited something important: "Keep my hand along the right wall to avoid the fallen rocks." So dark, so long, she should be using her torch, but finally her hand felt round a corner just as it said in the little red book. A shimmering curtain of rainbow colours ahead of her lit the way for the next fifty yards. She was too stunned to approach. It was in the book, definitely, and you must walk through it. Her heart pounded, yet she knew this led to Regency

England and that was a long way from *him*. And she could return to the twenty-first century and her old life any time at all, exactly as Laura had. "Courage Libby, courage." She heard the voice again, increasingly forceful, then diminishing as it echoed around the tunnel. That man who went to the café was chasing her – she'd been seen.

She scrambled over a few rocks and, clutching her handbag and bulky backpack with her right hand, she leapt into the curtain, steadying herself by holding her hand against the left wall. Not light and airy, it stole her breath, and fear, boiling fear bubbled up. She remembered Laura's words and whispered them. "It's heavy, as if the light of centuries has been condensed." So I must push through and when I reach the other side, I will be in 1814. Liberty concentrated on putting one foot in front of the other which wasn't half as difficult as Laura's notes stated. Quicker than she'd expected, she felt the sandy floor beneath her feet, and daylight lay ahead. Overwhelming relief flooded through her veins. Filling her lungs with pure sea air, she scrambled over more rocks towards the light at the end of the tunnel.

Her long black velvet skirt and embroidered white cotton blouse appeared to be practically new. She looked down and dusted the sand off her hem. "What am I doing here? Why am I clutching a backpack?" She sat on a rock and undid the zip. A bottle of water, an apple, chocolate bars, a very useful long, warm scarf – or was it a shawl? A little red book caught her eye. Hmm... This book is important, that I do remember. Liberty ate the apple and read the book. It contained instructions and it jogged her memory. She must look for the seventy-seven steps and keeping to the right along the beach, she would find them. This was like a treasure hunt and the fun was only just beginning. Damned cold though. She wrapped the shawl around herself, found a tight fitting cap adorned with a floppy, felt flower, stuffed her hair into it and gingerly began walking. She glanced back towards the cave entrance.

Several people were picking their way across the rocks and coming towards her and the women were wearing trousers – how very odd.

She called out to them. "Excuse me, please, am I going the right way for the seventy-seven steps?"

The little group all looked baffled until one girl piped up, "Ah you mean 'The Thirty-Nine Steps' – John Buchan's book?"

Liberty wanted to say she didn't, however her confidence deserted her. "Um..."

The girl pointed to the headland. "It's around there, in the bay. There's many more than that, or so I'm told, but everyone calls them the thirty-nine steps. I'm not sure if they're locked though because they're on a private beach and they lead up to a private estate."

Liberty became extremely worried. She *must* use the steps to reach the top of the cliff, of this she was sure.

"You might be better to go past there and on to Stoney Bay. There's plenty of access to the prom and... ah, yes, I think you might mean the steps which run from the prom to the main road. There's probably seventy-seven of those."

This sounded reassuring. "Thank you." She tried a little curtsey but it wasn't very successful and she lost her balance.

"Here, let me help you with that backpack," said one of the men. He lifted it up and helped her put her arms through the straps. "That'll make things easier for you." He stood back to look at her. "You'd better hurry, the tide is coming in and it will cut you off. Go carefully."

She wrapped her shawl around her shoulders and over the top of the backpack. She thanked them and wished she hadn't overheard their comments about her sanity. What about theirs? No respectable woman wore trousers in 1814.

Anna Faversham

Chapter Seven
An adventure together

At the top of the steps, Liberty knew for sure this was not 1814. The houses were clearly built much later, the 1930s perhaps. She sat down on the top step and consulted the little red book. She spat out a torrent of angry words as she realized where she'd gone wrong. She should have kept her right hand on the right wall as she went through the curtain of light. In her haste to get away from... from what? The voice. What voice? Whatever! In her haste, she'd put her left hand on the left wall and ended up in some other time. But what time? It didn't matter, all she needed to do was turn round and go back again. She had hammered that into her head so if things went wrong, that was what should be done.

Tired and despondent, Liberty dashed down the steps to the promenade and looked towards the north where she knew the cave and her old life awaited her. A vague recollection of a feeling of adventure broke into her growing desperation, lifting her from confusion and despair to hope. Alas, the roar of the surging sea, foaming as it broke against the rocks, smashed her budding confidence because slogging around the headland was no longer an option. The incoming tide showed no concern for her fate; it obeyed the moon and, as King Canute demonstrated, no man could stop it. She bit her lip: how come she could remember an eleventh century Danish king yet not what she did yesterday? Or the day before.

She'd have to wait. After much muttering, Liberty sat on the promenade and swung her legs over the side. Staring at the beach being stolen minute by minute by incoming waves, she realized how very cold she was. "How stupid can I be?" she murmured as she searched for something warmer than a shawl. How senseless I must look – a long velvet skirt, a blouse and a shawl on the beach on a freezing day. "Go on, rain." The universe was against her so it might as well rain and finish its work. Nothing as useful as a cardigan or coat came to light. However, an A5 blue silk, Chinese patterned notebook aroused her curiosity. She stared at the first page. "Objectives." She read just the first sentence and felt her heart break. "To arrive in Regency England, and assess the possibility of establishing myself as a wealthy lady." In brackets were the words "Sell jewellery in handbag for immediate needs." A lone tear ran down her face, swiftly followed by another.

"Do you need any help?"

Hastily, Liberty wiped her face with one of the many tissues she had stuffed up the sleeves of her blouse. She looked up to see a young woman about the same age as her with curly, chestnut hair and a round, kind face, and a Dachshund patiently looking up at her too. Liberty scrambled up as she said, "Um... I think I'm lost." *Oh honestly, is that the best I can think of to say?*

"Where have you come from and where are you trying to go?"

A sensible, straightforward type. She'd give a straight answer. "I'm trying to go around the headland but the tide has cut it off." *Rats! That was different from being lost; she must get her story worked out.* "I think I'm a bit lost." She sneezed.

The young woman did not bat an eyelid. "While you wait for the tide to go out again would you like to come to my grandmother's and you can get warmed up and have a cup of tea?"

Liberty frowned. *How strange. Was this something the girl usually did?*

"My name's Gemma, and I'm staying with her for a few days. She won't mind," she said, inclining her head.

Liberty feigned a smile. "I would love to come back with you. I'm frozen."

"Follow me." Gemma started walking towards the steps as she said, "By the way, this is Granny's dog, William."

"Hello, William." Liberty walked slowly behind Gemma and the dog which looked perplexed. She became aware that she ought to give her name but she couldn't remember it. Had she written it in the little blue book?

Gemma glanced over her shoulder regularly as she watched Liberty agonizing over her predicament. At the top of the steps, she waited for her. "Don't worry, here we are, this is my grandmother's flat." She opened the gate and closed it behind Liberty. There were two doors and Gemma let them through one of them with the key. "It's a ground floor flat, Granny likes it because it has a nice garden at the back." She called out to her grandmother who came into the hallway to take the dog. "Granny this is a lady who has got a bit lost and I promised to give her a hot drink while she figures out what to do."

Liberty caught the look in the grandmother's eye and read it as 'have you brought home another of your waifs and strays?'

"I'm so sorry to intrude. I think I've lost my memory as well as lost where I am."

Gemma's Granny was exactly how every grandmother should be, with a round face, wavy white hair, spectacles and a welcoming smile.

"Sit down here in the front room, love." She took the lead off the dog. "His name's William after my father, he loved Dachshunds." She bustled round plumping up cushions, removing her knitting and making her visitor feel comfortable. "I'll put the fire on, love." She bent over and switched on an electric fire. "There, we'll have two bars on, shall we, as it's so cold?" She picked up a pink, frilled pinafore from the sofa and, putting it on, said, "How do you like your tea? With milk? Sugar?"

Liberty wasn't at all sure so she said she didn't mind. She wondered what she should call the grandmother and that reminded her to dive down into the backpack to find the little blue book. Not there. Ah, the handbag. Yes, there it sat on top of some jewellery, not a lot but stunning. She picked out the book and closed the bag quickly. Here was her lifeline. On the first page she'd detailed her objectives. The next page had a heading of 'Personal History'. Her name was Liberty Taffet and she was born in 1999 which made her, um... She lived in Middleston, Kent, England. Her brother lived in Australia, her father had recently died and her mother died some years ago. A further page gave details on what the backpack contained and why, and the explanation she was to give for owning the jewellery. She had no currency so she should sell the jewellery.

Gemma returned from hanging up her coat in the hall after having a quick conversation with her grandmother in the kitchen. She was wearing a flowery, green dress with a hemline at least four inches above her knees. Could this be the 1960s? "Do you mind if I ask you the date?"

"It's Sunday 24th of March," Gemma said with a smile.

Sunday? That didn't sound right. She consulted the little blue book – she'd left on Tuesday 24th March. "What year is it?"

Gemma raised her eyebrows. "1968."

Yay! The Beatles, the Rolling Stones, the Hollies, this could turn out to be a fantastic adventure. How did she know this? She didn't know about herself yet she remembered history, musical history anyway and perhaps that was because...

"You look very happy. Has it rung any bells?"

"I'd expected it to be..." Yikes, she mustn't say 1814. She'd definitely be locked away somewhere. She changed the subject. "I'm sorry, I haven't told you my name. It's Liberty Taffet. I couldn't remember it but it is written in my notebook." That sounded a bit daft, so she added, "Old school habits die hard. I still write my name in... oh everything really." It would be better if she kept her mouth shut.

Granny came in with three cups and saucers and a large teapot. She poured out tea into all three cups and suggested Liberty help herself to milk and sugar. She then put a yellow tea cosy on the pot.

Liberty began to smile. This was like something on the TV and she loved it until Granny said, "Now tell us as much as you can remember, Liberty, and let's see if we can let your family know where you are."

"Family? My parents have both recently died and my brother lives in Australia."

"Australia?" Gemma perked up. "I'd love to go there."

"I hope to visit him some time." Grief! He wouldn't have been born if she tried to visit him now.

"Don't you worry at all, my dear. Have you somewhere to stay tonight?"

"When the tide goes out, I can walk back..." No, she must not mention the caves. "Where is this?"

"This is Bradstowe," said Gemma.

Granny stood up to pull the curtains. "It's beginning to rain and the wind is getting stronger. Would you like to stay here tonight? We can take you to the doctor tomorrow if you wish. Memories often return. You've probably had a stressful problem or a bump on the head, and this amnesia will only be temporary." She smiled gently and added, "Sometimes it helps to forget what it is you've forgotten."

Gemma chimed in quickly. "Yes, start afresh until your memory returns."

Liberty frowned. Perhaps this was wise. At least enjoy the adventure for a short while, and if everything went wrong, there was also the option to return through the cave – the little red book made that very clear.

"Please stay, Liberty. Shall I make up a bed for you?"

Liberty took a deep breath, enormously relieved. Gemma didn't wait for an answer. When she returned, she suggested Liberty follow her to the little box room. "It's titchy, stuffed full of old suitcases, books and other things Granny no longer uses." She sighed. "And the bed is old and lumpy, so sorry. Put your bags down and make yourself at home."

"Home?" Liberty couldn't remember her home.

"It'll all come back to you soon. Granny used to be a nurse during the war and she whispered to me in the kitchen that she'd seen a lot of this back then." She paused to give a comforting smile. "Come back to the front room when you're ready." Gemma tentatively smiled and disappeared.

Moments later, Granny put her head around the door, "Would you like a bit of fish for supper? I've got some smoked haddock in."

"That would be wonderful. Thank you so much."

Once on her own, Liberty tipped everything out from the backpack, hoping to find something more suited to the 60s to wear. Success, well, partially. She'd packed a granddad style pink shirt which could have been worn as all-in-one underwear in 1814. It came down almost to her knees and if she tied the multi-coloured long silk scarf around her waist, it might pass. A purple velvet jacket with gold buttons would have to do as a coat. And she'd wear the spare pair of tights with her sandals. Embarrassing but better suited to the times than the long skirt and shawl.

~

After the smoked haddock, potatoes and peas, they all sat around the fire. Liberty asked Gemma where she lived.

"I'm supposed to be starting a new job very shortly," she took a deep breath, "but I've nowhere to live yet. Tomorrow I'm taking the train up to London to look at a couple of bedsits which I've seen advertised." She handed Liberty a newspaper and pointed out two. "They go very quickly, so I'll have to make a quick decision."

Liberty attempted to read them out. "Bedsit in family home. Use of bathroom and kitchen. £2 and is that ten shillings?" She pointed to £2 10/- at the end of the advert. She hoped she hadn't made a fool of herself.

"Yes, that's right. It doesn't sound ideal. I don't fancy sharing a kitchen and bathroom. The other one is better."

Liberty took a look. "Yes, this sounds a little better as it has its own kitchenette. More expensive though. And what about the area?"

"They're both in south London, Norwood, to be precise. There's a frequent train service into central London from there."

"There's another one here." Liberty pointed to an advert and read out, "Second floor flat. Bedroom, lounge, kitchen, Heron Hill, £5 per week."

Gemma wasn't so sure. "I'm not sure I can afford £5."

Granny tilted her head and offered her opinion. "If I were you, I'd find out the cost of commuting from Norwood and compare it with Heron Hill. Your own little flat would be better than a room in a family house. You don't know what the family will be like, skinheads maybe. Be careful."

"Skinheads? Oh I know about those," Liberty blurted. "And mods and rockers too. They had motorbikes and Vespa scooters."

Granny and Gemma laughed in delight. "Some of them still have," said Gemma.

"Would you mind if I come to London with you tomorrow? I'll find a hostel to stay in until I remember where I live."

Granny looked alarmed. "Be careful who you mix with, Liberty, people judge you by your friends."

While Liberty's eyes grew larger, Gemma jumped in with, "I'll look after her until her memory returns, Granny."

"My dear, I would expect nothing less." Then in the lowest voice she could manage, she added, "From a very small child, you always helped the underdog. Maybe find a doctor?"

The following day, on the way to the station, they passed a small jeweller. "Forgive me, Gemma, I have to pop in here." Gemma looked as though she might follow her, so Liberty said, "I'll only be a minute or two."

And so it was that Liberty and Gemma caught the train from Bradstow to London on the Monday morning. Two young ladies on an adventure together.

Two young men, separately, also boarded the train.

Chapter Eight
Liberty smelt a rat

"We must have been meant to meet," said Gemma. "Sharing a flat is the obvious answer."

"It's saved us time looking at bedsits," replied Liberty. "A memory has come back to me! Wherever I've come from, I needed to find a flat. Isn't it strange? I was living in a loft, no that's not quite right. Oh drat! The memory has disappeared."

"It's progress though. Maybe that memory will return again. What did the loft look like?"

"It was only small and I needed somewhere different. I just can't grasp why." She shrugged.

The two young women increased their pace as they walked along to the address they'd seen in the newspaper for the accommodation agency. However, the agency turned out to be only a small flat in a dilapidated house in a run-down neighbourhood.

Gemma checked the address. "329b Alberta Road." She took a deep breath. "There's only one way to find out." She rang the bell.

A scrawny, middle aged man answered. "You wantin' the flat?"

Gemma looked concerned yet bravely answered, "Yes. May we see it please?"

Half an hour later, viewing the second floor of a poorly maintained, Victorian end of terrace house, Gemma said to Liberty, "Are we sure about this?"

"The pros are: one, cheap rent; two, it's near the station; three, the rooms are big; four..." and there Liberty stopped and giggled.

"The cons are: one, there's a hole in the floor underneath the big chair; two, the furniture is very old; three, there's no bathroom."

"If you ain't got a tin bath, there's the public baths down the road," muttered the agent, "next to the launderette. The toilet's downstairs, on the ground floor."

"We've nothing much to compare it with," whispered Gemma. "There's so few flats available and I've run out of time. Perhaps my mum and dad will help out with getting set up properly." She tried to look hopeful.

The scrawny man waved his key. "Four weeks' rent up front, cash, then weekly in advance. You wannit or not?"

In a low voice Liberty said, "We might not see that deposit again."

Gemma's eyes widened. "Yet there aren't any other flats available immediately and it'll save us a hotel bill, though Granny says we can both go back to her."

The scrawny man eyed Gemma's suitcase. "Git a move on. You ain't the only ones viewin' today."

Conferring with Gemma, Liberty said, "Shall we take it?" Liberty knew she had sufficient money, though she'd been surprised at the sapphire brooch and matching bracelet only raising £65 from the High Street jeweller. A hundred and one thoughts whirled. Yet she heard herself say in conclusion, "Okay."

She watched the skinny legged man shuffle off in shoes so big and ill-fitting they looked like clogs.

~

The forms were signed; the flat was possibly legally theirs. Liberty smelt a rat, but perhaps this was how things were done in 1968. £25 having been handed over to the scrawny chap, they were now allowed to live there.

The large bedroom was furnished only with two single beds and two wardrobes each with a drawer at the bottom. Faded red lino covered most of the floor. While Gemma carefully unpacked, Liberty contemplated buying some suitable clothes. She'd spent nearly £2 on the train ticket and a shilling bus fare to the flat agency, and £12/10/- as her share of the flat deposit and then another £2/10/- on the first week's rent. Gemma had some tinned food in her suitcase for the two of them, courtesy of her Granny, sufficient for tonight so food shopping could wait.

"Gemma, I absolutely must go clothes shopping."

"Do you want me to come with you?"

"Yes, that would be great."

An hour later, Gemma was showing Liberty all the delights of Swinging London from the top of a red, double-decker bus. "Quick, get off here. C & A has just about everything you'll need and it's very reasonably priced."

Within another hour, Liberty had bought a navy blue coat, a pair of navy blue shoes, a matching long-sleeved red jersey and skirt, five pairs of knickers and two pairs of tights.

"I still need another outfit. I can't wear the same clothes every day." The pink shirt and purple velvet jacket were embarrassing.

"You have your beautiful embroidered blouse you could wear with the red skirt."

"Hmm..." Liberty noticed a black skirt for £2/2/6. "This is the very thing. It will go with anything else I buy and I love the way it's all twirly."

"That's a bargain. Snap it up. Hope you don't mind, I'm going to get it in green."

"Of course not, you go ahead."

Clutching their shopping bags, they headed for the bus stop. And then it rained. Liberty could stand it no longer and began rummaging in her shopping bags. A purple velvet jacket over a grandad shirt was no match for a downpour.

"Here, take this umbrella."

Liberty whirled around. She thought she recognized the voice, but who was this man smiling amiably at them both?

Gemma came to her rescue. "Thanks. But what about you? You'll get wet now."

"Only for a minute or two. Look here comes your bus."

Liberty wondered how he knew this was their bus. Five different routes stopped here. He shepherded them onto the bus, took his umbrella, stood back and walked away as the bus departed.

"How very kind," said Gemma.

Chapter Nine
Surprise

"Right," said Liberty the morning after sleeping directly on the mattress, fully clothed, with no bedclothes, covered only by strategically placed garments, topped by her coat. "We need to do some urgent shopping. I'm frozen."

Gemma looked as if she hadn't slept a wink and mumbled. "I'm frozen and famished and I don't have a lot of money, I've really only got enough to get myself through my first week until I get paid. I wasn't expecting to pay such a large deposit. And I thought I'd be getting a furnished bedsit."

Liberty rootled around in her handbag for her purse. She found a little over £25 which for some unfathomable reason sounded a very small amount with which to purchase some bedding. She pulled out twenty £1 notes. "Have I got enough to get us set up here in the bedroom which is the main thing?"

Gemma tipped her head slightly.

"Let's make a 'to do' list," Liberty suggested brightly.

"Um... What do we need for that?"

Liberty blinked. She supposed a pattern cutter wouldn't need one of those. Surely though, she must have heard... She pulled out her little blue book and a ball point pen. "I'll write it in here."

Within five minutes, Liberty concocted a list with costings supplied by Gemma. "We'll start with a trip to the corner shop and get some food. Are you all right if we don't have a shower this morning?"

"We can go to the baths later today, I don't mind, or we can just have a wash in the kitchen and go tomorrow," Gemma said.

A wash in the kitchen? A shiver scuttled down Liberty's back. She'd endured washes in the kitchen before. Where?

"We can take turns." Gemma waited for a response. "Or–"

Interrupting, Liberty said, "Suits me."

After their quick trip to buy food, Liberty said, "At least there's a useful kitchen cabinet," as she stacked tins of baked beans and soup, bread and milk in the cupboard.

Gemma seized a tin of spam and tucked it under the sink. "This can be our 'Joseph Store' until we find somewhere better."

Liberty blinked. "Our what?"

"Our 'Joseph Store'. It's one of Granny's life lessons. You know, wisdom handed down the generations. A 'Joseph Store' works on the basis of every time you go food shopping, you put one item away for a rainy day, and only when you have enough for a week stashed away are you allowed to use up the oldest items when you can give yourself a treat and use several in one week. You go on replacing them–"

"Ad infinitum," interrupted Liberty, catching on to what she considered a brilliant idea. "And then, if you get low on money, you've got some reserves – it's like money in the bank. Wow! Was Joseph someone in your family?"

"No. It refers to Joseph, Jacob's favourite son. You know, the one who was given a coat of many colours and was sold by his brothers into slavery. He stored up food before a famine. It's in the Old Testament."

"Ah," said Liberty, none the wiser; the Old Testament was not her strong point. Her tummy rumbled. Embarrassed, she announced, "I'll make us some scrambled eggs on toast for breakfast before we tackle the second item on our 'to do' list."

"Liberty," began Gemma.

"Call me Libby."

"Libby," began Gemma again, "do you suppose you did some sort of office work? An administrator or something? You're very organized."

"Possibly, it seems to come naturally," she said as she whisked the eggs.

"This electric stove is pretty ancient," said Gemma, "it's going to take a long time to toast a couple of slices of bread in the grill. At least there's two saucepans in the bottom cupboard." She pulled one out and put it on the stove for the scrambled eggs and she filled the other one with water to boil for making the tea. "Do you think we made a mistake coming here?"

After a few seconds, Liberty replied, "I've been thinking the same but, on the whole, I think it will work well. Look," she said kicking the cardboard boxes they'd acquired at the shop, "if we put them on top of one another, with the open side of the top one facing out, it will make a little cupboard or dressing table for the bedroom."

Gemma's forlorn expression was not improved by Liberty's demonstration, but a hot breakfast was a mood-lifter.

Deciding to skip lunch, they set off for the shops and it wasn't long before the two shoppers returned home each with a haul of a pillow, two sheets, two pillow slips and two blankets. As they staggered up the stairs, they noticed the door to the flat beneath theirs stood ajar. A woman put her skinny hand around the door and coughed.

"Excuse me," she said as her head appeared. "Someone's been in your flat while you were out."

Both Liberty and Gemma simply stared at the middle-aged woman with straggly, long brown hair.

"Upstairs. I heard him moving around. He went in all the rooms, one after the other."

"Did you see him?" asked Liberty.

"No, sorry."

"Thank you very much for telling us." Gemma smiled at the head.

Liberty continued walking up the stairs. "Yes, thank you, we'll have to be careful."

The two friends entered their flat cautiously and looked around.

"I can't see anything's missing."

Liberty chuckled. "Nothing much to take," then hastily added, "Have you checked your wardrobe?"

Gemma looked inside. "Seems all right."

"Odd," said Liberty. "Mine's not been touched either. Perhaps it's the landlord inspecting the property – such as it is!"

"I was going to have a snooze," muttered Gemma, "but I don't feel like it now. I don't feel safe."

"We can put a chair under the front door handle tonight and maybe get a new lock put on soon."

"I'm completely out of money. I feel awful, you've paid for everything. I'll pay you back as soon as I can but I've got hardly anything until I get paid."

"You have me," laughed Liberty. "Mad, potty me."

Much later Liberty realized that without her, Gemma would not have been in this dreadful, barely furnished flat and without any money.

The following day, Liberty consulted her 'to do' list. She ticked off a few items which they'd crammed in the previous afternoon and moved on to 'find a job' even though she possessed no identification nor various other requirements for employment. At least she now had an address and smart clothes. Standing in front of Gemma, in her red jumper, matching skirt, navy coat and chubby-heeled sling back shoes, she asked, "How do I look?"

"Very stylish."

Liberty had noticed several employment agencies in the local High Street when they were shopping. She'd start at the first one she came across and by the time she reached the last, maybe she'd have had enough practice at interviews to get a job as one of those ladies who wheeled trolleys around offices pouring out teas for the employees. They existed, of this she was sure, she'd seen them on

TV. Television? Where was this television? They didn't have one. Was her memory returning? She must have had a television before she came here. Came from where? She shivered. I'm just cold, she told herself as she pushed open the door of the first employment agency.

"Good morning," said the lady behind the big desk at the back of the office. Her tiny skirt was more like a wide belt and her long, auburn hair was completely straight, not a kink nor a curl to be seen. "Please take a seat and tell me what you are looking for."

"I'm not sure. What vacancies do you have?"

"A vast number, as you probably know. Did you see anything in the window to suit? It's really up to you to choose something. Or perhaps you could become a temp?"

A temp? This is the answer. "Actually, temporary work would suit me fine. Thank you." Oh no. Liberty noticed a sign on the wall with the name of the agency – 'Office Assistance'. She reassured herself by realizing tea ladies might come into such a category. "I don't mind what I do. I'd happily be a tea lady." Liberty winced. Was that what they were called?

The interviewer smiled dismissively and said, "Pop over there and type out this." She handed Liberty a card with a few sentences on it. "You can choose the manual Imperial or the IBM Selectric."

Liberty began to feel slightly sick as she stared at them. What could she say?

The interviewer wandered over to the electric typewriter and switched it on. "Here, have a go on this. Have you used a Selectric before?"

"No. No I haven't."

"This little golf ball whizzes round instead of the normal striking keys. Don't let it worry you."

Consoling herself with the fact that nobody knew who she was and there were several other agencies within walking distance, Liberty chose the whizzing golf ball. She placed her fingers on the keyboard and began typing, copying from the card. Oh boy, it really did whizz and it clattered like a well shod horse galloping on cobbles. What fun.

"You can touch-type," said the interviewer as if dreaming of imminent empire building. "I can find a place for you. Let's do a spelling test. I'll say the word, you type it. Is that all right with you?"

"Yes." Definitely yes.

"Allergies." The Selectric clattered. The interviewer paused. "Amnesia."

Liberty lifted her head to stare at the interviewer; did she suspect?

"Amnesia," she repeated. Liberty typed. "Anaemic, bacteria, cyst." Another thirteen medically related words followed until she finished triumphantly with "whooping cough."

Liberty swivelled on the typing chair and asked, "Why are they all medical terms?"

"Because, if you are ready, I can get you started tomorrow. How does that sound?"

Liberty bit her lip, thought of her nearly empty purse and said, "Wonderful!"

"Well, you know of course that the National Health Service is terribly understaffed administratively, and I've been trying to find someone suitable for almost a week now. They'll welcome you with open arms."

Struck dumb, Liberty couldn't bring herself to ask how much money, which hospital and other pertinent questions, so she felt relieved as the woman sat behind her desk and indicated to Liberty to sit opposite. She tried not to look desperate.

"Now if you fill in this form, I'll write all the details you'll need." She handed Liberty a form and a biro and began talking as she wrote down the details. "I don't know what you've been earning up till now but you'll be pleased to hear we pay extra for medical secretaries. I had a hunch you'd be a good speller. Have you ever worked in a hospital before?"

Probably not, thought Liberty. "No," she said diffidently and carried on figuring out how to fill in the form. She knew her name and her address, though little else and so handed back an incomplete form. "I'm sorry I hadn't expected to be asked for–"

"Don't worry, we can always fill those details in later. Now, do you know where Guy's Hospital is?"

Liberty whipped back, "I've never needed a hospital yet."

Laughing, the interviewer gave her all the details she'd written out including the pay. "Nine shillings an hour," she announced. "Remember, you don't get paid for lunch breaks."

Liberty frowned as she puzzled over whether to get excited or offended.

"Rises to ten shillings once we know you can do the job."

~

And so it was that Liberty walked through the huge, ornate gates of Guy's Hospital on the following morning not knowing she was earning more than most other girls of her age. She introduced herself to the Personnel Department as Miss Liberty Taffet and subsequently found herself in a tiny office adjoining that of the Consultant Radiologist, Professor Hans Schmidt. She felt at home while exploring the filing cabinet and typing some scribbled letters she'd found on her desk.

Around midday, she ran out of things to do so she left a note on the typewriter, wandered around the grounds, and felt ecstatically happy. A dingy flat, but a fine friend and a job which would pay the bills. And then she saw a dark haired man sitting on a bench reading a file, with a briefcase beside him.

He looked up, smiled and stood to greet her. "Hello Libby."

"Hello," responded Liberty politely, "do I know you?"

He showed her a photo he was holding in his hand. "You do, and to prove it, I have your photo."

He's gorgeous, thought Liberty. In her whole life she'd never seen anyone who immediately filled her with a warm, fuzzy feeling, a desire to know him, to love him, to be with him forever. Yet how did he get my photo? She became suspicious. It must be easy for someone so good-looking to chat up passing girls. Or, maybe he's connected with the employment agency; is he checking up on her? Sneaky. She was going off him.

"Think, Miss Libby Taffet, if I know your name and I have your photo I am likely to know you and therefore you might know me."

"Well I don't." This is not the sort of problem she wanted to encounter on her first day and she turned around and walked swiftly back to the security of her office. Yet she would really like to see him again. "Perhaps he'll think I'm playing hard to get," she whispered to her typewriter. "And that might be good." She patted her new friend, the Selectric, and sat up straight.

She hadn't yet met the Professor, he'd been lecturing all morning, so she was pleased when he knocked on her door and welcomed her to his department.

"My apologies for not having removed my permanent secretary's personal belongings. She left in rather a hurry." Professor Schmidt spoke with no trace of German accent and his white coat looked immaculate.

"Oh," said Liberty, her eyes wide.

"Forgive me, I didn't mean to alarm you. It's a sad and disturbing tale. The photos pinned to the little board behind you are of her sister. Her sister answered an advertisement in a newspaper for a personal assistant to Count someone or the other. 'Must be able to travel' it said. A fabulous salary was offered. £2,000 a year, I believe."

Liberty swivelled around to see three photos and a newspaper cutting.

"To cut a long story short, within the first week her sister accompanied the so-called Count overseas and has never been seen again. The family hired a detective who traced her to North Africa and he managed to take a photo of her leaning out of the window of a house of ill repute; she had a chain around her wrist. We await further news."

"That's terrible. I hope they can bring her home."

Professor Schmidt stared solemnly at Liberty. "Research thoroughly. Don't go accepting any posts which sound too good to be true. Apparently white slavery didn't stop with the Barbary pirates."

Liberty wanted to say and don't go accepting secretaries who haven't been properly vetted. Instead, she said, "I hope I will prove acceptable until your secretary returns." She smiled, wondering where her growing poise came from; was she always used to dealing with strangers and top professional men, boffins even? But what exactly were Barbary pirates?

On her way home, she spotted a small jeweller near the railway station. She noticed a discreet sign in the window offering to buy antique or second-hand jewellery. Useful. Liberty hurried back to the flat.

"I haven't told your friend yet," said the skinny woman in the flat beneath theirs. "When she was out, he got in again." She pointed upwards. "I heard him, see, 'cos you've got a hole in the floor, haven't you?"

"Indeed we have. Did you see him or her this time?"

"Nah, he must tiptoe down the stairs. He was lucky too cos your friend came back soon after."

"Thanks for telling me."

As she opened her front door a man's voice called out, "Surprise."

Chapter Ten
Semi-house-trained big puppy

Clutching a small television under one arm, a tall, chubby chap grinned at Liberty. He attempted a bow and said in a low, conspiratorial tone, "Bond, Jon Bond. I'm delighted to greet you."

It was impossible not to laugh. So theatrical, such panache, and with the TV under his arm, highly comical.

Gemma stood behind him beaming. "Please excuse my big brother doing his party piece. He so wants to be a famous spy like James Bond."

"If I have to have such a short, sharp name, I might as well make the most of it."

Gemma took a step back and tugged Jon's jersey. "Let Liberty in, Jonathan, let her in." She feigned exasperation and explained, "He's just arrived."

"Oh good. I might have thought he always went around with a television under one arm."

Jon stood back to let Liberty in. "I can think of better things to grasp with my arms."

"Don't take any notice of him, Libby, he's full of cheek."

"And here I am, the dashing hero, clutching a gift of momentous importance, and where's the gratitude, the respect, the joy at seeing me once again?" Mockingly he added, "Are you going to keep me standing in this hall all night, little sis?"

"Sorry," said Gemma, "come into the lounge–"

"Sitting room, Gemma, how many times must I tell you it's not a place for lounging? Sitting room or living room."

Gemma sighed. "Okay, just put it on the floor in the *sitting room*."

It took him only a few seconds to decide where on the floor to put it, adjust the aerial and turn it on. "Notice with what speed and efficiency a television is installed." He began sniffing in an exaggerated fashion and stared at the offending small, faded rug. "Musty. Dreadful. Get it aired. Hang it out of the window. Beat the dust out. Sling it – but definitely do *something*. It's unhealthy."

Gemma glared. "Jon we know it's musty and I promise I'll do something in the coming week."

"Promise?"

"Yes."

Satisfied, Jon tackled something else. "All these bare light bulbs – haven't you heard of lamp shades? Go to a jumble sale if you must but get something up soon. I want to see this flat looking tickety boo."

Liberty thought that not in a million years could they get this ropey old place looking 'tickety boo', whatever that meant. Still, it's cheap.

Jon turned the television off. "Not needed tonight, we're going out."

"*We're* going out?" In a tone conveying long-suffering, Gemma asked, "What plans have you got for me now?"

"You'll soon find out. First you must introduce this young lady."

As fast as a racing greyhound from its starting trap, Liberty announced, "I'm Liberty Taffet. Your sister and I are sharing this flat."

"Miss Taffet, you are courageous in the extreme. I wish you well." He bowed as if to the Queen. "Get your glad rags on pronto, we are off to seek our destinies."

Gemma shooed the riveted Liberty into the bedroom.

"Is he always like this? Or is he on something?"

Gemma sighed, "He's always like this, unstoppable. Sorry."

"No need to apologize. At least I don't have to decide what to wear. It'll be the black swirly skirt and my white embroidered blouse." She threw her purple, velvet jacket around her shoulders.

"I haven't got much to choose from either," Gemma said as she picked out a grey skirt, pink blouse and black jacket. "These will have to do."

Jon knocked on the door. "Ready girls?"

"And is he always in a hurry?"

"Always. Actually, he's brilliant and accomplishes more in a day than I will in a lifetime."

"Chop chop."

The girls dutifully followed Jon out to his car: a red Triumph Spitfire with only two seats.

"We're going out on the town," he said. "A delectable dinner first, then on to mingle at 'The Market.'"

"Jon, stop it, slow down. How are we both supposed to sit in the one seat?"

"Miss Liberty Taffet sits in the one seat and you sit up on the boot," he said as he took the top down. "Here, have my scarf. Keep your feet behind the seats and hold on tight."

And so they roared around the streets with Gemma clutching the backs of the seats until they reached Westminster Bridge when they were called to a halt by a policeman.

"I'm afraid, young lady," said the policeman standing in front of them. "It is against the law for you to sit out of the cockpit and very dangerous too."

"Can we both sit in this front seat?" suggested Liberty.

The policeman raised his eyebrows, turned and strode back to his patrol car.

"Right," said Jon, "squeeze in together. It'll keep you warm."

"At last," responded Gemma.

Jon zoomed into the courtyard of the St Ermin's Hotel, gave his car keys to the commissionaire and, finally slowing down, he ushered the two girls through the open door.

"Wait here a second." Jon approached the Reception desk and had a quiet word. Liberty heard the receptionist respond by saying she'd arrange for an extra place to be laid.

During dinner, Jon entertained them with tales of the hotel having been used during the war by MI6 and the much respected Special Operations Executive. His final flourish was his whisper of the rumoured secret tunnel into Parliament.

Gemma explained to Liberty that Jon collected all sorts of potentially interesting information for his work. Liberty wanted to know more but he turned the conversation to asking how Liberty met his sister.

"I can only tell you that I am extremely embarrassed because I've lost my memory and Gemma has kindly taken me under her wing."

As serious as an owl, Jon nodded. "Gemma is the most wonderful girl in the world. Bit of a square perhaps but life in Swinging London will soon fix that." He winked at Liberty. "She's got very big wings and all waifs and strays flock to her. Injured birds in particular."

"Stop it, Jon. We are not 'birds'." She turned to Liberty. "I'm sorry, he needs training." Then she turned to her brother and said forcefully, "Libby is not injured."

"Indubitably. My apologies, Miss Taffet. I was not referring to you but as her big brother, I've noticed how from the age of seven upwards, she would bring home pigeons with broken wings and expect me to fix them. Then there was the duck with–"

"My giddy aunt, Jon, you get worse as you get older."

Jon grinned mischievously. "She keeps me in check, see, I told you she is wonderful." He winked at Gemma and whispered, "Your new friend should see a doctor."

Suddenly Liberty remembered she hadn't told Gemma about their unwanted visitor to the flat. Should she tell her now? She didn't want to spoil the evening so she decided to wait. Flashing through her mind came the image of the man who said he knew her. He had her photograph. How? Was he...? Later, not now.

Their next stop was at 'The Market' a nightclub in Soho.

"Famous," said Jon; though on being told he'd have to join at a considerable price, he declared it to be infamous. Nevertheless, not wishing to disappoint, he joined and brought in his two guests and bought them drinks. Gemma asked for an orange juice and Liberty thought it best to have the same. He shepherded them to a dark green banquette overlooking a small dance floor. "Mindboggling," he said with disgust. "I'd no idea the patrons would be from another planet." He glanced around to another section of the club. "And they're all chickling out of their minds."

"Chickling?"

"Jon's way of saying chicks giggling. Sorry, Liberty, I should have warned you."

Chicks? Ah... girls.

Gemma's eyes were now on stalks. Liberty's eyes were on the lolling, semi-dressed members of this so-called club. The members' eyes were unable to focus on anybody or anything.

"Undeniably infamous," Jon growled. "When you've finished your drink, we'll try a club where they're on the same planet as us." He squeezed his sister's hand. "Can't let you sit in this stink, you could get as high as the stars in minutes." He smacked his hand. "Bad choice, my abject apologies. I'll beat Brian up for recommending this. The skunk."

They set off along Oxford Street. Jon, wearing a dark green and yellow striped jacket over a light green shirt with matching trousers blended in well with Swinging London's colourful society. Despite her best efforts, Liberty felt as small and drab as a sparrow among peacocks. Her attention was caught by the many Mini Coopers parading past, and she was ecstatic to see three E-Type Jaguars in a row, each with a long haired, colourfully dressed girl in the passenger seat. It was like a Buy British show, she decided. Cool Britannia. And then five Vespa motor scooters paraded past, each with a girl riding pillion. A couple of street musicians, both playing enthusiastically on their violins added to the bustle and gaiety. As they approached, the fiddlers struck up the 'Can Can'. Jon grabbed the girls' hands and swung them into the road facing the oncoming traffic currently held up at the traffic lights. "Come on Liberty, you can do the Can Can with those long legs, come on, higher. Gemma, get cracking girl. This is Swinging London remember; you're not in rural Hampshire now."

As well as dancing, Jon started singing, if lah-lahing can be called singing, and Gemma and Liberty flung their legs in the air in time to the rhythm of the Can Can, almost falling over and laughing. The traffic lights changed to green. A red double decker bus pulled up in front of them and the driver started clapping his hands to the beat. Despite the cold night air, passengers hung off the platform at the back and clapped and swayed. When the fiddlers stopped, Jon, still holding the girls' hands bowed low, and Gemma and Liberty curtsied. Then, raising his right hand to the sky, Jon took another bow and finally clapped the clappers before dragging the girls to the safety of the pavement and flinging some coins into the fiddlers' upturned hat.

"Look, I see it!" he declared seconds later.

"What?" said Gemma, puffing after her unaccustomed exertion.

"The famous 'Cage Club'. Down that side road."

"'*Cage* Club'? Oh no, not another hole like the last one. No, I don't want to go."

"Listen to your big brother, you've arrived in the centre of the universe and all you've done is rent a grotty flat, rotten, literally. It's time to live, sis, live. When do you start work?"

"Next week."

"Then you have a few days to play in the playground. Come on, in to the Cage we go."

Jon paid with a small, plastic card and Gemma appeared worried. "What's that?"

"A Barclaycard. You should get one. No need to carry so much cash. Everyone will have one soon."

Gemma shook her head. Liberty, on the other hand, recalled the strange plastic card she'd found in the zipped pocket of her handbag. She'd examine it closely later; nothing should slow this exciting excursion to the sights and sounds of a world she'd never known existed. Or had she?

The 'Cage Club' was markedly different from 'The Market'. Hanging from the ceiling were huge bird cages. Inside each, a fashionably clad girl danced to the music. Tom Jones belted out 'Delilah' and Jon turned to Gemma and said, "See, straight from the Bible, what more could you ask?"

Gemma whispered to Libby, "It's impossible not to like him, though I sometimes want to wring his neck."

Meanwhile, Jon was creatively describing various people's dancing. "Pink flamingo struck by lightning," he said of a jerking, skinny legged fellow in a billowing pink shirt and red trousers. "And look at those two, flapping like fat pigeons taking off in flight."

The disc jockey announced, "And now for all you love-birds, this is Louis Armstrong riding high in the charts with 'What a Wonderful World'. Okay you cool guys, grab a groovy girl and give her a moment to remember."

Jon didn't grab Liberty, he asked her so politely she hadn't the heart to decline. A moment to remember? How could anyone forget such a bouncing, cuddly, semi-house-trained big puppy?

Chapter Eleven
Pink nylon sheets

"He says he knows me, Gemma, and he has a photo of me." Liberty had intended only to say goodbye before setting off to go to work but the man in the hospital grounds had surfaced in her worried mind again.

"So why didn't you find out more?"

"Because he looked too good to be true." And hadn't the professor just warned her?

"Too good to be true?" echoed Gemma who appeared to think Liberty was missing a great opportunity. "You must find out more. As I'm not working yet, shall I meet you for lunch and we can see if he turns up?"

"Would you? Oh that would be wonderful."

"What time would you like me to come?"

"One o'clock? By the hospital gates?"

"I'll bring sandwiches and an umbrella, just in case, and maybe we'll see him if we sit on the same bench." Gemma paused. "And don't forget, Jon is taking us to see 'Oliver' tonight."

Liberty hadn't forgotten; she might have forgotten who she was but she wouldn't forget a trip to the theatre with Jon. "I might be a little later home, will it be a problem?"

"He's picking us up at seven. I'll have something ready to eat at six thirty. Okay?"

Liberty thought hard. "I can just about do that. Rats! I nearly forgot. The woman downstairs told me on Tuesday night that someone had been in our flat again."

"Oh no." Gemma frowned in concentration. "But there was no sign of anything being taken."

"I didn't notice anything missing either. I'm wondering if it's the man with my photo. I'm afraid he might be a stalker."

"A what?"

"You know, one of those people who follows you around all the time with ill intent." Liberty made her best vampire face and turned her hands into claws.

Gemma laughed. "Do you believe her?"

"Oh," said Liberty, "it hadn't occurred to me she might not be all there." She tapped her forehead. Worry crept over her face. Miss Liberty Taffet was not 'all there'. Much was unquestionably missing. "I must go, I don't want to be late."

She managed to find a seat on the bus and pushed her worries away. Today would be a good day. And, once seated in her warm office, with nothing very much to do, she took a look at the ring she had slipped into her handbag. A sapphire and diamond ring should provide enough to buy something nice to wear tonight, something for work and there might even be enough left over for another sheet, one would be enough to start with. Each week she'd put the top sheet on the bottom and the clean sheet on the top. Did people do that? Well, she would. Needs must. Her thoughts drifted to Jon and wondered where he lived and whether he had a girlfriend.

At one o'clock precisely, Liberty met Gemma at the gates and they both wandered over to the bench where Liberty first saw the man with her photo.

Gemma offered her flatmate a cheese sandwich. "One day I'm going to be able to afford pickle too," she mused.

"Your brother seems to have done well for himself, what does he do?"

"He tells everyone he's a manager in 'invisible exports'. This, he says, keeps people guessing as to what could be exported invisibly."

"Well, it makes me wonder what he's up to, that's for sure."

"Oh, he's straight as a die."

"Sorry, Gemma, I didn't mean... I'm sure he's..."

Gemma helped out. "He's done rather well. Within five years at the same company, he has a team of seven and he tells me he's a vital part of the economy." Gemma giggled. "Have you guessed yet?"

"No. I'll..." Liberty trailed away as she noticed the possible stalker appear from one of the buildings. He'd seen her. "Gemma, the tall man with the photo of me – don't look now, he's over there." She inclined her head to indicate the direction.

From behind the bench, a different man put his head between the two of them. "Got any spare sandwiches for me?" He then whipped round and squeezed his way on to the bench next to Liberty. "You're Liberty Taffet, aren't you?"

Stunned, Liberty turned to face the stranger and Gemma leaned forward to see him better.

"Are you from the employment agency?"

"I am not!"

Suddenly the gingery, whiskery creature, now recoiling like an imperilled squirrel, leapt up and scarpered behind some nearby trees. The two girls watched as the other man, narrowed his eyes, changed direction and followed him.

"Ooh..." said Liberty with relish. "This has livened up the day."

"You know where we've seen the ginger fellow before?" said Gemma.

"No."

"He's the man who held the umbrella over us and knew which bus we needed to catch."

"Are you sure?"

"Think so. He's about the right height. Is it possible you really do know him? And the other man?"

Liberty finished her sandwich before answering. "I suppose I ought to find out more about them. I think I've been spooked by what's happened to the secretary I've replaced."

An enquiring look from Gemma encouraged Liberty to elaborate.

"Her sister answered an advertisement for a particularly good job. Something like double the normal pay and with foreign travel thrown in. Now the sister hasn't been seen since."

"White slavery!" gasped Gemma. "I've heard it's happening a lot."

"How very worrying. Anyway, my replacement has gone to North Africa where her sister was last seen. I'm a bit worried for *her* too."

"She's probably not gone alone," Gemma said reassuringly.

"Yes, I suppose you're right." Her thoughts returned to the present situation. "But when I've only been in London for such a short time it doesn't sound possible that these two men could know me."

"Remember, I found you on the beach; perhaps you came from London?"

Liberty shrugged her shoulders, bewildered.

"Libby, I'm going to scoot off. I want to find out the best way to travel to my new job. I daren't be late on my first day. Be careful."

"I'll see you at six thirty. Bye. Thanks for the sandwich."

Liberty watched her friend go, took a quick look over her shoulder to ensure she would not be followed and then headed towards the jeweller. The twenty-five minutes left of her lunch hour might usefully be filled by selling the ring. She looked at similar rings in the window and most were priced over £100. The jeweller, curious about the ring, said it appeared to be new. Liberty had silently rehearsed saying it belonged to her mother who'd died and left it to her and now that she was orphaned, she was trying to furnish a small flat. She said it faultlessly and the jeweller seemed satisfied. She now possessed £70 to keep her going until her first pay. A horrible thought crossed her mind. Would they pay her in cash? She needed cash until she opened a bank account. Perhaps she already had a bank account?

Once she returned to her office, she decided to read the little blue book tucked in her handbag. Maybe she'd have time for the red one too. One thing was certain, these were the key to her lost memory which seemed to be getting worse.

Unfortunately, Professor Schmidt burst into her office and announced, "Come with me. I want you to take notes during a short meeting I'm having with Personnel. Can you do that?"

She was not at all sure but she nodded enthusiastically and, after stuffing her handbag in a drawer, she grabbed a notebook and pencil and followed the professor.

Professor Schmidt, delighted when an hour after the meeting she handed him a typed copy of her notes, said, "Look, I don't need you for the rest of the afternoon. Many another temporary secretary would not have been so efficient, so you go home and I'll complete your time sheet to five o'clock. Just this once, mind."

Liberty was thrilled – a whole extra hour to do some shopping. She went to the recommended C & A and bought a long-sleeved, burnt orange mini dress, a pencil slim, dark grey skirt, a warm jersey for work and an even warmer one for keeping out the cold in the unheated flat. That reminded her to get another blanket and two towels. She'd have liked to buy one for Gemma too but couldn't carry anything more.

A huge clock hanging from one of the shops chimed six. Liberty, clutching her bags, managed a trot to the bus stop just as her bus arrived.

Over one of Gemma's frugal concoctions – sardine spaghetti – the two girls swapped stories of the day's highlights and Liberty, filled with unnecessary guilt, apologized for not buying Gemma anything.

"You mustn't worry, Libby, my mum's been this afternoon. Jon telephoned her this morning and she immediately caught the train. She brought a suitcase with most of my clothes and a hot water bottle. My eiderdown took up the rest of the space."

"A hot water bottle!" gasped Liberty. "Why didn't I think of that?"

"She marched me off to the High Street where we bought the electric fire, two bars it's got, and now she knows you're a 'respectable girl' she bought you a hot water bottle too. And we have a kettle – no more boiling the water in those ancient saucepans."

"Oh wow!"

"And," continued Gemma, "I have a set of pink nylon sheets and pillow cases."

Liberty looked horrified. Nylon sheets? Nylon? She managed a smile to say "How very kind of her."

"They're so easy to wash and dry," Gemma enthused. "We'd better get ready," said Gemma clearing both plates into the sink. "I'll have to wash those up later."

Liberty, suddenly energized, leapt up and headed for the bedroom with Gemma hurrying behind declaring her mother was appalled at our "living conditions." While putting on her selected white trouser suit, she added, "And I got a lecture about not being brought up to live in a slum."

Liberty defended. "Did she realize you have hardly any money until you get paid at the end of next week?"

Gemma looked sheepish. "I did mention it." In her mother's defence, she waved two pound notes. "Dad sent me this to tide me over. He's just had to give up work; he was diagnosed with advanced cancer. And," she took a deep breath, "they were flooded out a couple of weeks ago – which is why I went to stay at Granny's. Dad wanted me out of the way." She smiled, a little shakily. "Well, that's what he said. Really they were worried about me not having found anywhere to stay in London. They kept insisting on the YWCA hostel." Gemma sighed loudly. "I'll miss him."

"The hostel would probably have been a lot warmer than this."

"Bit by bit we can make this flat as cosy as a bird's nest, we can even put something over the hole so long as no-one stands on it," said Gemma.

Both girls gave a hollow laugh and Liberty followed hers with thoughts of birds' nests being a bit chilly, uncomfortable and providing no shelter from the rain.

Many knocks on the door let them know Jon was impatient, as always, to get on with life.

"Been shopping at Biba?" Jon said, nodding approvingly at Liberty's new, orange dress. "I'll bring you a feather boa to go with it next time."

While Liberty puzzled over where Biba was, Jon shooed his sister towards the door. "There's room to put a bathroom in this hallway," he remarked casually as he scowled at the bare space.

"I wish," Liberty whispered to Gemma.

~

Leaving the Piccadilly Theatre, Liberty felt as if she'd been given the key to Heaven. "Oliver", the musical, was fantastic, she told Jon as she thanked him profusely, feeling almost overwhelmed at the sights, sounds and smells of London at night.

"Chestnuts," said Gemma, "I smell chestnuts."

Jon rubbed his hands together. "The very thing. This way." He grabbed Liberty's hand, indicated she should seize Gemma's, and pulled them along like an enthusiastic puppy straining at the leash. The dallying, departing theatre-goers were rapidly left behind, unable to compete with the puppy's eager energy whisking them towards Piccadilly Circus and the aroma of roasting chestnuts.

Perched on the base of the statue of the winged archer in Piccadilly Circus, Jon steered their eyes to a couple of men having a contretemps with a group of merry girls.

"The plan is that in fifty years' time," bellowed the swarthy looking man with the bushy, black beard, "we'll be running your country."

"Rubbish," shouted one of the girls, swaying precariously on her exceptionally high heels.

"And we'll be running all your commerce," said the smaller, oriental man with the inscrutable face.

The group of girls linked arms and started singing "Cool Britannia, Britannia rules the waves," and collapsed giggling when they tried but failed to remember the rest of the verse.

Jon roared laughing. "Ignore those fellows, there's too few of these agitators to worry about." Munching the last chestnut, he offered another thought. "Of course, they could be the cuckoo in our nest." He pulled his shoulders back and said, "However, I think it's the Russians we need to keep an eye on." He took a deep breath. "Enough of this – we're supposed to welcome strangers and we shall." He chuckled. "It's even my job to do just that!" Appearing to have buried his qualms, he said hastily, "I must fetch the car. Pick you up outside Fortnum and Mason."

Waiting outside what Gemma called "The Queen's Grocer", she asked Liberty if she agreed with the two men.

Liberty had been mulling over that very question. "Something tells me they're not far wrong. The bearded one..." She tailed off, a puzzled frown fleetingly crossing her face. She resumed with gusto. "The Chinese people are entrepreneurial, committed to succeeding and they work very hard, we could learn a lot from them." Catching Gemma's astonished stare, she added, "I must have read that somewhere, no seen..." she stalled. "I'm not sure but then I'm not sure of anything anymore."

Chapter Twelve
The chattering surrendered

Professor Hans Schmidt put his head around Liberty's office door. "Pop into my office will you, please?"

Had she done something wrong? She straightened her new grey skirt and stylish jumper, and relief flooded through her – at least she looked smart. She walked in, looking confident.

"Next week I have to attend a conference in Swansea. Only for the first three days so I can't justify paying you for the full week. I don't want to lose you though and I'd like you to return. Will you be able to return on Thursday?"

Reassured she wasn't about to lose her source of income totally, she smiled and said it was fine.

"I do, however, have a task which will keep you busy today. You see the stack of folders by the window?"

Liberty nodded and walked towards them.

"All thirty-two of them are applications for the position of Registrar." He raised an eyebrow quizzically and, meeting no response from Liberty, he explained about the six months rotational junior doctor's position. "I'm looking for someone sociable who will fit in with the department and perhaps have additional useful skills. They'll all be intelligent so I need you to sort through and recommend six for interviews beginning on Thursday morning. Assess their interests. And will they fit in with the rest of us? When you've made your selection, take all the files to Dr Fox and she'll handle it from there." He sauntered over to the pile and picked it up. "It's heavy, shall I carry it through to your office?"

"Um..." Did he really expect her to choose the next doctor? "Yes please, that will be helpful."

Professor Schmidt dumped the pile on her desk. "If you need any help, speak to Dr Fox or Personnel. I'm giving lectures until late afternoon, then I'm afraid I have an important appointment." He smiled and cleared his throat theatrically. "I'm the umpire for the inter-hospital cricket match. Bart's is playing King's College Hospital." He grinned. "We shall be playing the winner. We're in need of a couple of extra players really." He pursed his lips. "A good spin bowler would help." He raised his eyebrows, allowing her time to comment but she couldn't find anything sensible to say. "Any questions before I go?"

Liberty was sure she'd find some the moment he'd left the office but for now, she had none. "Thank you, no. I'll get on with this immediately," she said, glancing at the clock on the wall as Professor Schmidt disappeared into his office.

She rubbed her hands together, then gingerly picked up her first file. "My giddy aunt." She chuckled, she'd picked that phrase up from Gemma. This first file was a likely candidate. Nine 'O' levels – were they the same as GCSEs? Where did she get the name GCSE from? What did it stand for? She ignored her doubts and carried on. All the 'O' levels were grade A. He also had four 'A' levels, all grade A too. Hobbies: painting, reading, rugby. What a strange combination. Clearly well qualified, she put his file in her 'approved' pile.

The next file also impressed her. This candidate boasted fourteen 'O' levels and seven 'A' levels. All grade A. Worrying. Did he do anything other than study?

All of the first fifteen files now lay in the approved pile. This was ridiculous; she'd never come across such well-qualified applicants. She frowned. Of course she hadn't, she'd never worked in a hospital before. Or had she? She must concentrate or she'd not get through the pile. She picked up the fifteen approved files and whittled them down to one by looking at their hobbies and other interests as well as their qualifications and work history. She must not be swayed by their photographs, well, not a lot. She ought to choose some female candidates; outnumbered, if they were as good as the men, they deserved a chance.

By mid afternoon, she had chosen six suitable contenders. The one on top of the pile was her first choice. A note from Personnel, attached to the file, indicated huffily that he'd been very late in applying and he hadn't included a photograph. However, Liberty saw he was not only well qualified, but also a spin bowler for a cricket club. Yet being late in applying and not following the rules might go against him. She moved his file down to the fourth choice. She commandeered a trolley, loaded it up and took all the files to Dr Fox who thanked her for sparing her from having to wade through thirty-two applications.

~

Friday night was quiet for the two flatmates.
"Jon's got to work this weekend," Gemma said with a sigh. She busied herself with cooking another of her frugal concoctions: cottage pie – mostly vegetables with a few ounces of minced beef and a lot of potato topping. "I'm sorry," she said, "I thought I'd better save some mince for tomorrow."

Liberty frowned. Her purse contained at least enough money to pay for several weeks' food but she didn't want to seem rich when Gemma was struggling. Her guilt was assuaged by the thought that she would insist on paying for the next load of shopping saying it was because Gemma's brother had given them a television. Another expense entered her mind. "Do we have to pay to go to the public bath place?"

"I think so," replied Gemma. "It won't be much though. Shall we go tomorrow? Saturday... hmm... I hope it won't be too busy."

"Yes, let's be brave. What's it like?"

"I've never been, but as far as I understand, you are shown to a cubicle with a toilet and a proper bath. Some call it a wash house."

"Is there a shower? I usually wash my hair in the shower." It tripped off her tongue easily and she knew what a shower was, so she must have had one. But where? Memory was a strange thing.

"I doubt it. Maybe. We'll have to see. There'll be a hand basin, I expect."

Unbidden, a quotation from Cicero gently floated through Liberty's weary thoughts. "Cannot people realize how large an income is thrift?" How very true. Being thrifty had brought them through the first difficult week. Well... that and her mother's ill-gotten jewellery, and Jon and his treats and Gemma's father's sacrifice of his own meagre resources. What did people do who didn't have those assets? And who the heck was Cicero?

~

Early on Sunday morning, Liberty learned something about Gemma she'd never suspected.

Lazing in her finally warm bed, still topped with her coat, she was not keen to face the icy cold flat. Gemma, however, was getting dressed in some sort of uniform. Black nylon stockings, slimline navy blue skirt, and good grief, what was that black bonnet thing on her bed? Was she really intending to wear it?

Gemma smiled. "You look puzzled. You can come too, if you like."

"Where?"

"The Salvation Army. The Sunday morning meeting starts at eleven o'clock. There's time for us to have breakfast and it's within walking distance if you fancy coming."

Stone the crows, you must be joking. However, Liberty propped herself up on one elbow and asked, "What do you do at these meetings?"

Gemma laughed. "The Salvation Army is a church, just like any other mainstream church. The services start with a song, a hymn that is, then there might be a prayer and we have a choir. Why don't you come along and see?"

Liberty managed not to say what she thought and slumped back in bed.

"I haven't been to one in London before, so I don't know anyone, I'd love you to come with me."

Liberty closed her eyes. Hymns, prayers – not quite up her street. "How long do these meetings last?"

"Only an hour or so."

A silent sigh, a moment of indecision, a pronouncement: "Okay, I'll come." Panicking, she pointed and added, "I don't have that uniform and certainly not one of those bonnets."

Gemma laughed. "You don't need one, anyone can come, it's just that I decided to nail my colours to the mast." Walking into the kitchen she called out, "Egg on toast all right for you?"

"Yes, thanks." Liberty sighed loudly this time. Why oh why did she agree to go to some crackpot church? And what did nailing her colours to the mast mean? Ah... perhaps she's happy for all to see what she believes in. Yes, of course, it would be like flying a flag from a boat. "I suppose," she mumbled under the covers, "I owe it to her." How would she have managed without her and her beliefs? And she's done all the cooking. She put her feet on the floor and began the first steps of a Sunday like no other she'd experienced before, not that she could remember.

At ten minutes to eleven, Gemma led Liberty through the double doors of a converted, disused primary school. It was warm, welcoming, and therefore worth coming. Gemma exchanged greetings with several friendly, interested people, though Liberty thought they veered towards being inquisitive. Liberty was introduced as "My friend, Libby." Nothing more and that was fine with her.

They chose a couple of seats next to a family with two children who were busy with colouring books. A brass band of at least thirty people burst into life and the chattering surrendered. A choir, introduced as 'the Songsters', followed this with a meditative piece called, 'Someone Cares.' Liberty's eyes filled with tears as the words of the first line seemed to talk to her directly.

"Do you sometimes feel that no one truly knows you?"

And the tune turned the words into a gentle whisper in her ears. She dived into her handbag for a tissue, only there weren't any. Without a word, Gemma handed her a cotton handkerchief.

The sermon was, to Liberty's great relief, short. It seemed to be about the burden of being rich and some young man not wanting to give up his money. Quite right too, who would? The only thing Liberty approved of was that it was taken from Matthew chapter 19. She liked the name. If she had a son, she'd call him Matthew.

At the end of the meeting, a middle-aged Indian woman in a Salvation Army uniform, complete with black straw bonnet and its big bow, asked if they'd like to come for Sunday lunch.

The girls exchanged glances and knew the right thing to do, obviously, was to accept.

~

Gemma's watch said ten o'clock when they returned to their cold flat, tired but happy after a roast beef lunch, spotted dick pudding and custard, a walk in the park, and for afternoon tea – cheese and cucumber sandwiches and a Victoria sponge cake. There'd also been another meeting at six o'clock and the evening finished with the 'Youth Group' gathering in someone's big house with more cakes and cordial. Liberty couldn't help but think that she and Gemma were finally very well fed, if only for a day.

"It was so kind of Paul to run us home. I think he likes you, Gemma."

Gemma laughed, "I thought he liked you! But yes, it was good to get a lift home."

"Nice car."

"Yes, green's my favourite colour and the Cortina has room for his double bass and guitar."

Liberty thought a nod was in order. Paul, the son of the Indian lady, was one of the bandsmen, and he had been particularly friendly. "I don't think I've met such hospitable people, apart from you, of course, but you're one of *them*."

"Yes, and very pleased to be so. It doesn't matter where you go in the world, you'll always get a welcome. Or so I'm told." She laughed and went into the kitchen and put the kettle on. "Hot water bottle and bed for me. Tomorrow, do you mind if I have first use of the kitchen sink? I'll need to leave by eight o'clock to be sure of getting to work on time, I don't want to be late on my first day."

"Fine by me, you go ahead. I don't have to go to work until Thursday." Liberty decided that in the morning, she'd take a look at the little blue book she always carried in her handbag.

Chapter Thirteen
The line went dead

A Monday morning, not required at the hospital and nothing much to do. Liberty sat at the rickety kitchen table sipping her tea as she pondered all that had happened since she'd arrived on the beach at Bradstow. Thank goodness Gemma happened to speak to her. "Happened," she said aloud. It felt more like fate. Without Gemma and her wonderful grandmother, she'd have had nowhere to sleep on a bitterly cold March night. If Gemma hadn't been so slow in looking for accommodation, she would never have met her. "Accommodation? Huh!" It was a start, a poor start though. Such a relief to find saleable jewellery in her handbag – why was that? Without it, she'd have starved. "Handbag!" She dashed into the bedroom and rummaged through the bag. She pulled out the two notebooks and threw them on the bed. She'd look at those later. She still retained a pair of diamond earrings to sell and a sapphire and diamond brooch. They would help to furnish this hell-hole and that would make life in here so very much better. What a time she'd had. Fancy doing the Can Can in one of the most famous streets in the world and bringing the traffic to a halt! Jonathan was fantastic. Life was fantastic. To be in Swinging London was even more fantastic.

    She made another cup of tea, took it into the freezing living room, switched on the two bar electric fire, curled up on the old, faux leather sofa, and took a look at the blue notebook. The electric fire promptly faded. "Rats!" She rushed back to the bedroom and searched for shillings in her purse – none. She looked at the electricity meter to see if it took anything other than shillings. It didn't. What a stupid system. She would finish her tea and then go shopping and get some shillings. She flicked through the blue book and noticed a heading in capital letters 'HOW TO RETURN'. Her eyes widened as she read the instructions in her own handwriting. Of course – this would bring back her memory, this was the rescue package. She abandoned her tea, scribbled a note to Gemma, hid the jewels in a paper bag under her mattress, stuffed the keys labelled 'office, keep with you at all times' in her backpack and set off for the train to Bradstow, leaving the smoggy air of London behind.

~

Liberty stood on the rocky beach at the entrance to a familiar cave and consulted the blue book. At the light curtain, whatever that was, she must reverse the hand she used to guide her through. Reverse? Ah, she vaguely recalled coming out of the cave with her left hand touching the side. That would be correct, because she always carried her handbag in her right hand. She switched it over. She trailed her right hand along the white chalk wall, scrambled over some rocks, presumably designed to keep people out, turned a corner and there it was – the light curtain. A sheen of rainbow colours, shimmering, drawing her towards it. Was it safe? She used its light to consult her blue book. Yes, this is right. These were notes she'd made for herself after reading the red notebook. She checked her notes and wished she'd explained things better. She became aware of the sound of absolute silence. Could there be such a thing? She ought to be able to hear herself breathe. Unable to take more than shallow breaths, she heard nothing. Had she gone deaf? She took stock for a moment; it was, she declared, "An ominous silence." What relief: she could hear herself. The moment of control soon died, replaced by panic, which led to trembling. Her hand shook as she fed it into the hungry light. She stepped forward, compelled to be swallowed. It glowed as if all the light of the years travelling from a distant star was condensed into this quavering mass of radiance. Squinting, she shielded her eyes and pushed on until her hand disappeared out of the light and then her foot and finally her whole body broke through to the other side. All her memories flooded back and the cavernous silence was broken by a rat scarpering.

In one of the zip-up compartments in her backpack there'd be a small, wind-up torch. Located, it helped her find her way to the entrance to the caves. She hastened towards her way out and was overwhelmingly relieved to see the emergency exit doors would open when she lifted the bar. She hesitated. Suppose there were people on the other side? What could she say? She concocted a story about doing a safety check and, feeling highly apprehensive, she lifted the bar and slid into 2020, just remembering to jam the door ever so slightly ajar. She wanted to shout 'hurrah' because her memory had most definitely returned.

There was not a soul to be seen. Not a car on the road, nothing. Sheer terror flooded through her: something had gone wrong. Falteringly, she approached the road. "Oh," she whispered, "everyone is dead." She clutched her handbag and sat down on a wall. Perhaps she should turn round and go straight back? No. She was determined to get to her office and bring back what she needed for her new life in 1968. Yet how would she get to her office, fifty miles away? "Stupid, stupid," she announced. She'd left her car keys in 1968, stashed away in the wardrobe. Deciding to walk as far as Merrygate railway station to see if somebody somewhere was alive, she set off, singing at the top of her voice. "I see trees of green, red roses too." No, 'What a Wonderful World' was not appropriate even if the gardens she passed were full of colourful flowers. She surreptitiously glanced in some windows but saw nothing; then she worried that if she did see something, it might be a dead body. Could all this have happened in the short time she'd been away? Was this the end of the world? Rubbish! Memories of Nick explaining about something called 'Covid' flooded through her relieved brain. The priority was to get to her office and she could find out more then.

Mistake in Time

The clock in the station said two forty-five and, with huge relief, she saw a woman behind the ticket counter, reading. She found some 2020 currency in one of the pockets of her backpack and, gaining confidence, she approached, asked when the next train to London would be coming and waited for an answer which never came. She coughed loudly and tried again. "Excuse me, when is the next train to London due?" Was the woman deaf? Is this something to do with that virus? Is this how it affected people?

Liberty was saved from making a song and dance about it by hearing the sizzle of the train tracks. Panicking she rushed onto the platform and watched it arrive. The overhead information said it was for London, Victoria, the very train she needed.

The carriages were almost empty and few people boarded at stations along the line. Nobody spoke. Unnerving was the word which kept coming to mind. At Bromley South, she alighted and crossed to the platform for the Middleston train, travelling without paying. Brilliant!

In just over an hour, she was walking along the deserted streets of Middleston towards her office and, thanking her lucky stars, she slumped in her swivel chair. This was her real life, even though she had not yet found a house to buy. Her office was so much more comfortable and warmer than Gemma's flat. This reminded her that Gemma would return to find the electric meter needed feeding with shillings. Poor Gemma. "Hope she's got some," she whispered. Then she felt guilty about wasting money here in her office. She shouldn't have left the heating on. She took a deep breath and muttered, "Can't get everything right," followed by the excuse that she hadn't intended to be away very long. Much more important was the thought of everything she could look forward to. The 1960s were great, and Gemma's brother was great fun, the type of man she'd like to see a whole lot more of. Very different from Nick though. Oh Nick, I fell in love with you, but you belong to someone else. She sighed and conjured up his image in her mind. Those dark, Italian locks, those eyes that narrowed when he clocked someone. "It hurts; hurts more than I ever knew love could." She indulged in exquisite pain a little longer, remembering when he first noticed her. He'd eyed her up and down in an instant and yet, his eyes being narrowed slightly, it was difficult to read his thoughts. She must stop thinking of the man fate denied her.

She wrenched her thoughts away to focus on opening the blinds and spending a few moments planning her future life. Here, in 2020, she had money; she'd be able to choose a stunning flat overlooking the river or even a small house. She had a job she enjoyed which just about paid the bills with a little left over. She'd expand, open offices in other parts of the country, and if she couldn't have Nick, she'd wait for the right man to come along. She'd find him. She'd return to 1968, help Gemma find a new flatmate, leave her some money and explain. She'd be able to return any time she liked and enjoy Swinging London for a weekend. Seeping into her mind was a fact which could not be ignored here and now: where are all the people? The pandemic!

She opened her laptop, found the latest news from the BBC, and gasped. No wonder the streets were deserted. The whole country was in something called 'lockdown'. She read on and found that she had been disobeying the rules. Since when had there been rules to say you mustn't leave your home except for essential food shopping and a bit of exercise? What was this country coming to? This wasn't the middle ages with their raging plagues. Maybe she should go back to 1968 until the government sorted things out. It needed a lot of thought. "But," she announced, "I can go backwards and forwards when I like." She smiled: her equilibrium was restored.

She could not ignore the flashing of the landline answerphone any longer. The agency had been neglected while she had enjoyed the challenges and great social life of the 1960s. Recalling dancing the Can Can in Oxford Street refreshed her and she pressed the answerphone. The first message was from Nick, left before she'd departed on her adventure to the caves. Why hadn't she seen it then? Ah, she'd gone to bed very early for a change and not bothered to check the phone the following morning – her focus was on the adventure ahead. Rather than his usual nonchalant, dreamy, deep voice, a stern tone greeted her.

"Libby, it's Nick. If you are planning to go to the caves again, don't go." Liberty thought she might play this several times once he'd finished. "Remember you told me about the red book which you thought might have been written by Laura Redfern? You were right, it was. I contacted her husband, Matthew Redfern, you know, the psychologist in Harley Street and told him how you'd found Laura's notes and that we'd taken a tour of the caves." Liberty's heart thumped. "Whatever you do, and this is the most important message you will ever have in your life, *do not go into the caves*." Oh, he is so masterful. She'd never heard him like this. "I'll be on your doorstep at eight tomorrow morning. Sleep well, there's nothing to worry about so long as you don't go into the caves." Why on earth had he been so worried?

Liberty was overcome with the remembrance of his smile. She hugged herself, he cared, he really cared. What a good doctor he makes. She realized then that she had left before eight o'clock and he'd missed her. She listened again, twice.

On locating her mobile, she played her messages. "Libby, I'm chasing you down the M2. If you get this message, pull over onto the hard shoulder."

Gosh, he's all fired up about the caves.

The third message was even more demanding. "You're driving way too fast and I'm flashing my headlights. Pull over, stop, do not go into the caves."

A fourth message: "Libby, I know you've sneaked into the caves and I'm right behind you. It's my voice you can hear shouting your name. Stop, do not go through a shimmering light." There was a silence except for the sound of his exhausted breathing. "Please, Libby, please answer your phone."

So that echoing voice was Nick's, not the angry cave employee. Her stomach turned over. She checked for more messages but that was the last. She reasoned there'd be no signal further into the caves.

He'd given up. And she never heard him because she'd left her mobile in her office because, why the heck would she take it to Regency times? Not that she made it to Regency times.

She'd ring him on his mobile. No answer, not even the usual invitation to leave a message.

"It's Monday, I have a whole three days here before I need to return," Liberty muttered, opening her diary. She read the quotation at the top of the page: "First day of April, when winter, having run its course, hands the baton over to spring." She smiled as she visualised her thoughts and stared at the page. "It's a Wednesday here." She scratched her head and counted the days she'd been away. "Is it ten? No. Yes. Oh who cares. However, if it's a Wednesday, it's likely he'll be at the hospital." She rang the switchboard. It was ages before they answered. This terrible mess could soon be rectified.

"Dr Nylander, please."

"Hello, hello."

Liberty raised her voice. "Dr Nylander."

"I'm sorry, I can't hear you."

"DR NYLANDER," shouted Libby.

"I cannot hear you. If you are in urgent need, please dial 999 and call for an ambulance."

The line went dead.

Chapter Fourteen
Toddling like a penguin

Early that evening, Liberty realized she could not see herself when she looked in the mirror.

The small mirror above the kitchen sink reflected the doorway to the office but not Liberty standing in front of it. Weird. Impossible. She'd try another mirror. There would be a small one in her handbag. It didn't reflect her face. She stared down at her feet: she could see herself. Creeping into her mind came the picture of the woman in the ticket office at Merrygate. She had shown no recognition of her being there at all and the woman could not hear her, neither could the telephonist who answered the phone at the hospital when she'd tried to contact Nick. Not only was she invisible to others, she was also unable to make herself heard. She was a ghost.

She hurried back to the comfort of her office chair and closed her eyes. She couldn't be a ghost – she wasn't dead. Or was she? How might she test this out? She felt hungry; ghosts don't feel hungry nor do they eat. She raided the fridge. Half a loaf of bread looked on the verge of going mouldy. She hadn't time to find out for sure and moved on to an unopened packet of Wensleydale cheese with cranberries which was still in date. She ripped it open, cut off a chunk, and ate it. "See," she said to the nearby mirror, "I am here; I am not a ghost." There were some currant buns too. She examined the packet, only just out-of-date, maybe they'd be all right if she toasted them.

Within ten minutes, she was seated at her desk again with a tray of buttered buns, the packet of cheese and a mug of black tea. The answers to her predicament surely lay in the red and blue books which she now pored over impatiently as she ate. With frayed nerves, she compared the two – had her notes in the blue book omitted an important fact?

She raced through to the end of the red book then closed her eyes; she could not bear to read again the last paragraph, but she must and she read it aloud:

"It is with great regret that I must record that one can never see into the future. After the shipwreck, when I fortuitously landed on the beach at Bradstow in 1814 and found my way to the cave, I travelled through the light curtain and into 2009. I could remember everything about my life in 1814 and before. However," Liberty noticed the emphasis, "when I returned from 2009 to my past life, I was unable to remember anything at all of my new life in the twenty-first century. Hence the need for these notes."

With her head in her hands, Liberty repeated, "...one can never see into the future." And here she sat, in what had become the future. It was perfectly clear why she could remember Gemma because her life with Gemma was in the chronological past. When she was in 1968, 2020 was the forbidden future and that's why she appeared to have lost her memory. She sat bolt upright. There was no mention of being like a ghost. She supposed it was something so awful that Laura had not needed to remind herself. "Nick! That's what Nick found out from Laura's husband and he'd tried to warn her. She immediately realized that nobody in their right mind, having conferred with Matt Redfern, would elect to become a ghost in their own time. He must be here in 2020 still. She crossed her arms on the desktop, put her head down and sobbed. Unwilling to contemplate the repercussions of her folly, Liberty climbed the stairs and fell into bed. She slept for ten hours, in the comfort blanket of darkness.

Dappled daylight penetrated her dream of floating. She stirred and felt the unwelcome scene drift away. Unable to capture it, she took a deep breath and resolved to plod through the day. She was dressed, she was hungry, she was alive. Leaving the shadowy loft, she decided to make a mug of tea and eat whatever might still be edible in the fridge. If only she'd taken some things out of the freezer last night. Smoked salmon slices, a currant loaf, and all sorts of treats were pulled out and put in the fridge to defrost. The microwave, the wonderful microwave transformed several slices of the currant loaf into a warm breakfast.

Somehow she must pull herself together. Not so long ago, she'd been a respected business woman, running her own successful company. She'd also been a manager in the National Health Service. She *must* concentrate on the present. It was obvious now – she could not return to her life in 2020. A tear rolled down her face to her chin where it stubbornly refused to fall off. Nick would not be able to see her even if she did find him. She brushed the tear away and rootled around in the desk's bottom drawer for her box of tissues.

"Where's Nick?" If only Nick were here with her. Where can he be? Perhaps she should go to the hospital to look for him. He would understand her predicament. She started a 'to do' list on her computer.

1. Send text to Nick.
2. If no response, write an explanatory note and locate Nick.
3. If can't find Nick, draw up a

There was a gaping blank. She shook off her rising panic – she could do number one on the list. She sent a text. Now all she had to do was wait.

After ten minutes she irrationally tried to smarten herself; she washed, oh how she longed for a shower or bath. She changed her clothes for trousers and put her warmest jacket on. Perhaps Laura had got it wrong; perhaps after a while, one became visible again.

Two more texts, one more mug of tea and one hour later, she gave up waiting and went to the hospital where staff were manically rushing around. She searched and listened but found no sign of Nick. She decided to impersonate a doctor by leaving a signed note at the Reception desk asking them to call Dr Nicolo Nylander over the tannoy, requesting him to report urgently to Dr Smith at Reception. One of the receptionists picked up the note and, puzzled, read it aloud to the other. They agreed it should be read over the tannoy. It was. Three times. All it produced was an irate Dr Smith declaring his signature had been forged. In Human Resources she waited for a woman to leave her desk and when she did, she sneaked over to her computer and typed frantically. This caused chaos when one of the staff noticed what she declared as "remote access" when she saw the mouse whizzing around the screen and the keyboard moving of its own accord. She called out to everyone to shut down their computers as there was a security breach. Liberty returned to her office, despondent.

Living in 2020 was unlikely to be viable. However, she had learnt something: if she could write something down, someone could read it aloud and if she had her mobile with her, she could leave a message for Nick. She charged her mobile.

She set about concocting a message. It would have to start with a reason for the person to read it aloud. Could she pretend it was part of a treasure hunt or something similar and this might be the next clue, to be read out by a stranger? "Problem," she muttered. "Nobody's around." She decided she ought to watch the one 'o clock news. "My giddy aunt," she declared as the graphs of hospital admissions and deaths were shown on screen.

Becoming more depressed, she tried to think of another idea to get someone to read out a message to Nick. "Aha! This might work."

She wrote out a message, put her jacket back on and grabbed her handbag and phone.

Now where do the homeless people hang out? Near the river. Not a soul was in sight. "Shops," she whispered, "food shops are open and there will be people."

Passing a newsagent which also sold food, she went in, placed the message in front of the man behind the counter. It only took a couple of seconds for the man to see the message.

"Anisha," the man called out. From behind a curtained doorway, a lady in a colourful sari came out and squinted at the piece of paper. "You put this here?"

"No," said the lady. "Read it out, I can't see it."

The man sighed, "You wanna wear those glasses, else how you gonna know if customers give you the right money?"

The lady sighed. "So what does it say?"

"It says if I read this out, something good will happen: I will come into money."

The lady looked ecstatic. "Money? We do need some. We got no customers now. Go on, it's kismet."

Clutching her mobile, Liberty set it to record.

The man held the paper firmly and read. "Nick, it's Libby. I am invisible, and you can't hear me. A kind person is reading this for me. I have to return to 1968. I hope you will be very happy. Thank you for what you have tried to do for me. Come to me quickly while I am still in 2020."

The Indian lady sniffed. "It's a girl speaking to her lost love, she feels he doesn't see her."

"It's a trick. 1968? 2020? It's some kind of code. Quick, you look. Is anyone in the shop, someone listening somewhere?"

"Now it's you who needs glasses, there's nobody, nobody anywhere. But you have been kind, and now karma will look after you."

"Karma? You and your kismet and karma. I keep telling you, you make your own fate – work hard that's the way."

Liberty was delighted. It had all gone to plan. She found her purse, took out a £10 note and let it flutter down onto the counter. As the invisible note left her hands, it appeared as if by magic. The man stepped away and clutched his chest with both hands. The lady picked up the £10 note and hurried through the door behind her.

"What did I tell you?" she called over her shoulder. "You never listen."

Liberty, highly amused, returned hastily to her office, immediately dialled Nick's number on her landline but there was no sound at all. She sat stock-still afterwards, rigid, almost in a trance, until her right eye let go of a tear. Something was wrong. Or was he just busy with patients? She'd ring his home landline. She had it somewhere, she'd secretly written it down – yes, in the back of her diary. She dialled, there was an answerphone message, she played the message on her mobile and now, all she could do was hope.

Floating into her mind was the echoing voice calling out her name when she was in the cave. It was Nick's voice. Maybe, just maybe, Nick followed her through into the light curtain. She sat bolt upright. "That's it!" she said, punching the air. If only she'd known it was Nick calling out, she would have waited for him, he would have stopped her and none of this would have happened. What a mess. Understatement of the year. Regardless of what he's found out, he's in 1968 with his mobile which won't be picking up any messages. It had taken her all this time to realize what had happened and why Nick wouldn't be answering his phone. She was what Nick would call a 'dunderhead'. That thought was reinforced when she realized that the man with her photo in the hospital grounds in 1968 was Nick. All she had to do was return safely and he'd be there waiting for her.

But now that she was in 2020, she decided to make the most of the opportunity to stock up with useful things for 1968. A smile crossed her face – she could come back here whenever she wanted. She grabbed a pen and ticked off number one on the 'to do' list – she had located Nick and she'd be returning to him very shortly. She crossed out number two – now she knew where to find him, it was irrelevant. She was returning to her normal, efficient self and set about finishing the 'to do' list.

4. Get 2020 currency from the NatWest ATM. Walk into shops, grab a trolley and it will become invisible. Remember not to let go of it.

5. Stock up on long-lasting food. Tins etc. Put straight into my canvas shopping bags in the supermarket trolley.

Liberty paused. She didn't want to become a thief. She detested shop-lifters, selfish lot. How could she pay? She hunted for a couple of envelopes in her top drawer and addressed both to 'The Manager'. She might not need two but better to be safe than sorry. She felt invigorated to be back to her old, efficient self.

6. Estimate cost and put cash into envelope. Leave envelope at the check-out.

She hurriedly added to each envelope: 'For the attention of the Manager, strictly private.' When the Manager found the tills were short, he'd know that the apparent shop-lifter had a conscience and had paid.
A useful idea occurred to her and she added:

7. Buy one of those shopping trolley things, with wheels.
8. Return to office, charge mobile.
9. Make a list of useful items other than food to take back to 1968 and go shopping for them.
10. Pack my new shopping trolley, the canvas bag and backpack with clothes, some jewellery, make-up and the useful items.
11. Make notes of what I might need to remember about 2020. Eat, TV, sleep.
12. Friday morning, turn off heating, etc. lock up, return to the cave with as much as I can carry.

She printed off the list.

~

Liberty followed the plan rigidly, set off from her Middleston office on the Friday and arrived back at the London flat on Wednesday 3rd

April, 1968, toddling like a penguin wearing several extra layers of clothes.

Chapter Fifteen
The fate of six people

Liberty put her key in the lock and pushed open the door. Home at last. Only it didn't look quite the same as she'd remembered. Instead of the large, square hall, a partition had been installed with a door and draped across the doorway was an aqua feather boa.

Jon leapt out from the living room. "Welcome home. We have a surprise for you." Then, seeing her stuffed penguin act, he rushed to help. "Are you so cold as to need to wear your entire wardrobe at the same time?" Before Liberty thought of anything sensible to say, he added, "You have your own personal pot-bellied stove here." He stuck out his ample midriff. "It's always warm and you may cosy up any time."

Liberty giggled. Jon lit up a room, a situation, everything, wherever he was.

He took her shopping trolley and pulled it into the kitchen. "Three months of shopping?"

Despite feeling drained, Liberty couldn't help laughing. She was about to respond when he whipped her canvas shopping bag off her. Seeing the clothes on the top, he said, "May I have permission to enter madam's boudoir?"

Liberty tipped her head with a smile. "You may; just put it on my bed, please."

Jon pretended not to know which bed was hers when Liberty followed him in.

"The one without the huge teddy bear." Where had that bear come from? It was at least four feet tall and probably had the same waist measurement.

Jon shouted, "I see mother has been visiting you again, Gemma."

Gemma put her head around the door. "Oh, Jon Bear. Yes, Dad too; so good to see him. They brought the bear and some other stuff in the car."

Liberty asked incredulously, "You've named him after your brother?"

"Of course. Don't you think they look alike?"

Jon took it in his stride. "Oh it gets worse. Mother wrote a poem about it," he pointed to the bear, "composed to console Gemma when I went off to boarding school."

"He was awarded a scholarship," chipped in Gemma.

Jon grabbed the bear, held it in front of him and, in a gruff bear voice, he began:

I was born in the woods on a foggy, foggy day
I am not sure when but it was long before May.
It was cold in the woods and I began to cry,
No home for me, nowhere for me to lie.
Then from afar, I thought I heard you say,
"I shall miss my brother on the day he goes away."
So I said to myself, what no brother?
Leave it to me it will be no bother
To walk all the way from the foggy, foggy downs
Into your arms, chase away your frowns.
When your brother's gone, you need not fret,
I will play with you, you'll be glad we met.

Jon took a bow as Liberty clapped.

Gemma limited her appreciation to a smile; there were more practical matters on her mind. "Have you eaten? I've got some spam fritters keeping warm in the oven. We were just about to eat."

Spam fritters again, oh grief, could there be anything worse? "Only if you have enough, thank you."

Still in the bedroom, Liberty peeled off her coat, a cardigan, a colourful wool jersey and a pair of trousers. "There, that's better," she said triumphantly revealing a second pair underneath and a thin jersey on top. Then she grabbed the cardigan and put it back on again,

Gemma barely concealed her amusement, whereas Jon enquired, straight-faced, about her trip to the North Pole, swiftly followed by the reminder that they had a ceremony to attend. He grabbed her hand and pulled her towards the partition in the hall.

Gemma called out, "Paul, come and watch this."

Liberty recognized Paul as the young man who had given them a lift home after that unusual yet enjoyable Sunday at The Salvation Army.

"Now, you are not allowed to cut the 'ribbon', ahem, the feather boa. It's my gift to you from Biba." Jon leaned forward and pecked her on the cheek. "You may wrap it around your neck and then open the door."

"What?" said Liberty, eyes wide as she looked inside. "How?"

Gemma explained. "Jon has friends, hundreds of them and a whole heap turned up while I was at work, slipped the lock–"

"With my Barclaycard," interjected Jon.

Gemma continued as if she'd not been interrupted, "and began installing this bathroom."

"Wow!" Gemma looked at the full-sized bath, clearly second-hand yet usable, a proper lavatory with a high cistern and chain, and a non-matching hand basin in pink.

"All plumbed in, proper-like," said Jon, imitating one of his friends.

Paul laughed, but Liberty looked worried. "What will the landlord say?"

"Libby, my love," Jon put his arm around her shoulders, "he'll probably never know. The sort who owns flats like this owns them by the hundred, and so long as you pay your rent, you'll not see him from one year to the next. And, if he does turn up, he'll think he installed it and has forgotten, or he'll just be pleased because he'll be able to rent it out for more when you leave." He grinned.

Liberty chuckled; it was hard to fault his logic. She gave him a hug. "What a wonderful big brother and friend you are."

Gemma whispered, "It's free. One of his friends is a farmer and he found all this stuff, and more, tipped over his fence."

"He was glad to get rid of it," added Jon.

Gemma shooed them all into the living room, mumbling about Jon's plumber friends breaking into her flat. At this point Liberty realized there was no light in the bathroom. A small matter that would be rectified with a supply of candles.

Liberty sat in the armchair above the hole, or so she thought.

"It's safe to sit there now," said Gemma as she brought in a plate of spam fritters. "Jon's nailed some wood over the top. We need to remember not to try and move the chair."

"Temporary fix," said Jon.

They munched their way through six fritters, Liberty and Gemma insisting that one was more than enough. Nobody had asked her where she'd been which was just as well as she had no idea, remembering only being on the beach at Bradstow and finding her way back to London, slowly but surely.

"How did your first few days at work go, Gemma?"

"Um..." she hesitated, "I suppose I could say all right. The first steps on the ladder, that's the main thing. Cutting out endless dress patterns doesn't pay too well and it's a bit boring."

Liberty shrugged her shoulders. "As you say, it's only a starting point."

"Paul's also hoping to branch out on his own, aren't you?" said Gemma turning to Paul.

"I am, I am. I'm currently sous chef in a hotel."

Liberty wondered what he thought of spam fritters but thought it best not to ask. Instead, she said, "Wow! So how will you branch out from that?"

Jon could not stay quiet for long. "Oh this guy is real cool. His ideas rate higher than groovy. Tell her, Paul."

"Happy to do so, another time perhaps? I can see Liberty is very tired and, after I've assisted Gemma with the washing up, I'll be off. Got an early start in the morning."

Thank God for observant men. "It's true, I'm whacked, and I need to unpack." If only all men were saints. Hmm… perhaps not.

"It's all this shopping and careering round the country. You must tell us all about it sometime soon," said Jon giving Liberty a cheeky smile.

~

Professor Schmidt beckoned Liberty into his office and sat at his desk.

"I trust you enjoyed your days at home?"

She smiled, he was so thoughtful. "I did a little shopping." There – that wasn't a lie. Not the whole truth though, but she didn't need to mention her trip to and from the caves and it was true that she had done some shopping somewhere, though where exactly was beyond recall. She frowned. She really must make notes of everything that happens on the other side of the light curtain.

Professor Schmidt also frowned. "Is everything all right, Liberty?"

Liberty regained her composure. "Absolutely." She sounded like Jon – his style was catching. "And I'm looking forward to helping in any way I can."

"Good, good. We have three interviews today and three tomorrow. We've gone with the six you chose. Here's their files, in order of their interviews. Now what I'd like you to do is this." He pointed to the chair on the other side of his desk. "Sit down. I don't think you'll need to take any notes," he said, catching sight of the notebook she'd brought with her. "The receptionist at the main Reception desk will telephone you when the first applicant arrives. I want you to meet each one, bring them back to your office, sit them down and get them talking and relaxing. Ask them about their journey

– as the Queen does. That sort of thing. Then," he emphasized, "I want you to jot down any notes on how they respond to *you*."

Liberty blinked, her eyebrows raised.

"I want you to ensure they'll fit in with the staff and put our patients at ease. I think you'll be able to suss out more than I can as they'll be on their best behaviour when I see them." He gave her a wink. "I'll collect them after a few minutes and you should then hand me their file with your notes inside." The telephone in her office rang. "That'll be our first applicant, I hope. Away you go."

Professor Schmidt was right and Liberty took a quick look at the top file before escorting Dr Cynnie Symonds to the chair in her office.

"Have you come far?" Liberty enquired pretending she didn't know.

"Terrible journey. Absolutely ghastly. Sat next to a frightful bore on the train, rambling on about the crossword to the man opposite and puffing away on his pipe – appalling pong."

Liberty chuckled and knew exactly what she meant. "I hate the rush hour."

"Oh rather. To be avoided at all costs."

Liberty thought it better not to ask how she planned to get to the hospital each morning. Chauffeur driven car perhaps? She scribbled a note. 'Moans a lot, though might mean she has high standards' and tucked it into the file before handing it to the Professor.

The next candidate, Dr Turtle, was equally difficult to envisage as being suited to Professor Schmidt's team. Immaculately dressed, he strode in after her and sat down without an invitation to do so in *her* office. 'Sense of entitlement,' scribbled Liberty as she sniffed the strong smell of a compulsive smoker.

"Have you come far?" enquired Liberty with a smile. She knew his current address was near the Welsh border.

"No."

Probably stayed overnight in a hotel so perhaps that's true.

Not knowing what else to talk about she resorted to the English tried and trusted standby. "Well you've chosen a nice day for an interview." Liberty waved her hand towards the window. "However, I'm told it's going to rain later."

"Yes." He didn't deign to look at her and brushed some invisible dust off his sleeve.

Perhaps he's nervous. "Professor Schmidt is very good to work for, I find."

"Really?"

That's your lot, thought Liberty. This stuffed shirt can't be bothered. 'Condescending, not a conversationalist,' she added to her note, as Dr Turtle pulled out a book and began to read it.

The third candidate arrived after lunch and bounced along after her into the office. An optimist, thought Liberty, a useful quality. "Have you come far?" She was finding it interesting to see how differently that question could be answered.

"Not at all. I live in Westminster, across the river, which means I'm unlikely to be late."

Punctual. Liberty frowned. He'd need to offer more than that. It was the bow tie that concerned her. Quite a few of the *Consultants* wore bow ties, she'd noticed, but not the junior doctors. Nevertheless, she soldiered on with the conversation. "Do I detect a Glasgow accent?" She shouldn't have asked: it just slipped out.

"Most certainly not." The accent grew stronger. "I'm Edinburgh born and bred, so don't confuse me with..." he tailed off, drew in a deep breath and crossed his legs.

Liberty smiled. "I'm sorry, I'm not very good at recognizing accents. I often mistake the Scottish for the Irish and vice versa."

"You'll *no* be popular for that."

The accent appeared stronger; she must defuse the situation. "I expect you know that an Edinburgh accent is considered one of the most attractive in the world."

"Aye, I do." Then in a perfect English accent, he asked, "Does the Professor play golf?"

"I'm not at all sure. I'm sure he loves..." she stopped, she would not give away his love of cricket, not to this chameleon, "most sports."

She was greatly relieved when Professor Schmidt knocked on the door, introduced himself and shepherded the prickly Scot into his office.

'Chameleon' she wrote, slipping the note into the file.

Over an hour later, the Professor emerged, having shown the chameleon out through his other office door.

"So, Miss Liberty Taffet, what's the verdict so far? Not too impressed?"

"Obviously they're all highly qualified but perhaps not 'patient friendly' in one way or another."

"I want you to pay particular attention to tomorrow's first interviewee. Take a thorough look at the file and grill him before I see him." He looked at his watch. "It's nearly five o'clock, so you may as well slip away after you've tidied up here. Lock the files away, won't you."

"Yes indeed I will. Thank you."

Liberty sat at her desk to glance at the top file. Nine a.m. tomorrow. The one without a photo. She logged in her brain the thought that he was somewhat unprepared. Mustn't judge before I have all the facts, maybe he has good reason, and his CV is impeccable. She'd leave scrutinizing it until tomorrow. If she dashed out immediately, she'd be able to catch the earlier train. She scooped up the files and locked them in her desk drawer. The fate of six people would be decided tomorrow.

Chapter Sixteen
Hungry for more

"Good morning, Dr Nylander. I'm Professor Schmidt's secretary. Follow me please."

Liberty, having steeled herself, led the smartly dressed prospective new doctor up to her office and gestured towards the chair. "Professor Schmidt will see you soon."

Liberty felt prickles all down her spine – this was the guy in the hospital grounds who'd shown her a photograph of herself. Had he been trying to ingratiate himself before this interview? If so, he was going about it the wrong way. Yet, when she arrived to collect him from Reception, he had given no indication that he had spoken to her before. She would not treat him any differently from the other candidates until she knew more about him.

"Have you come far?" She decided a mini smile would be in order at this point. She gestured towards the chair opposite hers.

"From Dulwich, not far at all."

Dulwich? She didn't know London well yet she knew it wasn't far from her flat. She ought to ask questions relevant to his application so said, "Why are you applying for this vacancy?"

"Ultimately, I intend to become an orthopaedic surgeon. I think a six month rotational appointment in radiology would be extremely useful to learn about diagnosis."

She became aware of his dark, wide eyes, and of a tingling deep within, almost as if her very bones were responding to his dreamy, soft voice, calling her to remember, remember. Was this man from her forgotten past? She really must consult that little blue book more. She blinked several times to restore herself to the real world, the world of this delectable male seated and waiting for her to say something. But what?

He came to her rescue. "Have you worked here long?"

An easy question, but why did he want to know? "No, I'm here temporarily until the permanent secretary returns." She was the one supposed to be asking the questions.

"Do you live locally?" If her train hadn't been late, she'd have studied his file better.

With a completely straight face, he repeated what he'd told her earlier. "Yes, Dulwich is quite close. I live in the part they call Dulwich Village. I like it there; you'd hardly know it's in London."

"How long have you lived there?" Damn, damn, damn. These were not the sort of questions she should be asking.

"Long enough to find they have a cricket team in need of a spin bowler, so I have volunteered my services."

Ah yes, she had noticed this in his file, if little else, and it might recommend him to the professor. Her thoughts were captured by his devastating smile, but at last the professional side of her won – cricket was something she should emphasize to the professor. She scribbled a note and slipped it inside Dr Nylander's file. He would be pleased. Silence filled the room with expectation of further so-called conversation. She thought about asking him where he studied – but it would be in his file. Why oh why did her train have to be late this morning? Ah, she could ask about where he grew up. No, that was too intrusive. Her head drooped as she pretended to be distracted by something in her drawer. Then she hit upon a possibly relevant question. "What interests do you have other than medicine?" Oh drat, now it sounded as if she were trying to interview him. This was all going wrong.

"I love history and the way it has shaped how we are today." He talked of Georgian and Victorian influences and expressed approval of Charles Dickens' work in revealing the plight of the poor. "And Shakespeare, I love Shakespeare – so incisive, and ahead of his time."

Liberty listened intently, hungry for more yet she breathed a sigh of relief when Professor Schmidt took him away. It was definitely the man who showed her a photograph of herself and this was creepy. Perhaps she should make a note of this for the professor? She wrote, 'I can't pinpoint it but something is not right about this eminently suitable candidate.' That was a fair comment and she'd hand it to him after the interview hoping it would be ignored.

After Dr Nylander left, her boss came into her office and did a little dance.

Liberty laughed. "Was it the spin bowling?"

"No, no, no," he said as he punched the air. "How could you suspect such a thing?"

Liberty laughed.

"Merely the icing on the cake. However," he returned to his serious demeanour, "we have two more excellent applicants to see today." He handed her Dr Nylander's file. "He was impressed with what he'd seen of my department – as you are all he's seen, I must conclude that he approves of the secretary I have appointed. Which reminds me, if my permanent one is unable to return soon, would you consider staying on for some considerable time? Her mother has contacted me and they've had some difficult news."

Liberty felt her heart pounding. A reliable income with the possibility of seeing... no, she mustn't jump the gun. "I'd be pleased to. Thank you."

The telephone rang. The penultimate applicant awaited. She did not deliver the warning note.

~

Gemma and Paul were at the ten pin bowling alley. Liberty didn't mind at all being alone in the flat. She would wash her hair, have a long bath, and mull over the interviewing of Dr Nylander. Dr *Nicolo* Nylander.

As the bath water could only be described as lukewarm, she abandoned the planned half-hour soak-and-dream in the romantic light of the fat candle she'd bought on her way home. Wrapped in a towel, she tipped out the remaining contents of the canvas bag onto the bed. "Pyjamas. Hurrah!" It was far too cold to wander around in just cotton nightwear, so she popped a jersey on over the top and slipped her feet into the sheepskin slippers. Bliss. She retrieved the half-empty shopping trolley from the kitchen and tipped that out too. She should have done this yesterday instead of watching the TV. She forgave herself because it had been a very tiring day. A mini hairdryer was a great find, so she attended first to the cold, wet hair hanging around her neck. She wondered if she could keep the hairdryer on to warm the bedroom up a bit. "Good idea," she said, then decided a better idea would be to get something to eat.

Liberty reached up to the shelf where she'd crammed a load of tinned foods and put one in the Joseph Store. No wonder the shopping trolley was heavy. She didn't remember ever having a shopping trolley before. I must read the notebooks, all the answers are in there and, with a bit of luck, the answer to where this Nicolo Nylander had found her photo would be there too.

She emptied a can of something called 'Big Soup' into a saucepan and while it slowly warmed, she found several packs of 'Aunty's Chocolate Sponge Puddings'. She wrenched one little pot from the cardboard and read the instructions: microwave for 30 seconds or steam for 25 minutes. Liberty frowned. "We haven't got a microwave, whatever that is, and I can't wait 25 minutes." A tin of creamed rice, warmed in the other saucepan, would do instead.

No longer hungry, she made a mug of tea.

The kitchen remained cold, oh so very cold, even with the fleeting warmth of the stove. Might as well go straight to bed but first the pile of belongings on her bed needed to be sorted.

What were these coins? A little plastic bag full of coins was labelled 'ten pence coins'. She rushed to see if they would fit in the electric meter. She saw a one shilling coin left on top of the meter and measured them against the ten pence ones. The shilling coins were marginally smaller. Nevertheless, she'd try these coins. Jon said some landlords fiddled the tenants by setting the amount of electricity lower than they were entitled to, therefore she rammed the slightly bigger ten pence coins into the slot and felt no guilt. She fed the meter with twenty of them and hoped it would be many months before anyone found them and then she could plead guilty and replace them with shillings.

Next, she noticed two strange plastic things which appeared to be some kind of plug to go into electric sockets. She tried one in the socket near her bed and purred with gratitude for the warmth radiating from the little gadget. And she had two. She'd put one near Gemma's bed. No socket. She dashed into the living room and found a spare socket. Together with the two-bar electric fire, the room might eventually become warm enough to watch the TV without blankets from their beds.

Gemma and Paul clumped up the bare wooden stairs and called out, "Hello."

Liberty didn't fancy being seen in her pyjamas so she rushed into the bedroom and left the door ajar.

"I'm in the bedroom, I'm having an early night. Hope you had a good time."

Gemma peeped in. "We did. Do you mind if we invite Paul and Jon for dinner on Saturday evening?"

"That's fine, you go ahead."

Gemma disappeared sporting a smile, seemingly oblivious to the pile of things on Liberty's bed.

Liberty found it difficult to know where to put everything. The four coathangers already in the wardrobe were insufficient and the drawer at the bottom was becoming full. She found a pack of Post-it notes and scribbled down 'shopping list – coathangers x 6'. Maybe get an extra couple for Gemma.

At the very bottom of the pile on her bed, she found a book. A book, a wonderful book. She gazed around the room, there was nowhere to put such a thing. She folded up the canvas bag and the backpack, stuffed them into the shopping trolley and put it under her bed. Time to settle down with the book. Oh drat! She'd forgotten to put the kettle on for her hot water bottle; she couldn't let Paul see her like this. She looked at the book: 'Where There's a Will'. She turned it over and read 'A bold, daylight kidnapping shocks Branton and leaves Nathan Stone with a tough case'. She'd go without the hot water bottle and curl up with the book. A real treat. She felt as if her own life had become like a suspense thriller – though she could do without a kidnapping.

Gemma came in, handed a hot water bottle to Liberty and, without a word, went out again.

Chapter Seventeen
Food for thought

The bouncing puppy, otherwise known as Gemma's brother, arrived for dinner a few minutes after eight, clutching a big bunch of daffodils, two bottles of sparkling drink and a radio. He held his cheek out for a kiss from Liberty, and who could refuse?

"We haven't got any vases, Jon," said Gemma with a sigh.

"That's why I brought daffodils: they're easy to snip down to size for any container you do have."

"The tin cans," said Liberty to Gemma, "we can use those." She dashed into the kitchen and retrieved two from the rubbish bin, washed them and plonked them on the draining board. "And when we open the tin of garden peas, there'll be a third." With a broad smile, she took the flowers from his arms while Gemma kissed him with thanks for the radio too.

Gemma led the way. "Paul's already here, come through."

Paul leapt to his feet to shake hands with Jon, and Gemma began handing around tiny home-made pancakes with added chopped apple and raisins.

"Blini," announced Jon, "suitable for dolls' houses."

Gemma hit him playfully and left the plate near Paul who promptly took another one. "Delicious."

"Crawler," said Jon.

Paul laughed. "Being a *sous*-chef, I've had plenty of practice. But I genuinely think Gemma's been very inventive and they've turned out well."

The kitchen table had been brought into the living room with the two chairs and Paul had provided two fold-up canvas garden chairs.

White plates contrasted well with the deep red paper napkins Gemma had used, in the absence of a table cloth, to cover the table. A bottle of sparkling white grape juice stood to one side of the lit candle originally bought for the bathroom. Surely there'd be some wine, what was a dinner party without wine?

Liberty returned to the kitchen to attend to the flowers. She was suddenly overcome with a memory: tables set with candles, flowers, sparkling drinking glasses and pristine white tablecloths. There was a man. Where had she seen this? A restaurant somewhere, but where? A memory from her past – it had to be. Was she recovering?

She took the arranged daffodils into the living room and placed them on the floor either side of the two bar electric fire. It was at least warmer due to the addition of her plug-in electric fan heaters.

Jon poured out his sparkling elderflower drink into the four small glasses, raised his own and said, "Chin-chin, you lovely people. Here's to success."

Liberty hadn't the slightest idea what 'chin-chin' meant but raised hers and, though tempted to say 'cheers', she diffidently joined with Paul and Gemma and said, "Chin-chin".

By the time they'd finished their main course of tinned creamed chicken casserole – courtesy of Liberty's trip through the cave – the conversation was becoming far too absorbing for the girls to bring in the next course.

Each told of how they saw themselves in five years' time.

Gemma, encouraged by Jon, spoke first. "Like God–"

"Well that's a conversation stopper if ever I heard one," interrupted Jon.

With a dramatic exasperated sigh, Gemma continued. "I hope to have my own shop selling clothes I have designed and made."

Paul clapped and Liberty joined in.

"So what's this got to do with God?"

"All I mean, Jon, is that God designed and created, and he inspires us to design and create too. Anything that doesn't sell, even in a sale, I'll give to one of our charity shops."

"*Our* charity shops?" Liberty queried. "You're going to set up charity shops too?"

"No," said Gemma with a smile. "The Salvation Army was a pioneer way back in the nineteenth century and now has many shops around the country."

"Think of the poor in Charles Dickens' books. That's who The Salvation Army set out to help," added Jon.

Was there no getting away from this Army? Liberty's grumpy thoughts lifted when she remembered that Dr Nicolo Nylander was a fan of Charles Dickens.

Paul nodded slowly and, grinning, he said, "That's certainly given me food for thought."

Jon couldn't resist. "Do you always have food on your mind?"

Paul laughed. "I was thinking that it's difficult to be generous if you've not got much yourself. If you are successful, you can definitely be more generous."

Gemma added, "Until then, I shall be generous with my smiles."

Nobody mentioned that Gemma was not one for flashing smiles about.

"Okay Jon, it's your turn," said Gemma with a determined look.

"Unlike my saintly sister, I currently head up a department which not only provides the right guide for every tour but also vets hotels for visiting Americans on tours around Europe. Some Americans, not having been so crushed by the war, expect higher standards than some European countries, including Britain, are able to provide. I have to manage the expectation of Americans, used to luxury, with the ability of other countries to provide acceptable standards. In five years' time, I'd like to have my own chain of travel agencies." He grinned, then looked at Liberty and across to Gemma. "I see tourism, particularly touring poor countries, as a transfer of money from the rich to the poor." He allowed a few seconds before continuing. "At the moment it is the Americans who are doing most of the travelling and every time they stay in a hotel, let's say in a London one, they bring their dollars and spend them here. When they start travelling, say to some African countries, their dollars are needed even more. We British are now beginning to travel a lot more and we are spreading a little relief to countries in greater need than we are. And, of course, the travellers get to have a great time."

Liberty's eyes widened as she looked around their poorly furnished living room. Jon noticed.

"It's true many of the British are suffering from the long-lasting effects of the war. For example, the money the country had to borrow to buy planes and tanks and so on, all needs to be paid back before we can spend enough on replacing our bombed housing stock." He clocked their nods. Liberty decided to nod too; she was learning a lot. Satisfied, he continued. "So in five years' time I should like to be part of an industry that spreads money from the richer to the poorer. I want my own chain of travel agents bringing people into Britain and sending our richer people to countries which need an injection of money to feed and house their own."

"But won't the public want to go to rich countries too?"

"Yes, that's true, Paul, and maybe they'll bring back ideas on how to do things better here."

Encouraging comments flew around. Liberty, although cringing at the saintliness of those around her, realized it all made sense. Almost against her will, she vowed to remember these good tips – she'd write them in her Chinese silk blue book.

Gemma asked Paul if he'd mind if they served the pudding before he had his turn.

"A very good idea," he said.

Liberty inwardly groaned but couldn't help but agree.

Gemma went into the kitchen while Liberty cleared the plates and dishes. It didn't take long for all four to finish the bread and butter pudding served with Liberty's much complimented Ambrosia tinned custard, and for Liberty to make the coffee.

Still sitting around the table and drinking coffee in the light of only the one candle plus the street lighting, Paul began by saying, "My plan begins this July. In five years' time, I also see myself as having a chain – a chain of restaurants."

"Now that's a good idea," said Jon.

"I have been planning this for some time which means I can spell out to you how my first restaurant will operate."

"Operate?" said Jon.

"You'll see. I am going to take over the lease of 'Jojo's' in King Street." He held his finger up to show he had much more to tell. "Instead of a menu, chefs having heart attacks, and long waits for the meal to arrive, I am going to offer no choice whatsoever." He frowned. "Perhaps I might offer one alternative – an omelette."

Jon looked dubious, so did Liberty. Gemma sat in awe.

Paul grinned. "Every day there would be a different dish served. For example, Mondays might be steak pie, chips and peas with bread and butter pudding with custard to follow, or trifle. Trifle will always be available – it's so easy, and popular." He grinned at Gemma. "Tuesdays might be an Indian meal. My mother says she'll help with that, bless her."

Liberty saw Paul with new eyes. Of course, he was half Indian; his skin was a lovely shade of light brown, as if he had a bit of a tan all year round and his fabulous black hair shone. He had a slight Liverpudlian accent, like his father's.

"Imagine the ease in the kitchen." He paused for effect. "The kitchen can be smaller, leaving more space for tables."

Liberty began to feel that saints had their uses.

"Imagine the ease of ordering the ingredients. Imagine the diners being served within five minutes. It will be cheap for the diner and cheaper for me and there will be much less waste. Where I work now, it's heart breaking."

"Paul, I congratulate you," said Jon who began to clap loudly.

Paul held up his forefinger again. "I haven't finished." He grinned. "So that I can attract good staff who will want to work there, I'm going to encourage good manners."

Liberty blinked, Jon barely managed to hold back a scoff and Gemma cupped her chin and leaned forward.

"There will be a sign saying the price of coffee is 1/6d, but for a 'coffee please' it will be 1/3d. For a 'coffee please' followed by a 'thank you' when it is served, it will be 1/-. Tea would be cheaper, of course. I might change the prices, I'll have to check the competition, but I think you can see what I'm trying for. What do you think?"

"My giddy aunt," said Gemma, "What a brilliant idea. And I can imagine the customers laughing and joking about the lessons in manners!"

Liberty wasn't sure what to think.

"I have one more idea which may or may not work. I haven't thought it through. I wondered about providing a free meal for some who will then give their labour in return." Seeing his friends' puzzled faces, he continued. "They would wash up."

"Not sure about that one, Paul," Jon said earnestly. "However, the rest is brilliant." Jon banged his teaspoon on the table and Liberty and Gemma clapped. "Absolutely, indubitably brilliant. And how many restaurants do you hope to have altogether?"

"In five years' time? About fifteen. In ten years' time I'm hoping for fifty. They need to be strategically placed. The idea won't work in Knightsbridge, will it?" Paul chuckled.

Jon responded. "Probably not, yet fashion's a funny thing – who can tell."

"Let's just say the rich are not my intended market. I'm hoping to cut out waste and provide excellent, affordable food to all and thereby make a profit."

"Roast Sunday lunch?"

"Of course." Paul quickly turned to Liberty. "Sorry Libby, we boys have been monopolizing the conversation. Now it's your turn, where do you see yourself in five years' time?"

Liberty sat in silence, her eyes growing larger.

Gemma quickly explained, "Paul, Libby's lost her memory. She can only remember the last few weeks." Surreptitiously, she pulled a handkerchief from up her sleeve and slid it under the table to Liberty.

"I'm so sorry. I had no idea. Have you seen a doctor, Libby?"

Liberty sniffed quietly. "I'm temping for one at the moment, a radiologist and he hasn't suspected. I daren't say anything in case I lose the job."

"If you're currently able to do the job you're paid to do, I expect you will be all right. He might recommend someone to you and doctors are honour bound to keep your confidence."

"I don't even know my National Insurance number. I keep waiting for my agency to sack me."

"We'll all rally round if you have a problem," said Gemma, glancing at the men for their approval.

All eyes moved back to Liberty; if she didn't find a way to divert the conversation, she'd cry. "Thank you." She had no plans to match these annoying goody-two-shoes until, like lightning, a thought occurred to rescue her. "Have we told you about the people in the flat below? They're the sort of people who need help right away by the looks of it." She'd been evasive and had spoken sharply; she needed to make a quick exit. "I'll refill the coffee pot while you tell them, Gemma." Liberty listened while she attended to the coffee.

"There's not a lot to say really except the woman has told us someone comes into our flat while we're out."

"Do you think it's true?" queried Jon.

"That's what I wondered. Nothing's gone missing. And it's odd, I've only seen her hand coming round the door followed by her head."

Jon tapped his forehead. "Bit doolally perhaps?"

"Don't know. It's a bit unnerving being told someone is using our flat while we are out. And your friends who did the bathroom got in easily enough, so someone else could."

Jon pulled his mea culpa face. "We could put a new lock on but until then I'll have a word with Tom, and ask him to station a Panda car outside sometimes when you're at work."

Gemma explained to Paul, "Tom is a Detective Inspector and he'll probably tell some new constable that he needs the house to be watched for a criminal hiding out or something."

"He won't arrest anyone, will he?"

"No, Gemma, he'll simply report back to Tom. Tom fancies you anyway, so he'll be pleased to help." Then his eyes flicked to Paul and he coughed. "He's met someone now, getting engaged soon, but I'm sure he'll help."

Fortunately, Liberty came in with a fresh pot of coffee and the Cadbury's Milk Tray chocolates that Paul had brought. "Any ideas on how to help them?"

"Who?"

"Oh Jon – the couple downstairs. They don't seem to work and it's very kind of them to let us know what's going on."

Punching the air, Jon said, "Project Rescue the Odd Couple. What do you think?"

Paul nodded in assent. "Perhaps we should check they're not in hiding from the police, or that downstairs is not a safe house, or something."

"Won't be a safe house; wrong sort of area." Turning to Gemma Jon said, "Sorry old girl but you're slap bang in the middle of the wrong end of town, surrounded by–"

"Don't call me 'old girl'. I've told you before, I'm younger than you by seven years."

Paul laughed. "Never mind the 'wrong end of town', it's the 'old girl' that worries you!"

A clanking sound and shouting drew their attention to the back of the flat. They all poured out of the door and down the stairs to the window. An ancient caravan was being towed by what Jon called a prehistoric car to the small square of concrete which had once been the foundations of a house but was now a bombed out, overgrown, pot-holed patch of no use to man nor beast except these three elderly, scruffy chaps.

"Nice new neighbours moving in, Gemma." Jon beamed.

Chapter Eighteen
Sneaky things, thoughts

"Mornin' ladies."

"Good morning," chorused the two young women.

"Mornin'," called another man from across the street.

Gemma and Liberty smiled, nodded and carried on walking towards the main road, Gemma in her Salvation Army uniform, complete with black bonnet, and Liberty in what Gemma called her 'Sunday best'.

"Call in any time you like for a cabbage, luv, my man grows 'em."

"Thank you," said Gemma to the elderly lady. "That's very kind."

"Your lot helped us when we needed it so now we've got a roof over our heads and a garden too, we can pay you back." The woman appeared to have another think. "Well, not quite that, but we've got enough cabbages to spare you one or two sometimes."

By the time they got to the end of the street, they'd spoken to seven of their neighbours.

"It's a sign of spring, perhaps, with them all out having a natter in their front gardens. Or it could be the uniform," said Gemma. "Perhaps they saw us last Sunday morning and looked out for us today."

"And here we are." Liberty smiled brightly. "I suppose the black bonnet with such a big bow is quite distinctive." She managed to refrain from asking if Gemma felt a clot wearing it. Liberty hadn't been aware The Salvation Army even existed. Or perhaps it was another thing she'd forgotten. "What did they mean about us lot helping them?"

"Not sure but The Army has hostels for the homeless. Who knows?"

Liberty shrugged her shoulders and changed the subject. "Good of Paul's parents to ask us to lunch and tea again. Are you beginning to fall for Paul?"

Gemma looked aghast. "Fall for him? Well, he's rather nice. I quite like him."

Is that all? "Early days, Gemma. I think he's dead keen on you though."

They reached the door of the converted school just in time to hear the band playing so they quickly found two seats together.

"You realize it's Palm Sunday, do you?"

Liberty frowned. Palm Sunday. She turned the words over in her mind. Good grief, was it nearly Easter? "Ah, that's the day when Jesus rode into Jerusalem."

"Yes, on a donkey."

"Got it, thanks." She doubted she'd known much about the Bible even before she lost her memory.

The first song they sang was all about Jesus riding on the donkey. Liberty didn't know the tune, so she glued her eyes to the song book and mimed. Gemma however, with a beautiful, low voice, sang in harmony with the congregation. Oh how Liberty wished she knew the songs and could sing.

It was an odd sort of service, informal, people smiling, and it became even more easy-going when Paul and three young men made their way to the front, picked up guitars, with one on drums, and began to play like a backing group to three girls lined up to lead the singing for the next song. Why didn't they call them hymns?

"Did you know that Paul's seen the Beatles live in the Cavern Club in Liverpool?"

Cavern Club? Gemma appeared to think Liberty should know about this. Liberty phrased her reply carefully. "No, I didn't. Of course, I do know he's from somewhere near Liverpool. I heard him tell Jon that London's not the only place that might be called swinging."

"I'm always telling Jon off about that."

Liberty noticed that all had gone quiet and so she shut up. The man leading the service, or meeting as Gemma kept calling it, mansplained. Liberty wondered where she'd remembered such an inelegant word from. The guitar group were going to 'lead our thoughts to Calvary' whatever that might be. He elaborated. On and on. But then the lead guitarist struck a chord, the girls sang, and the whole atmosphere changed, yet not as Liberty expected.

Liberty wished she'd listened better to the mansplainer. This was all about Jesus, that irrelevant figure from so long ago, giving up his life for those he loved. Who does that nowadays? Only nutters or the misguided. She shut "or heroes" out of her mind. Sneaky things, thoughts. Another verse was being sung.

> See, from his head, his hands, his feet,
> Sorrow and love flow mingled down;
> Did e'er such love and sorrow meet,
> Or thorns compose so rich a crown?

This hurt. The gift of a life for those who neither knew nor cared hit hard. Liberty snuffled as quietly as possible into her hanky and then spent most of the meeting staring at her feet.

Towards the end of the meeting, her wish was granted: she knew the words and the tune for 'There is a green hill far away,' and she sang heartily at first, then the meaning of the words kicked in and by the time they sang verse three, she sang with an overwhelming sense of respect and something like a pain in her heart.

> He died that we might be forgiven,

He died to make us good,
That we might go at last to Heaven,
Saved by his precious blood.

Liberty wondered who'd written such simple, yet powerful words, words which brought back a memory now evaporating into the air, if only she could catch it.

She was relieved when the brass band struck up a tune and as they finished, people started to leave the building. She glanced over her shoulder to the doorway teeming with people. Who was the dark-haired man in a long coat now disappearing through the gateway? She must stop thinking she was being followed. Not all dark haired men were the new doctor.

Gemma and Liberty joined the queue shuffling to the exit.

"Hello, lovely to see you again." The uniformed mansplainer stood in the doorway shaking hands with the congregation as they left. "We must have a chat some time."

Gemma looked enthusiastic, well as much as Gemma ever did. Liberty preferred to offer only the slightest of smiles; she wasn't very keen on having this man explaining everything he thought she should know.

~

Late in the afternoon, Paul's family, Gemma and Liberty were helping themselves to a buffet tea in the comfortable lounge of a comfortable home.

Paul's father rubbed his hands together. "Fine spread, my dear, very fine." He turned to Gemma and said, "My wife loves having people for lunch and a spot of tea on Sundays. We tend to be too busy, too involved, during the week."

Gemma responded with thanks and Liberty added hers effusively.

"Has Paul told you of his plans?" Paul's mother handed round a plate of little pastries.

"About the restaurant?"

"Ah, no, Gemma. I meant about the cottage. Obviously not. Come on, Paul, this is important." With no response coming from the munching Paul, his mother found this useful gap to add a little boast. "He went to one of the best Grammar Schools in the country, Head Boy, he was."

"Mother! That's enough."

"It's given you all the tools for life, Paul," his father added earnestly.

Liberty watched Paul closely. A driving force in the community, as was his family, she decided.

"I've got permission from the Officer–"

"That's what we call our church minister, because we're an 'Army'," whispered Gemma to Liberty.

"Sorry, Libby, yes, I've got permission to turn the cottage attached to the hall into a night club."

"What!" Paul's father pretended to be cross.

"More of a discotheque."

"Have another go."

"Okay, Dad, a dedicated building for a youth club."

Paul's mother gave his father a look which spoke of long-resigned, affectionate tolerance.

"There'll be live guitar groups. There's enough Christian groups around. Our group will kick-off, of course. We're going to knock down one of the non-supporting walls to make a room big enough for dancing and the adjacent room will become a cosy bar–"

"Serving non-alcoholic drinks."

"Yes Dad, and donated snacks; mum says she'll do some baking on Fridays for the Friday and Saturday night stints. Thanks Mum. The idea is that young people will have a safe place to enjoy the music they love without being surrounded by the drunk and the stoned. During the week, we'll use it for things like Bible Studies for young people, many other things too for all the congregation. Anyway, that's the gist of it. It's going to be real groovy."

Paul's mother gently explained that a lot of money needed to be raised and added, "If God is behind this project, He'll provide the money."

Liberty frowned.

"Financing is the first hurdle," said Paul's father.

"Well Dad, we can do some things ourselves."

Gemma suddenly spoke up. "Jon! My brother Jon has friends who could help tackle the project." She turned to Paul's mother. "They installed a bathroom for us in just a couple of days. Four of them turned up and, well, I think they'll get it finished in a jiffy."

Paul's mother giggled like a teenager and his father's face fell into a smile at his wife's delight. "How fortuitous. Do you think they'll come?" he asked.

"Almost certainly," said Gemma. "I'll ask." Anything to do with Jon instantly happened.

"Mum is arranging a Jumble Sale for next Saturday morning and that will give us a few more pounds in the kitty."

Liberty, having sat quietly curious, suddenly blurted, "I'd like to arrange an Auction of Promises."

Silence. Perhaps such things were not allowed. What could be wrong?

"A what?" said Paul with a gentle smile.

Liberty began slowly. "An Auction of Promises is where, say," she clutched her chin until she came up with, "I could promise to babysit for an evening. The auctioneer asks for bids starting at," she paused, "perhaps one shilling."

"Two shillings at the very least," said Paul's mother.

"Double that," chipped in Paul.

"Aha... you see how it goes?"

They did. And it wasn't long before they'd compiled a list of five promises.

"If you ask around, you'll probably collect many more ideas and volunteers and then you arrange a bit of a party at the hall." Would it be allowed? "And someone would be the auctioneer and everyone can bid and the proceeds go to the youth group."

"Where did you hear about such a thing?" Paul's mother asked. "It sounds fun and might make quite a bit of money."

Liberty couldn't remember. Had she arranged such an event in her former life?

"Not to worry, dear, we don't have time for further ideas now anyway; we'll be late for the meeting – it's gone half past five."

Sitting in the back of Paul's car, Liberty's attention began to wander: would the man in the navy blue coat be at the meeting?

Chapter Nineteen
Preferably forever

"Good morning, Miss Taffet. Come into my office will you please. Bring your notebook."

Liberty picked up her pad and pen and hurried into her boss's office.

"Sit down."

She felt somewhat anxious and put on her professional face. Ready, raring to go.

"I've had a chat with the other Consultants in Radiology and they are in agreement with my choice of Dr Nicolo Nylander, who has an impressive CV." Sitting back in his comfortable, swivel armchair, he steepled his fingers and tapped his lips.

And can play cricket, thought Liberty.

"He looks like a good fit for the department. Thank you for pointing out his cricketing experience as it might have been overlooked. He's polite and modest; sound traits in a young doctor."

Liberty wondered if she dared ask when he would be starting. She decided it was unwise to appear too interested.

"Personnel will handle all the paperwork, though I'd like you to take down this personal letter. Ah, I think you said you don't take shorthand. Not to worry, I'll use the Dictaphone, I'll sign it this morning please. Make sure it's posted tonight as I'd like to see him again before he starts."

Starts when? Oh, come on. Tell me. Maybe it would be mentioned in the letter she'd type. It wasn't.

And that was as close as Liberty Taffet got to knowing more about the man who made her nerves quake.

~

After dinner, while pigeons played kiss chase, Gemma and Liberty hung the faded, threadbare greeny/grey rug out of the stairway window and with one holding one corner and the other holding another, they shook it as violently as they dared. Liberty broke a nail and Gemma coughed and spluttered. They hauled it in, noticing the three old guys in the caravan watching with some amusement. Liberty waved before slamming down the sash window and locking it. They noticed the woman in the flat beneath them peep out and shut the door quickly.

Once they'd laid the rug down, they rummaged in the larder, neither explaining why.

"What about these chocolates that we didn't have after dinner last Saturday?"

"We won't miss them, Gemma, not as we've just pigged out on Paul's box."

Gemma smiled hesitantly. "But what can we say?"

"We need only thank them for keeping an eye on the place."

Both took a deep breath and descended the stairs diffidently.

Gemma stood behind Liberty who knocked gently on the door. The hand came around the door and the head followed.

Liberty smiled her best, encouraging smile. "We wanted to thank you for telling us about the intruder and so we hope you like chocolates." She held out the box towards the door.

"Thanks, luv," said the woman. "No need. Just put them on the floor."

Liberty looked a little bemused. Had she heard right? She held out the box towards the door then, as the woman shuffled to get her one arm at the best angle to receive the present without opening the door further, Liberty wished she'd done as she was told. With some difficulty, the one-armed woman clutched the box. Liberty tried hard not to stare at the slack sleeve hanging down her left side.

Gemma came to the rescue. "We don't know what we'd do without you."

Liberty thought that was a bit over the top but managed to stay silent.

"We'd never have known someone's coming in uninvited. My brother is asking a friend to look out for who it might be. We thought we'd make you aware he might be in a Panda car."

From inside, the man called out in a slurred voice, "Police car? Outside here? Cor, that'll be the day. He'll end up with no tyres even while he's sitting there."

"He's not joking, luv."

Liberty caught a glimpse of a disfigured face and the skinny, one-armed woman whispered, "Shrapnel, luv, in the war. He don't like people seein' him."

"Thank you so much, for looking out for us. If there's anything we can do for you, please let us know."

"We're all right, luv. We've got each other. Thanks for the chocolates."

Liberty and Gemma nodded, turned away and slowly climbed the stairs.

In the privacy of their flat, Gemma and Liberty exchanged troubled glances.

~

On the Tuesday morning, Liberty chose to wear a smart, light green suit with a white blouse. The skirt was short though it didn't make the grade to be granted the status of miniskirt, anyway she'd rather look professional than trendy. After all, this was the day Dr Nylander would receive the letter and he might visit the Professor immediately. He'd been asked to telephone to make arrangements.

On the Wednesday morning, Liberty, still hoping he might be seeing the Professor, wore the suit again with a peppermint green and white striped blouse.

On the Thursday morning, she wore it again with a navy blue polo neck, not quite the look she was trying for but it did go well with her navy blue shoes and the handbag she'd brought back from... from the cave. The cave was the source of so many good things, she couldn't stop the slight smile taking up residence on her face.

"Dr Nylander is due to pop in any minute now but I have an urgent case to assess. Perhaps you could show him around the department, just what's where, no need to go into details, simply keep him busy and introduce him to anyone you bump into." Professor Schmidt smiled with a hint of a wink.

As the professor hurried away, sparrows sang and danced along the guttering above her window. The telephone rang. Dr Nylander was in Reception.

As instructed, Liberty showed Dr Nylander what he called the professor's 'kingdom'. Liberty wondered what Professor Schmidt would make of his audacity should it leak out.

"The tardy-gaited nurse – is she kept as a pet?"

Liberty suffocated a giggle at his description of the slowest walker in the department. "Are you asking for all the gossip?" She indicated the chair for him to sit and sat behind her own desk, almost opposite.

"Heaven forfend! You've seen straight through me."

"I think you must be referring to Nurse Williams. She's actually extremely good at comforting the very sick from the wards or our nervous patients." Liberty began to breathe heavily. Dare she ask him the question uppermost in her mind? She hesitated.

"I wanted to ask you something," said Dr Nylander.

She'd missed her chance. That's why he was a doctor and she was just a temp. She gave him an encouraging smile and hoped to prolong the time together.

"Are you having a little trouble remembering?"

Horrified, she said, "Why do you ask?"

Why oh why did the professor suddenly appear in the doorway? Drat, drat, drat. Now she'd have to wait longer to find out how he knew her – he clearly did.

"I do apologize for keeping you waiting, Dr Nylander." He held open his office door and tossed Liberty a thank you. As Dr Nylander left her office, he too tossed her a thank you with a look and a smile she would cherish until the next time they met, but preferably forever.

Chapter Twenty
Groovy, baby, real groovy

On Good Friday morning, Gemma went to The Salvation Army: Liberty did not. There was only so much religion she could take. She reproached herself for such a thought yet didn't change her mind. Besides, it would give Gemma and Paul a little more time to themselves without her hanging around. Into her head came the words, 'Rubbish' and 'Excuses'. She came up with a better excuse: the envelope she'd picked up yesterday from Reception.

Flopping on the sofa with a cup of tea next to her feet, she reread the worrying message.

"Don't trust Nylander. He's not what he seems."

She studied the handwriting: words squashed together, barely legible. Disguised maybe? Who would send her something like this? Another candidate? And why would they send it to her? Why not send it directly to the Professor? She answered the last question with the thought that it must be only she who needed to be wary. Maybe she'd tell Gemma. Or Jon. Yes, Jon would know what to do. There again, maybe it came from the ginger-haired man that Dr Nylander had more or less chased away when she was sitting on the bench at the hospital. That's likely. Does he know something about Dr Nylander? Or is he jealous?

She busied herself with cooking an exceptionally tasty lunch for Gemma and thought about Dr Nylander and the question he'd asked, turning them over and over until she burnt the sauce.

~

Late on the Saturday morning, the two girls stirred. Gemma declared it was too cold to get up, yet bravely put her feet on the floor to the sound of Liberty cheering her on. Liberty's contribution to starting the day was to lean across to the electric socket and turn on the little plug-in heater.

"I'll get up in five minutes," she declared.

"I'll put the kettle on."

To their surprise, the sun shone in the south-facing kitchen and the living room, sending its donation to warming two grateful girls. Gemma put their new radio on which merrily encouraged everyone to 'buy British'.

"That's a novel idea."

"Yes, and a great one. Don't you remember?"

Liberty shook her head.

"You know the country's in deep debt, do you?" Not receiving a reply, Gemma continued. "Some inspired chap, can't remember his name, suggested that if we all worked an extra half day a week, the country would bounce back to being the wealthiest country in the world. Ring any bells?"

Liberty concentrated on pouring some milk on her cereal and, taking a mouthful, she once again shook her head – wealthiest? That's some target.

"Five secretaries in his company," Gemma frowned, "can't remember what the company did, but they all came in half an hour early every day without getting extra pay. The idea snowballed and it's rolling out all over the country. All the politicians have backed it – amazing, eh?"

"When was this?"

"End of last year, I think. Not sure."

"And is it making any difference?"

"Don't know. I do know the Trade Unions are against it. Shooting themselves in the foot, as usual."

"So do you go in early?"

"My boss says we can if we want to and I think it's a good idea, so I'm going to start doing that. Paul and Jon both do."

Oh, the goody-two-shoes brigade again. She gulped down her tea and felt slightly more with-it. "So when we go shopping this morning–"

"Afternoon," interrupted Gemma.

"Er... yes, I suppose it will be. Should we look out for food produced in Britain?"

"We can try." Gemma seemed thoughtful.

At this point, the electricity ran out. Again.

Some hours later, after Liberty had collected her pay and breathed a sigh of relief that they still hadn't questioned her about her National Insurance number, Liberty and Gemma unpacked their shopping bags and each fed the electricity meter with shilling coins.

"That should keep us going," said Gemma triumphantly. "And now it's getting warmer and we're both working, things should get better. Oh, we didn't buy something for the couple downstairs. We should have bought them an Easter egg at least. Shall I run down to the corner shop and buy one?"

Liberty fished in her purse. "I'll pay for it, the Agency told me I'm getting a rise in pay. Here's a florin, hope it's enough."

And so the day went on, with nothing much to get excited about until at half past seven in the evening there was a knock on the door.

"Surprise," yelled Jon, with Paul grinning behind him.

Both clutched large chocolate Easter eggs and Liberty, instead of feeling hugely grateful for two good men with luxury treats arriving, felt mortified. The egg she and Gemma left by the door of the couple downstairs wasn't even half the size.

That night, sitting up in bed, Liberty started a journal.

The following morning, Easter Sunday, she decided she would go to the meeting and then on for lunch and tea at Paul's. Again, she felt not quite mortified, but maybe a little ashamed that she was only going because of the good company, and the fine food and warm, comfortable home that came with it.

The meeting itself turned out to be remarkably entertaining, inspirational even. Never before had she seen such joy, almost tangible, glowing and infecting everyone. Children clutching tambourines didn't just bash or shake them during choruses, they played them in time to the music, flinging their arms around and clearly enjoying every minute. And when the congregation sang "Up from the grave he arose, with a mighty triumph o'er his foes," it felt like a reunion party. Even placid Gemma shone and clapped.

There was no sign of the dark-haired man she'd caught a glimpse of the week before.

In her journal that night, Liberty wrote, "If only I could remember if I'd ever felt like this before. It has nothing to do with a man, not Jon, not the new doctor, it's as if I'm beginning to find myself, a better self." There followed a point by point detailing of the 'day's doings', ending with a promise to herself to go back through the cave at the next opportunity and bring the poor couple downstairs something nice, though she'd no idea what.

~

For Bank Holiday Monday, it had been decided, enthusiastically by Jon, to go to Dreamland, an amusement park in Merrygate. At ten o'clock they were steaming down the new M2 motorway and when Paul reached eighty miles an hour and rising, Gemma appeared very uncomfortable and made a little noise in her throat. Paul slowed, Jon prodded Gemma from behind and Liberty merely smiled. She was in the company of friends, friends like she'd never had before, friends who enriched her life and she never, ever wanted to lose them.

"The Big Dipper – that's the one to start with," said Jon, sniffing the smell of the sea air mixed with all kinds of delicious indulgences as they walked through the entrance.

Liberty laughed. She had predicted his choice.

"Big brother, we need a coffee and cake first. Don't you agree, Libby?"

"Oh yes," Liberty said loyally, concealing her eagerness to try some of the rides first.

Paul took Gemma's hand and squeezed it slightly. "Over there," he whispered, "next to the ice cream kiosk." He tugged her hand and led the way. "Come on Jon, feedies first."

"I suppose that's your motto."

"Of course. We chefs think of nothing else."

"I love the smell of fairs," said Gemma, "can you smell hot dogs?"

"Hot chestnuts too. Loads of things," responded Jon. "And listen to all the stimulating chatter; the sound of families enjoying making the economy work."

Gemma sighed. "I suppose this is your world, Jon, the world of holidays."

"Yup. And your world is shown by all the colourful gear the girls are wearing. And look at you two. Liberty in white trousers and a floaty red top and you in a floral, green dress with touches of purple. Groovy, baby, real groovy."

Exasperated, Gemma said, "I'm not your baby."

"Yes you are, you're my baby sister and you're providing people with clothes made in England and therefore providing work and an income." He turned to Paul and in a pretend whisper he said, "And giving us plenty to ogle."

"He's right," said Paul, grinning but saying nothing about Jon's comment. "Our country needs us to put it back together again and if we can do it by having fun, it can't be bad."

Liberty could not remember anyone else talking like these two. Was it normal? She supposed it was a good thing; she'd heard worse conversations. As the two men continued putting the world right, Liberty turned to Gemma. "What do you want to go on next?"

"I don't mind. If there's something you particularly want to do, speak up and bash Jon into submission, it's easily done by the way."

"I'm content for the moment to do what you want to do. I love it all." A little girl rushed by clutching an ice cream cone and fell over. Her anxious grandmother ran to help. "Did you come here with your grandmother, Gemma?"

Jon flung the answer over his shoulder. "We did, we did. With her living so close to here, we had some great times, didn't we, old girl?"

Because they were standing near the iconic noise of the roundabout's hurdy gurdy, Gemma merely nodded.

Coffees and doughnuts, devoured quickly by Jon and less so by the others, were followed by a ride on the Ghost Train.

Jon nudged Paul. "You get your girl on her own, afraid and in the dark – what more could a man want?"

Instantly Paul replied, "A kiss?"

Jon roared laughing and Liberty, having overheard, thought how wonderfully innocent this all was, such a contrast with... with what? Where had she been where things felt so very different?

The dizzying Big Dipper and the rattling and whooshing of the Scenic Railway were followed by quieter pursuits. The shooting gallery, where Jon and Paul competed and came away with identical scores, was fun but no prizes were won. Jon moseyed through the crowds with Libby's arm in his. "Don't want to lose you," he said with a wink. "Let's see if we can win a prize here."

"Jonathan – this is for children and it's got a big sign overhead, 'A Prize Every Time'."

"And what is it that you keep calling me? A big kid! Come on, the swimming ducks are a must for any amusement park and only two shillings for all four of us – what a bargain."

As promised, each came away with a prize. Jon won a comb, Paul won a ball-point pen, Gemma, a tiny cuddly bear and Libby won a bookmark.

"Daylight robbery," muttered Jon, laughing. "Time for the Floating Tubs."

Liberty, laughing, stared at Jon. "The what?"

"Floating Tubs. They're great. We'll have two big tubs which get pushed off with a splash and then they float serenely around the channels of water. A different scene round every corner, all lit up." He winked at Paul. "Very romantic."

Two hours later, after fish and chips and more rides, they were on the motorway driving towards London. Gemma asked, "Has it brought back any memories?"

"The smells and sounds seemed familiar yet I can't explain why." The only picture that deigned to grace her brain was that of Dr Nylander enquiring if she had trouble remembering.

Chapter Twenty-One
We adopted them

Disappointed? More like devastated. The note said Dr Nylander would not be starting until next week. At least this was a short working week following Easter Monday, and what a day that was. The only other consolation Liberty found in this one sentence from the Professor was that she did not have to consider any action regarding the anonymous warning not to trust Dr Nylander. She would put it out of her mind and knuckle down to the pile of work the Professor had left on her desk.

To console herself, she worked through her lunch hour and left work a little early so that she could go shopping before going home. She walked across London Bridge and caught a bus to Piccadilly. She'd shop at nothing less than the grocer to the Queen – Fortnum and Mason. Before entering, she stopped to look in the windows. What a treat. This was more like it. This, she felt sure, was what she had been used to in her forgotten past. Tourists were looking upwards and pointing, so she followed their gaze. An ornate clock told her it was nearly five o'clock. Time to hurry inside where there were groceries galore. The fabulous eau de nil signature colour added to the feeling of being in a magical world. This must be how Alice felt in Wonderland. She wandered around and wouldn't have been surprised to find the Cheshire Cat grinning from a shelf. She reminded herself that there was no time for silly thoughts – what would she buy? Maybe something for the couple downstairs; if only she knew their names. What would they like? Something useful. A special jam maybe? She didn't want to get too close; somehow the neat shelves inspired respect. She took a look at the prices. A pot of jam was... how much! She bought it anyway and spent another twenty minutes wandering around looking at foods she'd never be able to afford.

On the way home, she stopped at the corner shop, bought two jars of jam and left them outside the door of the tenants below. Half the price and double the quantity of the Fortnum's jam, surely that was the right thing to do.

"Look what I've got," she said to Gemma who was finishing cooking spaghetti bolognaise.

"Jam," said Gemma with a straight face.

"*Fortnum and Mason* jam," responded Liberty.

"To eat?"

"Of course. Maybe though, just a thought, maybe we could display it here." She leant over the little table to put it on the window sill. "This will show we're making financial progress."

Gemma laughed.

"Only until the boys come over for afternoon tea. What do you think?"

Gemma's face lit up even more. "Scones, jam and cream."

"And cakes."

~

The following evening, Gemma tentatively said, "Paul phoned me at work, I'm not supposed to have calls, but fortunately the boss happened to be out. He asked me what I was doing tonight. Anyway, to cut a long story short, I'm going to help with getting the cottage decorated. Much of the building work's been done and he said he could do with another pair of hands, or even two pairs, he said."

Liberty agreed. There was nothing much to do on a Wednesday evening and so they both changed into old clothes and set off for the cottage next to The Salvation Army. To their horror, they found it covered in graffiti and Paul busy scrubbing it off.

"Hi girls. Good to see you. I'm sorry, I didn't know this had happened."

Gemma looked forlorn. Liberty looked angry and pointed to the words 'Chapel of Hate' daubed across the door. "What on Earth...?"

"My father says there's a converted chapel not far from here which encourages people to attend and curse those they hate."

Liberty's eyes nearly popped out of their sockets. "What! How awful."

There's more to it, of course but, I ask you, is there a more offensive thing to set up in a former chapel?" Paul sighed and carried on scrubbing. "A Chapel of Hate is mentioned in a book, written years ago and some newcomer to the area has started what he calls 'An alternative to boring church'. He left a pile of pamphlets in the doorway with the name 'Chapel of Hate' on the front page. I've dumped them in the dustbin."

Oh shame, thought Liberty, she'd liked to have read one.

"Do you know who he is?"

"No, though it should be easy to find out."

Paul showed Liberty and Gemma through to the kitchen and for the next hour or so, they all scrubbed away at the door and the brickwork until it began to look quite smart. "He's done us a favour – I'd no idea this old place would scrub up so well. A lick of paint on the front door and it will be much more attractive. We need to think of a name. I don't fancy calling it 'The Youth Club', as the officer suggested."

Liberty nudged Gemma when Paul went back to the kitchen. "I think I saw the ginger squirrel around that corner," she pointed across the road, "just as we arrived."

"Ginger squirrel?"

"The man who spoke to us when we were both sitting on the bench at the hospital."

"Oh... the one who held his umbrella over us and knew which bus we needed?"

"That's the one." Liberty took a deep breath and wiped the palms of her hands down her trousers. "I think he's stalking me."

"Stalking? What do you mean?"

Grief, was she naïve or what? "Stalking, you know, obsessively following me."

"I've not heard of it before, well, not using that word. I use it for stalking a wild animal stealthily, like a deer or something."

"That's what a stalker does, only in this case, he's stalking a person, me, and I reckon he's the one who's getting into our flat."

"Ooh creepy," said Gemma. "I'm glad Paul said he'd give us a lift home. I don't fancy walking home in the dark with him around."

After they finished at the cottage, they all returned to the flat. Paul declined their offer of coffee. "Gotta be up early. If you fancy helping out any time, that'll be great. I'd intended to start on the coffee bar tonight, but it'll have to wait."

As the girls climbed the stairs, a hand came around the door of the flat below theirs and a head followed. This time she allowed a little more of herself to be seen.

"He's been upstairs again. You've just missed him."

"Are you sure it's a man?"

"I got a glimpse of him; built like a man, not too tall, more sort of stocky. Had a hood up."

Liberty desperately tried to remember what the ginger squirrel had been wearing. A t-shirt came to mind, yellow. She asked.

"Nah, couldn't see. He had a dirty brown jacket on." She looked apologetic, then perked up. "Thanks for the jams, you didn't need to do that."

"I bought too many," lied Liberty.

She seemed a simple sort of woman though not so daft as to believe all she heard. Liberty felt silly. Why couldn't she have said something like 'it's a thank you pressie.'?

"Come in and meet my husband. He don't like visitors usually."

Liberty and Gemma felt privileged: they doubted many people got past the front door.

"I'm Tom," said the man silhouetted against the light of the street lamps.

"I'm Mary. And I know you're Libby and Gemma," she gave a shy smile.

The girls' eyes strayed to the walls. Every inch was covered with pictures of the Queen and Prince Philip, except where a tin bath hung with a towel over the top.

"We buy newspapers if they've got some pictures," Mary explained, "and cut them out."

"Better than the wallpaper in here," said Tom.

Liberty decided to nod and smile in agreement.

"Sit down for a moment," said Mary, pointing to a large, somewhat dilapidated sofa. She disappeared for a moment and returned with a plate of plain biscuits, then went back for a jug of water, finally bringing four cups. "We ain't got any fancy stuff, but if you'd like a drop of water, I'll pour you some."

Liberty took a deep breath. She thought she and Gemma were on the breadline but this showed poverty in its extreme. The two girls were dumbstruck and tried valiantly to hide their thoughts.

Tom came to their rescue, still as a silhouette in the unlit room. "We were both orphans, you see. In the same children's home. When you get to sixteen, they chuck you out. Happens in all of them. I had to leave a couple of weeks before Mary."

Looking pained, Mary said, "We was on the streets for a week or two and then, so we looked respectable, we got married; it took all the money we'd saved up. Wasn't easy, but..." she tailed off.

"We did it though, didn't we, love?" Tom took over while Mary handed the biscuits around with her one hand. "Lost it as a baby," he pointed to her arm, "but I got a job, good one too, sweeping the streets – they always need street sweepers, don't they?"

Gemma and Liberty nodded; it was, after all, true.

"We could afford a room of our own then. No more sleeping under bridges. No parents, but we done it." Without warning, Tom announced, "Mary found out she'd been dumped in a dustbin."

Liberty couldn't stop her gasp and Gemma swallowed hard.

"I told her not to worry. I didn't know *where* I came from."

Mary and Tom smiled and their eyes shone as they looked at each other. Mary switched on a lamp with the lowest wattage possible and Tom explained they didn't have curtains as the street lights helped to keep the electricity costs down. As he limped over to sit by a small table, Liberty saw his horrendously disfigured face. "The war came, I got injured, couldn't work. It's been a struggle. I get around better now but no-one wants to employ someone looking like me." Without a trace of self-pity, he stated, "Mary cried when she found your jam. We ain't got no relations that we know of. No one cares. I don't go out, we don't meet anyone. You're the first people I've talked to in ages."

Mary chipped in. "But what we have got is our Queen and Prince Philip. We adopted them as our mum and dad."

In the solemn silence that followed, a tear ran down Liberty's cheeks.

"I go down to do a bit of shopping and if I see a picture of them on the front page, I always buy the paper." She pointed to a colourful souvenir tea towel hanging on the wall. "We got that on her coronation." Her pride glowed and she looked almost beautiful.

"So you see," said Tom, "we wanted to say a big thank you."

For two jars of jam.

~

"Can you sleep," whispered Liberty.

Gemma turned over in bed. "Not a wink."

"I'll get them something else on my way home from work."

"Shall we get them a little each week?"

"Good thinking," muttered Liberty as she rolled over, finally feeling gentle sleep easing out her troubles.

Chapter Twenty-Two
Pilgrim's Progress

On the following warm, spring evening, Gemma and Liberty sat quietly watching the television while Gemma sewed a small cotton cushion cover. She enquired if Liberty had any laddered tights that she couldn't wear any more.

"Don't throw them away. I'll wash them and I can make Tom and Mary a cushion from these offcuts of material. I thought I'd make us one but I don't think these bright pinks and yellows are quite right for in here," she waved her arm around the room's ancient furniture, "whereas it will brighten up downstairs. Fancy not having even one cushion." Gemma appeared unfazed by the fact that they currently had none either.

"So you need the tights for what exactly?"

"I'll cut them up into small pieces and use them as stuffing. Not the best of materials but we might as well use what we've got."

Liberty wasn't too sure. "It'll take ages to collect enough old tights."

"We might find other things to use as stuffing too. If I wasn't so new at work, I'd ask around but I've already been given these off cuts of cotton and I don't want to look too much like a scrounger."

Liberty understood and what was worse, Gemma must now wait a whole month before her next pay day. At least, working as a temp, she was paid weekly. Quite well too. "Gemma, I've been thinking."

"Does it hurt?"

Liberty felt too absorbed to enjoy any leg-pulling. "Yes, it does."

"Not the answer I expected, sorry Libby. Are you all right?"

Liberty nodded. "You know the song the choir sang? 'Someone Cares', I think it's called."

"Yes, it's from a Salvation Army musical. You know, like 'The Sound of Music' by Rogers and Hammerstein. Well, two Salvation Army officers wrote 'Take Over Bid' and it's great fun. 'Someone Cares' was written especially for it. However, we all like it so much that we sing it a lot, even in meetings – or what you call services."

Liberty didn't need its history. "Have you got the words?"

"I can remember most of them but we can check on Sunday."

"Thanks." The words were haunting her. Did anybody care? Care about her? Care about the couple downstairs? Liberty picked up her book; she had almost finished it and she didn't feel like watching the boring television, neither did she want to fall into John Bunyan's slough of despond, that deep, boggy place from which it was so hard to extricate yourself.

Gemma also lost interest in the TV and, continuing her sewing, she voiced her thoughts. "Do you suppose..."

Liberty glanced up.

"Do you suppose God placed us here in this flat for a reason?"

"To punish us?" The words slipped out and couldn't be retrieved.

"I was thinking more along the lines of the couple downstairs needing help. The Bible says something, well quite a lot about helping our neighbours."

Liberty looked blank. She knew too little of the Bible. Yet she could quote from an old tome like Bunyan's Pilgrim's Progress. "I was rather pleased to find they were not criminals holed up."

Gemma laughed. "Yes, I'm glad we got to know them better."

Liberty began formulating a bit of a plan. "I think I might spend the weekend trying to find out more about myself."

Gemma made assenting noises and nodded. "I hope you can, and it's a good time too as Jon is escorting a group of American tourists around London on Saturday and then Oxford on Sunday."

"I thought his job consisted of monitoring hotels."

"Oh it does, but he sometimes takes the London and Oxford tours if they're at weekends. He'd be very good at it, don't you think?"

Liberty caught Gemma's amusement. "Yes, I can imagine him throwing in a hundred and one tales of dastardly deeds in days gone by." She paused, thinking of the fun they'd had together and how much he'd improved their first weeks in London. "I'm sorry; when I said God sent us here 'to punish us' I didn't mean that I wish I wasn't here. I can't imagine what my life would have been like if you hadn't found me. And now we have our own bathroom, it's beginning to be a real bargain."

"And if I hadn't met you, I wouldn't have met Paul."

With a smile of relief, Liberty decided to have an early night, tucked up with the last chapter of her crime novel and the little blue book of secrets, as she had decided to call her notebook. It was imperative that she take it with her to the cave so she made notes of a few things to bring back home. "Home," she whispered. "I think of this as home now. How odd."

~

After work on Friday, she went straight back to the flat to do the weekly shopping, as arranged with Gemma.

"Should we buy them a luxury item, chocolates perhaps, or something healthier?" There was no need for Liberty to explain who 'them' were.

"They're both in need of some nourishing food, I think."

Scrawny, chillingly skinny, like something out of... she shivered. "Something healthy it is then. Oranges maybe?"

"There's not many about, they're not in season and they're expensive. What about a box of eggs?"

"Oh Gemma, that's brilliant." Since when had a box of eggs qualified as a brilliant idea? "Right. Two boxes, one for them and one for us." It didn't seem much, yet Gemma once again needed to eke out the little money she possessed and, learning slowly, Liberty kept her mouth shut.

Liberty cooked a quick dinner of minced beef, tinned peas and potatoes while Gemma changed into some old clothes, ready to help Paul at the cottage.

"I'm sorry I'm not offering to help tonight. I just don't feel like it. I want to..." how could she say she wanted to absorb the little red book and read her blue book of secrets more thoroughly. The answers were all in there, she knew that much.

Once on her own, she began to read. Within an hour, she could no longer deny her suspicions.

Chapter Twenty-Three
You are not a ghost

Liberty unlocked the door to her agency office in Middleston. The journey to 2020 had gone without a hitch and she'd remembered to keep hold of her backpack into which she'd packed her rolled-up trolley bag, with its useful little wheels, and the canvas one too. This time she knew she was invisible and that the backpack would only remain invisible if she held on to it, and that was essential – she didn't want to spook anyone. This is the most amazing adventure, she thought. I am a time-traveller. She stood rigid as she stared at her office. She'd brought her car keys but decided that a car seen speeding along without a driver was likely to cause a stir, so she'd travelled by train and spent the time thinking of Nick. Dr Nylander would be starting this coming week in 1968 at Guy's hospital and she would see him. She must make notes because when she returned, she'd forget she'd known him in her past. Oh joy, sweet, sweet, joy. She punched the air and shouted, "Yay." How could it possibly be that the doctor she'd see on Monday morning would be the man she'd had dinner with just before they left to explore the caves? It was all clear to her now: he'd followed her through and... oh Nick, I'm so sorry, I didn't know I'd forget 2020 and become invisible if I returned. I'm so very sorry you followed me.

Then she panicked, flung her backpack on the floor and rushed to her desk. How could she be sure of the year? It might be 2021 or even 2030!

"Stupid, stupid," she said aloud with the assurance of knowing that even if she were in a crowd, nobody would be able to hear her. It was unlikely her office would be looking the same in 2030. Her mind flicked back to the woman in the train ticket office. She'd marched up to the counter and called out 'Oy bonzo!'; there had been no reaction whatsoever, just like the first time when she'd tried to buy a ticket. Yes, it was 2020; she saw almost no-one on the way here. She looked out of the window – not a soul in what should be a bustling thoroughfare. A huge smile crossed her face – 'thoroughfare', such an old-fashioned word. She put the kettle on, raided the fridge, switched on the television and made herself comfortable on her office chair. Her clock on the shelf said half past ten. The TV seemed to be showing nothing but news of the Coronavirus. She sniffed her yoghurt – the date on it said it should be used by 20th April. It smelt all right, so she ate it. There was also some cheese which seemed to be okay too. The bread was stale, yet not mouldy and she made a honey sandwich. This would do for the moment. The words of the weather forecaster penetrated her thoughts.

"As we start what used to be called the working week..."

"It's Monday," shouted Liberty, punching the air.

"...we can expect the temperatures to rise a little, but don't expect too much, May is still a little way off..."

Liberty heard no more; she was engrossed in her desk diary. "It's Monday 20th April and that's right because, because..." She consulted her blue book. "I left very, very early on Saturday 20th April, 1968. So..." she frowned in concentration, "the date remains the same but the day changes. Got it!" The time on the TV didn't agree with her clock on the wall. Why is everything...? Ah... I know. It's no longer Greenwich Mean Time, it's now British Summer Time. She leapt up and put the clock forward an hour. Why didn't she notice it last time she was here? She thought back to her last visit to her agency office and the startling realization that she was invisible. No wonder she hadn't thought about a lost hour, she'd lost far more than that.

The television news focused endlessly on the virus. "Good grief, the Prime Minister has been in hospital." She wondered if she could catch it. Well, she wouldn't be here long and then she'd return to the safety of *home* – how very odd. She swivelled in her chair. Her priorities were... she referred to her incomplete, hastily prepared list in her blue book. She'd scribbled down some exciting things to buy, and decided that, as there were a few tins of food in the cupboard, she'd leave shopping until the afternoon. She heated a tin of soup in the microwave then took it to her desk and sipped it from her mug.

It wasn't the most important task, and perhaps she shouldn't do this first but she searched the Internet for The Salvation Army. "Fascinating," she declared. "It's not just a Sunday church, there are loads of things going on. There's even a free food bank up the road from here." She carried on reading, with occasional outbursts. "It's in 132 countries." She wondered how many countries there were altogether but disciplined herself not to get distracted, well, not any more than she already was. She noted it ran shelters for the homeless, it operated disaster relief, and humanitarian aid in developing countries and hospitals, schools and much more. This Wikipedia site – what a terrific source of information, she must remember to donate to it again. Hang on... the Salvation Army also ran refuges for those in need and what else? "Aha..." she read aloud, "the relief of poverty and other charitable objectives beneficial to society or the community of mankind as a whole." She pondered and remembered the last service. She'd been more interested in the Sunday lunches with Paul's parents than she was with what anyone said. Except... 'Someone Cares'. She flipped over to the official site of The Salvation Army and after spending a little time marvelling at all the things she'd never known in life, she did a search for the words which led her to the Gifts page and there it was: a tea towel with the words of Someone Cares.

Do you sometimes feel that no one truly knows you,
And that no one understands or really cares?

Through his people, God himself is close beside you,
And through them he plans to answer all your prayers.
Someone cares, someone cares,
Someone knows your deepest need, your burden shares;
Someone cares, someone cares,
God himself will hear the whisper of your prayers.

Tears filled her eyes. Not in her whole life had she ever felt so alone, alone and in a predicament. Time travelling might seem a great adventure but in 1968 she lived in a dump, relying on selling her mother's ill-gotten gains. She had no career path with a secure salary, no exciting business of her own. She rummaged around in her handbag for a tissue but found none. Surely they'd been invented by the sixties? Or were they too expensive? She sniffed as she pulled out a forgotten leaflet which Gemma had given her. It was a Salvation Army publication and flicking through it, she came across some words that drove her to despair.

"Sometimes the only fighting we need to do is to stand still and hold our shield over someone else as they weep."

Liberty's tears increased – she had no-one to hold a shield over her. Not a soul. She wasn't even a proper ghost. Here in her own time, there was nobody to care for her and no-one for her to care for. There was no point in being here at all, except to raid her belongings. Habit made her pull open her desk drawer and take a handful of tissues from the box. She dried her eyes, sniffed, and stared at the screen. 'Someone cares.' "Do you care, God? Do you?" Her hand shook slightly as she began to read the leaflet. The founder of The Salvation Army was ranting on about fighting back in the nineteenth century.

"While women weep as they do now, I'll fight. While little children go hungry, as they do now, I'll fight. While men go to prison, in and out, in and out, I'll fight. While there is a drunkard left, while there is a poor lost girl upon the streets, while there remains one dark soul without the light of God, I'll fight. I'll fight to the very end!"

She stood up and punched the air. "I'll fight too. My life in 1968 is not that bad. In fact, I love it!"

She marched out to the kitchen, drank a glass of water and returned to her desk invigorated. What should she do about the agency? No need to panic. The pandemic wrapped it in cotton wool to preserve it until better times. Until then, she could use her office as a sanctuary, a place where her presence was unlikely to be detected and from where she could acquire all sorts of goodies.

She was about to close her screen when she wondered how she could get her hands on one of those tea towels? Easy. Order one online, pay by credit card, have it delivered here and she'd collect it next time. She ordered two and hoped the package would be small enough to go in her post box.

"Post box!" She ran down to street level and opened it. Only three letters, phew. The first thanked her for all she'd done for one of her clients. The second was a shirty note cancelling membership and referring to the virus as if it were Liberty's fault. Hmm... No wonder no-one wanted to go out with her. The third... She'd reached the top of the stairs and closed the door behind her. The third had almost indecipherable handwriting; honestly, some people! How's a postman supposed to deliver...

Something clattered at the window. She turned and saw a stone dash against the pane. Carefully she stood beside the window and peeked out. Nothing and no-one to see. Whatever made her try to hide? No-one could see her. Did a bird drop something? She ignored it. A third stone clattered on the window. Secure in the knowledge that nobody could see her, she ventured down into the hallway, opened the front door slightly and peeped out. Not a soul. She opened the door wide and stepped outside. Nothing, nobody hiding in doorways either. Could it be Nick? Invisible Nick? Swiftly she returned, closed the door behind her, dashed up the stairs and rushed to the window to see if someone might now be seen. Another little stone hit the window. This time it had been thrown from the inside.

Instinctively she shouted, "Who are you?"

No reply because, of course, they couldn't hear her. She dashed to her desk, wrote a note and left it lying on top. She put the pen down. It appeared and disappeared in an instant.

Some minutes later, a long, angry spiel appeared on the sheet of paper.

You damn bitch. I wanted me and you to run the agency together. I'd got plans for it. Not just this hell-hole of an office, I'd have made it country wide. With bespoke services for singles. Finally I get to come through that weird cave, following you yet again, and you disappear. Not a sign of you and when I find someone to ask, they can't see, hear or feel me. I'm a ghost.

Gregor Hode had followed her from 1968! Was he sleeping on her doorstep? Creepy. She frowned, picked up a different pen and replied.

You are not a ghost. Ghosts can walk through doors – you can't. I am not a bitch. You are a scheming squirrel she crossed out 'squirrel' and wrote *rat. Now get out of my office and...* She hesitated. He probably didn't realize he could return to 1968 and be visible again; she decided not to tell him. *...make the best of what 2020 can offer. Go back to your house and sit out the pandemic. You can eat, sleep and do everything as before, you just can't be seen or heard.* Not a bad thing – better not write that.

Just can't be seen or heard? <u>Just</u>!!!!!! I might as well be dead. You murdering slut. I saw you with two men. You've been there less than a month and you've got two slavering dogs after you. Well you've lost them now and you might as well be dead too. Look, let's bury the hatchet and help each other out.

Grief! From calling her a slut to asking for help in a few short sentences. I should cocoa. She smiled at her 1968 slang which gave her courage. Not in a million years would she help him out.

You can make a start by setting up your own house with all that you need in the way of food. You can watch the television, listen to the radio, do some gardening and amaze everyone by making changes while they stare yet can't see anybody.

Gregor's scrawl appeared. *You mean I should become a poltergeist instead of a ghost? Not a bad idea. Might be fun. I'll be back.*

I meant you could do some nice things for people. She put the pen down, she saw it for a second before it disappeared then reappeared – flying through the air until it hit the door.

Liberty picked up the pen, went down the stairs and opened the door to the street for the nasty, scheming rat. An unwelcome feeling of guilt disturbed her for a few seconds.

Could she be sure he'd gone? No, not yet. She'd have to wait and watch. Dratted nuisance. She reminded herself not to go near her hidden jewels and the gold until she was sure, nor would she check her bank account yet. She must ignore him and concentrate. The best thing to do would be to close her agency now, send out emails to all her clients suggesting that in one month's time they all meet up outside the Riverside Restaurant in the park. She couldn't be there, of course, but they'd have a chance to pick up the pieces and make arrangements for themselves. She drafted an email, changed the wording from 'one month' to 'three months' and decided to send it to all her clients later today. She then ensured she'd logged out so it was password protected. She wrote a note: *All clients' email addresses are on the computer.* She carefully placed a towel over the top of the keyboard and the mouse, marking exactly where it lay and laid the note on top. Time to go shopping.

She returned an hour later with food and not much else. The endless information about the lockdown on the TV assumed she knew everything previously communicated. The fact that only essential shops were open had not sunk in. As far as she was concerned, all shops are essential. Her trolley bag was full of food, and she'd remembered not to take too many things that needed to be kept in a fridge or freezer. 1968's flat was pretty basic. Nevertheless, as she stored the fresh food in her fridge, the one she'd chosen with Nick, she patted the six packets of smoked salmon. Two were for Tom and Mary. Oh how good it will feel to hand those over. She smiled as she reflected on the astonishment of the check-out woman when an envelope full of cash appeared beside her. Liberty knew she didn't have to do that but she never wanted to be like Gregor Hode.

The towel over the keyboard and mouse lay undisturbed. Gregor rat was not here.

Decisions, decisions. She sat down with a cup of frothy coffee and a ready meal. She inhaled the delicious smell of cooked chicken and dumplings. Having checked they could be cooked in an oven as well as a microwave, she'd bought another four to take back to '68. So long as she could keep coming back here, she could alleviate their poverty in Swinging London. Creeping through her mind was the vision of who she now knew was Nick standing at the back of The Salvation Army one Sunday morning, like a guardian angel. "Stop it!" she shouted. "Concentrate."

She completed her list of things to do which included sending out the emails, and contacting Companies House and other mundane closing-down-the-company matters. She would put a sign in the window of the front door saying the agency had closed, then when Gregor rat came knocking, maybe he'd think she'd left.

Rather more important was to decide what to do with the gold bars and the jewellery. She searched the Internet for the price of gold now and the price of gold in 1968. Yikes! It had been so cheap back then. What to do? If gold was over £1,700 per ounce now, though only $35 per ounce in 1968, it didn't seem like a good idea to sell the forty gold bars in the past. She tried not to get side-tracked on the Internet yet again by the fascinating intrigues of world banks to control the price at that time. However, she would try to find out how much one dollar was worth in pounds sterling in 1968. She gave up. Whatever the answer, no way should she sell her gold in 1968. She mustn't get distracted; time had a nasty habit of running out. She'd leave the gold here; she'd found a hiding place in the loft and there it would stay until she could keep it safe in her new life. Dealing in gold without being able to open a bank account could cause problems.

She wanted to go back to Gemma. She'd even come to like The Salvation Army – of all things. Into her head shot the name 'Matthew' and the words of the sermon based on the story of the burden of being rich. "Takes up a lot of time," she whispered.

Her thoughts swirled and became darker as she worried about going through the cave and landing in the wrong period. She revised her previous decision: she must always, always have some jewellery with her; it acted like currency in whatever time she landed. Making herself comfortable at her desk, she decided to have a short nap. She put her head on her hands, sleepily pleased with permanently ridding herself of Gregor, and drifted off to sleep, perchance to dream of Nick.

Chapter Twenty-Four
Damned by a rampaging virus

The first thing Liberty noticed when she stirred was the letter she hadn't opened. Another moaning client throwing in the towel, no doubt. Stiff from falling asleep on her desk, she stretched, stood and stared at the clock. Four o'clock. It should be Monday still, surely. Must hang on to where I am and when. Hah! Only a time traveller would think like that. Or someone disorientated. Or going mad. A strong mug of tea would bring her round and only afterwards would she tackle the letter.

While the kettle boiled, her mind flicked through all that had happened since she found the little red book in the filing cabinet. Immediately it hopped over to the evening in the restaurant when she had shown Nick the book. They'd visited the caves together and the Guide had warned everyone that it had been known for people to go missing in them – never to be seen again. Liberty smiled: she was one of them. Nick was another. She remembered her mad dash to have an adventure: the idea of exploring Regency times beckoned and Laura's little red book made it sound so simple. Her stupid lack of preparation caused her to emerge in 1968. Now she knew that Nick and the rat, that awful Gregor Hode, had followed her. The kettle boiled and while the tea bag brewed, she thought of how fortuitous it was that she'd met Gemma. How could Nick have been so brave, foolhardy even? Fancy following her when he'd known that returning to an ordinary life in 2020 was impossible. Yet life in 1968 was a whole lot more interesting, exciting even, than her comfortable life here at the agency. Yes, she'd enjoyed arranging events for single people, but...

Taking the mug back to her desk she allowed herself a few more jumbled memories of the flat they'd found, meeting Jon and Paul and all the fun they'd had in Swinging London. She couldn't imagine dancing the Can Can in Oxford Street now. She took a deep breath and smiled broadly; she loved her time travel life.

Liberty glared at the letter's scrawly handwriting. It could wait until she tackled the job of closing down the agency. At least it wasn't a brown envelope from something like the Inland Revenue. She tried to brush away the growing fear that it was from the rat until opening it became preferable to finishing the depressing task of wrapping up her livelihood. She made a second cup of tea.

"Procrastinate. That's what I do." In between sips, she spoke to the wall. "I'm absolutely hopeless. Not only do I put things off, I also fling out bad ideas, my thoughts are often terrible. Look at what I told, or rather didn't tell the rat. And Gemma wouldn't call anyone a rat. Or would she? See, I even think bad things about her. And Jon. Jon's a dark horse. He comes and goes whenever he chooses." A flood of kind things that Jon had done for her and Gemma surfaced in her mind. "See, I can't even stay on a *bad* track. I have the attention span of a goldfish, if that. He's been fantastic. I love him dearly." She indulged her procrastination with several slow sips. He'd never tried to kiss her, not properly. Why not? Was he like Nick, with a fiancée tucked away somewhere? He's brilliant to have around. As for going back to 1968 or remaining here, am I making the right decision? Of course. It would be awful to live as a ghost. She chuckled a little as she thought of Gregor not knowing he'd be able to return to normal by finding his way back to 1968. "Normal? What is normal? Look at this damned world. Damned, yes damned by a rampaging virus. Why would anyone want to stay here?" The Internet, convenience foods, and many other advantages crowded her thoughts; eventually she voiced them. "I am so lucky. See – I'm all over the place, I just don't know what to do. Ever. I'm always like this. Rubbish. I love 1968 and

I can, at least for some considerable time, keep using the Internet and bring back nice things for everyone. I ought to bring Jon something back, and Gemma. And Nick. Right. I'll tackle the mini job of opening a little letter, then I'll finish closing down the agency. I'll sleep and I'll continue tomorrow." She noted this down in her 'to do' list, now called an 'Order of Battle' thanks to Jon. "But what about going back to 1814? I've almost forgotten and it was my attempt to go there that's landed me in this predicament. Yet if I hadn't gone through the light curtain in the cave, I'd still be here with a broken business and a deserted world." She turned away from talking to the wall and referred to her 'Order of Battle'. She would stay on track, be organized and rip open and read the letter.

Dear Libby,
My apologies for not being able to personally deliver this hastily typed letter. I tried; I'd hoped you might be here for Easter too. I returned to my home and, as you will know, I am invisible. Fortunately, I lived alone, so I am not startling anyone. Though I can think of a few folks I'd like to spook. Might do that another time.
After much agonizing, I have written to my parents saying I have a terminal illness (partially true as this invisibility is incurable). I have written a Will and I'll ask two people from 1968, who are still alive now in 2020, to witness my signature and then return the Will to 2020. As I can't provide a dead body as proof, the beneficiaries of the Will might have to wait some time before I shall be declared dead. I am taking back with me to 1968 some useful medical text books, medicines and other books which will prove helpful for what we shall have to face while we are living there. I am telling you this in case you return here to 2020 so that you have a chance to prepare your departure from this period in time.
Yes, departure. I contacted Matt Redfern the night before you and I travelled through the curtain of light in the cave. The little

red book of Laura's notes neglects to mention that too many journeys through the curtain result in invisibility in *both* times. Laura has had a permanently invisible toe since her last return journey. Again I emphasize we cannot keep travelling back and forth.

If you find they've locked the door to the caves again, I've drawn a map on the back of this letter to show you another way in. Use it to return to 1968.

There is still the possibility of travelling to Regency times. I will explain more when I see you. You must take this letter back with you so that you remember who I am. Wherever you are, I will find you.

Liberty's eyes were on stalks. The letter ended with his name and a kiss. Why hadn't she opened it first? Why was she such a scatterbrain? She'd been a manager in the National Health Service and she'd never been like this back then. Was it the time travelling? Love? Was she in love? And what about the danger of becoming invisible in 2020 *and* 1968? This must take priority.

She took a deep breath, tucked the letter in her handbag and set about following the Order of Battle. "Nick will approve."

By noon on the following day, Liberty reckoned she had done all she could to close her company satisfactorily and had put most of her personal affairs in good order. She still needed to email her friends with some sort of explanation as to why they'd never hear from her again. Also, she had no idea how to write a Will, but did her best to leave her estate, excluding the goods she still had in storage, to her brother. He'd not want the bother of those. She wrote to him and, following Nick's example, she explained she had little time left, and that in her desk was a copy of her Will. He'd have to visit and deal with matters. Yet wouldn't he be wondering where she was, or at least where her dead body was? She'd take the Will to Aurora and Grandpapa and ask them to witness her signature. Perhaps they'd help her rewrite it properly. When her Will was found in 2020, Aurora and

Grandpapa would still be alive. Nick knew that because he saw them regularly as older people before he went through the light curtain and returned – invisible. His grandparents would be able to help fudge over the difficult details of their disappearance because in 2020, they would remember them in 1968 as time travellers. Oh this was getting too complicated. She put the letter she'd written to her brother in her top drawer to post next time she came. It was too early at the moment; she didn't want him turning up before she'd 'gone'.

Finally she felt ready to pack. Not being able to return safely to 2020 on a regular basis changed her plans. She thought of Nick's priorities: medical books. She owned no equivalent but two unread books by her bedside caught her eye and she guiltily packed them. An 18-carat white gold diamond bracelet was all she took from her secret store; a tiny ticket attached told her the price: £4,500. She grinned with satisfaction; it should improve her life in the flat considerably. She would be sure to ask a good price for it. She snatched up her calculator, a battery-operated tiny alarm clock and carefully packed them and stuffed AA and triple A batteries into every nook and cranny. Gemma won't need to wake me up in the mornings anymore. Unable to resist, she put the matching diamond ring in her handbag. Once she had found somewhere to hide a good stash of jewellery and gold, she'd take it all.

At four o'clock she knew she ought to be leaving. She locked her desk and emptied the kettle, and then snatched a loose fitting, alpaca blend cape which she hung through the straps of her handbag. "No more cold nights," she said triumphantly. "Must buy some coathangers."

As she staggered up the hill to the station, she couldn't help but smile: she could travel anywhere, totally free. Next time, and she would insist on a next time, even if her toe became invisible, she might be able to stay for a week or so. Perhaps she and Nick might travel by train together and see all the spring blossoms from the comfort of first class? One thing was certain, Jaelyn was now a thing of the past.

Unfortunately, another thought quickly followed: how would she explain arriving back at the flat with another haul of goodies?

Chapter Twenty-Five
Wet feet

On the train to work on Monday morning, Liberty worried about Gemma's reaction to all the extra food in the cupboard and the pile of clothes in her wardrobe, too many to be able to hang up. The alarm clock had startled Gemma even though she was already awake and in the bathroom. Liberty had tried to explain that her memory was returning and that she'd found her old address in the blue book she carried around. She'd told Gemma the landlord said she could come back and empty the flat whenever she liked as he was not going to rent it until after his summer holidays in August. The lie convinced Gemma who hoped her memory would return fully soon. Liberty hoped Jon and Paul wouldn't try to be helpful. That concern paled into insignificance when the professor called her into his office.

"Miss Taffet, I have been so pleased to have you work for me; your cheerfulness and efficiency have contributed in no small way to the running of my department."

Liberty's mouth smiled: her eyes showed concern.

Of all the days for the Professor's permanent secretary to return to her job, she chose the day on which Dr Nicolo Nylander was due to begin work in the Radiology Department. What were the chances of her job coming to an abrupt end on the very day that held all, well some, of the answers? The Professor introduced them to each other and asked Liberty to bring his permanent secretary up-to-date. "We'll pay you for today, Miss Taffet, but you may leave as soon as Susan is comfortable." If her flat had a telephone, she'd have received a message, the Professor had said apologetically.

Around midday she enquired as nonchalantly as possible if Dr Nylander would be in the department today.

"The new doctor? An absolute darling, isn't he? The last one was a complete noodle." Clearly dreaming of exciting times ahead, it took a slight clearing of Liberty's throat to return Susan to the matter in hand. Dismissively the secretary said, "Yes, he came earlier, looked shocked, in the nicest possible way and disappeared. I suppose he was expecting to see you. Anyway, he's attending a lecture this morning."

So he'd be in later. Liberty hesitated too long and only managed to get her mouth open.

"He starts in the department tomorrow."

She might just as well have finished with the flourish, 'When you won't be here.' Liberty decided not to respond, then changed her mind though only got as far as "Would you tell..." Noting the raised eyebrows and stony stare of the secretary, Liberty shrugged her shoulders and said, "It doesn't matter." She smiled and said goodbye feeling a complete noodle, a phrase stolen from the secretary whose intention to steal Nick was quite apparent.

She'd call in at her agency on the way home and see if there was hope of another job. First, she'd find a West End jeweller and sell the bracelet; she might need the money.

Bond Street, that'd be the place to go. It wasn't. She'd been stopped at the door by a liveried doorman at both jewellers she'd tried. They'd eyed her with disdain. No, they didn't buy second-hand jewellery. How embarrassing. Eventually a window shopper referred her to the Hatton Garden district where she might find an interested jeweller.

The first one she came across shattered her rising hopes of not being broke. "£100?" She frowned. She'd imagined twice that amount. "Thank you, but no thank you."

She tried another. "£75? No thank you, I've been offered more elsewhere."

The young man shook his head. "I'll make it one hundred and twenty-five." Steely dark eyes surveyed her.

She should have gone to her usual jeweller close to the hospital. Now Liberty shook her head.

The jeweller sniffed. "One hundred and fifty – my final offer."

"I need more. Sorry." Then she thought again. If she could lose her job without even any notification, she'd be unwise to turn down £150. She mentally calculated how many weeks she'd need to work to earn that money – approximately nine weeks.

"Where did you get the bracelet?"

Liberty stopped. Was there a chance? "From my mother." Fleetingly, she wondered if Gemma would count that as a lie. She wouldn't. It wasn't a lie.

"Bring it here and I'll take a closer look." He did. He took out what appeared to be a special kind of magnifying glass and held it to his eye. "Your mother's?"

"Yes. I wouldn't sell it but my temporary work has unexpectedly finished."

"It's particularly fine. The colour and clarity are exceptional." He put the bracelet on the counter and stared at her.

"Do you have more of your mother's jewellery?"

Ooh. Smartie pants. He was investigating if it was worth his while to tempt her into being a loyal customer. She'd play along. "I do. I have the matching ring but I need £200 immediately."

He began to write out a cheque.

"I need the money in cash, sorry."

"You're not in any trouble, are you?"

"Oh no. Nothing like that. It's just that," she hesitated, "this is my first time in London and I've had to pay cash for the deposit on a grotty flat and I have to pay the rent in cash too and now the permanent secretary has returned, I don't have a job." Inside, she groaned, then added, "I've been temping." She tossed her long, dark hair and did her best to look distressed.

Mistake in Time

The guy behind the counter raised his eyebrows and scratched his forehead before relenting. "I'll pay you in notes. Look, you don't need to worry about getting another job if you're a secretary. London's crying out for them. Wait there." He came back with a bundle of bank notes and began counting them out. "Ten, twenty..."

With a promise to bring him more, Liberty left Hatton Garden with nearly three months' pay. She caught a bus to the employment agency where, indeed, another job awaited her. She would start on Wednesday.

Climbing the stairs to her front door, she remembered she hadn't given Tom and Mary the goodies she'd brought them from... well, wherever she'd got them from.

Slumping onto her bed, she opened her handbag and counted the bank notes. She rubbed her hands together until she realized she resembled Scrooge. An unexpected tear ran down her face. The radio, put the radio on. Radio Caroline burst into life, cheering, chatty – everything she needed. She imagined the DJ sitting in a dark studio on board an old boat far out to sea. A broad smile crept over her face. "Pirate radio." How wonderful. Jon said they played what young people wanted to hear and that the BBC should catch up. He was right, of course. And then he'd gone on to say we should remember them on dark and stormy nights in their old tub of a boat, rocking and rolling with their music. The memory of Jon's brilliant wit boosted her spirits. She listened as Aretha Franklin sang 'I say a little prayer,' and Liberty thought how appropriate for the DJs on this windy day.

Rummaging in her handbag for a hanky, she found some tissues and a letter. It was from Nick and signed with a kiss. She didn't fully understand what he'd written but instinctively she knew his guidance was important and she could not keep going through the caves if she didn't want to lose a toe, or more. She read on to the end and her smile grew. "Wherever you are, I will find you." Dr Nicolo Nylander would find her. How wonderful to have someone who understood her dilemma.

She leapt up. Into her mind flooded an abundance of good intentions, the first of which was to take Tom and Mary two hermetically sealed packs of smoked salmon, a cheese and bacon flan and an extra large slab of Cadbury's milk chocolate. She knocked on their door and with a well-meant smile, she handed over the food, which unexpectedly seemed much less than she'd intended. She hurried away, embarrassed, but flung a cheery, "Enjoy!"

"Thank you," called Mary to Liberty's disappearing back.

Liberty read the letter yet again, this time picturing the invisible Nick attempting to write what he could not see. She giggled as she read about his idea of spooking some deserving persons. At the part where he'd mentioned they were both time travellers, she clutched it to her heart. "No-one will believe us, Nick." This brief letter sent her into ecstasy. Now she knew why her body sizzled when he came close – he was special to her in her real time. "No, this is my real time: 1968." She read on. Action was needed. She must return and bring everything of worth here. "Not the most secure place to stash gold and jewels," she mumbled. She searched and thought hard but all plans were obscured by the vision of Dr Nicolo Nylander in a just below knee length navy coat when every other man wore a shorter style. No wonder he stood out from the crowd.

She heard Gemma's key in the door. "Hi Gemma, you're home early."

"Ah... We're all going out so it's a good job you're home too."

"Out? Out where?"

"Jon rang me at work, I wish he wouldn't, my boss doesn't like it. Anyway, Paul and he are in league and luckily for us, they're taking us to a Chinese restaurant somewhere uptown. Jon's driving to Paul and then they'll call for us. Jon says he's not leaving his car outside here all evening."

"I don't blame him. What time are they coming?"

"Seven o'clock."

"I need to wash my hair and have a bath."

"Will it dry in time? Your hair I mean."

Liberty's eyes lit up. "Guess what I've got?"

Gemma shook her head.

Liberty grinned and dashed to her wardrobe, rootled around and produced a hair dryer.

Gemma looked puzzled. "Does it work? I used to have one and it took ages. In fact, I gave up using it."

"I think it does. Anyway, I'll try it and if it's too slow, I'll sit in front of our little plug-in socket fan heater."

"Good luck with that," laughed Gemma. "It'll take forever."

Gemma laid out various outfits on her bed. "Which one do you think?" She bent over to straighten out her short, swirly green skirt. "What was that?" She looked at the ceiling. "I thought I felt a spot of water."

Liberty stared upwards. "I can't see anything. Check if it happens again."

It didn't, so the girls busied themselves with choosing outfits and they both decided to wear the swirly skirts and in between their decisions, Liberty told Gemma about the secretary returning.

"Have they found her sister then?"

"Apparently not. She's come back defeated for the moment but she had news that a girl answering the description of her sister has been seen on the top floor of a block of high rise flats, in north Africa somewhere. She was waving a scarf and calling out. Now that there's a bit of a lead, the police are taking over."

"What were they waiting for?"

"Don't know. That's all she said and I didn't have time to listen to any more. We must be sure *we* don't answer advertisements which seem too good to be true."

"The poor girl. White slavery is an awful thing. Any kind is and I can't believe it's still happening, not these days. I feel so sorry for her and her poor sister."

Liberty sat on her bed. What was wrong with her? Why wasn't she like Gemma? Why hadn't she felt any sympathy for the secretary?

Was she so self-centred? Whatever must Gemma think of her? She must change. She'd work on it.

At seven o'clock precisely, Jon hammered on the door. "Ready, steady, go!" He corralled them both down the stairs, like an eager sheepdog, slammed the flat door shut, leaving his daily newspaper outside Tom and Mary's door. "Gotta keep the neighbours in touch with the world," he whispered to his sister.

"You're wonderful," she responded, "most of the time." She pulled a face and pointed to his orange trousers.

Once in central London, Paul parked his car 'somewhere safe', took Gemma's hand and led the way.

"I hope you like Chinese," he called back to Liberty. "It's a bit of a walk from here."

"Which allows time for these two country girls to get in the swing of things. Look, Libby, here's Carnaby Street. Have you been here before?"

Liberty doubted it and as she turned the corner, she knew she definitely hadn't.

"Feast your eyes. You have before you, colourful clobber par excellence," Jon quietly said to Gemma and Liberty. "No grotty gear."

Jon was wearing a red jacket with his orange trousers. Liberty's embarrassment faded now that she understood why. She loved the trendy look and was relieved she'd grabbed her aqua feather boa to enliven her all black outfit.

Paul's look remained understated: peacock fashions were not for him. He confidently carried off jeans and a heavy white polo neck.

The thrilling atmosphere was almost tangible. Music spilled from record shops, the sounds of the Beatles, the Rolling Stones, Gerry and the Pacemakers and others sizzled through the air. The clatter of steel tipped stiletto heels, and cast iron segs on the heels of men's colourful, two-tone shoes gave a metallic drumbeat to Swinging London.

What once were plain brown brick buildings were now multi-coloured towers. Directly ahead stood one with pale blue bricks on the first floor, a pink second floor and purple window frames throughout attempting to provide co-ordination, all atop a shop where the windows were decorated with rainbows and stars. A young man in a purple shirt and orange tie stepped outside with a stick-thin girl on his arm. With her dark fringe almost covering her eyes, her yellow dress short enough to have passed for a well-fitted long vest, and knee-high white boots, she captured eyes until the next vision came into view.

A man in top hat and tails played a grand piano in the road. Pink trousers and matching shirt were the only clue he was in Carnaby Street and not the Royal Albert Hall.

A red MGB cruised gracefully past. The occupants, enjoying the ride with the roof down, wore matching red tops and navy caps.

"Groovy," Jon said to Paul. "If you see one of those caps for sale here, let me know."

Paul nodded enthusiastically. "Might get one myself. It'd go well with this polo neck."

"How many Union flags have you counted?"

Gemma whispered to Paul, "Union Jacks, he means."

Jon shot back, "I do not. Union is the right word; Union Jack is for when it's flown at sea."

"Sorry Paul, my fault; he's the fount of all knowledge, not me."

In a low voice, Paul said, "Though perhaps not the fount of all *wisdom*." He winked at Gemma and squeezed her hand as he answered Jon. "At least a dozen, maybe twenty or more."

"I'd like a hat too," said Liberty. "One like that." She inclined her head towards a tall, slim girl, dressed all in white except for pink chubby heeled sling-back shoes and a pink, wide-brimmed, floppy hat.

"Where would you wear it?" Gemma enquired.

"Everywhere." Privately she knew she wouldn't wear it anywhere.

"See where the Rolls-Royce is parked?" Paul turned to Jon. "That's the Chinese restaurant behind."

~

At a quarter to midnight, they arrived back at the flat.

"We'll just see you to your front door," said Paul.

"And can I use your loo, please?" asked Jon.

"As you arranged for it to be here, how could we possibly say no," teased Gemma.

Paul and Gemma waited for Jon in the living room while Liberty flung her handbag onto her bed. The flat smells musty, she thought. Tomorrow she had no work to go to and she'd give it a good airing. She heard dripping. Above Gemma's bed was a brown patch with the ceiling paper hanging down slightly.

"Gemma, Gemma, quickly." She whipped off the bedclothes and flung them on the floor, then took the bottom sheet and the pillow too. All sopping wet. "Gemma!"

Gemma and Paul sauntered in from the living room looking a little flustered.

"Look." Liberty pointed to the ceiling and Paul swung into action.

"Where's your loft hatch?"

"Um... oh... in the bathroom," answered Gemma.

"What's all the fuss?" enquired Jon, returning from the bathroom.

"Any minute now," said Paul, there's going to be one helluva flood. Quick grab that end of the bed and shift it into the middle."

Within seconds, the water dribbled directly onto the lino and Liberty placed the washing up bowl to catch the increasing trickle.

"I can probably climb into the loft if the loo is in the right place."

"It is," said Jon. "I'll give you a hand up."

Liberty hastily rescued her backpack and treasures from under the bed and put them in the wardrobe.

"I suppose we might sleep in the living room," Gemma murmured. "I'll put this wet bedding in the bath when the boys finish in there."

They took Liberty's dry bedclothes carefully into the living room and put them on top of the sofa, then watched Paul and Jon from the doorway.

"It's the tank, Jon. The bottom edge at the back has rusted badly. I can't see too well with just this candle but I'd say it's unsafe and getting worse. The girls need to get out." Paul clambered down onto the bathroom floor and went straight to tell the girls. "You two shouldn't stay here tonight. The base of the tank is unsafe and the washing up bowl isn't going to hold the flood. Come home with me and you can stay in our spare bedroom. We'll sort this out in the morning. Take everything of yours out of the bedroom and stick it in the living room somewhere up off the floor."

"I'll tell the couple downstairs," said Jon, "as it's possible it will flood through to them if it does give way."

"Have you got your landlord's address?"

"Oh Paul, thank you." Gemma hugged him. "We've only got the agent's address and phone number."

"That will do. If I could have plugged the leak, I would have. Now bring your overnight things with you and we'll go back to mine."

As they went down the stairs, Jon was trying to convince Mary they should move everything from directly underneath the possible collapse of the water tank.

"He's right, Mary. We wouldn't disturb you at this time of night if we didn't have to."

Mary nodded and waved goodbye as, under the weight of water, the ceiling upstairs gave way to the deluge now steadily flowing down the stairs leaving them all with wet feet.

Chapter Twenty-Six
Auction of Promises

This would be her second day at The National Hospital and all she could do was hope. Hope that it would be better than her first day. As temporary secretary to the General Manager, a man with a distinguished war record, she'd shot into the hospital yesterday, late, reported to Personnel and been introduced to a tall man of military bearing. Introductions over, she was keen to make up for being late and assumed the door in his office led to hers. It didn't; it was the General Manager's personal bathroom. She'd decided to slow her pace from thereon. The lady from Personnel had introduced her to the two other secretaries who shared the spacious office next door and Liberty just smiled and tipped her head as she'd walked towards a huge desk at the back and sat down. Apparently, this assumption was wrong too and the secretaries clearly didn't take to her.

So on this Thursday morning things had to get better. She adopted the strategy of not speaking unless spoken to, yet this had led to her mistakes. Maybe she should rethink...

Sir Arthur Hollingbourne padded across to her, placed his forefinger on her desk and appeared to be tapping out a tune. She looked up with a bright smile.

"Meeting this morning. Twelve, all from London hospitals. We'll require refreshments at eleven."

Liberty nodded cheerfully while her heart thumped. Where would she find the necessary tea cups? Or did they want coffee? What sort of refreshments?

The older secretary took pity on her and showed her the kitchen. "There's a tin of biscuits in the top cupboard."

Biscuits? Huh! A half packet of Rich Tea. She glanced at the clock on the wall and made a decision.

Within fifteen minutes, she had purchased shortbread biscuits, chocolate biscuits, custard creams and bourbon creams. When the time came, she knocked on the door and wheeled across to the back of the room a trolley of two coffee pots, a large teapot, a jug of milk and two large plates of biscuits. Into her head came the words 'serve to the left, take from the right'.

The visitors continued to debate while she served, simply asking each in a whisper if they required tea or coffee. Everything came to a halt when she put the plates of biscuits along the centre of the large, rectangular table. Approving murmurs lifted her spirits.

About an hour later, Sir Arthur silently crossed the room to her desk.

"Please come with me, Miss Taffet."

Liberty took a deep breath and followed him.

In his office, he showed her to a chair on the other side of his impressive desk.

"Tell me about yourself."

She must be very careful and decided not to mention that she was practically homeless. Should she invent her history? Perhaps not this time. "Until a month or so ago, I could have told you anything you needed to know. However," she took another deep breath, "I'm afraid I have lost my memory and I can only remember my life in the last few weeks."

"Loss of memory? And here you are – assigned to a hospital for neurology."

She must maintain control. Hers was not the normal sort of loss of memory, this much she now knew, and if she'd known The National Hospital specialized in neurology, she'd have turned down the assignment. She frowned. How did she know a neurologist might help with memory loss? Most people wouldn't know that, would they? Had she worked in a hospital? Was she a nurse? No, definitely not a nurse – not with all that blood.

Sir Arthur watched her range of expressions.

"I think it is returning of its own accord. I hope I'll not need treatment though if I do, I'll know who to ask." Her smile was radiant to compensate for her assertive pose. She must make this knight in shining armour decide she didn't need his help, just a job.

"How long ago did this occur?"

"I can remember back clearly as far as the end of March but before that, at the moment, I only get snatches. It doesn't bother me at all."

Sir Arthur leant across the desk as if to examine her more closely. "I hope you will enjoy your work here. Regarding your loss of memory, you may have legal problems at some point. I am here to help, if necessary." He changed tack. "I wanted to thank you. Splendid service. Impressively correct."

Of course, being a knight he would know what's right from wrong in the dizzy heights of serving tea and biscuits. She pursed her lips in case her amusement spilt out.

"Thank you, Sir Arthur. It was my pleasure." She surprised herself by realizing it was true.

"Right, tally ho, it's off to work we go."

Liberty took this to mean she should stand up and get on with clearing the table, which she did.

"Did he offer you the job?" Four eyes followed her to her desk.

"I think I'm expected to come in to work tomorrow."

The eyes squinted.

~

The bouncing Tigger arrived at Paul's house on Friday night and was welcomed into the lounge. Liberty had decided Jon was due a promotion from puppy to the lively tiger fondly known as Tigger in Winnie the Pooh. When he announced his news of an available flat to Gemma, Paul and herself, she knew he was worth the promotion.

"It's not far from here; you'll still be able to catch the same train to work, and it's a bit closer to The Salvation Army." Gemma and Paul were delighted. "It's not vacant until next Saturday, but I can give you a hand with the moving. I think it would be sensible if you immediately moved everything out of the old flat. I assume you have located the landlord?"

Gemma looked as vague as Liberty.

"What's the problem?"

Gemma answered. "We don't know who he is. We've only met the agent and we pay rent to him when he comes round each week."

"He won't be collecting any more rent from you. The landlord has defaulted on his responsibilities."

"We'll lose our deposit, Jon. Shouldn't we ask for it back?"

"We could try, Gemma. Where's your rent book?"

Gemma seemed distressed. "We've never had one."

"So you just paid a man a large deposit and several weeks' rent in cash?"

"Yes."

"I doubt you'll even be able to find the man. It's a well-known trick. They find empty properties, advertise, take a deposit, and collect rent for as long as they can get away with it. If the landlord turns up, you either don't know the name of the man or he's given a false one, and his address is probably another of the empty properties, which he'll move out of and into another." He tutted loudly before adding, "At least in this case the real landlord gets a free bathroom."

Crestfallen, Liberty said nothing. She certainly could not improve on silence. They'd been paying a crook and the benefits of Jon's sterling efforts installing a bathroom were short-lived.

Tigger had lost his bounce too and came close to snarling. "Before any more time passes and someone raids your flat, we must retrieve all your belongings, and I mean now." He turned to Paul, "I hope you don't mind. I know this is usually the night you spend converting the cottage, but it won't take long as the girls haven't got much clobber anyway."

Paul leapt up. "Let's go. I'm pretty sure mum won't mind storing your gear. We can put some in the garage or the shed if necessary. Better let her know first though then we can whizz over and clear the way. See you all by the car."

As soon as Paul left the room, Jon said to Gemma, "You've got a good one there, hang on to him."

"I know, Jon, I know." Her face gave away that she loved her big brother even though he was sometimes exasperating. She then nudged Liberty and whispered, "When we're packing up perhaps we can look out for something to leave Tom and Mary."

"Good idea. Remind me, won't you?"

~

The next morning, Liberty woke up early, courtesy of the bright sun shining through a gap in the drawn curtains. She lay on her back and considered. They'd left Mary a cardigan and a woollen scarf for Tom. She blinked and pursed her lips as she realized he never went out. Still, they'd also left a tin of corned beef, two tins of sardines and a tin of pilchards. Oh, and half a loaf of bread. She recalled Mary's face. She'd opened the door wide enough for them to see Tom's silhouette in the background and hear him making approving noises. Silently she made a promise. For the rest of her life, well maybe for at least a year, she would visit monthly with a bag of food, or something. Perhaps The Salvation Army would find them a better place to live. They did things like that. Or the local council surely should help.

It would be a busy day. First, they would take a look at the flat Jon had found for them. And in the evening, the Auction of Promises was being held at The Salvation Army. She peeped at the clock. Half past six. Perhaps she'd sit up and read the paperback she'd stuffed in her handbag. As quietly as possible, she pulled out 'Songbird'. A slight smile blossomed as she turned to Chapter One. She read a few lines, then flicked to the back to learn about the author: Julia Bell. She snuggled down and started again.

After a full English breakfast, which Paul said his Indian mother proudly produced every Saturday, they waited for Jon. On arrival, Jon, in full bounce and a smart blue and grey striped jacket, produced a map and an address. During the drive, from the front passenger seat, he took the trouble to rehearse the girls in what they should say. He didn't get far.

"Stop it, Jon!" Gemma sounded like an exasperated mother scolding her toddler. "You're making me nervous. I get the picture: it's in a good area, it's big, it has a garden and the owner lives upstairs."

"It's more expensive," Jon said, ignoring his sister. "Try to look as though you're not surprised and that it is worth the price she's asking. We'll soon see if it isn't."

Gemma sighed loudly.

Paul slowed the car as he turned into a long, straight road, bordered by trees in blossom. "This is the road, I think."

Jon peered around. "It is, it is."

At the front door of the imposing semi-detached three storey Edwardian house, Gemma introduced herself and Liberty and, as Jon insisted on seeing the flat too, she introduced him. "My brother," she smiled and added, "He won't be living here."

The flat was worth every penny of its £8 weekly rental, and even had a telephone in the hall, yet Gemma seemed concerned and whispered to Jon to ask if a deposit needed to be paid.

"What's a big brother for? Stop worrying, smile and say you'll take it." He turned to Liberty, raised his eyebrows and surreptitiously gave her an enquiring thumbs up.

Liberty grinned and returned the gesture with gusto. Her only worry was that it was quite a long way south of central London – not good for commuting.

The owner of the house, Mrs Tualin, explained she'd be interviewing three other prospective tenants and she'd let them know as soon as she'd made up her mind.

This was the first indication Liberty had that it was *they* who were being interviewed. It didn't occur to her there might be competition. Yet it should have done, it was obvious that housing stock was in short supply. "Thank you so much for your time, Mrs Tualin. We both appreciate it very much and I can assure you we shall look after the lovely flat you are providing, should we be chosen." Liberty meant every word.

"I need you to understand that as I shall be living above you in the same house, I don't want noisy parties." She tried a little laugh. "I'm past that now." She turned to look at Jon. "Thank you for your telephone number, I'll call you tomorrow."

Liberty spent the afternoon sorting through her possessions at Paul's house. She was enormously relieved that they had been able to leave most of them in the bedroom they'd been given by Paul's mum. Satisfied she would not be disturbed, she took out the letter from her handbag. He'd said he'd find her but he hadn't. Where was he? Why hadn't he come? It was obvious, of course. She no longer worked at the same hospital as him and, if he'd found out where she lived, she was no longer there. If he didn't come soon, she'd have to go to Guy's and ask to see him. Suppose that secretary had already stolen him? She frowned. She'd ask to leave The National Hospital early and go to Guy's on Monday afternoon.

That evening, Gemma and Liberty sorted through their clothes to find something dressy to wear for the Auction of Promises.

"Do you think this is smart enough?"

Gemma considered Liberty's grey, pencil skirt and bright orange jumper.

"Definitely. It looks super."

Half an hour later, they arrived with Paul at The Salvation Army which welcomed them at little tables as if it were a café. Paul showed them to a table with five seats. The smell of coffee and baking wafted out from the kitchen at the back.

"The other seats are for my parents and Jon." He tipped the chairs forward to show they were reserved. He raised his arm to two ladies standing near a hatch. They hurried over with a little teapot and a tray of cupcakes.

"This is such a treat, Paul," said Liberty appreciatively.

Paul and his mother had collected twenty-five promises to be auctioned which were on a card in the centre of each table as if it were a menu.

"Look at these, Gemma. Is there anything there we might bid for?"

"I think I'll be outbid for everything."

"Mrs Samuels is offering to do five Sunday lunches for up to four people each time. Isn't she fantastic? Paul's so lucky."

Liberty reeled off several other promises: a drive around the country lanes of Surrey with afternoon tea at the end, car washing, and Gemma's offer to design and make a skirt. Liberty became aware she'd contributed nothing. She'd been too busy. She had nothing to offer. At the very least she could have promised to babysit. She made up her mind to bid for at least some of the items, reckoning that those who gave their talents needed to be balanced by those who had money to spend, and with that thought, she settled into enjoying the evening.

She was jolted out of her relaxed mood when a man politely asked if there was room for another at the table.

Chapter Twenty-Seven
The exquisitely English art

"May I sit here?" He placed the chair he'd been carrying, next to Liberty.

Nick looked so casual yet smart in his blue check shirt, cream trousers and dark blue jacket, not Sixties Cool but Forever Cool. Liberty melted as his eyes spoke to her heart; she blinked and nodded.

Paul banged the wooden gavel on the table he'd placed at the front of the hall and faced the hundred or more eager, potential buyers. "I hope you have examined the menu of promises on offer and decided you'd like them all." His infectious grin and his manner were decidedly more assertive than usual. "If you would like to bid, please raise your hand."

All were attentive and most stopped munching and sipping.

"Our first promise comes from Rosemary who is offering to bake a cake for every Sunday in May. She'll bring it to the morning meeting for you to collect. If you're not sure if Rosemary's cakes are worth a fortune – sample her cupcakes tonight. For all your successful bids, you can pay at the end of the auction." Paul held up a pink card and said, "Here is the promise for cakes." He grinned. "Now who will bid one shilling?"

Several hands shot up.

"Two shillings?"

The hands remained in the air.

"Ten shillings?"

Two hands remained, waving.

"Eleven shillings for four delicious, big cakes?"
Both hands remained in the air.
"Twelve shillings?"
One hand went down.
"Going, going to Mrs Mazibuko – gone!" Paul slammed the gavel down and his mother collected the pink card, wrote on it, and delivered it to the delighted Mrs Mazibuko.

Nick whispered, "May I see you after this – alone?"

Liberty turned, every bone sizzling as she stared into his dark eyes. She must keep cool. "Yes, I can see you afterwards but we are temporarily living with Mrs Samuels, she's the lady delivering the cards. I'll have to leave when she does."

Mr Samuels, seated next to Gemma, coughed gently though his hint to pay attention was wasted by the arrival of a repentant Tigger.

"Sorry, sorry, sorry. I didn't mean to be so late." Jon glanced across to Nick, glared at him and raised his eyebrows at Liberty.

Liberty smiled brightly. Nick assessed the latecomer.

Paul banged his gavel gently several times and held up a blue card. "Five shillings for a car wash and polish? You choose the time, the place will be our car park at the back. We have the Zungo twins to thank for this."

Hands were in the air.

"Six shillings? Anyone?" He looked around. "Ah Mr Samuels, thank you."

Nick seized the opportunity of another lull in the proceedings and hurriedly whispered, "Give me your address and I'll collect you tomorrow afternoon if that suits?"

Liberty scribbled down her details and slipped it to Nick. "Three o'clock should be fine. I'll explain..."

Paul gently banged the gavel to call for silence; Nick and Liberty were not the only ones snatching an opportunity to chatter in between each auctioned item.

"Here's a good one. A lift to and from a supermarket of your choice, once a week for a month. Who'll start me with one shilling?"

A grey-haired lady of about ninety, by Liberty's reckoning, was the winner at one shilling and ninepence. Liberty turned to Gemma. "He raised the price in pennies. That's so kind."

Gemma glowed yet said nothing; her whole focus remained on the auctioneer.

Liberty paid one pound two shillings for Gemma to make her a skirt. Jon paid £3 for a Sunday lunch for four at Mrs Samuels.

Nick paid £3 for a flower arrangement for every Sunday in May. "To be presented to Mrs Samuels," he whispered, "for looking after you."

Nick also paid £2/10/- for a bottle of Coty's L'Aimant perfume. "For you."

Liberty shone with joy. What a treat. It wasn't a 'promise' like the other auctioned items but it held the promise of time together.

When the auction finished, Jon moved his chair to sit next to Nick. "Hello, I've not seen you before."

Nick volleyed back. "And when I've been, I've not seen you."

"Touché," responded Jon with a half-smile.

Liberty intervened. "Nick, this is Jon, he's the best friend a girl could have."

"How do you do," each said to the other.

"Nick is a doctor at the hospital where I worked – Guy's."

Jon raised an eyebrow. "Really? Yet you no longer work there." He glanced over to Liberty before resuming his interrogation of the interloper. "So do you come here often?"

Liberty felt the tension yet worried she might laugh at their sparring.

Nick turned on a little charm and played the sympathy card. "I am a stranger to this part of London and I have few friends here. I decided to try a church which is new to me – The Salvation Army. Everyone has been so friendly."

The words 'until now', though unspoken, hung in the air.

"It's most kind of you to contribute so generously," mediated Mr Samuels, nodding approvingly.

"Indubitably," smiled Jon. "We need people like you."

Liberty winced. Jon's words were kind, if a little showy, but the tone... and he'd sneaked in a dagger in his so-called smile. She sighed.

Mrs Samuels, now pouring out some tea at their table, whispered to her husband, "Ah, this is the exquisitely English art."

He frowned.

"Each is insulting the other but no-one would know."

Mr Samuels shook his head. "I don't think they've got started yet, this is just the warm-up." He and his wife chuckled.

Liberty stood and patted Nick on the shoulder, unseen, she hoped. To Gemma she said, "I'll wait for you outside."

"Good idea," Gemma responded.

Nick followed Liberty to the gate. "A very successful evening, I hear it was your idea. I'm sorry your friend and I didn't take to each other." He glanced over his shoulder. "Your minder is already coming this way. I'm grateful you have someone doing my job for me, so I'll try not to antagonize him too much. I'll pick you up from the address you gave me at three o'clock tomorrow. It's important, so don't be persuaded otherwise." He touched her arm and left.

So masterful. It was what she needed. Tramlines. Something to stop her being so scatty.

"Left you standing?" Jon stood next to Liberty. "Don't worry; as soon as Paul's parents leave, I'll drive you home."

"I'm so very pleased to have met you and Gemma. I don't know what I'd have done without you."

"I'll always be here for you. Friend for life – that's me."

When all had returned to the Samuels' home and were relaxing in their lounge reflecting on the success of the evening, Jon mentioned Nick. Mrs Samuels glanced up from her knitting.

Mr Samuels asked Liberty a few questions, few of which she could answer, well, not without using the information in his personnel file which must remain confidential.

"He's a doctor." Surely recommendation enough: they have standards.

Jon shot back. "So was Crippen."

"Crippen? Who do you mean?"

"Dr Crippen was an infamous murderer."

Liberty chuckled. "Oh no, Nick is not a murderer, far from it."

"Yet you seem to know so little about him."

Gemma waded in. "My giddy aunt, Jon. Of course Libby doesn't know much about him. She realizes she's met him before and they were just beginning to find out about each other when she changed jobs."

Mrs Samuels bit her lip yet the words escaped anyway. "There's something not quite right about him. Have you noticed, Libby dear?"

Nick had warned her. He knew they'd try to persuade her not to have anything to do with him. "I think I should tell you that I have arranged to meet him tomorrow afternoon. I hope you don't mind, Mrs Samuels?"

"Not at all, my dear. Simply tell us where you're going so we don't have to worry."

Mr Samuels cleared his throat and touched his wife's arm. "Come, come. Liberty is old enough and not irresponsible. She's no doubt aware this man is a little different. Intelligent men often are."

Time travellers were particularly different. Liberty thought it would be best to change the subject but how? Ah... "I have something for you, Jon. I keep forgetting to give it to you." She dashed upstairs and returned with 'The Big Book of Silly Jokes'. "I've had this for a while. It's not new but I thought you'd like it."

Jon took it and flicked through, reading out some of what he thought were the pick of the bunch. "Excellent, excellent!" he roared. "Looks like an American author. Carole P. Roman." He read out a joke. "Jolly good collection." Then he frowned. "Misprint here." He showed Paul. "Copyright says 2019."

Gemma sat with her hand propped up over her mouth as, eyes wide, she stared at Liberty's confused face.

Suddenly, Liberty smiled confidently: Jon had provided the answer himself. "Yes, it must be a misprint and that's probably why

I was given it." Maybe that was true or maybe not. She couldn't remember.

Chapter Twenty-Eight
Trouble makers or potty

"Liberty, let me introduce you to my family. This is my grandmother, I call her Nonna, Italian for Granny."

"My name is Aurora, please you call me Aurora." An exceptionally beautiful woman with long, jet black hair with a hint of a curl and a delightful accent, smiled graciously.

"Nonna is Italian and came to England after the war."

"I captured her and brought her home," declared a jovial man in his forties, wearing red trousers and a cream jersey.

Nick, watching Liberty closely, said, "Grandpapa is a war hero, he single-handedly liberated Europe."

Grandpapa gave Nick an affectionate punch on the arm. "Take no notice of him, Liberty, he exaggerates. I liberated only Italy."

Aurora was laughing. "This is all for your benefit, Liberty. One day I tell you truth."

The genial atmosphere spread to Liberty who felt completely at home. She tried to think of her parents' home but nothing came to mind.

"Come, we go to the drawing room and we have the English afternoon tea."

"Nick," Liberty sidled up to him, "How can your grandparents accept you as their grandson when they are probably less than twenty years older than you?" Her eyes grew large and her mouth dropped open. "You've told them?"

"Yes. And the remarkable thing is, they believe me. Grandpapa is a historian but is surprisingly interested in science fiction. He's of the opinion that much of the fiction he reads will one day, soon even, be true. You can relax, they understand what we are."

"We do indeed," said Grandpapa, surreptitiously listening in, "and we shall do all we can to help you settle into the Swinging Sixties."

Liberty turned the phrase over and over – Swinging Sixties – it had a zing about it.

The drawing room was furnished in art deco style with a small, circular table in one corner. On the table stood a silver cross with the crucified Jesus. Of course, Aurora, being Italian, was a Catholic.

"You like?" Aurora inclined her head towards the foot-high crucifix. "You believe?"

What could she say? She took a deep breath before summoning up the courage to say, "If I didn't before, I am beginning to believe now." She frowned, wondering if that was exactly true.

Aurora smiled, turned and pointed out a portrait of a man in Regency dress. "See, this painting was saved from the old house. It is Nicolo's ancestor on Grandpapa's side. Nicolo's father is, of course, our son. It is big puzzle, yes?"

Liberty nodded; mystifying but true.

"We do not wish to confuse our son, he's only eight years old and is at boarding school so we can talk freely. We have told him a cousin of his is staying with us, nothing more; we cannot say Nick is our grandson."

"I'm hoping I'll at least catch a glimpse of my father as a child." Nick smiled broadly. "Of course, I call Grandpapa 'Grandie' so that when he returns, I'll not slip up. You can help me with that, Libby, especially if you call him 'Grandie' too."

"I am amazed," an understatement, "you both believe Nick and I are time travellers?"

"Indeed, indeed," Grandpapa said enthusiastically. "I have long suspected it is possible and now I have proof – in my own family too."

He punched the air, then added, "It's a great pity that I must keep this secret; however, I shall."

"Grandie believes that needing to keep things secret means we are not allowing the truth to surface, but for our sakes, he will not say a word."

Liberty thanked him profusely then could not resist asking, "Do you believe in UFOs?"

"Absolutely. Let me tell you of the unidentified flying object I saw over the Northumberland coast."

"Not now, my darling, it is the time for the tea."

Right on cue, just as they sat on the two sofas either side of the fireplace, a lady with a wrinkled face wheeled in a trolley. Aurora spoke to her in Italian and the lady smiled at Liberty in welcome.

"She used to be my nanny and my wonderful husband let me bring her here to my new land."

Liberty decided the only acceptable response was a delighted smile.

From a silver teapot, Aurora poured tea and encouraged her guests to help themselves to egg and cress, and smoked salmon sandwiches.

"Tell us about yourself, Liberty," said Nick's disconcertingly young grandmother.

Liberty put her tea cup down and tucked her long hair behind her ears. "My first memories of arriving in 1968 are walking along the Bradstow shore, with the wind in my hair, the scent of the sea and feeling utterly lost when I saw women wearing trousers. You see, I'd intended to travel back to 1814." She hesitated. "Then Gemma," she turned to look at Nick, "Gemma took me back to her grandmother's." Liberty realized there were now two fortuitously placed grandmothers.

Nick explained, "Gemma is the young lady with whom Liberty is sharing a flat."

"I didn't realize I was a time traveller; I thought I'd only lost my memory. I'd brought a change of clothing with me and the all-important notebook which told me how to return to 2020 but I was fascinated with the life and the characters I was meeting. I financed the deposit for the flat and the rent by selling some of my mother's jewellery which I'd brought with me."

"Oh my dear," said Aurora, "how painful for you."

Liberty warmed to this lady with every sentence she uttered. Acknowledging Aurora's concern, she continued. "I found work by going to a recruitment agency, though I have no National Insurance number nor any other essential identification. It seemed they were very short of medical secretaries so they tested my typing and spelling of medical words and didn't bother with anything else. Hence my first job happened to be at Guy's hospital, where I met Nick." She hurriedly added, "Again."

Nick consulted his large leather notebook. "In 2020, Libby was a manager in the National Health Service and that is where I *first* met her."

Liberty felt a shiver. She'd worked in a hospital – yes – there was a woman, she couldn't remember her name nor even picture her, yet she knew she didn't like her.

"We had dinner together one night and Libby showed me a book she'd found in her office."

Liberty looked astonished. "I don't remember any of this."

"Neither do I," laughed Nick, his dark eyes shining. "It's the reason why I made copious notes when I went back to 2020." He turned to his grandparents. "Obviously, in 2020 I knew that Grandie, Nonna, my parents and even I lived in this house before I went to university."

"We're so happy that you did," said Aurora crossing her arms over her chest and rocking as if she were cuddling Nick.

"Go on, go on," said Grandpapa. "What about the book Liberty showed you?"

Nick smiled. "We pored over a little red book with notes which the previous owner of the agency had written. Liberty had bought the agency when she left the hospital and that's where she found the book. Caves were mentioned." He turned to look at Liberty sitting by his side on the sofa. "Do you remember any of this?"

"No."

"Neither do I." He laughed and turned over a few pages. "We both visited the caves and noticed some were cordoned off."

Liberty searched her handbag. "I've got Laura's little red book with me."

"You do?" Grandpapa appeared delighted.

Liberty scrabbled around in the dark depths of her bag and came up with both the red and her own blue notebook. "I carry these two with me everywhere I go because I don't want to leave them lying around for somebody else to find."

"And it is the returning that I must warn you about," said Nick.

"I love returning." She consulted her blue notebook. "Look at all the things I have brought back." She showed Nick and then began to read some out to the bemusement of his grandparents. "And returning has been essential because my jewellery, and other important things are securely stored there." Best not to mention the gold yet.

Nick took hold of her hand and squeezed it gently. "Do you also have my letter in your handbag, perchance?"

"Liberty smiled broadly. "Of course." She produced it with a flourish.

"In it, I explained to you that one of Laura's toes became invisible after several trips back and forth. Dr Matt Redfern, her husband, made clear to me that it is likely to happen to us too and will probably spread to other areas of the body if we continue to visit." He glanced across to his grandparents, raised his eyebrows then returned to looking at Liberty. "Remember I spoke to Matt before you went through the cave into the light curtain the first time."

Liberty's hand flew to her mouth. "Did you..." She took a deep breath and let her hand fall to her side. "Nick, did you follow me through the light curtain knowing you would only be able to return to 2020 as a ghost?" Had she neglected to write this down in her blue notebook?

Nick remained silent.

Aurora didn't. "Oh my true Italian child." She flew across to sit beside him and hug him. "Such love. You knew what you'd be giving up. You knew..." Her tears spilled down her cheeks.

Liberty's tears did too while Aurora said, 'such love' over and over again.

Nick offered each a cotton hanky. "We must not look back to 2020, we must look forward." He grinned, indicating he was aware of the irony of his words. "This is a wonderful time to be living. My notes tell me that, in the coming years, the UK will not be involved in any serious wars apart from a violent skirmish in the South Atlantic and we had troops in Europe at one point." He hastily added, "Lives, good lives were lost, but it was nothing like the Second World War."

Grandpapa frowned, "Exactly which countries or who or what are you describing?"

"This I must leave unsaid. Nothing for you to worry about."

Liberty saw him underline the words 'rampant inflation in the 70s' and 'three day week – shortage of electricity – miners' strike'. She caught on. His grandparents might be seen as troublemakers or potty if they tried to warn of battles to come. Or even, perhaps, the future might be changed? Could it be possible? If so..? She'd let Nick do the talking.

He did. "2020, however is in the grip of what appears to be a pandemic." He glanced across to his grandparents. "It is not wise for you to know the future and I do not wish to place you at a disadvantage by giving you too much information about the twenty-first century. All I will say is that when I returned to early 2020 a hitherto unknown virus was rampaging through the world population and we cannot discern the outcome. There are those who say it will wipe out billions. There have been many theories including the unbelievable one that the Chinese actually created it to wipe out their elderly because the one child policy means there is an insufficient number of young people to support the elderly in their retirement." He sighed loudly.

"One child policy?" queried Grandpapa.

"I have said too much. If that rumour were to be true, it has backfired. It's spread around the world, mostly to the elderly it's true, and there is no vaccine yet and certainly no cure. 1968 looks good to me." He squeezed her hand again, grinned and said, "You may have saved my life."

Not that either of them knew anything much about the virus at the time, thought Liberty, yet he credited her with the deed. Dumbstruck, she basked in the overwhelming flow of love sweeping through her.

"Personally, I think our scientists will create a vaccine but it takes time." He took a deep breath. "Enough of viruses and wild theories, I have brought you here today, Liberty, not only to explain about the dangers of returning but also to provide you with acceptable credentials for life here and now. Grandie was imprisoned by the Nazis in the early years of the war. He learnt from a former forger, also imprisoned, how to... well you know." He raised his eyebrows and winked. "This aided his escape back to Britain and has been a huge help with creating the right credentials for me to practice as a doctor here."

"I'll help you too, Liberty. It is, for me, an honour to assist my time travelling grandson and his special lady. Also, I shall be roping my brother into helping. He's a Civil Servant and his department, well, I'll say no more except that, between the two of us we can *fix* things."

Aurora passed the plate of little cakes around.

Nick took one. Liberty shook her head. She needed to concentrate, not eat cakes. Did Aurora have cotton wool in her ears?

"It's hard to take it all in, isn't it?" As Liberty seemed unable to answer, Nick swallowed the little cake, closed his notebook, rose to his feet and pulled her up. "Come, I'll show you the grounds."

Grounds, thought Liberty, they have grounds not a garden.

Stepping onto the terrace at the back of the house, Liberty took a deep breath. Meeting Nick's grandparents was wonderful but she was left feeling confused. Her thoughts were wiped away when she saw two dogs racing towards them.

"Hope you like dogs?"

"Oh yes." Of that she was sure.

The dogs were upon them, panting, tails wagging, and inspections of Liberty being made.

"Sit." The dogs sat. "Quiet yet stern is the modus operandi for training these two." He turned to the dogs. "Introduce yourselves." Both lifted one paw. "Do you mind shaking paws, Libby? They'll be lifelong friends if you do."

Libby bent down and dutifully shook their paws. "They're adorable. Are they Labradors?"

"Yes, golden Labradors, couple of softies, they are. When Grandie complains he's cold at night, I've heard Nonna shout, "Well put another dog on the bed.""

Liberty shook with laughter. "You are joking, surely?"

"No, really, it's true. I think it's Nonna's way of turning down a bit of nooky. The dogs have beds in the hall allowing them to patrol at night if they hear a noise but one of them sometimes sneaks onto Grandie's bed." Turning to the dogs, he said, "Heel," and stepped onto the lawn. "Their names are Sun and Sirius. I tend to say Sunny and Siri, unless they're misbehaving."

Again, Liberty found herself laughing almost uncontrollably with the relief of returning to uncomplicated real life.

"The German Shepherd, the guard dog with his own little house by the annexe, died the week I arrived. He was elderly. He'll be replaced once they stop mourning. Until then, apparently, Grandie sees me as the interim territorial guardian. I come home at all hours of the day and night, pick up the cricket bat and do a circuit."

"Cricket bat?"

"Next best thing to a guard dog."

Yet again, Liberty laughed with not a care in the world. "I find this whole setup unbelievable. Your grandparents actually believe us and, by the looks of it, so do the dogs."

"Ah... as these two assess everything by smell and the number of treats, I made sure I had smelly treats in my pockets for the first few weeks, just in case they were suspicious. It must have worked."

"Man is still superior to dog then." She chuckled as Nick gave Sun and Sirius permission to roam again.

"I should warn you that Grandie swears prolifically, not that you'd know it. He has a vocabulary stuffed with invented words to use when he deems it necessary to let off steam. Unfortunately, these words have run down the generations. I remember my father using them – he's too young to use them now, of course. I've tried to ditch the habit and you must give me a stern look if I explode."

Liberty giggled. "Except if you explode with righteous indignation, when I might excuse you."

"Righteous indignation? All my explosions are such."

Liberty grinned. He hadn't cottoned on to the 1968 way of speech, in fact, he sounded as if he were from the eighteen hundreds. And this she really, really, liked.

As they strolled towards the perimeter of the property, Nick became serious. "What we must both do is make a short record of our lives from birth to 2020 and we can only do this by returning one last time. We'll plan this another day." He smiled and introduced what for him was a sure reality: we are welcome here, we can improve the lives of those around us, we have talents and experience to offer; there is much we can do." He took her in his arms and kissed her on the cheek. "We'll make a great team, and we can stay for many years before there'll be complications and then we'll revert to Plan A."

Liberty had already thought of a few complications but didn't want to spoil the moment. A kiss on the cheek prevented her from questioning him on 'plan A'. For many, a single touch would not be enough, but for her the warmth of his arms, the gentle touch to her face, and his words, all sent a shiver of delight through her entire body.

He released her and pointed. "Do you see the old house?"

Liberty peered across the lawns to the ruins of what must once have been a fine Georgian house. Its grey stone walls were barely visible. "It's almost strangled by ivy."

"And there's a small tree growing inside it now." He smiled and raised his eyebrows. "It was bombed in the First World War, a zeppelin raid apparently. It was a direct, unexpected hit; all were killed. Fortunately, Colonel James Nylander was with his regiment in France. He was my great grandfather."

"Was?"

"Yes he died just a few years ago, in the early 1960s. It was he who built what we now call 'the new house' in 1920. Grandie said he sold some land, sketched out the design of five reception rooms, twelve bedrooms, the usual others, and here you have the finished article." He waved his arm. "Of course, they're a bit light on bathrooms. I have to walk down the hall to one. We can soon alter that though. Might have to give up a bedroom or four but it will be worth it. There's the annexe too, though that is currently unused." Almost inaudibly, he repeated, "Currently." He took hold of her hand. "Another time, I'll take you down to explore. The woods beyond are ours too."

Turning her slightly to face the new house, he said, "Grandie has a powerful telescope. He searches the stars, convinced aliens will one day visit."

Alarmed, Liberty said, "Do *you* think that?"

Nick chuckled. "No; but who knows? Would you have believed in time travelling last Christmas?"

Liberty shook her head. "No way."

"He's one of those gloriously British creatures – an eccentric and appealingly unaware of it."

"Do you know if they are still alive in 2020?"

"Yes, they are both in their nineties and living in the annexe. My parents live in the main house. Don't say a word about that, please." His eyes reinforced his request. "I can only tell you because I made a note of it. It's strange that, having come from the future, we are not allowed to *remember* it and there's only so much I can note down. Paper outlasts modern technology, otherwise I'd take back a Dictaphone." He returned to the subject of telescopes. "Grandie keeps track of UFOs. Loads of them, apparently." He spread his arms wide to demonstrate 'loads'."

"Really? Or are they just comets?"

Nick grinned. "Only time will tell."

Liberty smiled in agreement. "Do you like living here?"

"Immensely. The little place I had was fine for when I first arrived but fortunately I discovered my parents' address tucked away in my wallet as being my next of kin. I followed it up and found my grandparents living here. Nonna was wary at first but Grandie declared I looked Italian, like Nonna, and it was obvious I was a family member. It didn't take him long to recognize I was what he called 'out of my time'. To cut a long story short, he was over the moon to have some of his wacky theories proved true."

It took Liberty a while to fathom how all this could be correct. Eventually she was satisfied and declared that she understood but it sure did hurt her brain. She never wanted to leave this place – it had an atmosphere of peace and calm yet there appeared to be a house full of life and love set in its midst.

Nick took her hand and began to walk back to his home. "I cannot return next weekend as my shift doesn't finish until seven on Sunday night, but if you can arrange to be free for the following weekend, I think that would be the time for us both to go back and collect everything we need."

"I think it will be all right," she said hesitantly. "I can't come next weekend anyway as it's when we move into our new flat. Jon rang Gemma at lunch time to say we were successful."

~

That evening, just before ten o'clock, Nick knocked quietly on the front door of the Samuels' house. Paul opened the door.

"Come in, come in," he stood aside to let them both in.

"Thanks, but I'll shoot off home; I've an early start tomorrow morning and I guess you have too."

Liberty thanked Nick with a kiss on the cheek and watched him drive away.

There'd be rather a lot to write in her journal tonight.

Chapter Twenty-Nine
Locked away from inquisitive eyes

Nick borrowed his grandfather's car to pick up Liberty from Paul's house on the Tuesday evening.

"What do you think? Like it?"

"Oh wow! It's a Morgan, isn't it?"

"Yup. Suits him, don't you think?"

"Definitely," Liberty laughed. "It looks like something out of the 1920s."

"That's the idea; but goes like a rocket. You might want to put this on." He pointed to the hat he'd placed on the passenger seat.

Nick opened the low, passenger door and Liberty slid in, clutching the hat, saying "There's quite an art to getting in, isn't there?"

"It would be even more difficult if I had the hood up." Nick didn't bother with opening the door and slipped over the top easily. "It's a knack," he said with a smile. "The hat looks great on you. It's Nonna's Breton cap she wears sailing."

As they roared away, Liberty pulled the hat down tightly.

"I hope you don't mind, Libby, I decided we could talk more easily if we didn't go to a restaurant. Nonna's organizing something for the summer house. It's close to the woods and the bluebells are in bud."

The summer house was small, cosy and well furnished. It boasted a table near the window, laid for two, with a low, round bowl of flowers to one side. An elderly butler, in full fig, brought two baskets laden with food and began setting it out.

"Your Nonna is wonderful," whispered Liberty.

"She's prepared the food herself. She wanted you to taste some authentic Italian dishes."

The butler lit a candle and, dismissed and thanked, he returned to the house.

"Does he live here?"

"The butler? No, not any more. He's nearly eighty. Nonna found him a little place of his own and he comes when required."

Sitting opposite each other, Nick raised his glass of wine. Liberty raised hers and together they said, "Chin-chin." His loving eyes said a lot more and Liberty revelled in the tingle of goosebumps. While he took a sip, she reflected on how he often showed his feelings, imperceptible to most, in his eyes. She remembered the times she'd caught his eyes narrowing slightly as he assessed people, the way they flashed when something amused him, and the steel in them when he disapproved. Now she saw concentration; eyes that spoke of determination, purpose and grit. Somehow, his strength of character showed perfectly in two delectable, dark eyes.

"Penny for them."

Liberty chuckled. "It's strange to think that a penny would actually buy something in this time."

"Your answer is as good as a politician's."

She grinned; he'd not missed that she'd avoided answering his request.

After the butler cleared the dishes and brought a pot of coffee, milk and tiny coffee cups, they sacrificed savouring their time together and started working on what they should bring back from their final trip to 2020.

"Nick, were you able to visit this house in 2020 as a ghost and see how everyone was?"

"According to my notes, yes. I delivered my letters here. I popped them through the letter box but I also went around to the back door and slipped in. I noted how strange to see that little had changed except the art deco furniture had been shifted from the main sitting room to the library."

"You have a library big enough...?"

"Have to have one, I'm afraid. There are so many books to house. Now let's crack on." He took a deep breath. "While we are there, we must each gather as much information on our personal lives as possible. I'll collect together some more medical text books and also records detailing recent history encompassing the sixties onwards."

Liberty didn't need him to explain why; she imagined them being able to see into the future. What a gift. He continued with various other useful items and Liberty added, "Photographs. I'd like to take actual printed photos."

"All of these things must be locked away from inquisitive eyes."

Another hour passed in debating and mentally packing things into two backpacks and suitcases on wheels which could be carried through the caves, in particular – the light curtain.

As the sun set in pink and purple glory, he turned his full attention to Liberty, a rare form of generosity from a man whose mind is raided by so many other people and problems. Then she saw it again – the smile that would melt Antarctica and certainly her heart.

~

Moving day arrived and Jon's red Spitfire had the roof down which enabled the girls to pack more into it than might have been wise. Gemma's huge teddy bear sat in the front seat with a large bag on his lap, much to the amusement of many pedestrians. Paul's car was also full to the brim, not only with a suitcase and boxes in the boot but also with tins of Mrs Samuel's baking. They set off in convoy towards the new flat with Jon at his Tiggerish best.

At the agreed time of eleven o'clock, they rang the doorbell of their new home and Mrs Tualin opened the door.

"I have some bad news. I'm afraid, I needed to remortgage the house. I won't go into the details; however, I advise you never to get married. Men! I've been left high and dry."

"Judas!" exclaimed Jon, visibly shocked at what this news would surely mean for the girls.

Undeterred, Mrs Tualin continued. "I've been paying six per cent interest but as from next month, I have to pay nearly eight per cent. It's a considerable difference which I hadn't anticipated and can ill afford. With much regret, and my apologies, I must ask you for another £3 each week."

This news was greeted with stunned silence from all except Jon. "Is there something extra you're able to offer for this money? Something, perhaps, that costs you nothing but which benefits Miss Bond and Miss Taffet?"

"Come in and we can discuss this. I am deeply embarrassed and I do apologize. Don't leave your bags in the open car, Mr Bond, bring them in, especially your bear. Let us think positively – we *can* solve this." She added in a whisper, "I hope."

Liberty stepped in first. She glanced at the large double bedroom, the small yet adequate kitchen, the dining room, the bathroom and separate loo. By the time she was shown into the sitting room with its comfortable sofa, armchairs and French windows opening onto the garden – their garden, she knew she'd not give it up. "Mrs Tualin, I wonder if we could turn the dining room into another bedroom?"

"Wonderful, wonderful. The thought had occurred to me, though..."

Jon regained his bounce. "I can provide a bed and a..." he dashed to the dining room and called out, "a single wardrobe and maybe a chest of drawers too." He returned to the sitting room. "How does that sound?"

"Wonderful, undeniably wonderful." Mrs Tualin smiled broadly in relief. "We can put the little dining table and chairs in that corner." She pointed to a space to the left of the French windows. "There's no curtains in the dining room though."

"I can do that," said Gemma.

"So you just need to find a third girl?" said Paul who'd been visually approving the new flat.

Gemma sighed. "That will be the difficult part."

Mrs Tualin looked delighted despite the obvious difficulty. "I can keep your rent at £8 a week for the next two weeks but after that I shall find myself heading into debt. I've dismissed the gardener already so if you want to help out at all, I'd be very grateful."

"Can do," said Paul.

Liberty glanced at Paul in his dark blue, open neck shirt and jeans and wondered how he always managed to be so nice. Nice, yes that's the word. And kind. And to top it all, he's good-looking with a trendy Liverpool accent. She glanced at Gemma who glowed. Liberty pursed her lips. How and why had she fallen through time into a corral of saints? And did she envy their effortless niceness? Quite possibly. If only she… Concentrate.

"I'll leave you to settle in." Mrs Tualin held out her hand to take the envelope Jon offered her.

Unpacking didn't take long. Trying to pay Jon back for the deposit and first week's rent would take a little longer. In the kitchen, Gemma was peering into Mrs Samuel's tins.

"Look at all this. She's made enough sandwiches for the four of us and there's chocolate cake too. And in this tin there's a Tupperware container of..." she sniffed it, "beef stew, delicious. We can have it for lunch tomorrow."

Liberty was stacking the cupboard with all the supplies Mrs Samuels provided. A horrible, empty feeling crawled into her stomach. Tom and Mary seemed to have nobody who cared about them and here she was, having arrived in 1968 like a beached whale, surrounded by rescuers galore. A sniff and a few blinks stopped the tears.

"All right?" enquired Gemma.

"Very much so, thank you. It's only that I thought of poor Tom and Mary."

"What's the hold-up?" Jon put his head around the door.

"Libby's wondering how Tom and Mary are."

"I'll come to the meeting tomorrow and on the way back we can call in. I promise this is not a ruse to be invited for Sunday lunch. I'll clear off afterwards."

Liberty brightened immediately and put aside a tin of ham from the cupboard.

In between enjoying the sandwiches and cake, Paul brought them up-to-date on the youth club plans. Suddenly he changed tack. "You know, I have so much to be grateful for. I haven't told you before but my parents adopted me."

What to say? Libby tried and failed.

"I was found..." Paul closed his eyes before spitting out, "in a tin bathtub just about floating in the river Mersey."

Silence; all were stunned.

Gemma touched his hand, "You don't have to tell us, Paul."

"I've never told anyone else but I want you to know how much you all mean to me. I was only a few hours old. Because I was a little more brown than most, well, half-caste, I was adopted by my Indian mother and English father." He perked up. "Ready-made they were."

All smiled.

"They gave me a very good life, still do." He paused in reflection. "I've just wanted to give something back so they will feel it was worthwhile taking me on."

Gemma gently said, "I'm sure they've loved having you as their own. Every moment."

Liberty nodded and Jon said, "Of all people, Paul, you are someone who never stops giving."

Paul appeared not to have heard. "Without them, I wouldn't have met you." He gave a determined smile, topped up everyone's glasses with sparkling grape juice and raised his glass. "To good friends, to happiness in your new home and to finding a first-class new flatmate."

Chapter Thirty
Marks out of ten

"Hello, I'm Chloe Campbell. Thanks for seeing me."

Liberty's immediate assessment was favourable. On the doorstep stood a petite girl, with glorious, long red hair, dressed conservatively in a brown, pencil skirt with a beige patterned jersey on top. A huge sense of relief flooded through her. "Come in." She showed her into the sitting room. The newspaper advertisement produced a huge response but they'd whittled it down to three possible candidates. The two seen so far were given eight and seven out of ten marks. Chloe might make it to a nine.

"Hello," said Gemma, visibly impressed. "You can ask us any questions you like and we've got a few for you."

"Thanks. I'm happy for you to ask me anything you like."

Gemma and Liberty sat next to each other on the sofa, exchanged approving glances and suggested Chloe sit in the armchair facing them and the garden.

Liberty's managerial skills came to the fore, surprising herself and Gemma at the same time.

"Tell us about yourself: where you come from, where you live now, where you work, anything you like."

Chloe obliged. She was seventeen and worked as a shop assistant in Swan and Edgar in Piccadilly Circus. "I'm a bit of a duffer really."

"Working in Piccadilly? It's the centre of the Universe, you'd have to be good," said Gemma encouragingly.

"And on Saturday evenings I work as a waitress not far from there. I know there's a bus direct from here to Piccadilly." Her hopeful eyes touched their hearts.

"Yes, that's right," said Liberty mentally racking up the points because the candidate had done her homework and was also likely to be able to afford the rent. "Where are you living now?"

"In the YWCA hostel near Oxford Street." At this point, Chloe looked flustered and mentioned difficulties in her parents' marriage.

A sure shutdown for further background questioning, thought Liberty. Yet it was likely Gemma's sympathetic heart would give her ten points. "Would you like to have a look at the flat?"

"Yeah, that'd be cool, thanks."

When looking at what would become Chloe's bedroom, Gemma explained that curtains would also be hung. "Might take another week or so."

Whereas the other two possible candidates looked concerned about this, Chloe said she understood and would just turn the lights off. At the end of the tour, they offered her a cup of tea or coffee and both went to the kitchen out of her earshot.

"Marks out of ten?"

Gemma said, "Ten. I think the poor girl might be in dire need. If you agree, shall we say she can move in as soon as she likes?"

"I'd give her nine. I think your 'poor girl' might be a good little actress. Nevertheless, she seems, as you say, the neediest." Liberty thought hard. A tussle began: she'd need to make sure her jewellery and gold bars were well hidden, yet it seemed the poor kid could do with a break.

"Is it a yes?"

Liberty took a deep breath. "Yes. It's good to see our new flatmate is happy about no boyfriends staying overnight, no parties, and sharing the chores and payment for the shopping. She didn't flinch at all. I'll check with her again, I think."

"And shall we keep our split of the rent at £4 each and she need only pay £3?"

It sounded fair as Chloe would have the smallest room, although Gemma and Liberty shared, it was a large, light room. Liberty took another deep breath. "Yes, if you say so. Remember though, she hasn't had to pay a deposit."

"It just means she doesn't get anything back from it whereas we do. We hope."

"Not if she wrecks the place." Liberty smiled. "Only kidding." Returning to the sitting room, she asked Chloe to confirm there would be no boyfriends staying overnight and no parties without everyone's agreement. A couple of other rules also got a nod of assent from Chloe and an enthusiastic confirmation. Gemma heaved a sigh of relief.

"When would you like to move in," asked Liberty.

"Would Thursday be too soon?"

"It would have to be in the evening," Gemma responded.

"I only have a suitcase so there's no hassle."

~

True to his word, within a few days of declaring he'd find a bed, wardrobe and chest of drawers, Jon and his 'friend with van' arrived with two out of three, promising to bring a wardrobe very soon.

And so, less than two weeks after the girls moved in, they had found another flatmate. Mrs Tualin, delighted, said Chloe needn't pay rent until the Saturday though she'd charge her for cutting another key.

Chloe did have only one suitcase but also a large backpack and a holdall. A black, London taxi cab pulled away from across the road. Had Chloe arrived in a taxi? Surely not. Just a coincidence.

Paul called in later on the Thursday evening. "Band Practice is cancelled," he said, not missing the chance to give a short explanation to Chloe about The Salvation Army's brass bands. Nor did he miss the opportunity to advertise the youth club. "We need all the help we can get to add the finishing touches to our new club house. You'd be very welcome to come too, Chloe. Friday night, I'll come and collect you all. Wear some old clothes."

"Friday evening? Yeah, that'd be cool."

While Chloe watched the television, Paul, Gemma and Liberty sat outside in the fading sunlight. Liberty noticed a caravan parked in the field at the back of next door's garden. It was only just visible behind the hedge. "I'm going to take a look around," she told them. Not wishing to appear nosy, she stopped to smell the roses; most were in bud but a few were in bloom and Liberty's nose nearly collided with an industrious bee working overtime. She decided it would be better to walk straight to the end and take a look from there. She stood by the gate and peered over. The caravan seemed to be the same size as the one near their old flat although the curtains were different and this one sported a light green stripe on the side. Into her mind shot a conversation with Gemma about the terrible shortage of housing. Most likely this was yet another homeless household and she didn't need to worry. Anyway, why would anybody be following them? She turned around, strolled back to Gemma and Paul, and decided to be diplomatic and leave the two lovebirds alone. "It's getting chilly out here, I think I'll go inside and watch TV."

Chloe, wearing the same clothes she'd worn at her interview with the girls, had stretched out on the sofa watching a Western. "John Wayne," was all she said.

Gemma always sat on the sofa and Liberty's chosen seat was the armchair facing the garden. A third person, unaware of custom, might upset the unspoken rules. Nevertheless, Liberty kindly said, "If you've not got some old clothes for tomorrow night, I can lend you some."

"Thanks, that'd be great."

Liberty made a mental note to go to the jumble sale on Saturday afternoon. A frisson of joy seeped through her. Looking after Chloe would be like having a younger sister. Maybe there'd be some suitable curtains on sale too. She mustn't, however, forget Tom and Mary. She smiled at the memory of them just as John Wayne shot someone dead.

Chapter Thirty-One
Bleakheath Bozos

Liberty began to unpack their Saturday shopping, sighed and said, "Poor Jon, it's always happening to him. He's a star, Gemma. Whenever he enters a room, it's as if a light has been turned on." Liberty couldn't stop her thoughts contrasting this with Nick entering a room: he radiated a sense of presence without saying or doing anything except being there. She frowned; she was supposed to be focussing on Jon. "Jon is extraordinary, truly. The best friend anyone could ever have and I hope always to be friends with him. I would miss him terribly if he didn't come to see us." Both were kind, both knew how to put people at their ease, although Nick could be razor sharp, like the Queen's consort, Prince Philip. Probably better not to mention Nick, nor Prince Philip.

Gemma noticed Liberty's faraway expression and waited before she said, "Jon will still come to see us, even though Nick's more on the scene now. He's a great brother, but probably won't come so often."

"He's helped us so much. What would we have done without him?"

"He's always been there for me."

Liberty continued to unpack their shopping bags while Gemma started cleaning the sink. "I haven't said anything like 'I don't want to go out with you again, because I'd be happy to do so. He's never tried anything on, Gemma, he's a real gentleman and only kissed me on the cheek in all the time I've known him. I thought he might have a proper girlfriend tucked away somewhere. I even began to feel guilty in case I was taking him away from her."

"He's never mentioned anyone in particular, so I don't think so. He did ask about a foursome with Paul again sometime."

"What did you say?"

"Only that we were going to the jumble sale and then we'd both got separate plans for later." Gemma whispered, "Where's Chloe? I thought she was meant to be cleaning the kitchen while we did the shopping."

Liberty shrugged and switched on Radio Caroline. The Beatles were belting out 'Taxman', displacing all worries about Chloe who, she hoped, would soon get the hang of flat-sharing. Life doesn't get much better. Nick would be here later to whisk her away to paradise.

Even the afternoon jumble sale seemed fun. Chloe bought a long black cardigan with a button missing for threepence, Liberty bought Mary a flower-patterned skirt with an elasticated waist, a nearly new T-shirt for Tom and they all clubbed together to pay three shillings for a pair of red and white striped curtains which would probably fit Chloe's bedroom window. Paul's mother was selling some refreshments and he treated them all. Chloe thanked him profusely which made the other two girls smile. On the whole, she'd settled in well, paid her rent and seemed pleased to have found a safe haven.

"Going to get some sleep before my shift tonight," Chloe announced. "I think I know the way."

"We'll be quiet when we get back," Gemma responded.

"Here's your curtains, Chloe. We've got rather a lot to carry."

On their way home, they called in at the corner shop and then their old, deserted flat. Mary opened the door her customary few inches before welcoming them in to a damp-smelling flat.

"Did the landlord come and attend to the leak?" asked Liberty.

"He's foreign and doesn't speak much English. He looked mad about you living in the flat upstairs. He kept saying, 'No rent, no rent'."

"But we did pay rent," said Liberty. "We paid £5 a week and the man we rented it from collected it every Monday night."

Gemma and Liberty glanced at each other and the penny dropped. "It's what Jon said," she turned to Tom and Mary, "my brother told us there were swindles like this going on."

"I told him the flood wasn't your fault and you'd paid your rent in good faith," Tom said. "I made sure he knew my Mary heard the rent man coming up the stairs every Monday. A landlord should pay more attention to his business."

"Thank you both so much," said Liberty. "I hope he's pleased with the free bathroom he's acquired."

"He didn't mention it." Tom sighed loudly and stuffed his hands in his trouser pockets. "He gave us an electric fire and told us to open our windows. He also gave us ten shillings for the meter."

"To help dry it out, see," said Mary.

Liberty immediately rummaged in her purse and found another two shillings which she left on their table while they were busy talking to Gemma.

"My brother might be able to find you alternative accommodation."

"I don't think we can afford more," sighed Mary. "We only pay £3 and we've got a bedroom, kitchen, lounge and our own toilet. And you mustn't worry about us, we're all right, honest. London's bound to be expensive, we know that, but we ain't getting enough money that's all. It was different before the war, when we worked. We had our good times then." Mary turned to Tom who gave her a wink and a lop-sided smile. In return, she gave him a smile and sparkling eyes.

While Mary talked, Liberty placed on the table two tins of soup, a tin of ham, the colourful skirt for Mary and the T-shirt for Tom and felt gutted it wasn't a great deal more.

"You're so kind," said Tom, who didn't miss a thing.

On the bare sofa, Gemma placed her home-made cushion, stuffed with laddered, cut-up tights donated by the girls at work. "Bye for now. We miss you."

Later that day, Nonna said, "Are you enjoying living in the Swinging London, Libby?" She linked up with Liberty's arm as they both gazed out of the window across the grounds towards the ruin.

"I am, definitely. I love the music; absolutely great. I heard a Beatles' song on the radio which I'd never heard before."

"Which one?"

"Taxman."

Nonna dropped Liberty's arm and faced her. "Zut! As my dear husband would say. Those are the good men. They tell the world about our very bad Mr Wilson. Zut! He is taking our money and we can't afford to repair the roof. It leaks in the annexe and... I must stop. Forgive me."

Liberty realized she hadn't paid any tax, not yet anyway. She began to worry about the lack of proper 'paperwork'. "The song made it sound like they paid 95% of their income in tax."

"Those Beatles might also have been bled dry by agents, managers, hangers on of all kinds," said Grandpapa joining in zealously. "And then to have to pay 95% tax on the rest. How demoralising. We don't pay as much of course, but it is more than most."

"What are we supposed to do?" said Nonna. "Let a fine house like this become a ruin too?"

As Grandpapa handed his wife a large book, Liberty sensed the close presence of Nick and turned as he said, "I have a plan, Nonna, which I have been outlining to Grandie. Come, let's all sit down and I'll tell you all about it."

Nonna held up her hand. "No, no, don't tell me if it would make me criminal."

"Aurora, Nick is like an angel come to rescue us: he brings the gift of knowledge."

"No, not if it is knowledge of the future. I will sit on the garden bench with Liberty. You men have your secrets and we shall be the angels."

Liberty came close to laughing at the thought of being an angel, just managing to hold it back to a smile which Nick mirrored.

Aurora led the way to the garden. "You might like to see what I have here." Her conspiratorial grin was infectious as she gratefully put the hefty tome on the bench. "You sit close and I will reveal all the secrets. Our secrets, they are the best."

For almost an hour, they giggled, groaned and nearly cried at the tales held within the huge book of family history. Each generation chronicled life as they experienced it. Some added opinions, some added words of lasting wisdom and others resorted to yarns and rumours. The custom was to write no more than four pages so some writing was tiny and others ignored the custom, much to the disgust of Aurora.

"May I see the family history in the Regency era?"

Aurora found the early nineteenth century and handed the heavy book to Liberty who could barely hold it on her lap. Aurora stood, straightened her skirt and said, "I will see what our men are doing and I'll bring back some lemonade. Yes?"

"Oh yes please."

Liberty carefully turned the pages to the middle years of the Regency and became riveted as she read entry after entry. There was one particular sentence which she wondered if Nick had read. She'd be able to ask him right away because he and Grandpapa were walking towards her.

"We've been sent out here," Grandpapa said with a defeated expression.

"Aha! I see you have volume four of the book of secrets, Libby. Page one of volume one is the best." Nick assumed a Shakespearian actor's comportment and ranged back and forth. "In the year eleven-hundred-and- fifty-one, I, Arthur–"

Liberty giggled helplessly. All hope of showing him the significant sentence evaporated.

"He lists the number of his cows, sheep, chickens, and children – in that order. And from that acorn grew a mighty oak." Nick waved his arm in the direction of the oak tree standing near the ruin.

Grandpapa chipped in. "It's true. About the tree, I mean. Reckoned to be over eight hundred years old." While Liberty marvelled, Grandpapa muttered, "Needs felling. Another good storm and it'll come crashing down. I ought to euthanize it." He muttered on until he spotted his wife approaching. "Ah, my darling wife brings us sustenance."

And while Aurora poured out home-made lemonade, Nick manhandled the great book safely inside and returned.

"So, you big boys, you will tell us about the cricket you've been planning?"

"This year," began Grandpapa in a serious tone, "this year is the bicentenary of the Regency Cricket Match with the Bleakheath Bozos."

"Grandie! That's not factual and you told me they usually win."

Aurora tapped her husband on his knee, "You are very bad. Nick is right, you must call them the Bleakheath Regency Cricket Club."

"They have some excellent players so I must undermine their confidence."

Nick jumped in, explaining that the club dated back two hundred years and the first match they played was against the staff and family of the original Bleakheath Hall.

Grandpapa added, "The problem we face is that we have very few staff with this smaller house and most of them are women."

Aurora hastily interjected, "And women don't play cricket."

Nick, as an aside to Liberty, said, "I've yet to update them on this – it could come as a bit of a shock."

"Update? Why?"

In a low voice he said, "I have a photo of the England Women's Cricket Team in my room. It's to remind me that women can do so much more than they're allowed to in this era. As in many countries, our country in 1968 isn't utilizing one of its greatest resources." He continued aloud, "We can field nine at the moment. Do you think Paul and Jon will play? If so, we have a full team."

"If you will supply me with their telephone numbers, Liberty, I will ask them," said Grandpapa.

Liberty offered to find out and let him know.

It was nearly midnight when Nick and Liberty left. On the drive home, Liberty asked what else Grandie talked about. "Surely not just cricket? For a whole hour?"

"Most of the time." Nick slowed down. "We also talked about finance. I had to wait a long time for my first month's salary. Until I located my grandparents, I had only my wits to feed me and my priority was to ensure I knew where you were. Fortunately, it didn't take long." He reached across and squeezed her knee. "I would not have followed you through a time portal just to lose you when I got here."

Liberty glowed and wanted to fall into his arms, but he was driving. She'd have to make do with a knee squeeze.

"I needed to pawn my watch to give me enough to tide me over before finding them. The night before we both left 2020, Matt Redfern tipped me off to have something readily saleable, which was my Omega watch, because I might be spending longer in 1968 than anticipated. He was right. Luckily, it worked out."

He slowed the car and parked outside Liberty's new flat. "When I returned to 2020 at Easter, I made notes about which shares flourished from the late sixties up to around 1990. I couldn't spend all my time on it but I came up with eight, sound picks."

"Which ones?"

Nick's reply was simply to smile conspiratorially. "I've just given him the name and information on one financial company. He'll buy five thousand shares now, keep them until a certain date when they reach a temporary peak – I've been able to give him dates to look out for, then sell. He can buy them back when the price has fallen. Each time he does it, he'll make money."

"What! Surely that's illegal?"

"Who will believe him when he says a time traveller gave him some financial advice?"

"It's morally wrong though."

"All it has done is remove the element of risk. I've told him to keep some until at least 1985 if he can." He picked up her hand and held it to his lips. A loving kiss was followed by, "What *you* are doing is illegal: working without the right paperwork and not paying tax. I am at least paying tax."

Liberty was aghast. Yet what else could she do?

"How else could I repay him and help with the upkeep of the house?" As Liberty didn't reply, Nick continued. "I've given him the list of the other seven picks and told him the best time to buy and sell."

"Will he follow your advice?"

"I'm pretty certain he will because in 2020, during my Easter trip back to my little house near Middleston hospital, I remembered he'd shown me his share portfolio a couple of years before. He said how well it performed over the years and how much he owed me for keeping the family afloat. Of course, at the time, real time," he emphasized, "as he was in his nineties, I thought he might be going doolally and so I didn't take any notice of his musings about a dark stranger from a time afar having knowledge of the future. Now, of course, I know that I was the dark stranger. He refrained from telling me the full story – something I would never have believed. He probably worried that we'd send him to a nursing home for the delusional if he elaborated further." He chuckled.

Liberty held back from suggesting it was fate. Such a trite comment. Maybe one of Gemma's overused phrases would be right for this occasion. "God moves in mysterious ways." She instantly regretted it; surely God didn't... wouldn't... She did voice another thought though. "How do you remember all that happened in 2020? Are you writing it all down in case it's useful now in 1968?"

"I keep telling you, yes, I am and you should be too. I wish we had mobile phones; it would save me a lot of time."

"Mobile what?"

"Don't try to figure it all out at the moment. However, when we return, you must make notes galore so that you know who you were and what you achieved." He grinned then opened the car door and went around to Liberty's door to hold it for her. "Don't forget to warn Paul and Jon about Grandie's invitation to play cricket. They might wonder who he is, so remember to say he is my distant cousin not my grandfather – he's only forty-two and therefore it's impossible for him to be my grandfather and we don't want to be thought liars, do we?" Grinning broadly, he walked her to the door, stood with his back towards it, took her in his arms and kissed her. Her knees went weak, she slipped down slowly, prevented from falling further only by his strong arms holding her up.

He took her key, turned it in the door, stood aside and let her in. He might have followed but for the midnight silence broken by the sound of gentle sniffling within.

Chapter Thirty-Two
Clay-brained fleshmonger

A whole week flew by. Gemma tormented herself with worries, which she declined to reveal, and Liberty's anxiety grew each time she saw her boss, Sir Arthur Hollingbourne. Like Gemma, she also dared not discuss her fears. How kind of Sir Arthur to want to refer her to a doctor who could help recover her memory: how risky if she allowed him. Yet could she fob him off with just cheerful smiles of being content without it? Fortunately, there was no time for gloom and doom because Paul would soon be here. As he'd be taking Gemma, he'd volunteered to take all three girls to the Regency Cricket Match at Bleakheath Hall.

When the doorbell rang, Chloe raced to open the door.

"Come in, come in," she enthused. "We're nearly ready."

Liberty wasn't so sure. Whereas she and Gemma had done their best to dress in Regency style, as advised, Chloe's short dress looked more like a lace petticoat. Transparent too. Should this be pointed out? Perhaps she'd done her best. Perhaps she had no idea what Regency dress looked like. Difficult. She'd used far too much make-up and scent too.

Gemma appeared, wearing a long, polyester, high-waisted dress in a pretty shade of green. "To match your car, Paul."

Paul moved forward and kissed her on her cheek. Chloe claimed one for herself. "Only fair," she said, tossing her glorious red hair.

Paul gave her a hasty peck on the cheek. Chloe looked smug. Paul turned and whispered to Gemma, "I think she's lonely."

Liberty was not convinced. Gemma drew back from Paul and Liberty now knew why Gemma slept so poorly all last week: this wasn't Chloe's first advance.

Romance matters turned worse when Chloe asked to sit in the front seat of Paul's Cortina. "I'm sorry," she said to Gemma, "but I get car sick if I sit in the back."

"Is that all right, Gemma?" queried Paul.

Liberty unobtrusively shook her head and pursed her lips. Gemma, however, produced a bright smile which didn't quite reach her eyes. "Of course. I'm happy sitting next to Liberty."

As Chloe stood by the car door, apparently helplessly, Paul opened her door first before doing the same for Gemma and Liberty. Gemma looked crushed and Liberty gritted her teeth as they listened to their new flatmate asking Paul which bus to catch for Piccadilly that evening. As Paul wasn't sure, he said he'd run her to the bus terminus near Bleakheath when the time came for her to leave. Chloe rummaged in her red handbag, pulled out a slip of paper, tossed it on the floor and continued rooting. Liberty exchanged suspicious glances with Gemma.

"If you don't have your bus fare, Chloe, I'll lend you some money."

"Oh, um... no, I've got enough somewhere in here, thanks, Libby."

Something would have to be done.

On arrival at Bleakheath Hall, Paul parked where Grandpapa directed.

"Welcome, welcome. So good of you to rescue us."

"Our pleasure," said Paul.

"My name's Maximilian, but do call me Max." He stood tall, immaculately dressed and as warm and welcoming as the day's summer breeze. "Meet the dogs. This is Sun, and Sirius is over there inspecting all entrants to his territory."

"What does he do if he doesn't like you?" Chloe looked worried.

"During an event like this, he'll only sit by your feet and give a low warning growl. For instance, everyone knows not to bring drugs anywhere near Bleakheath Hall."

Chloe looked relieved.

Nick joined them and his inscrutable face clocked Chloe. Liberty watched his eyes narrow as he viewed her from head to toe. How astute; it's impossible to read eyes you cannot see but she did hear him mutter, "Something wicked this way comes."

Grandpapa positioned himself in front of Nick so that Chloe's attempt to introduce herself became impossible. Swishing her long red hair, she tried to outmanoeuvre him but failed. "Come with me, young lady, and I'll introduce you to my wife – the greatest privilege you'll ever have. Look and learn."

Paul's eyebrows collided with his floppy hair, Liberty grinned and Gemma stood rooted.

Nick, immaculately yet casually dressed, took Liberty's hand and planted a kiss. His eyes spoke of promise. Swiftly, he turned the subject from Chloe. "Nonna has a Regency dress set aside for you in case you'd like to try it. I like your blouse and long skirt as they are, yet to please her, you might want to take a look."

"I'd love to, thank you. Maybe I should wait until Gr... um, Max has finished educating Chloe." Oh, if she could swallow unwise words, she would have swallowed those, yet Paul and Gemma grinned. Nick, with a mere glimmer of a smile, visibly refrained from one of his barbs.

"Follow me," said Nick to the little group. "I'll take you down to the pitch." He turned to Liberty. "It's the flat ground in front of the ruin. Only just big enough, but we manage."

Bunting and balloons were everywhere and the scent of blossoming bluebells filled the air. The sun shone in a cloudless sky and conversations about 'perfect summer's afternoon' were the prevailing exchanges. Green garden chairs were laid out on the gently sloping land beside the cricket pitch and Nick led them to four on the front row with reserved signs. "Nonna will sit on the end which enables her to jump up and down a lot." He clarified this with "Attending to the refreshments in the summer house and late arrivals." As an aside, he said to Paul, "We Gentlemen, when not fielding, congregate by the ruin. There's a stack of folding, canvas chairs for batsmen." Nick took Liberty's hand. "Right, let's head back and get togged up."

Half-an-hour later, resplendent in a cream Regency-style dress with pink satin ribbons around the high waist, Liberty walked with Aurora towards the gathering crowds on the lawn overlooking the cricket pitch. She'd left her handbag in the new house and carried a matching pink velvet reticule with cream ribbons. Her bonnet also matched, being pink with cream ribbons and a flourish of red rose blooms. A matching parasol rested on her shoulder. As the spectators took their seats, the team captains were tossing a coin.

"Max has won the toss," exclaimed Aurora. "He always prefers to bat first."

Liberty's eyes were wide. Nick was opening the batting. The bowler took a few paces back and bowled: underarm. "Surely that's not allowed?" she whispered to Aurora.

"They play by the 1809 rules. Most things are the same as today, just a few changes have been made. You notice there are no boundaries?"

"I didn't think to look." Her eyes were fixed on Nick who hit what might have been a 'four' by modern rules. She turned to Gemma. "Where's Jon?"

"He arrived when you were changing. You look terrific, by the way."

"Thank you, so do you."

Chloe, sitting next to Gemma, stuck her head into the conversation. "Don't the men look sexy in their old costumes?"

Gemma chuckled and leaned forward to ask Aurora, "Did they really wear top hats while playing cricket?"

Aurora obliged with a wealth of detail including confirming they did, indeed, wear hats, often top hats, or military ones. "And pantaloons," she said grinning. "They look grand, you think?" While all nodded, she added, "Some are not dressed, how you say, authentically, but close enough."

Grandpapa was caught out on his third ball. The spectators politely applauded as he took an elaborate bow. Paul took his place and together with Nick, they formed a strong partnership, racking up fifty runs in less than an hour. So that other members of the team had a chance to bat, they both retired, leaving the way for Jon and the elderly butler to take their places.

Chloe watched Jon's every move. "Your brother's a big chap, isn't he, Gemma? He looks more like a rugby player."

"He does play rugby too," Gemma said proudly.

After two hours, team Gentlemen declared with a total of ninety-seven runs.

Aurora explained that in Georgian times, they didn't stop for refreshments, so today they would wait until the game finished. When two of the Players strolled towards the wicket, the crowd of a hundred or more, quietened to a respectful hush and the game resumed.

"Is Players the name of the team?" Chloe whispered to Gemma.

"No idea," replied Gemma. Liberty shrugged her shoulders. Aurora had excused herself to take a look at the arrangements in the summer house.

Two hours later, the game ended with the Players having made ninety-two runs.

The crowd clapped as the Gentlemen were awarded a small silver cup. A few at a time strolled towards the summer house, some taking their chairs with them, ready to enjoy the feast prepared by Aurora's team of helpers.

Liberty and Nick noticed Chloe attempting to catch up with Paul as he walked with Gemma.

"Clay-brained fleshmonger, you have there."

"Nick, I can only think you mean that Chloe is stupid and rather concerned with matters of the flesh."

"Close enough, but Shakespeare said it more succinctly. She's made several attempts, not only throwing herself at me but to find out all about you." He drew a deep breath before choosing to say, "Grandie warned me to beware of what I let over my doorstep; it seems a wanton lass has crossed yours."

Liberty sighed. "Paul's promised to drive her to the bus station in time for her to go to work."

"Work? Saturday night?"

"We think she needs the money. She works as a waitress some evenings."

They helped themselves from the buffet, took a drink and a plate of food away from the celebrating crowd and sat on the wall near the house.

"Was Grandpapa pleased you won?"

"Over the moon, he said, and he thanks you for bringing your friends. The Players kindly allowed them to be a part of our team. 'This year only,' they said. As you can see, most of our team are in their sixties and are easily run out. However," he squeezed her hand, "we triumphed. First time in five years, apparently."

"I love the old English traditions," she said wistfully.

Nick's attention focused on Chloe. "She's chatting up Jon now."

They both watched as Jon checked his watch then nodded at Chloe. He took another bite of the sausage from the barbecue, nodded again, finished the sausage and walked with Chloe to speak to Liberty, only Chloe beat him to it.

"Libby, Jon's gonna take me to work. Kind, isn't he?" This was said as if no-one else was.

"Chloe's got a difficult journey, change of buses and all that lark, so I'll take her straight there."

Chloe glowed. "No need to take me any further than Piccadilly. I can walk from there and the streets get narrow..." she stopped abruptly.

"Whatever you say," said Jon, blowing a kiss to Gemma. And off he went with Chloe linking arms.

All were silent as they listened to the Triumph Spitfire's engine roar away.

Chapter Thirty-Three
Spurting like Vesuvius

Chloe slept late, far too late to tag along with Gemma and Liberty to The Salvation Army's Sunday morning open air service. Liberty's emotions were torn: did the poor girl, forced to work nights to earn extra money, deserve to be pitied? She'd had a difficult upbringing, didn't earn much, had been living in a hostel and seemingly had no friends. Or was she a schemer? Liberty really wanted to believe the former. Yet there was also the possibility that her background was a pack of lies. After all, she herself had concocted a false personal history in order to stay here in 1968. There wasn't time for all this thinking, she must be ready in five minutes if she was to accompany Gemma.

As she tucked a handkerchief in her pocket, her fingers found a piece of paper. Some old shopping list probably.

"We need to hurry, Libby," whispered Gemma, trying not to wake Chloe.

Liberty stuffed the paper back in her pocket.

They arrived in the grounds of the local hospital and caught sight of the brass band gathering in the small garden in front of the wards.

"What are we supposed to do?"

Gemma smiled. "The usual. Sing along to the songs mainly. The patients like to hear us, we're a welcome distraction."

Liberty wondered if that was all they were. All this rushing around to get here, just to be a welcome distraction? At least the sun shone brightly and tomorrow was a Bank Holiday and they could both sleep late.

The band struck up with what the Captain called a well-known Welsh hymn which Liberty did not recognize. He then prayed in a surprisingly booming voice and the dozen or so Songsters sang a short song heartily.

The matron appeared, thanked everyone for coming and handed the Bandmaster a slip of paper.

"Requests from the patients," said Gemma.

"Have you been to these things before?"

"Yes, lots of times back home. I quite like them. It's nice to know we're cheering up the patients. Staff too, apparently."

Gemma, in her dark navy uniform suit and black bonnet, delved into her handbag for her song book. "I know most of the words, but just in case, we can use this."

One of the Songster's toddlers approached them. "Mummy says I can stand with you."

Gemma looked up and saw the mother giving her a thumbs up and a hopeful smile just as the little girl sneezed. Liberty pulled her hanky from her pocket, Gemma took it and attended to her new fan. The folded paper had dropped on the ground and immediately the little girl picked it up.

In the sweetest voice she said, "This dwopped fwom your pocket."

Enchanted, Liberty thanked her and was about to stuff it back where it came from when she chanced to glance at it again. It wasn't a shopping list. It was from Nick.

"We have a request from Nurse Perkins for "What a Friend We Have in Jesus."

Gemma hurriedly flicked the pages over of the song book while Liberty, shocked to her core read, "I'll not be available for a while, will tell you why later. Take good care." Her stomach lurched as if she were on a fairground roller coaster. He was involved in something dangerous. Or maybe he'd been found out. Someone knew his curriculum vitae wasn't genuine. Something had happened to Nonna or Grandie. Something... Then she frowned. When did he slip it into her jacket pocket? It must have been when he took her home. Why didn't he simply tell her? And why should she take care?

The band started playing and Gemma held the song book in front of Liberty with one hand and held the toddler's with the other. Loudly, clearly, she sang:

What a friend we have in Jesus
All our sins and griefs to bear
What a privilege to carry
Everything to God in prayer.
Oh, what peace we often forfeit
Oh, what needless pain we bear
All because we do not carry
Everything to God in prayer.

Have we trials and temptations?
Is there trouble anywhere?
We should never be discouraged
Take it to the Lord in prayer.
Can we find a friend so faithful
Who will all our sorrows share?
Jesus knows our every weakness
Take it to the Lord in prayer.

It seemed familiar and Liberty joined in tentatively. Strangely comforted, she took a deep breath. All would be well. Or would it? Maybe she'd pray about Nick tonight after Gemma was asleep. If she did, it would be the first time in... Well, she couldn't remember.

As Paul's mother was hosting some winners of the Auction of Promises for Sunday lunch, after the morning meeting at the hall Gemma and Liberty returned to the flat. There was no sign of Chloe, so Gemma and Liberty ate Sunday lunch on their own and saved her some on a plate. Liberty went into the garden and read her note from Nick again. Should she phone?

Gemma brought out two mugs of tea. "Paul says the youth club is practically finished, thanks to lots of people rallying round, and he's planning an opening ceremony." Gemma chuckled as she said, "He's asked me to think of a name for it. Got any ideas?"

Liberty shrugged her shoulders. "No, sorry."

"Anything wrong, Libby, you've been very quiet?"

Before Libby could think how to answer, the doorbell rang and Gemma sauntered inside to answer it. She reappeared, followed by Jon. "I'll get you a tea."

"Thanks." Jon sat down on Gemma's chair. "I'm glad I've got you on your own, Libby. I can't believe what happened last night."

"Last night? With Chloe?"

"Yes. She glowed all the way to London, touching my arm, smiling coquettishly, asking me to come to her work."

"Her work? What? A restaurant?"

"No, it's a night club."

Liberty appeared puzzled, then tried to find some good in this tale. "So she's a hard-up girl needing to be a waitress in a nightclub in the wrong part of town?"

"Something didn't feel right. I dropped her off, followed her, a man walked out of a doorway and tapped his watch. Rolex, it was."

"Jon, you couldn't have seen that."

"I know a Rolex when I see one – they're as rare as wings on a walrus." He paused. "Well, almost. Anyway, Chloe was apparently late and he became angry. I didn't like the look of him. Head to toe dressed in black. Well his cap was black, hair was ginger."

Gemma appeared with a mug of tea.

"Sorry, old girl, I've stolen your chair. I'll bring another." As soon as he'd grabbed another dining chair, he sat down and resumed. "Nick and I had a chat after our innings and we were both a little concerned about your new flatmate. I said I'd take her to where she worked so Paul needn't get involved. Nick said she'd made a play for him too, which you didn't see, so that was Paul, him and me all in a very short time. Flattered as we might have been, it seemed forced."

"Oh Jon, she's just naïve, poor girl. Probably desperate to find a boyfriend."

"And doesn't care if she snatches yours? Gemma, dear, you're far too kind." It seemed Gemma was the naïve one.

"We need to be careful of her, is that what you're saying?"

"Yes Libby. I phoned Nick early this morning and gave him the low-down. He says he's exceptionally busy at the moment but he thinks there's more to it than that."

"You're making it sound ominous, Jon," Gemma gave him her best glare. "You're frightening us."

"Judas! So you should be."

Liberty frowned.

Gemma whispered, "Jon reckons it's not right to use 'Jesus' as a swear word."

"Indubitably. Why should the good guy have his name used? Let's use the bad guy's name instead." He adjusted his tone to 'gentle'. "You've no need to be frightened. The fairies at the bottom of the garden are watching over you."

Gemma scoffed. "Stop it, Jon."

"I suppose you have noticed the caravan at the bottom of the garden?"

"Of course."

Liberty chimed in. "It's different from the one the old guys had at the other flat though."

"You think so?"

"Jon, if you have something to say, get on with it. You're scaring us." Gemma glared again.

"The caravan is the same, it's just been tarted up a bit. The guys are the same. They are three homeless ex-prisoners. I was concerned when you moved into that dreadful neighbourhood so I concocted a little plan. They'd look out for you in return for the caravan. So far, no-one's complained about them."

Gemma's alarm grew with every syllable and finally she burst, spurting like Vesuvius. "You did what? You've asked three criminals..."

Liberty watched in astonishment as Gemma continued to rain down boiling lava on her brother, and like the inhabitants of Pompeii, Jon's attempts at holding it back were futile.

Finally, Jon raised his voice. "Judas, old girl!"

"Don't you swear at me!"

Liberty couldn't help the growing smile almost bursting into a laugh and covered her mouth with her hand. A fearless kitten was taking on a British bulldog and winning.

The bulldog fought back. "They're the best! You couldn't ask for better protection. They scared away the man who kept breaking into your old flat. They know what to look out for and, and... I wasn't going to tell you but that sweet little Chloe has brought a man here while you've been at work. He didn't have a chance to stay more than a few minutes because they started hammering on your door. He fled out of the French windows, chased by one of the guys." He paused for breath. "Unfortunately, they're past sprinting so they lost him."

Gemma took a deep breath. "Why didn't you tell us?"

Liberty thought it was obvious why he didn't. She asked gently, "What did he look like?"

"Stocky, ginger hair. Didn't you suspect that chap you kept calling the ginger rat was the one sneaking into your old flat?"

Liberty froze visibly.

"Do you recognize him?" Jon demanded.

Liberty breathed heavily. "Possibly. Does Nick know?"

"I told him at the cricket match."

Was this why Nick wouldn't be available for a while? She didn't know what to say to Jon except to murmur, "Thank you."

Gently, Jon explained further. "They're not vicious criminals. They're old soldiers fallen on hard times."

Liberty thought it sounded like a well-used cliché until she remembered how many beggars there were on the streets of London wearing their medals. She'd asked one once, just to check he knew what the medals were for, and he proudly told her why he had been awarded them. She'd put a shilling in his upturned hat on the pavement, thanked him, and walked away. A shilling! Why not more? She knew why; some were being 'run' by gangs, others spent it all on booze. Next time she'd put an apple in the upturned hat; but she wouldn't have apples in her bag; maybe a bar of chocolate?

Gemma, having allowed Liberty time to be lost in her apparently troubling thoughts, decided to move things forward. "More tea, anyone?"

Both nodded. Liberty followed her friend.

"Stocky, ginger hair." Gemma raised her eyebrows.

"It can't be. That ginger squirrel followed..." She stopped. She could hardly say that Gregor Hode had followed her to 2020 and she'd left him there and she was very sure of this because she'd made notes. "It can't be. I've not seen him for ages."

Jon appeared in the doorway. "And the man whom Chloe met at that club – he had ginger hair, don't forget."

"So, big brother, you're saying that the man breaking into the old flat, the man where Chloe works in the evenings and the one she brought here are the same man?"

"Yes."

"And we can add," Gemma said, "that's he's the same man we saw at Guy's hospital when we were having lunch on the bench."

Liberty silently added he was the same man who had been annoying her in 2020.

"Should we confront Chloe?" Gemma asked.

"No, don't do that. Don't let her know what I've told you. Treat her as the young girl needing a safe place to live. We don't know why she is doing this yet. But we'll find out."

Chapter Thirty-Four
Don't scream

Early the following evening, Chloe waved goodbye to Liberty as she tip-tapped down the path in white, stiletto heeled shoes, fishnet tights and short, dark leather skirt.

"Extra shift tonight," Chloe called back with a cheery wave and grin.

As Gemma joined Liberty on the doorstep, Liberty said, "I suppose we should follow your brother's guidance to treat her as needing help."

"Jon's up to something, I'm sure. He and Nick seem to have struck up a friendship."

"I'm worried about Nick." Liberty daren't mention all the things which might be going wrong. Would his curriculum vitae be discovered as false? Even if, as he'd told her, he only altered the dates it would mean instant dismissal. Best to change the subject. "Jon is an amazing brother, you are so lucky. And to think that his old soldiers in the caravan managed to scare the ginger man away."

Gemma laughed. "Ginger man? I wonder if anyone calls me the chestnut girl." She chuckled. "We've certainly called him a few names since we first saw him."

"Rat," said Liberty. "That suits him best. Do you think we could take the guys in the caravan a thank you present?" They went to the kitchen looking for something special.

"The reality is," said a forlorn Liberty, "we don't have any luxuries."

"I can bake them some bread."

"Or cake? That might be a treat." Liberty pulled out the flour and the sugar while Gemma pulled out the butter from the fridge and the sultanas from the sparsely filled cupboards. "Do you have a recipe book somewhere?"

"I don't need one for a sultana cake. There's just one problem," Gemma said, searching for a suitable baking tray, "there isn't the right size tin. I'll have to use this roasting pan. It's not *too* big and we can cut the cake into squares."

By half past eight, the girls were knocking on the caravan door. There was no answer, yet the windows were open.

"We can't leave it outside, an animal might eat it."

Liberty peered through the windows. "Give it to me, I'll push the bag of cake inside."

The girls chuckled as they walked back to their garden flat and Liberty even stopped worrying about Nick. He was a brilliant doctor with good family back-up; he'd be all right, and she felt sure he'd not forget her. Both girls were unprepared to find Chloe angrily slamming around in her bedroom, spitting out words best not heard clearly but with a lot of 'nics' in them.

Gemma knocked on her door. "Anything we can do?"

The door was flung open and a furious Chloe glared at them both, Liberty in particular. "No. Nothing to do with you, Gemma. Sorry for making such a fuss."

Gemma enquired, "What happened?"

"Nothing, just didn't work out."

Liberty chipped in. "That's awful. Just when you think you'll be getting extra money too."

"The date changed, that's all. I'm going tomorrow."

Liberty decided not to telephone Nick from the flat.

The following day, from her office at the hospital, she telephoned Aurora at Bleakheath Hall.

"I don't suppose Nick is there, is he?"

"He is not," Aurora said in her attractive Italian accent. "Is it urgent you speak with him?"

"No, not really. I wanted to update him, that's all." She didn't like to mention her concern, yet Aurora detected it.

"You must not do the worrying, Libby. Nick is..."

Liberty couldn't concentrate on any more of Aurora's attempts to soothe her fears though she made what she called 'listening noises'.

"Thanks, Aurora. You've helped."

Replacing the telephone carefully, Liberty put her head in her hands. In Chloe's rant last night, there were a lot of unclear angry words ending in a nic. Or Nick.

That evening, Liberty watched as Chloe, dressed the same as the night before, set off for who knew where.

"Don't worry, Libby, Chloe's probably just being a little mischievous."

If ever there was a prize for understatement, Gemma would win it. She walked across to the open French windows and imagined Chloe meeting Nick on this beautiful spring evening. "Did you hear her last night? She poured out loads of words and stuck a 'Nick' on the end of each."

"Nick? I thought she said 'Mick'."

Liberty's spirit lifted for no longer than a second, then plunged. What if Nick found Chloe's indecorous dress attractive? What did she really know about him? Lately he'd divulged a little more about himself, but not much. And what if, like the lies he told to the hospital personnel department, he lied to her? She shook her head and plonked herself down on the sofa. And what about the anonymous note saying not to trust Nylander because he was not what he seemed? She'd almost forgotten receiving it. Was it from the rat? A single tear ran past her nose and she searched for a hanky. Finding none, she wiped it away with her sleeve.

Gemma, having changed from slippers to shoes, said, "It's Songster Practice, Libby. Sorry. I have to go. Will you be all right?"

"Yes, you go, I know you love it."

"I get to see Paul too." Gemma winced. "Sorry."

"I think Nick's meeting Chloe. Did you notice the triumphant look she gave me when she left?"

"I did. Don't let it bother you. You'll see Nick soon. He's a good man."

"You go, don't worry. I'll make a cup of tea."

Gemma left. Liberty didn't make any tea. Straightening her black, twirly skirt and her blue blouse, so different from Chloe's garb, she gazed at the blank television screen. He'd never said he loved her. He took her for granted. Secretive, he never shared anything personal. He didn't even mention his work. Liberty stopped to assess if that was true, couldn't remember, so carried on listing his perceived faults which she crowned with him seeing Chloe behind her back. A strange feeling came upon her. Déjà vu? Yes. He'd been seeing someone else. But where? When? She dashed into her bedroom, found the little notebooks, and took them back to the sofa. There in the blue one were the words "Engaged? To Jaelyn?" Dratted man. Why fall in love with someone like him? Why not Jon, the wonderful bouncing Tiger? She flicked through the pages and read that in 2020 Nick had taken her to a restaurant even though he was engaged to someone else. He clearly was not a man to be trusted. She tried to capture some memories of the restaurant. Why did he take her and where to? Nothing came. She'd have to make do with the brief notes. Not even a date to give her a clue.

Liberty stared at a pigeon on the lawn appearing to attack itself, picking out something from under its wing and apparently eating it. Once finished, it shook its feathers, recovered its dignity and strutted away. She sighed; even pigeons have their troubles.

She ambled into her bedroom, tucked the notebooks under her pillow, curled up facing the wall and wallowed in deep despair. Why couldn't she have fallen in love with uncomplicated Jon? The healing touch of sleep slowly enfolded her.

A hand clamped over her mouth.

"Don't scream; not if you value your life." Her head was pushed into the pillow, a knee rammed into the small of her back and her hands were being tied together. Her head was lifted from the pillow, she gasped before a white cloth with a strange smell covered her nose and mouth.

Chapter Thirty-Five
Against all the odds

Liberty's eyelids felt heavy; she closed them. Taking a deep breath, she experienced unwelcome cold, musty air in her nostrils. Startled, she tried opening her eyes again. It was dark except for a small pool of light a few yards away; she closed them once more and shivered.

"The bird stirs. About time too." Swearing profusely, her captor came closer and shone his torch onto her face. "Not such a pretty face now, eh? Feathers all dirty too."

Feathers? Reluctantly she opened her eyes and immediately protected them from the bright light with her hands. Hauling herself up from her horizontal position, she propped herself up on her elbow, glanced down at her clothes and began brushing the dust and dirt off them. How did they get like this?

As if he read her mind, he smirked, "I guess I should have cleaned my car boot before stuffing you in." He lowered his torch from her face and wafted it around, illuminating the golden bars of her cage. "Know where you are? Bet you don't."

Liberty stretched, sat up and looked around. This was a cage. Where had she seen...? Her memory coughed up that she was imprisoned like one of those dancers in the 'Cage Club', the club she'd been to with Jon and Gemma. While her captor whined on and on in his high-pitched, nasal voice, she focused on his supercilious smirk, like the grin of a shark made all the more menacing in the dim light, and suddenly realized who he was: Gregor Hode had definitely surfaced yet again.

"You cow. You outbid me for the agency. It should have been mine. Being a nice kind of guy, I would have *married* you even. Was it too much to ask? I already had a very successful career – plenty to offer you – building a booming empire, going to celebrity parties with you on my arm, but you've shattered my dream and here we are, back in the dark ages." Gregor strutted up and down. "Come on then – where are we?"

Liberty drew the woollen blanket she was sitting on around her legs. "It looks like an Underground station."

In a teeth clenching, staccato style he spat out, "Correct. Deep under London. And no train has run through here for over thirty years. Smell the mustiness; get used to it. You're in the cage which your flatmate danced in. Right bit of tat, she is." He scoffed, then grinned and continued like a squawking parrot performing its repertoire. "I own the 'Cage Club' now. Bet you didn't expect that, did you? I own it. Own it." He didn't wait for her answer but went on to describe the relatively easy way to rob shops of their cash. "All the tricks of the twenty-first century brought back to these innocents. So easy." He chortled. "And it's even easier back in 2020, nobody sees a so-called ghost and nobody sees what he's taken." He drew a gun from its holster and took aim at her.

Liberty, only partially recovered from her drugged stupor, stared stunned as he swivelled round, pulled the trigger and cackled as a bullet ricocheted off the wall and clanged as it hit a metal object in the darkness of the far tunnel. Now she was awake. She scrutinized him as he chuckled, scratched under his arm, threw back his shoulders and strutted around. She recalled the scrawny pigeon in their flat's garden. It had attacked an itch under its wing feathers, shuffled them, recovered its dignity, then strutted away.

Gregor stared at her. "What are you thinking? Own up."

"I'm thinking about a pigeon," she said defiantly. "How long have I been here?"

"It's Wednesday."

'Wednesday' didn't mean much to her. She put her head in her hands and mumbled. "So I've been here all night."

He took aim at her again and pretended to shoot. "You should have listened. See how quickly I've moved in on London life; you would have been my wife, looking down on the Chloes of this world being ogled for peanuts. Now look at you." He scoffed again. "She's not *your* friend. She's *my* slave and does what I tell her. You think you found a flatmate?" He followed with a torrent of swearing. "I sent her and she's been spying on you ever since. All I did was catch her out at something, sweeten her with a few pounds and she'd sold her soul." His shark smile was visible in the dim light of the torch he'd propped up against the white tiled wall.

Liberty's nerve began to fail; her stomach churned like a cement mixer. He rooted in the bag he'd brought and pushed a large packet of peanuts and a bottle of water through the bars. "You've missed your chance; now it's your turn to get peanuts." With an evil laugh, he turned, picked up his torch, flashed it around, jumped down onto the track and stomped off into the black hole, shouting back at her, "I'll get a good price for you."

Liberty felt cold to her bones and she couldn't move. She had to escape, absolutely had to. She remembered the tale of the secretary's sister lured into slavery. This would never happen to her. She'd fight him with everything she could muster. She took a deep breath of dank air, felt around for the water and peanuts and put them where she thought it easy to find them again. All this was because she'd outbid him for the agency? What agency? Something else she'd forgotten. She turned her thoughts to Chloe dancing in a cage, not waitressing. Had this rat owned the club when she'd visited with Jon and Gemma? She straightened out the blanket on the flat base of the cage, then began feeling the bars. There must be a door where the dancers entered. Feeling around the bars, she found something which felt like a latch and lifted it. What a relief. She pushed what must be the door but it didn't open more than an inch as it hit a wall. No problem, she'd wrench it inwards and push the cage back and squeeze out. A chain clanked. Padlocked. Defeated, she sat on the blanket, wrapped it around her feet and carefully opened the peanuts. How long did these need to last for? She hated the fact that she needed them as she tipped out a handful and ate them one at a time. A thought meandered through her mind. How did he get the cage here? She captured the thought, turning it over and over, hoping it might hold some answers. She drank some water and took another deep breath, then wished she hadn't; it was as if the air were centuries old, stale, musty, devoid of its life-giving properties. Her senses were returning in full. "How?" The one spoken word echoed. How can she escape? First, she must shout and the echo will carry it along the tunnel. If nothing happens then that's the time to think more.

She hollered, rattled the cage bars with one of her shoes, and let out a high-pitched scream. No response. She tried again. Still no answer. Time to think. The bars were more for glitzy show than to lock someone away. Maybe she could bend them enough to squeeze out. At least twenty minutes of wrenching achieved only sufficient space to get her arm and shoulder out. She found the peanuts and the water again and, eating one at a time, she wrestled again with how he might have manhandled this six foot high cage through the tunnel. He must have dismantled it. She felt around the bars, examining each one from top to bottom to see if there was some kind of clasp. Yes, this is how he'd moved it around. Every tenth bar was clipped to another. Could they be undone? If she had her handbag with her, her nail file would have been useful to prise open the clasps. Hope faded. This apology for a man had stalked her and was fixated enough to dismantle a cage and transport it to a disused station. What kind of person does something like that? She was up against an obsessive monster. How could she ever have noted in her blue book that she'd once thought he was cute? "I will not let my life be determined by this... this fiend." It wasn't a shout, it was a whisper, a motivating whisper.

She returned to work vigorously on the two bars she'd managed to wrench slightly apart. Recognizing that the gap was too high and needed to be low enough for her to get her legs and body through, she worked her way downwards. Surely the bars should have popped out of their fitting at the base of the cage. She attacked them, seething when they would not budge. The rat had thought this through rather better than she'd hoped: the cage looked flimsy but was built to safely hold high a gyrating, human body.

Liberty straightened out the blanket and felt around the base of the cage again. Her hand felt something plastic with a handle and a lid. Was there more food? It was empty. The significance of this made her realize the rat planned for her to be here for some time. If there was only enough water for a couple of days, he'd be back. If he'd wanted to kill her slowly here, he wouldn't have left peanuts, water and a bucket. Perhaps she could reason with him? What a stupid thought. She sat on the blanket and pulled it around her legs, hoping to retain some warmth and wishing she was dressed in something warmer than a mini skirt and blouse. Aloud she said, "Why aren't I like one of those tough girls in books?" Maybe she had been strong-minded and focused in her old life. She must have been. Although she couldn't remember what her work comprised, she must have been sensible with strategies, plans and people to deal with. Furthermore, she had founded and run her own company. The loss of her memory robbed her of all her life lessons. She could not think what the 'old' version of her would do now.

Instead, the 'new' Liberty thought of Nick. Where had he gone? Why? Where? When would he be back? Would he realize she'd been abducted? Would he fathom by who? "Whom," she announced, feeling pleased she'd corrected her grammar, surely that was evidence she was okay. Her thoughts returned to Nick and she yearned for him. Her heart was breaking, she could hardly bear to think of him in case he returned too late – or not at all; something was definitely wrong. She must escape. She scoffed a handful of nuts, took a swig of water and returned to what she called 'The Fight', working with all the strength she could muster to bend the bars. The thought of being sold spurred her on.

It was all to no avail and, hours later, not knowing the time and, arms aching, she decided to try to sleep and rolled herself in the one, inadequate blanket. She cleared her mind of plans to break out and thought only of treasured memories of Nick until the blessing of sleep enfolded her in its magic.

Unfortunately, the cold and the discomfort broke into her dreams only minutes later and, shivering, she wrapped the blanket tighter and stared into the dark. "Oh God, please don't let me cry." Everything, she would lose everything. She had tasted the joy of being in love and now... She hummed a tune; what tune? Some of the words filtered through and finally she managed enough to start singing.

Have we trials and temptations?
Is there trouble anywhere?

She couldn't remember all the words nor the tune so she hummed for a bit before picking up with:

Can we find a friend so faithful
Who will all our sorrows share?
Jesus knows our every weakness
Take it to the Lord in prayer.

Trials, temptations, trouble? Definitely. Liberty focused on her current temptation: shoving Gregor Hode under a train. Yes. She grinned. No. If she'd learnt anything in this new life, it was the power of good, no that wasn't the word. Racking her brain, she came up with the power of the knowledge of truth, the truth of who, ultimately, is governor of the universe and who would deal out vengeance. Hey, where did that come from? Had it seeped into her mind during one of those sermons, settled itself down in hiding, ready to pounce out when needed most? She chuckled, listened to the echo and chuckled again. She'd pray. For the first time in her life, well, maybe this was the second time, she would "take it to the Lord in prayer".

Once Liberty got started, she found it hard to stop. Whispering, she began with the overriding matter of being locked up. Almost as important was the problem of Nick being secretive; she knew something must be wrong. There was Gemma, probably getting worried, and what about Paul? She prayed they'd be happy together again. And Jon, amazing, dear Jon. She paused, quietly turning over thoughts about what might have happened with Jon if Nick hadn't been around. She resumed whispering, thanking God that Jon possessed many loyal and useful mates and maybe there would be someone special for him one day. She dwelt on this quietly for a moment then continued thinking what else ought to be prayed for. What about the terrible war in Vietnam; had she any right to pray for peace when she could do nothing about it herself? The words of the song came to her, 'Is there trouble anywhere'. Yes, there's trouble in Vietnam and all around there, so she took it to the Lord in a whispered prayer. Then she thanked God for the new flat. Ah yes, what about Tom and Mary? She prayed for them. She reasoned that as she had no-one else to talk to, she might as well continue. She did, until ending with a resounding rendition of the first lines of 'Land of Hope and Glory' causing her to laugh. "How disrespectful," she announced apologetically. Yet a warm glow had come over her and she decided that chatting to God in a friendly fashion must be allowed.

Against all the odds, Liberty fell asleep sitting up with a look of contentment on her face.

Chapter Thirty-Six
Rampallian rat

There were daggers in his treacherous eyes. Could Gregor be a killer? She'd rejected him, he had turned criminal – she *must* get out. Liberty had slept well, perhaps only for a short time – how could she tell? On waking, her brain kept turning over the memory of his smile as he gave her the peanuts and now it sent a bolt of energy – lightning sizzling through her. She stumbled towards the bars, found the gap she'd made, and wrenched them further apart. Yes! She could do this. Amazed at her new found strength, Liberty continued to make sufficient progress to get not only her arm through but also a leg. Just a little more work – freedom beckoned. Grunting aided her. Her sore hands did not. She picked up the blanket and wrapped it around her hands. The protection of the blanket enabled her to push very much harder. Five more minutes and she'd be out. Nothing could stop her now.

A noise from the direction of the tunnel alarmed her. Her whole body froze. Unmistakeably, the rails were rattling and a clickety clack sounded as if something was rolling along them. The rat was returning and he must be pushing some sort of cart. A picture of the dismantled golden cage being pushed along the rails flashed through her mind. "That's how he did it," she whispered. What would he be bringing this time? Or was it to cart her away? For sale.

Then hope – that always welcome feeling – welled up within her as she heard the unmistakeable sound of a Beatles' song.

"All you need is love, dum dididy dum. All you need is love, love. Love is all you need."

Surely it couldn't be the rat? Please, God, no. The man's voice grew louder, accompanied by increasing rattling. It didn't sound like Gregor, but a singer's voice often doesn't sound like their spoken voice. Hope froze. Listening intently, Liberty heard other voices, soft murmurs like boiling water in a pot. It can't be Gregor. "Help!" All sounds from the tunnel stopped. "Help! Help me!"

Noises clattered towards her, a powerful beam shone from the dark arc of the tunnel and a man in white overalls jumped up onto the platform and peered into the cage. He turned and roared, "Oy you lot, get up here quick."

She clung to the bars; her teeth felt as if they were vibrating, her knees were close to collapse but she felt the overwhelming joy of hope fulfilled.

Another three white-overalled men leapt up onto the platform and, without a word, wrenched open the already damaged bars and helped Liberty out. The singer grabbed the blanket and wrapped her shuddering body in it.

"Who's done this to you?" said one of the men.

"Gregor Hode," Liberty said firmly, shielding her eyes from the unaccustomed light of so many torches.

They were none the wiser but at least they had a name to follow-up. Two of the men dashed back into the tunnel and pumped their hand car and its trailer into the station, squealing brakes needlessly announcing its arrival.

"Get it emptied," said the singer, "I'll take her back up the line in the car and get an ambulance. You lot carry on with creating the set. The plans are in that briefcase." He pointed to a leather case on top of a pile of lights, cables and other necessities for filming. "The rest of the crew will be arriving at seven, so get moving. We've got a busy day ahead."

~

Sitting up, curtains pulled around her bed, Liberty listened to the kindly doctor.

"She's exhausted and cold but physically in good condition otherwise. It appears she's only been there overnight. I reckon that after a decent breakfast and another cup of tea, Miss Taffet will be well enough to be discharged." He scribbled his signature and handed the notes to the nurse. "Do you have anyone who can transport you home?"

Liberty looked forlorn. "I can't remember any telephone numbers."

The doctor pursed his lips. "Have the police been informed?"

The nurse nodded. "They want to interview her."

"Arrange for them to see her after her breakfast and gently insist they take her home. They'll likely want to ensure they're leaving her somewhere safe." He paused then said quietly, "Do you live alone?"

"No, I have two, er, well, one trusted flatmate and I have the telephone numbers of good friends at the flat." She took a deep breath. "I'll be all right if one of them can get home to ensure Gregor isn't around."

"The police won't leave you alone, not while your captor is at large." With a frown and pursed lips, he sighed, "As soon as you can, get some proper, healing sleep." He called the nurse aside, spoke to her, and then left the ward.

Liberty was just finishing her scrambled eggs on toast when the nurse introduced a detective and a uniformed policewoman. The woman sat on the chair facing her bed. The detective stood behind her.

"Now, young lady," he consulted his notebook. "Miss Taffet, isn't it?"

Liberty nodded, and defiantly sipped the last of her tea before putting the cup down.

"I'll take this for you," said the policewoman. She took the tray from Liberty's lap and placed it under the bed.

The detective went through his paces. When, how, why, what happened? He bristled with outrage when she mentioned Gregor Hode's threat of selling her. Once satisfied he had obtained all possible information, he tapped his pencil on his pad. "WPC Briggs will stay with you and arrange transport. She'll also stay with you at your flat until another officer arrives. Under no circumstances are you to be left alone with Miss Chloe Campbell. We shall be interviewing her and after that you must decide if she can continue to live with you. She sounds very impressionable and therefore it is important you are not alone with her while this Hode fellow is at large." He gave her a stern look.

Dutifully, Liberty nodded. "I understand. Thank you."

~

WPC Briggs drove Liberty to the flat, having first ascertained via a local policeman that Mrs Tualin would be there to let them in. Next, she checked it out, ensured all windows were shut and doors locked. Then she telephoned Gemma.

"I've suggested your friend remains at work as usual because I think you need to sleep. At least I've reassured her that you're not missing. When or if Miss Campbell arrives home, I will still be here."

Liberty thanked her and agreed a sleep in her own bed was definitely needed.

The telephone rang, the constable answered and returned to say that the detective had interviewed Miss Campbell and she had co-operated. "You can sleep soundly now. I'll wake you at six. Miss Bond said she'll be home around then. Best not to sleep longer, otherwise you won't sleep tonight."

"What day is it?"

WPC Briggs blinked. "It's Thursday, 30th May, and it's ten minutes past one."

Liberty studied the woman police constable. She wasn't much older than she was and managed to look quite feminine in her police uniform. "Thank you. There's milk in the fridge," she hesitated, "probably. Do make yourself a drink and if you can find anything to eat..."

"No need to concern yourself with me, Miss Taffet, you just curl up and sleep. All's well now."

At six o'clock precisely, Constable Briggs woke Liberty. "Your friend is home and there's no sign of Miss Campbell. Do you feel like getting up?"

Liberty nodded. "I'd like a bath and a change of clothes." She indicated her discarded clothes on a chair.

"A sensible thing to do. I'll speak to Miss Bond; she's busy in the kitchen at the moment."

Once she had washed away the grime of her imprisonment, Liberty dressed in a plain T-shirt, skirt and slippers, stripped the sheets off her bed.

"Shall we have trays on our laps?" Gemma asked with a tentative smile as Liberty came into the sitting room. "I'm making a chicken stew with dumplings."

Liberty took a long, deep breath. "Oh Gemma, it is so very good to be home with you again." She carefully sat down, as if the sofa might snap shut on her. "Dumplings. Yes please. Such a great comfort food."

"The police lady is stirring the pot at the moment; she's going to have some too. Apparently, there'll be another one doing the 'night shift'." Gemma seemed mortified as she continued, "I suppose I should have called the police when I found you weren't home. I'm so sorry but I thought you'd probably gone to Nick's."

"It's all right, Gemma, you weren't to know."

"I could kick myself." She paused, took a deep breath and said, "Would you like me to phone anyone for you?"

Liberty considered for a moment then announced, "Maybe I should ring Aurora."

"I can do that for you, if you give me the number."

"Thank you so much but I want what that rat did to me to make me stronger, so I'll ring."

Gemma stood aside as Liberty lurched towards the hall and snatched up the phone. Nick's grandparents' phone number was stored underneath; she dialled, fumbling a little. "Hello, may I speak to Aurora please?"

"Liberty, it's Nick. Don't you want to speak to me?"

"Nick, oh Nick. Sorry, I'm not very awake at the moment. I thought you'd still be away."

"Liberty, whatever is the matter?" As there was no reply, he announced, "I'll be there in half an hour. Are you at home?"

"Yes, Nick. Thank you." She put the phone down before she burst into tears."

Constable Briggs appeared in the hall and put her arm around Liberty. "Let it all out."

"I feel a complete noodle."

"Hardly that. You've been through an horrendous experience, one that, thankfully, few will have to endure. You escaped. Even if the film crew had not arrived, they told us you were almost out of the cage. You'd have been down that tunnel in no time. You had very little sleep and you are simply recovering. Tears are a good thing."

"My boyfriend is on his way. I'd better put some make-up on."

"You look fine without it, so may I suggest you come and eat Gemma's chicken stew first." It wasn't a question it was guidance, guidance that Liberty readily followed.

At ten minutes to seven, the doorbell rang and Liberty abandoned putting on her make-up and jumped up to answer it.

"Oh no," said WPC Briggs, "*I'll* open any doors which need opening."

Following a lot of whispering in the hall, Nick dashed into the sitting room. Restraining himself from hugging Liberty hard, he gently held her in his arms before guiding her back to the sofa.

A fleeting thought passed through her mind: *he sometimes behaves as a courting Regency gentleman would, as if I were a treasured china doll.*

Sitting alongside her, he asked, "Are you harmed in any way?"

"Not at all," she reassured him, "though I am still a little shaky. It's not something I'd want to go through again. Do you mind if I don't give you a detailed account at the moment?"

"Of course I don't mind. You can tell me in your own time. It's enough to know you're home – with protection from that rampallian rat."

The description brought forth a chuckle – her first in many hours. "Rampallian rat? Where do you get these words from?"

"From the great bard of the English language – Shakespeare, of course. And I've heard you mention the rat. I'm right, aren't I? Gregor Hode, from 2020, is the man you call 'the rat'.

"Shh... they might hear."

"Don't worry. Twenty twenty might mean anything, the name of a book, a play – anything." He slapped his knee. "As for the slimy slug, trailing behind her a sticky mess, it would be best if you distance yourself." He took her hand and raised it to his lips. "The rat's been very active, causing me difficulties too. For a start, he wrote the note, 'Don't trust Nylander', one of several inventive schemes."

Liberty remembered the envelope she'd picked up from the reception desk at the hospital where she worked. Her brow furrowed. "Nick, where have you been?"

Nick was saved by a tap on the door. "It's only me," said Gemma. "I thought you might like a cup of tea." She entered tentatively and added, "Or perhaps you'd like coffee, Nick? We have that too."

They both smiled, thanked Gemma, and Nick asked for coffee with milk. In the intervening moments, he kissed her. Initially it was a 'may I?' type kiss which met with approval. Then, arms around her, he hugged her tight, she was no china doll now, she was someone to be safeguarded and cherished. The kiss that followed heralded the giving of their hearts to each other, no holding back, pure ecstasy. Wherever Nick had been, she knew the rat's note lied.

Gemma put the tray on the coffee table and hurried out.

Chapter Thirty-Seven
If only

"I have some bad news, Liberty."

Liberty's eyes grew larger as they followed Nick pacing the drawing room in his grandparents' house. She had slept soundly in her flat the night before, secure in the knowledge that a policewoman stayed on watch. Nick had returned to collect her, guaranteeing her safety and mentioning trained guard dogs. Now his words set her heart pounding. What could the news possibly be? Gemma went off to work that morning – had the rat intercepted her? "Is Gemma safe?"

Nick spun round to face her on the sofa. "As far as I know, yes, she's safe. The police are still searching for Hode; he was probably scared off by the sight of the film crew and he'll know you'll have been rescued and will have identified him as your captor. No, it's something which affects *us*."

Something inside her didn't want to know so she put off hearing this bad news by saying, "By the way, WPC Briggs telephoned my boss and explained the situation. Apparently, he was very understanding and said he'd hold my job open for me until I'm fully recovered."

Nick tilted his head in recognition, yet did not smile.

"I'm not sure I can take any more bad news, Nick."

He took a deep breath and sat beside her. "Okay, it is something I do have to tell you but first let's talk about you."

"Stop sounding like I'm one of your patients."

Nick reached out for her hand. "I'm so sorry."

"It's just that I feel I'm all over the place. One minute I can save the world, the next I'm all at sea, like Boris Johnson."

"Who's Boris Johnson?"

"I've no idea. Could he be from 2020?"

"Imagine the chaos if it were possible to answer all such questions."

If he wasn't from 2020, perhaps he was from history. She could remember history up to the 1960s. She took a deep breath and ploughed on. "I can't believe I was like this in 2020. When I was in the cage, I remembered the words of a song about taking our troubles to Jesus in prayer. And I did, I prayed. It empowered me." She smiled at her 'business speak'. "Then, only hours later, even though I'd been rescued, I felt demoralized. I didn't care about anyone else or anything. Totally self-centred." She couldn't hold back her tears any longer and Nick wiped them away so tenderly that she started sobbing. "You see, look at me." She closed her eyes in shame and muttered, "I don't know where you've been." Suddenly she blurted, "Have you seen Chloe again?"

"Only to teach her a lesson. First, I stood her up. The next time I gave her a lecture on loyalty. She seemed contrite but I couldn't be sure." He sighed. "Don't you think I've agonized over this? If she hadn't come to meet me, leaving you on your own, you might not have been kidnapped."

"He'd have found a way. I wish you'd told me where you were going. I do trust you, I really do but not knowing where you've been worries me, especially this time. I know our time travelling will have consequences and I want to understand what they are."

"I will explain but now let's consider why you are now a worrier when once you were an enthusiastic rising star in our NHS, well able to keep your cool in a crisis." He reached out to touch the side of her face, stroked it until her eyes met his then let his hand fall. "Liberty, my only love, you have experienced a unique set of circumstances. You've lost both your parents early in your life. Your brother is ten thousand miles away. You courageously gave up a secure future in the NHS to become an entrepreneur, taking risks, working long hours, helping people to find friends, partners, new pathways in life and happiness.

"Then, not knowing the outcome, you set out on an adventure which did not end as you expected. Unable to return to 2020 without being invisible, you found yourself in a time for which you were totally unprepared, wholly reliant on strangers, and in danger of having no means of support should your status be found out. Without a National Insurance number nor a birth certificate, you have no right to state support, nor even secure employment. We are akin to being illegal immigrants." Nick took a deep breath. "Remember, you needed to relearn how to fit into society. You had no-one looking after you and your mind went into self-preservation mode. To cap it all, this rank-scented, viperous rat kidnaps you."

Liberty couldn't help but smile at yet another extravagant description of the malevolent Gregor Hode.

"I love it here in 1968, but you're right, deep within, I've known I am alone. Gemma has her wonderful brother, her parents and Paul; you have your grandparents."

"And you have me, Liberty."

"But I don't, do I? When I went back last time, I made notes about you and Jaelyn. You're engaged and look how you treated her. You took—"

Nick squeezed her hand. "I am not, nor have I ever been engaged to Jaelyn. Jaelyn is my father's goddaughter. I felt honour bound to keep an eye on her because she came from a one parent family and that parent has terminal cancer. She latched on to me. I also became aware that she had hopes for a future with me and she more or less talked herself into believing it to be true. I repeat – I am not engaged to her, nor would I have considered it. The only girl I have ever loved is you, though you always seemed to be keeping your distance. Unless I cornered you in your office, you'd shoot off in a different direction."

"Did I? I don't remember."

"Fortunately, neither do I. However, I always kept a diary and have done since I was twelve or so, still do. I've brought the latest ones back with me and they'd make interesting reading if I ever find the time."

Nick's face was serious yet Liberty began to smile. "So that's how you know so much more about 2020. I made notes when I returned but they were rather brief." The smile dropped as her doubts niggled at her again. "Where did you go, Nick?"

"This is what I want to talk to you about."

He leant forward and hugged her briefly which served only to make Liberty nervous despite the love that seemed to flow from him to her: the news must be terrible.

"First, I want you to remember that I followed you through the light curtain of my own volition. I knew the consequences – we would not be able to return to 2020. I'd spoken with Matt and Laura Redfern the night before. Laura, of course, having arrived from Regency times, understood the dangerous repercussions of travelling in time. She showed me her invisible toe as proof that she might have become invisible in both eras if she'd continued to go back and forth. The lesson went deep, so I knew what I was doing in following you."

"I am so terribly sorry, I had no idea..."

"There's no need to be sorry, I wanted to follow you. Hode did too but was unaware of the consequences." There was a moment of silence as they both dwelt on the rat having no idea where he was going. Nick resumed. "He'd always kept watch on your office and when you left in your car and I followed, he had to find out what was happening." Nick ensured Liberty wasn't too alarmed before continuing. "I'd felt chained to my responsibilities. To be a doctor can be a calling and, indeed, I... well, the point is, I knew I could not lose you. We'd only just begun. I want you to be with me always and I hope you feel the same."

She wanted to say that anywhere, anywhere at all, so long as she was with him it would be Heaven on Earth. Instead, she said simply, "I do, Nick, I do."

The kiss that followed was a taster of all she had ever hoped for and she drew strength from it. It was true she had experienced a unique set of circumstances, as Nick called her losses but now, being sure of his love, she felt differently – alive, ready to take on any difficulties which stood in the way of building a happy, successful future with someone deeply loved more each time she saw him.

Gently, he pushed her away. "There's more, Libby, the bad news is still to come."

Liberty wanted to nestle her head in his neck, but gazed directly in his strength-giving eyes. "I can take it now."

He kissed her forehead, focused his eyes on hers and locked them into her soul asking for so much more. The effect overwhelmed her and she felt as if panicked birds were attempting to take off from her stomach, fluttering and unable to escape. Gentle butterflies they were not.

Nick kissed her forehead again and continued. "Have you heard the story of the boiling frog?"

"Do you mean the one where if you put it into boiling water, it will immediately jump out, but if you put it in pleasantly warm water, it likes it?"

Nick nodded, his eyebrows raised. "That's the one. It fails to notice the water is being brought to the boil until, too late, it can't jump and is cooked."

Liberty's eyes stared as the meaning of this tale began to sink in.

"Not only did the rat target you, he also targeted me. Professor Schmidt received anonymous letters concerning both you and me. I only found out when a girl in Personnel warned me that 'somebody had it in for me'. As you know, doctors need to be squeaky clean – certainly not forging important documentation."

"If only that rat hadn't followed us."

Nick shrugged. That's not all. "Grandie's brother, the one he's roped in to help fix things for us, has been diagnosed with a brain tumour. I've visited him in Bart's, that is St Bartholomew's Hospital, and the operation is scheduled for next week. I know it will be successful, of course, because he lived to see the twenty-first century too and I'd mentioned it in my diary. However, this means our hope of him presenting us as asylum seekers or something similar, and therefore provided with all the necessary paperwork for a secure life here, has to be postponed for several months, maybe a year. Grandie and I have desperately tried to find another way to provide us with 'a past', birth certificates, qualifications and so on. I'm in full agreement that he should not attempt to contact contemptible criminals. Heaven only knows where that would lead us."

Liberty said wistfully, "I wish we could simply tell the truth."

Doggedly, he continued. "My time here has run out. I believe your time has too. Unfortunately, you have come to the notice of the police and the press are interested also and will dig into your background. We have enjoyed the warmth of our welcome but now we must recognize that things are hotting up and if we don't jump immediately, we may never be able to and *we* shall be branded as criminals." He kissed her hand. "As Wordsworth once said, 'Will you come, grow old with me'?"

She'd already decided. "Anywhere you say." The truth of his message had seeped into her bones before: the wonderful time she was having in the Swinging Sixties could not last.

"The best is yet to be. However, a few difficulties lie ahead. Personnel have made an appointment with the Professor for Monday afternoon and would like me to be in attendance. I know what will follow. I overheard the words 'posing as a doctor,' so I might be prosecuted for practising medicine illegally. The Medical Defence Union will not be able to help as the truth that we are time travellers would be an unacceptable defence." He paused and grinned. "My suspicion is that Gregor Hode is behind this and that is why we saw him in the grounds of Guy's Hospital and I saw him again, about a week ago. I'd changed the dates on various..." He pursed his lips. "You get the picture, I know. There is as much chance of being able to stay without being confronted by the forces of law and order, as there is for Germany to win the cricket world cup. To get to the point:

we need to leave 1968. We need to go to a time when we can thrive without the fear of being prosecuted." He paused. "You said you'd come anywhere but would you come to any *time*?"

Surprising herself, she whispered, "Anywhere, any time, so long as I am with you."

Nick allowed himself the shortest pause and the smallest smile. "Grandie and I have been poring over the history book of our family. Now this is the strangest of things: in 1814 there is a reference to a young couple... here, look at this." He handed her copies of some of the pages. "Grandie took these, what he calls Xerox copies, and said we should consider them carefully."

Liberty frowned in concentration. One of the pages was the very one that had caught her eye before. She'd never got round to mentioning it and besides, it appeared odd, almost other worldly. She read it aloud. "My husband and son lie cold in their graves and I am alone in Bleakheath Hall, icy cold, though it is June. It is a portent reminding me I must relinquish this abode of my husband's ancestors."

"Read on because a couple of weeks later she writes what I believe is pertinent to our future."

Liberty continued. "Stranger still is the arrival of a young couple. Their attire is unlike anything I would expect of visitors to Bleakheath, and they brought with them large metal cases on wheels. More peculiar still is their speech."

Liberty laughed. "This could be us."

"I thought the same."

She continued. "They handed me a letter. The seal bore our Coat of Arms. I invited them to sit in the drawing room with me while I perused the most unusual Letter of Introduction I have ever seen." Liberty glanced up to catch Nick staring at her. She read the rest of the entry in a whisper, her eyes wide. "They have appeared as if they were visitors from another planet, bringing with them the wisdom of the stars. I have come to the conclusion they are angels."

"You'll be relieved to know," said Nick, laughing, "that a few days later, she retracts her evaluation of 'us' and records her thought that we are 'strangers from another land'. Finally, she accepts that, being the spitting image of her husband, I am obviously his estranged brother 'of whom my dear husband never spoke'." He awaited a reply from Liberty which didn't come. "I admit I have been consuming this tome in the indiscriminate manner of a combine harvester but it has shown me a path – actually more than that – I believe it has shown me our destiny."

Liberty's eyes widened. "In short, Nick, you're saying we should prepare to leave this wonderful life before it collapses, and ensure we take with us some vital knowledge."

"Yes."

"And go to 1814?"

"Yes."

"When?"

"First we need to immediately tidy our lives here. Next we need to take back to 2020 anything we have here that we might need in our new life."

"Like my mother's jewellery, though most of it is still in 2020, I feel sure." There never seemed to be a good time to explain why her mother had so much. There was always something more important happening but one day she must find the right time.

Nick ran his fingers through his dark hair. "Yes, anything of value that would not be out of place in 1814. If we have articles of value which could be sold in 1814, we should take them with us as we shan't have a ready income when we arrive."

"My father left me some gold bars."

"He did? Where are they?"

"They're still in 2020 and I've noted down that if I sold them at the 2020 price, I might get relatively more than if I sold them in earlier times."

"Good. Your research will save valuable time. Somehow we need to turn 2020 money into portable valuables."

"Nick, what about Gemma?"

"Gemma will have a flat which she can't afford. We could give her a lump sum to tide her over until more people can be found, or maybe she could give notice and live at Paul's house or nearby."

"I have money I can give her. And Tom and Mary? I can't leave them without help. I committed to looking after them, well, at least alleviating their dire situation from time to time."

"I wonder if Nonna might find them something. They could refit one of the outbuildings and rehouse them, rent free if they can provide some services in some way. What do you think?"

"That would be wonderful, Nick."

"I'll give Grandie another stock market tip, enough to cover the cost of immediate refurbishment. He picked up her hand, kissed it and whispered, "We can do this."

Liberty's heart raced; she took a deep breath to steady her nerve and then a smile lit her face – Nick belonged in 1814. His plan must be expedited urgently. Her organizational skills were returning. "Do you think the rat is in hiding here or in 2020?"

He released her, stood and paced again. She could not help but admire his beautiful, lithe body as he patrolled the room.

"I don't know. *If* he is caught here, he'll end up in prison. However, he's as slippery as an eel and might move to a deserted island in the Outer Hebrides. I believe some are available for sale. One even has a colony of rare black rats."

Liberty laughed. "Poor Scotland! I doubt he could bear being invisible in 2020 for long, so I think you're probably right."

Chapter Thirty-Eight
I will

"We are going to miss you." Nonna dabbed her eyes with her white cotton handkerchief. "Yet go you must, it is your destino."

Liberty managed the smallest of smiles; she would miss this lovely lady's Italian accent and, although she had never before really believed in destiny, it sounded less frightening in Italian, positively alluring.

"The Regency costumes you wore for the cricket match shall be packed for you to take." Nonna thought for a moment. "Ah, I have also the shoes, you must have the shoes." There was another short silence. "And, and the reticule, you must have that. You must look, how you say...?"

"Authentic," said Grandpapa.

Aurora nodded in gratitude. "You have your signed Will?"

Liberty thanked Nick's grandparents for signing it. She sniffed – she'd done all she could.

"I must go."

Nick raised his hand to stop his grandmother rushing away. "When we go back in time to 1814," Nick put his arm around Liberty, "we shall not be able to remember you but you will both have made a colossal contribution to our lives and to history for which we cannot thank you enough."

Grandpapa beamed. "Never could I have imagined that all my theorising on time travel would be proved true. Such a pity I cannot dangle it in the faces of those who think I am mad."

"You are not mad, you are English," Aurora said proudly.

Grandpapa clenched his fists. "We will never forget you, never!" He handed Nick some parchment sheets. "Read it through, and if you agree, you can close these pages and seal them with the Nylander seal. Here you are, here's the wax, matches and seal. You can keep the matches; they might come in handy."

Sunny and Siri appeared at the window, standing on their hind legs with their snouts pressed against the glass and their eyes focused on Nick. He walked across the room and nodded a goodbye to his beloved dogs.

Liberty was relieved that he did not have to say goodbye to his eight-year-old father, though he left him a letter and a £5 note, something they both chuckled about.

Nick sat on the sofa, read each of the parchment sheets carefully and passed them on to Liberty for her approval. When both were satisfied with the tale of being travellers from an island off the coast of America, Nick strode purposefully to the desk in the corner and, watched by Grandpapa, he sealed the letter. "So I am to be the brother of the recently deceased, rightful heir of Bleakheath Hall. And Liberty is my wife. It therefore only remains for me to ask Liberty to make it true."

Startling Liberty, he knelt in front of her and said, "With all my heart, I love you, I have loved you from the moment we first met. I ask you to be my wife. I cannot offer you a white wedding, I can only offer you the promise of telling the fictitious tale of our marriage in a far island and a life which will fulfil our destiny." Still kneeling he pulled from the pocket of his jeans a little blue box, opened it and presented it to Liberty. "This antique ring dates back to the eighteenth century; the diamond is two carats and flawless. Will you accept it together with the promise of my everlasting love, wherever and whenever we may be?"

"I will." Liberty lifted her eyes to share her joy with Aurora and Grandie who both stood, almost to attention, as if fulfilling their duty as witnesses.

Nick placed the ring on her wedding finger, checked it fitted, and lifted her from the sofa. "I can't wait to introduce you as my wife," he said victoriously as he danced her around the room. "I shall ensure you have a gold wedding ring to wear before we present ourselves to 1814."

"Nick, I might have my mother's wedding ring. I've a note in my blue book to remind me not to sell it as my father left it to me. Would you allow me to wear that as *my* wedding ring? I would so love to have something to remember her by, even though I cannot recall even what she looks like."

"Of course, if you so wish."

He raised her left hand and kissed it.

A simple gesture which Liberty wished she could treasure for the rest of her life.

~

That same evening, having spent the day writing letters, which included her resignation from the employment agency and a short letter of thanks and apologies direct to Sir Arthur Hollingbourne, Liberty devoted herself to packing. Having packed the bare essentials, which for both Nick and Liberty included their daily journals and Xerox copies of several pages of the family history book, they felt able to attend the opening of the youth club.

Paul stood on the small stage and announced, "Thank you all for attending the opening of the Gateway Club. Many of you have helped in converting this grotty cottage into our cool Gateway." He pointed to the many coloured walls. "Coats of many colours were used." Only a few chuckled; the reference to Joseph's coat of many colours in the Bible was lost on most.

Liberty smiled gently at the choice of name for the club. Yes, it could be a gateway to a new, improved way of life. Paul was an irresistible force for good and, together with Gemma, they'd probably achieve their goals. How she loved cool Britannia, so warm, so friendly, so stimulating. If only she and Nick could stay forever, they would be part of this, this, what could she say? New, vibrant world? Paul's welcome speech continued while she ruminated on lost possibilities.

"You will find that upstairs there's table tennis and more, as well as our coffee bar. There is no charge for the coffee but it would be very helpful if you leave a contribution towards our costs in the yellow teapot at the bar. And if any of you wish to find out more about God, the universe or anything else – so long as it's not your maths homework – then don't hesitate to ask me. I might not know the answers but it'll be fun trying to find out. Hanging from the picture rails are boards with Bible quotations on them. If you're artistic and want to jazz them up a bit, just ask."

Liberty took in a deep breath and felt overwhelmed by gratitude to have found such inspirational people. She barely had time to let the thought settle before Nick whispered in her ear, "Sorry to spring this on you but it will be an excellent way to say our fond farewells." He grabbed her hand and pulled her on to the stage. "I wish you all to be the first to know: Liberty and I have today become engaged to be married."

As Liberty lifted her hand to show her ring, all eyes widened at the size of the diamond. Then everyone clapped and cheered, even those who had stepped inside for the very first time.

"I thank you all, and I apologize for gatecrashing." He bowed slightly and, with Liberty, he left the stage whispering to her that it wasn't wise to say too much.

Everyone clapped as they made their way towards the back of the room while Paul introduced the 'Good News', which unsurprisingly turned out to be the same group of young people who accompanied some of the songs during the Sunday meetings. The drummer began by beating every drum in the set, the guitars picked up the beat, Paul began singing, backed by two girls, and what had once been two downstairs rooms in an unloved cottage now rocked as a dance floor.

Gemma, wearing a newly made grey and yellow dress, came to congratulate Nick and Liberty but could hardly be heard. Liberty handed Gemma the letter she had written and followed Nick outside into the quieter, cool evening. Several people came out to congratulate them on their engagement.

Having read the letter, Gemma rushed outside. "You are leaving?" Forlorn, she added, "Where are you going?"

"It's all quite sudden, I realize, but Nick wants us to make a new life well away from Gregor Hode."

Gemma said, "But surely he'll be caught soon."

"We're leaving even the memory of him."

"When?"

"I'll collect my things from the flat tonight and leave the key as we'll be gone tomorrow. I am so very sorry to do this to you. The £100 is to cover my rent and other expenses and I hope you will be able to find two more flatmates. Can you do that?"

"Libby, that's far too much."

"Without you..." Liberty raised her eyebrows and grinned.

Gemma smiled graciously. "Did you notice Chloe in the club?"

"Chloe? Surely not."

"She turned up at the flat earlier today accompanied by a policewoman. She's been interviewed by them and they might need her to be a witness when they catch Gregor. She's apologized profusely and explained she was being blackmailed by the rat. He'd caught her shoplifting and he started controlling her. The police think Gregor has done a runner."

"I do hope they catch him. Is Chloe expecting to stay at the flat?"

"She's got nowhere else to go and Jon is going to sleep on the sofa tonight, just in case she's only returned to rob the place!" Gemma chuckled.

Liberty clutched Gemma's arm. "You are a wonderful person. Don't ever change."

A smile crept across Gemma's face. "As you are going away, I think I'm allowed to tell you that Paul has asked me to marry him."

"Oh how perfect. I'm so pleased for you." Liberty hugged her. "That's both of us. Wow!"

"So you see, I'll only need the flat for another six months or so," Gemma said disentangling herself from Liberty's arms. "And if the flat sharing doesn't work out, or we can't find a replacement for you, Jon and Paul will help me out, I'm sure, so please don't worry."

Liberty drew Gemma's attention to the rest of the letter. "You see I'm also asking that you somehow introduce Tom and Mary to Max and Aurora who will provide them with some light work and a place to live."

"Of course I will. Do you think they'll go?"

"If anyone can persuade them, it's you."

"And Jon," added Gemma.

Both girls grinned profusely, then hugged each other again.

"I can't think what I would have done without you, Gemma. You were like an angel sent from God."

Gemma laughed and, released from the hug, said, "I think the same about you!"

Jon bounced out to them. "What a day! I've just congratulated Nick on running off with the best girl on the planet, Gemma excluded, and Paul's got this project off to a rip-roaring start. I've counted thirty-six teenagers in there, that's not counting us oldies."

Had the engagement announcement hurt? If it did, he hardly showed it. She would miss her bouncing Tigger. Genes like his should be passed on, perhaps he'll find... her thoughts trailed off as he leant forward to kiss her on the cheek which then morphed into a bear hug.

"I am so going to miss you. I hope he's not taking you too far away. You'll come and see us, won't you?" Fortunately for Liberty, he didn't wait for an answer and continued. "Send us a postcard, we want to keep in touch."

"Jon," Liberty was about to say that she'd never forget him yet realized that she would because he would be way into what, from a Regency perspective, would be the future. She took a deep breath and started again. "Jon, you are a hero, the world needs more people like you, you light up the world with your, your..." And then she broke down and cried.

~

The following morning, a sunny Sunday, Grandie hid his feelings with talk of plans. "I shall continue my battle with squalor, poverty, idleness and ignorance, and rally the troops to provide more apprenticeships, to build a better world and—"

Sitting in the front seat of her husband's car, Nonna touched his arm lightly. "Hush, my darling, we all know you will fight on, now just concentrate, please I ask you, on the driving to Bradstow."

Nicolo and Liberty were holding hands on the back seat of the car. "I promise," said Nick solemnly, "that once we are settled in our new home," he hesitated then continued, "the new home being the old Bleakheath Hall," he smiled and squeezed her hand, "that I shall not be so preoccupied with matters of work and I shall spend my life dedicated to ensuring you are happy."

Liberty looked aghast. "I shall not keep you to such a promise. I like the way you have dedicated your life to making others healthy, so they have a chance to help others too. I like that you are serious, not flippant. My happiness will come when we are both fulfilling our potential to change our world for the better."

Nick, uncharacteristically, beamed. "Is that from one of The Salvation Army sermons?"

Liberty playfully punched his arm. "Yes, but it's worth remembering and I shall make it my own."

"At one stage I thought I'd lost you to the irresistible Mr Bond."

"He is so loveable, I agree. But..." she hesitated while searching for satisfactory words.

"You need say no more, the 'but' covers it all."

One hour later, parked in Stoney Bay, Grandie and Nick unloaded the two suitcases from the boot.

"I have packed you some cheese and home-made pickle sandwiches..." Nonna put her hand to her mouth, "Oh caro, I am so stupid, caro, caro, caro. Forgive me. I forget that you will be like ghosts and cannot eat."

Nick hugged his grandmother. "Nonna, we shall not be ghosts, just invisible and we can't be heard. We can certainly eat and with every bite we shall remember you both. All the time we are in 2020, you can stay in our hearts and minds, but if we successfully land in 1814, we shall not know the future – and you will not even have been born."

"I shall diligently look after our son, your father, and I shall know that he does grow up to have a son – you!"

Liberty watched, charmed, as they held each other tenderly. As they parted, she was pleased to be able to thank Aurora. "Sandwiches are exactly what we shall need on our journey. Thank you, Aurora. You have been so thoughtful and kind. I too shall miss you." Very, very much.

Aurora came forward and hugged her, surreptitiously whispering, "'The Lord shall preserve thy going out and thy coming in from this time forth and even for evermore.' It is from the Bible and it is meant for you, I am sure."

Liberty held back her tears. Parting was definitely not 'sweet sorrow', it was agony.

Grandie's feelings seeped out as he also thought of Shakespeare. "'Two of the fairest stars in all the heaven,' and they have blessed us with their mystery. And mystery it shall remain." Taking a deep breath, he picked up one of the cases. "Nick, let me carry one of these to the cave entrance."

"I can manage them both, Grandie, but thank you."

"I insist."

With a thin rope, Nick loosely tied himself to Liberty. "I'd hate to lose you once we become invisible."

And so it was, that in the mouth of the cave which would lead them to the future, Grandpapa, Nonna, Nicolo and Liberty said their heartbreaking farewells, unseen by all except a solitary seagull.

Chapter Thirty-Nine
A magical soundtrack

Nick and Liberty had agreed before they left Bleakheath Hall that they would have to use the secret, alternative exit from the caves, even though it would take longer. They'd also agreed to travel in Nick's Land Rover to Liberty's office despite the obvious hazard of causing alarm should anyone notice that it appeared to have no driver. All things considered, it was the better option and had the additional advantage of being able to untie themselves.

It took a while to get the car started but eventually they set off from Merrygate with their luggage in the boot and on the back seat. Silence reigned until Nick put the radio on. It was obvious that, since her last visit, people were no longer in what was generally called 'lockdown'. There was traffic on the roads, not as much as usual though. Listening to the news bulletin, it seemed that the only news was about Covid. They must be sure not to catch this nasty virus. She pursed her lips in defiance – the consequences were almost unimaginable.

In Liberty's office, Nick scribbled on the notepad on her desk. *"I love you too much to lose you so we must keep each other informed of everything we do and where we go. I'll obtain some surgical masks as soon as I can and we should wear them, just in case. I suspect they are useless but we must not jeopardize our health nor take the virus back to 1814."*

Liberty wrote a quick reply to his almost illegible message. *"I agree. We also need to be careful not to bump into each other."*

Seconds later the reply appeared. *"No, please do bump into me, all the time."*

Liberty laughed. But no-one heard. Writing their conversation took much longer than she'd imagined and soon Liberty's scrawl was being called inventive. She decided not to explain that if she appeared to be slow in replying it was because it took time to decipher his handwriting. She'd switch to using her laptop as soon as possible – they'd have to share it though. She scribbled a note to ask him to bring his laptop to the office.

An agreement was formed that they would stay in 2020 for no more than a week.

"On Tues 9th June we must complete our preparations for travelling to 1814 on the following morning. I now need a key to this office so that I can return to my place and say, or rather write, my farewells and divide the spoils of my hard work amongst those I care about."

Liberty found her spare key which appeared on the desk the moment she put it down. *"I shall miss you,"* she wrote.

"The sooner I go, the quicker I can return." Nick tipped out his case onto the table by the window and set his medical books to one side. *"Taking these as they might be useful,"* he scribbled. *"I'll wear this costume of Nonna's for our arrival at Bleakheath Hall in 1814. I hope!"* One by one, he put the Prussian blue tailcoat, the cream breeches and high-necked, fancy white shirt and cravat onto the chair and the black leather riding boots with the brown cuff beside it.

Liberty was mesmerized as each item appeared. She opened up what they'd called 'her' case on her desk and did the same on the other chair by the table. *"I'll wear the cream dress with the pink ribbons for arrival at BH."* As an afterthought, she scribbled, *"with the matching bonnet and I'll buy a pair of ankle boots to travel in."*

The pen disappeared from the desk and a message rocketed back. *"Also shop for shawls and those little ballet pump shoes. Remember you can only withdraw £300 a day, so plan to spread your shopping over the week."*

Liberty paused in her reading – was he mansplaining again? Or sharing the stress of remembering everything?

"Also remember we must buy the biggest suitcases, with four wheels, that we can find. Maybe wait until I'm with you so we can wheel them back without causing chaos. Look out for one of those garden trolleys with the canvas sides and big wheels, we'll need it to transport four cases through the light curtain. Charge your phone and I'll WhatsApp you."

"I'll start shopping after we've eaten A's cheese sandwiches. It's wonderful that we can recall everything from 68," responded Liberty.

"Yet we'll remember nothing at all when we reach 1814. We'll have only our wits and habits to help us. Muscle memory will help."

Liberty soon caught on to the meaning of muscle memory and hoped her ingrained, repetitive actions would be useful. She smiled broadly at the thought of Nick's carefully kept diaries being taken back to 1814; they'd be worth their weight. She placed Aurora's sandwiches on the table. One disappeared. She took one too, bit into the invisible food and chewed slowly, cherishing every mouthful.

Not being allowed to see into the future, she now knew, was one of God's rules. If only they could have stayed in Swinging London. Yet somehow she knew it was meant to be. "Meant to be," she whispered with a sense of satisfaction. Yes, being in 1968 had prepared her for going back in time even further. Not only had she learnt, at least to some extent, to live without all the advantages of the twenty-first century but, more importantly, she also learnt the power of having a purpose in life. Her three friends all had admirable principles, more than that – goals. She was glad Nick could not see her dithering – no, it was not dithering it was assessing. "It's the right thing to do. Research, plan, achieve." She couldn't share her whispers, not yet anyway. Their time in 1968 had many uses, yet Nick seemed to be out of time there. She remembered how he'd kissed her hand, when any other man would have been much more demonstrative. He would fit so well in a Regency lifestyle. This disinclination to expose his feelings charmed her. He was cool, with oodles of charisma. Eyes turned to him the moment he entered a room. How does anyone achieve that? He appeared to have been born with it. She imagined him sizing up all those he met, his dark eyes narrowing – her stomach turned over – that look! Oh how she'd like to capture it. Drat, drat, drat! Why hadn't she videoed it? She'd never be able to do that now and what would have been the point!

Suddenly excited, she delved into her open suitcase, finally finding the memory card from her camera. She'd go to Boots and use their self-service printing facility. She'd taken at least forty shots, surreptitiously, of course, otherwise Jon would have wanted to take the camera apart to see how it worked. Those photos would be so precious. She'd need to write on the back to say what they were.

Sandwiches eaten, black tea and coffee drunk, each went their separate ways. Liberty spent a treasured moment appreciating how Aurora had crammed in not only the costume she'd been given to wear for the cricket match but also another high-waisted, long, blue muslin dress with deep blue ribbon trims. Something she'd not be able to buy here in 2020.

Liberty took some envelopes from her drawer and emptied her petty cash tin. At the bank, she took out £300 from the ATM and went shopping for various items which were deemed essential. She wondered how long four pairs of pumps would last. Also from the shoe shop, she took two pairs of ankle boots. This exhausted the £300 she'd put in an envelope and left on the till. She walked out with the collection of footwear, leaving an astonished sales girl at the till. The limited amount of petty cash was spent on some favourite Marks and Spencer food.

Nick had said he'd not be back until tomorrow so she microwaved a ready meal, put the television on and fell asleep in her chair, oblivious of the constant news of a world-wide pandemic.

Around midnight, she woke up. Alone. Anxious. There was so much to do. Living in 1968 was like a practice run. She had learnt which items from the twenty-first century she thought were indispensable. Her journal faithfully recorded the fantastic time she'd had as well as life lessons – she'd never forget how Paul's mother described Gemma: she leaves traces of grace wherever she goes. Imagine being described like that! No way was she going to leave this inspirational account behind. Something else came to mind – her father's letter. She leapt up, put the light on and searched until she found it and the line that haunted her: "I leave you with my love and I expect you to be as good and kind as I meant to be." She placed it with the clothes which she'd be packing in the suitcases they hadn't yet bought – so much to do. First, find her mother's wedding ring. Second, check the post box downstairs to see if the 'Someone Cares' tea towels had been delivered. She'd never be able to give one to Tom and Mary now and that hurt. Had these thoughts been the cause of her sleeplessness? Reflecting, she thanked her brain. "Well done brain, you never sleep do you? There's always a bit of you occupied." Words can survive centuries, look at how often Nick quoted Shakespeare. Her father's words would guide her and the song's words would comfort her if needed. She also took her father's New International translation of the Bible from the bottom drawer of her desk and put this precious book out for packing too. As The Salvation Army said when a faithful Christian died, her parents had been 'promoted to glory'; of this she was now convinced. Satisfied, she drew in a deep breath, climbed the stairs to the loft and fell into a peaceful sleep.

She woke up late; her body clearly needed extra sleep, yet there was much to do. When Nick comes back, he must see progress, more than just a bottle of the 1968 L'Aimant scent tucked away in the little reticule and lots of shoes.

Raiding her wardrobe, she realized she could go out naked and no-one would know, yet wearing her yellow and blue floral dress and black, strappy sandals somehow gave her confidence and she experienced the joy of dressing up in fashionable 2020 clothes for the last time. Her wardrobe was also an unexpected treasure trove. An almost unworn black, velvet bolero would be so very useful in Regency times. What did they call it? Ah... a spencer. She'd wear it on the journey as it fastened right up to her neck. If they travelled on draughty coaches, this could be useful. "And," she said, "it will go with my long, black velvet skirt." She took a moment to remember wearing the skirt on the journey to 1968 when she thought she'd arrive in 1814: she was thankful she hadn't.

Opening her laptop, she started a list of things to pack in no particular order:

Ball point pens They wouldn't take up much space but would be easier to write with than goose feather quills.

Photos Which ones? Photos taken in her childhood of her family and the 1968 ones. Not too many as they're heavy.

Information on 1814 Nick would provide that.

Piano music Sounds silly yet imagine having a book of Beatles' songs for someone to play. What fun! Surely something inside her would be stirred and she'd feel invigorated even if she didn't know why. Or Vaughan Williams, or... she'd speak to Nick.

Books or information on farming techniques Nick would take care of that too.

Recipe book? Hmm... Heavy, not essential, might have a cook. She deleted it, then typed it back in again.

Nuts, Lots To keep us going if we take a while to get to Bleakheath Hall.

Chocolate Lots Definitely.

"This is a ridiculous list," she declared. "No not completely, but today I shall concentrate on buying underwear." She remembered how very cold it had been when she first arrived in 1968 and added jumpers, warm things to wear under and over those flimsy, flouncy clothes. "Tomorrow, I shall put the jewellery and the gold bars that are left in the to-be-packed pile." Nick had taken some of the gold bars in order to buy Regency currency and she estimated that just one of the smaller bars would exhaust some coin dealers' stock. She pictured him helping himself, unobserved, to the Regency coins and leaving behind an authenticated and packaged gold ingot. She giggled, imagining him following a dealer to his safe, or maybe even vault. She went stiff – suppose he was locked in? No, not Nick. She relaxed. He'd asked her if she had any rope. She hadn't. He said he'd buy some from the shop over the road. He also said he'd buy jewellery too. "Highly portable," he'd said. She imagined a few sales people being tied up with a gold ingot stuffed in their gag.

For some time, she felt better, more sensible, achieving much until an unwanted memory flitted across her brain. "Sparkles and rain," she said, remembering her thoughts before this adventure began and thinking they were omens. Gemma wouldn't approve of such mumbo jumbo. She smiled; dear Gemma. "I've learnt such a lot from her." With a deep sigh, she thought of how much she would miss her. But she must take action now, stop remembering, and not forget to post the letter to her brother and give him access to her bank account.

A mug of tea and breakfast set her up nicely for another round of shopping. Dashing into a clothes shop, she began to search for items suitable for wearing in Regency days. She knew she should stop her habit of looking at the instructions for washing – there'd be no washing machines in 1814 – however, something kept catching her eye. Most things were made in China and she reflected on the 'Buy British' campaign in the sixties and how China had become massively industrialised. No longer pitifully behind the times, it was supplying the world with consumer goods and very cheaply too. How much were the workers paid? Enough? Food must be cheaper. A shiver ran down her back as she remembered the scene in Piccadilly Circus when two men taunted a group of drunk girls with predictions. Their taunts were coming true, China, indeed the whole of the Far East was highly successful at supplying cheap goods for the Western world. And what was the other prediction which the guy with the bushy beard made? Something to do with governing the country?

Her train of thought was interrupted when she found herself jostled into a rack of dresses which crashed to the floor. She saw a distraught and confused woman attempting to pick it all up and several others assisting. It was her fault; her mind was too full of memories. However, that one incident cleared away the nagging doubt about leaving 2020. As much as she loved everything this time has to offer, being invisible ruined everything. Yet another ripple of anxiety ran through her. They must land in 1814 to be sure of slotting into history, as shown in Nick's family history book. What would happen if they made another mistake? How would they know if it was 1814 or not? She narrowly avoided a further mishap.

On returning to her office, she noticed a chair in the middle of the room. Nick was back. There was a note on the desk.

"Meeting Matt Redfern for more info. Then going to pull a few tigers' tails. I'll enjoy scaring the living daylights out of corrupt or malicious individuals."

Eyes wide, Liberty put a hand to her mouth. And then smiled.

~

Early on the Tuesday morning, Nick opened his laptop and wrote, *"We've completed all the tasks on our lists, and I'm so pleased you are leaving the agency to Laura. As the founder, she'll know what to do with it. The last thing we must do is restore our laptops to factory settings. Phones too. Also, have you made arrangements for the things you have in storage?"*

"I have." She decided not to rabbit on about how she'd posted the key through The Salvation Army's letterbox with a signed note for them to keep everything.

"And your car?"

"Dealt with." Probably not completely, but the DVLA always took ages...

"If you're satisfied that everything is as you'd like it to be, do you want to leave this disease ridden world today, one day ahead of schedule? Or do you want to spend the day finding out what happened to all those we met in 1968 and leave tomorrow, bang on schedule?"

"1968," typed Liberty.

"According to the history book recording when we arrive in June, we have time to do that."

"Then let's stay."

"I know what happened to my grandparents, my father and other relations so perhaps I can help you with the friends you made."

"Yes, please do. You find the men's history from 1968 to now and I'll do the girls."

Google appeared on their screens. As she had a separate, large screen, she could type on the invisible keyboard but see the untouched screen.

The first information to appear was Paul's. He married Gemma, they had three children and five grandchildren. He owned fifty-two restaurants, never changing from the plan of making them affordable to all. His signature dish was named 'Gem's Curry'. Now retired, he lived in Hertfordshire and was the bandmaster at his local Salvation Army.

Liberty found Gemma's history. She opened a bridal shop in Regent Street, London, and designed gowns for well-known celebrities until retiring to Hertfordshire with Paul.

Jon developed a chain of travel agencies, owned over fifty properties which he rented out, was a prominent philanthropist and had been awarded an OBE. He married, had two children, his wife died after seven years, and he has remained single.

"Chloe – there's no information, none at all. Perhaps she had another name?"

Nick typed, "Try s*earching on Microsoft Edge."*

Nothing was found for Chloe.

"I wonder what happened to the three men in the caravan."

"Unless you have their names, it's unlikely we'll ever know."

They did find something on the rat. Gregor Hode spent years going in and out of prison. He lost control of his business interests and was last heard of in Glasgow in 1998. Nothing further was known.

"I wonder what happened to him," typed Liberty. *"Odd that he should disappear completely."* She pictured him as a chameleon, blending in perfectly with wherever he pitched up.

"*Maybe he did go to a Scottish island or perhaps he's no longer with us.*"

Dead? Liberty bit her lip. She'd try to forgive him. There was no point carrying around hatred and spite – it only damaged her and those around her. Then she remembered, thank God, that in 1814 she wouldn't be able to remember him anyway.

"*I wish I could leave something good to Gemma, Paul, Jon, and Tom and Mary. To surprise them with unexpected gifts appearing on their doorstep and anonymous notes thanking...*" She hung her head. It was too late, they'd all made their own way in life and been successful too. If only she'd thought of this earlier in the week. There remained one thing she could do for them. She could pray for them while she was able to remember such kind friends. Friends once called 'goody-two-shoes' but now thought of as pure gold. "No, salt," she announced. The phrase had been in one of the officer's sermons: "You are the salt of the Earth," she whispered. While a shower of gratitude, love, affection and oh so much more flooded over her, she prayed, thanking God for the way she had met such people, who helped, guided...

Appearing on Nick's screen were the words, "*Found Tom and Mary. They did move to Bleakheath Hall. He became assistant gardener and Mary looked after the menagerie of animals which grew each year. They both died in 1978.*" A few moments later more words appeared. "*There's a plaque at the crematorium with the words 'Faithful to each other and faithful to those who loved them'.*"

Liberty began to sniffle and tears rolled down her cheeks. Nick and his family enabled her own promise to look after Tom and Mary to come true.

He searched for her hand and pulled her to her feet. He picked up her mother's wedding ring from the little box visible on her desk. He raised her hand to his lips, kissed it, found her ring finger, and slid the gold ring on until it hit her engagement ring. They clung to each other; words impossible. A blackbird, perched on a nearby branch, burst into its twilight song and created a magical soundtrack for two people in love.

Chapter Forty
Full of traps and pitfalls

The rainbow brilliance of the light curtain lay ahead. The sturdy garden trolley, on which stood all four suitcases, became visible when Nick stepped away from it. He turned off the torch he'd tied around his waist; its beam was no match for the light curtain. Liberty stretched out her hands but was unable to feel him; her heart began to thump. Then joy, oh joy, she sensed him close, and then his arms pulled her nearer and, shivering with delight as he snuffled around her ear searching for her lips, she guided him home. He held her tight as if this might be, God please forbid, their last kiss.

Some minutes later, Nick appeared to be shortening the rope so that she could stretch out her left hand and touch him. Nick placed her right hand on the right side of the chalky wall and pressed it there. All Liberty could do was hope that as the invisible Nick pushed through, he would bring them out in 1814. If Laura's instructions held true, they would arrive, as usual, on the same day of the month as today but over two centuries earlier.

Liberty felt the pull of the rope around her waist – Nick was entering the deceptively light and airy luminance; she kept hold of his shoulder with her left hand and left the smell of the musty cave behind. Despite being pulled by the taut rope and holding his shoulder, she needed all her strength to push through. This was different from her trips to 1968, now the light of centuries had condensed into an even heavier shimmer which stole her breath. This was what Laura had described; they were on the right path. With her eyes lowered to shield them from the brilliance, she continued putting one foot in front of the other and scraping her right hand along the rainbow-coloured chalk wall on the right. Sheer terror surged within her at the thought of arriving without Nick, only abating when she fell out of the force of the enveloping light to see her hand still holding Nick's shoulder. They were as one.

Nick rapidly untied them and the thought slipped away as he wrapped his arms around her breathing out a great sigh of relief and whispering, "It is so very good to *see* you again. Wherever we are, no matter what the date is, we are together and," he took a deep breath, "I know who you are."

Her heart thumping, Liberty threw her arms around him. This wonderful man loved her more than anything. Nothing, time nor place, mattered more than being together. And then, like waking from a dream, she wondered why she thought they might not be together and why the date was so important. It all slid away as she focused on the light at the end of the tunnel.

"It's time to leave this dark cave and see where we are. There's daylight ahead and I can hear the sea." Pushing the trolley, he headed towards the light. Liberty, freed from the rope, walked alongside.

They stayed in the privacy of the cave while Nick reviewed what they needed to do next. Liberty focused on her ring finger: she was married. She took both rings off and replaced them in the right order – wedding ring went on first, engagement ring went on after. Yes, she was definitely married to this dark, handsome man in the Prussian Blue tailcoat whose eyes were shining as he drew her closer.

"You look wonderful and I know you are my wife, and I know everything about you, though what we are doing pushing this trolley load of cases is something of a mystery." He wrapped his arms around her and kissed her as if she were the most precious girl in the world.

Liberty heard the sound of exuberant, dancing waves, leaping and clapping with joy. She revelled in feeling the same and breathed in the fresh sea air.

They held each other, not daring to let go until a seagull screeched overhead as it flew towards its fishing grounds.

When he released her, she pointed to what had been jabbing her hips. It appeared to be a book hanging from his belt.

He laughed. "I seem to have tied several things around my waist. I must investigate." The torch defeated his prodding until he pushed a button on its base.

"Curious," he said as he flashed the beam around, "but most useful."

Liberty tentatively peeped outside the cave. A summer breeze, warm and friendly, caressed her face in welcome. "We're safe, no-one is here and the tide is out." Why had she felt unsafe?

Nick was reading the notebook. "This appears to be a book of instructions, including what to do when we arrive in June 1814."

"1814? Is that the date?"

Nick shrugged. "According to these notes, which are in my own handwriting, we should turn right as we leave the cave and continue along until we find an almost invisible cave overgrown by bushes. There we shall find seventy-seven winding steps, hewn into the chalk, leading to the top of the cliff." He took a very deep breath and peered out. "This trolley of cases, I suppose they are important?"

"Does the book say anything about them?"

Nick turned a few pages. "Ah... it gives details of the contents some of which appear to be in gobbledegook."

Liberty walked over to them and tried to lift one. "They're too heavy to carry. I think we should hurry and push or pull the trolley as far as possible until we are on dry ground."

The smooth, damp sand was not perfect for pulling the trolley and rock beds were difficult to navigate. By the time they reached the seventy-seven steps, Liberty was exhausted even though Nick had been in charge of the trolley. "Would you mind if we rested awhile here?" Strapped to her wrist, she noticed a little bag with a drawstring and inside, a very small, glass bottle of water focused her attention. "Look, Nick! Water!"

"You drink it." He smiled in encouragement. "It will revive you."

Liberty drank half and insisted Nick drink the rest. He took a couple of sips and handed it back. "It's important you drink it. I can manage."

Liberty sat on the first of the steep steps and tried to scratch her arm; something was wrapped tightly around it. The cuff was too tight to pull up so she took her little black velvet jacket off. Along both arms were bracelets as far up as her elbow and around her neck were pearls and diamond necklaces.

Nick's eyes were wide until he rummaged through his notebook. "It's fine. They belonged to your mother and you are wearing some in case we lose our luggage."

"Does this mean we've packed these great, black cases ourselves?"

"Apparently. Yet I don't remember doing anything like that." Troubled, he tentatively patted one of them as if it were something from another planet.

Manoeuvring four heavy suitcases up seventy-seven winding steps proved time consuming though not impossible, as she had thought. The trolley folded up, much to their surprise.

At the top of the steps, they rested, unobserved, in a prison of high thorn bushes. Nick read aloud from his book. "One of these bushes is easily removed in order to reach the road." He glanced around. "Presumably, it's that tatty looking one." He pulled, it lifted, he smiled triumphantly. "Replace," he read after they squeezed through. He did, carefully pressing the thorny bush down and scraping the damp earth around the roots. No longer imprisoned, they took stock of their situation.

"Where are we trying to go?"

"Our destination is somewhere called..." he consulted the book and turned a few pages, "Bleakheath Hall."

"Is that close by?"

"The notes suggest we walk to Merrygate then catch a coach to Canterbury, stay overnight, then catch the London coach which passes close to Bleakheath Hall." He turned back a few pages and said, "We must walk straight ahead to the road, turn right and follow it to Merrygate."

"How do we pay for the coach and the accommodation?"

"Ah... all is well. I heard something jingling in my pockets as we came up the steps and upon inspection, I found it to be a golden guinea. I don't intend using that if at all possible. It was rattling against... look." He held out the palms of his hands to show ten pennies, three farthings, seven halfpennies, a number of shillings, two crowns and many sixpences. "These life-savers have been weighing me down and, if it really is 1814, then one of the shillings must not be used because..." he held up the offending shilling, "it declares itself to have been minted in 1815."

Puzzled, Liberty asked how that could possibly have happened.

Carefully returning the other coins to his pocket, he tucked the 1815 shilling into a different one. "I don't even care to guess. However, we should keep it until it can be used."

Progress slowed, due to hauling the big, green trolley along the dirt track and both feeling very thirsty. After another mile, and having seen no-one, they pulled the trolley off to the side of the road and sat down on the grass. A noise behind alarmed them and Nick stood to investigate. Liberty turned to see a scrawny girl, maybe fifteen or so, seemingly emerging from a hole in the ground; she appeared terrified.

Immediately, Liberty got up and rushed towards the scruffily dressed girl. Her face was dirty, her hands dirtier, everything about her was filthy. "Hello, are you okay?"

The girl looked startled. "Please madam, don't tell no-one, will yer?"

Was she a runaway? "Not if you don't want me to." She held out her hand to help the girl out of the hole. "What are you doing down a hole?"

The girl declined to leave but muttered, "I live 'ere."

"What!"

"It be nice, madam, honest it is. I pick up shells and I've got 'em all up the walls and on top so's it don't fall down on me." The beginning of a smile transformed her face. "I can show yer if yer like. There be plenty of room 'cos I been digging for ages."

The truth of this was verified by the mounds of mud and stones stretching back many yards, some were flattened and had become overgrown by long grass and weeds. Liberty would have liked to see this little shell home but her dress was already less than spotless. One thing she needed to know was the date.

"Do you know the...?" Of course she wouldn't. "What year is it?"

"Year madam? Why it be 1814."

Liberty contained her relief. "There's one thing you can do for us."

The girl nodded cautiously.

"We are very thirsty. Can you tell us where to get some water?"

"Down in Merrygate, madam. Go down the hill, it be not far. There be a stream, bit further, but best to go to the inn, they'll sell yer some ale."

Ale? Yes, of course. It's unwise to drink the water. What made her think that? "Thank you." She hurried back to Nick. "Have we some money to give this poor girl?"

He smiled. "I love you, Libby. I hope you will always help me to see..." He consulted his notebook. "A shilling would be nearly two days' pay for a housemaid, so that's good."

"But a maid has all her food and shelter provided. And what would one shilling buy this poor girl?"

"We don't have time to find out. Until we know what we need, let's give her this shilling."

"She also confirms we're in 1814. That's worth an extra shilling, don't you think? And this might be her one chance to buy sufficient food and drink. Shall we give her two?"

To her surprise, Nick handed her three.

They left the girl dumbstruck.

After refreshing themselves with ale and a large slice of venison pie, they boarded the coach to Canterbury. Their suitcases were removed from the trolley and all were strapped on top. It was their good fortune that no-one else travelled to Canterbury that afternoon which afforded them time to study their note books and take two hours' sleep.

The liveried guard blew his horn, then bellowed "Canterbury." The driver held the horses and the guard jumped down and opened the carriage door. "Finest inn in Canterbury," he said staring at the ground. While unloading the luggage, he said, "Come far, have yer?"

Nick gave one of his tight-faced smiles with a twitch of the lips and staring eyes and he and Liberty walked a few steps towards the inn.

A servant from the inn hurried out and Nick watched as a coin changed hands. He whispered to Liberty, "Be very careful. We don't want to lose anything. Wait here." Nick strode towards the coach, but the guard had already jumped on board while the driver whipped the horses and they galloped away. He returned to Liberty. "My humble apologies, I should have grabbed the reins. Pestiferous rascal."

If they hadn't been half asleep, they'd not have fallen for this nasty little trap. She looked around. The spire of the cathedral was about half a mile away and the coachmen were all the richer for dumping them too early.

After negotiating the price for a room and board and insisting they eat in the room, Nick supervised the suitcases being taken to their room at the top of the stairs. "Finest inn in Canterbury, huh." He turned to reassure Liberty whose breathing betrayed her anxiety. "I'm so sorry our first night together as a 'married'," he raised his eyebrows, "couple, is set in a reeky inn with a rascally host and fustilarian servant women bringing us our..." he hesitated, "dinner, if we're lucky."

Fustilarian? She loved his archaic insults. She'd follow this man, who made every minute amusing and enjoyable, to the ends of the Earth and she told him so. Though she remembered nothing of their past, she knew the very essence of Nick and basked in it. First night as a married couple? How come he knew that and she didn't?

Spirits lifted, food eaten, plates put outside the door, they both stared at the narrow bed opposite the two chairs they'd been sitting on.

"It's three foot six, and not an inch more."

Liberty laughed and pulled back a dirty blanket to reveal another discoloured blanket underneath. "Better luck tomorrow."

"Yes, let's leave the bed bugs to their hiding places and catch the early morning coach. I'm just going downstairs to tell the landlord we'll be leaving in the afternoon."

"Afternoon? Why?" After a flickering thought, she didn't need Nick's answer: their cases would make a good prize for an ambush by robbers in the know.

"I can see you've worked out why," he gave her a nod of respect. "The landlord at Merrygate mentioned a coach to London at half-past six each morning leaving from the cathedral. So let's quietly put the cases in the trolley and leave at dawn for the cathedral." He paused. "Joining history is full of traps and pitfalls. Yet 'sweet are the uses of adversity' as it will teach us much."

And so their first night together was spent sitting in two upright chairs, barring the door, with their sleepy heads on the rickety table, literally touching history.

Chapter Forty-One
Ooh, sneaky

Alighting from the Canterbury to London coach, Liberty gasped.

The coach driver grinned as he helped her down the step. "You not been here before?"

Nick answered for her. "My wife has not seen her new home until now." He turned to Liberty. "I hope you will like it."

Catching on to his look, she knew she should probably say no more than "I'm sure I shall," and smile.

Behind ornate iron gates, an exceptionally long driveway sloped slightly downwards towards a light grey stone house. Liberty's eyes were wide. For some unfathomable reason, she had imagined Bleakheath Hall to be the size of a small manor house, rather like... like what? She frowned. All she could remember was seeing Nick dragging these hard cases on the trolley across the beach, helping to manoeuvre them up steps onto the cliff top, Nick constantly consulting instructions in his book, feeling lost, and finding a poor child very much worse off than they were.

Nick stood beside her. "The coachman offered to drive us to the door but I declined. I'm not sure we can gain access and I didn't want them to see me try and possibly fail."

"I had no idea it would be so grand," Liberty said as she glanced at the soiled hem of her cream dress. Perhaps if she tied the ribbon on her bonnet in a neat bow, it would draw attention to her face rather than her dress. She tucked her hair behind her ears and hoped she'd made an improvement. "Did you notice Bleakheath village?" She didn't wait for an answer and continued. "It was... um..."

"Poverty stricken?"

"Yes. Scrawny infants in rags with no shoes, women in dirty clothes, and the men, the scruffy men were all just lolling around." Liberty blinked rapidly; this was no time to have her heart ripped apart.

Nick pushed one of the gates, which scraped the ground as if it hadn't been opened for some long time. He pursed his lips. "The perimeter hedges need trimming too and look at the length of the grass, it needs grazing animals. A few horses perhaps." Liberty thought of sheep, then thought again – not in front of the house; horses would look so much better. With the trolley rattling behind them, they walked slowly towards the steps leading up to the double doors. At the base of the steps, they studied the house carefully. Either side of the doors were eight windows in total and the house was three storeys high plus a semi-basement. He slowed to a halt and consulted his notebook. "Seven hundred acres, and I've noted that most of the land was sold after the house was bombed in the First World War to have funds to build a smaller house." He looked mystified. "First *World* War? It must be in the future."

"How far into the future?" queried Liberty as a worried frown crossed her face.

Nick flicked through a few pages. "I don't seem to have noted that down. Obviously, I must have thought it was so significant that I'd never forget the date. Maybe," he put his hand to his chin, "maybe there'll be more information further on or perhaps inside our cases. Leave all this aside for the moment or we'll concoct incorrect memories. I have written in several places that we are to remember we are time travellers. You and I have come from a different time."

Liberty was about to announce that this was impossible, instead she said, "What time?" She considered her dress, brushing off some dried dirt. "It must be quite recent as this dress is much like others

I've seen along the way." Travelling through time was highly unlikely but Nick's notebook had been right so far.

"Later today, I'll make sure I read more of my notes. For now, my instructions from my grandfather say I am to remember what our family history book says, and," he turned over some more pages, "we have a Letter of Introduction." He patted his still pristine Prussian Blue coat, until he found some parchment in the inside pocket. "Aha, this is it. According to these papers," he produced some from another inside pocket, "we shall be meeting the widow of the owner, who has also lost her only son quite recently." He began to read, "'My husband and son lie cold in their graves and I am alone in Bleakheath Hall, icy cold, though it is June. It is a portent reminding me I must relinquish this abode of my husband's ancestors.' Two weeks later, she writes, 'It is incumbent upon me to record the arrival of a young couple. Their attire is unlike anything I would expect of visitors to Bleakheath, and they brought with them large metal cases on wheels. More peculiar still is their speech.' Aha! It is more than our speech which is peculiar!" Nick took a deep breath. "We are to meet this widow and this is what will happen, 'They handed me a letter. The seal bore our Coat of Arms. I invited them to sit in the drawing room with me while I perused the most unusual Letter of Introduction I have ever seen. They have appeared as if they were visitors from another planet, bringing with them the wisdom of the stars. I have come to the conclusion they are angels.' You might be but I? I doubt anyone I know would call me that." He checked the letter for the Coat of Arms. They left the trolley of cases and climbed the steps. "I feel like we have been on a long sea voyage and now we are coming into harbour. In order to dock safely, we must act the part of a Regency married couple. Or angels," he grinned. "Are you ready?"

Liberty gazed up at the imposing double doors; there was no doubt – she was entering her own personal fairy tale. She quivered – she'd had this thought before. Why was this happening? Turning to Nick, she saw his encouraging, broad smile and answered.

"Definitely." And a nice mug of tea would be good. Mug? What a strange thought.

Nick pulled the bell. It clanged. No-one came. He pulled again.

Liberty glanced anxiously at her patient, capable husband and put her ear to the huge, oak door, a futile gesture, considering the likely thickness of it.

Nick pulled the bell for a third time. A middle-aged woman wearing a long, dark grey dress, a white cotton cap and a white apron peeped at them through the partially opened door. Apparently reassured, she opened it wide, yet still glared suspiciously.

"I wish to speak to your mistress. I have here a Letter of Introduction."

The woman eyed the folded parchment and relaxed when she saw the Coat of Arms. "Please come in, sir." She scrutinized Liberty, smiled and said, "And madam."

They followed her into a great hall. Liberty's eyes grew wide; she could be certain that never before had she seen such grandeur. Marble pillars supported a central dome above the circular hall and white stone stairs led up to a gallery with inset statues and sculpted friezes. Act naturally, she told herself while Nick gave his name solely as 'Nylander'.

The servant pointed to two shield-back, wooden arm chairs. "Please wait here." She ascended the stairs and turned to the left at the top, surreptitiously peering down upon them.

As Nick sat, he whispered, "Remember what the widow wrote in the book of the Nylander history: our attire is not quite right and we speak differently. We must try to be as formal as we can manage, despite how tired we feel. We should guide her into thinking we have travelled from another land, not from Heaven." He raised his eyebrows. "The letter says we have come from an island off America, though it doesn't give a name. We have endured an arduous journey and remember little of our home and travels. I'll indicate that we have survived misfortunes." He consulted his notebook again. "I introduced myself only as 'Nylander' because, it says here that although my real name is Nicolo Nylander, I am recorded in the book of the family history as Nicholas in Regency times." He gave Liberty a moment to absorb all he was imparting. "The book of history says she decides I am obviously her husband's estranged brother of whom he never spoke." He rummaged through his notebook. "I don't seem to have made a note of anything more in the Letter and I daren't break the wax seal." A noise of scurrying feet above put an end to his whispers.

The servant bobbed a curtsey before them. "My mistress says to wait here a moment longer and offers her apologies."

Nick nodded. The servant disappeared quickly and quietly into an adjacent room. Liberty listened at the door. "I can't hear anything except some sort of flapping." She put her ear to the door again. "I believe it's the sound of dust sheets being whipped off."

Nick concentrated on the almost silent footsteps making their way to the top of the stairs. He stood and motioned for Liberty to abandon her investigations and they both stood side by side as the lady of the house, about thirty years of age and wearing black, approached.

After the customary greetings of a bow from Nick and curtseys from the ladies, she said with a hint of a smile, "Good afternoon. I am Lady Nylander. Please follow me into the drawing room. My apologies for keeping you waiting."

The drawing room was sparsely furnished. Wooden armchairs with padded seats and backs were scattered around the room, the best being placed near an ornate fireplace where two footstools were positioned either side. Liberty noticed several portraits, ancestors she presumed. Significantly, there were gaps between them where the cream colour of the walls was slightly lighter. She glanced at Nick with raised eyebrows then flashed her eyes to the chandeliers neither of which possessed a full complement of candles. Nick nodded almost imperceptibly. Even the candelabra, strategically placed on twin nests of tables beside their chairs, had nothing more than stubs.

"I understand you have a Letter of Introduction for me." She motioned for them to sit down.

Nick handed the letter to her then sat next to Liberty. There was silence except for the sound of the letter being turned in the hands of Lady Nylander. Added to this came her increased rate of breathing almost as loud as the dusty bellows in the hearth once made.

Finally, having read it through at least three times, she took an even louder breath and announced, "I am unused to receiving visitors such as yourselves. Since Sir Arthur, my dear husband, passed to another realm, I, you may have noticed, have found it difficult..." She wiped away a tear with a lace handkerchief. "This letter introduces you as the lost brother of my husband. I'm afraid I don't recall any such person. Your apparel is as though you have travelled from afar. The fabric is..." She glanced at the telescope standing by the window. "The letter does not explain..." she tailed away.

"The seal, with our Coat of Arms, should reassure you we are of the same family as your husband. May I see the letter?"

Lady Nylander hesitated, scrutinized Nick from head to toe and did the same to Liberty. Clutching the letter tightly, she asked, "What are your names?"

"I am Nicholas Nylander and my wife's name is Liberty. We have travelled for many months."

She appeared reassured. "The letter," she hesitated again, "confirms you have travelled from across the ocean." Her eyes strayed to the telescope again. "My husband always thought..."

Liberty, taking courage, opened her mouth to speak, though merely smiled. Until she knew exactly what the letter said, it would be best to let Nick pick his way through the thistles.

"Forgive me, my dear," Lady Nylander said to Liberty, "you must think me most inhospitable. I shall call for some refreshment immediately." She put the letter on the table beside her and took the few steps to the tapestry bell-pull beside the fireplace.

As Lady Nylander turned to reseat herself, Nick said, "It has been many months since we left our home and we have crossed the Atlantic

Ocean to find my brother. Our journey was interrupted by a terrible storm of such ferocity that the ship put into a French harbour, delaying us for some considerable time."

Liberty nodded in confirmation.

"You do realize this letter is unsigned, I suppose?" Lady Nylander wafted the letter around.

"No," said Nick looking surprised.

"I exaggerate. The signature is illegible, that is all."

Nick was saved from more inventions when the servant opened the door and took a few steps towards them.

"Tea, a pot of tea," Lady Nylander rummaged in the invisible pocket in her dress and pulled out a tiny key, beckoned to her servant and nodded sternly, "and some seed cake, we have some, I'm sure?"

The servant appeared apprehensive but nodded, took the key, and waddled to the door. Hoping the strangers were not looking, she beckoned to Lady Nylander who silently swept towards her whispering, "What is it, Mrs Tottlebury?"

Liberty abandoned her pondering on why she needed a key to make a pot of tea and listened apprehensively.

"M'lady, the woman, she is covered from head to foot in jewels."

"What nonsense!" exclaimed Lady Nylander before recovering her poise. "What causes you to say such a thing?"

"While waiting in the hall, she started to unbutton her spencer and about her neck I saw many necklaces of pearls and jewels and they were up her arms too. Her husband forbad her to continue and she buttoned it up again."

Lady Nylander looked suspicious.

"Quickly! Look! I can see some around the back of her neck where her hair has parted."

Lady Nylander spun round, her eyes widened and she hurriedly whispered, "Bring the finest china, we must treat our guests with respect."

"M'lady, I think they may be angels and you know what the Bible says."

"I think you are being fanciful again, Mrs Tottlebury. Yet I am grateful for your concern. Yes, as the Bible says, 'Be not forgetful to entertain strangers'," Lady Nylander paused, breathed heavily and continued slowly and with trepidation, "'for thereby some have entertained angels unawares'." She regained her outward poise and whispered, "After you have served the tea, prepare the red room for them." Almost unheard, she muttered, "My dear husband said to be careful who we allow into our home. It is our fortress to keep out evil." She stared at her servant before whispering, "I hope we are welcoming angels and not those of evil intent."

Mrs Tottlebury agitatedly interrupted her mistress's thoughts and words. "M'lady they have strange metal boxes with handles and wheels – wheels!"

"Where?"

"Still at the bottom of the front steps."

"Bring them inside the hall."

"I tried; I can't lift them."

Lady Nylander closed her eyes momentarily and clenched her fist. "Concentrate on bringing us tea, the finest you can manage, then air and prepare the red room and we can, together maybe, bring in the boxes later."

She returned to her chair. "Forgive me, my housekeeper is no longer used to entertaining. I have asked her to prepare a room for you. I shall be honoured if you will stay and rest awhile."

Nick's smile was the broadest Liberty had seen for some time; it was as though all his qualms had vanished and he had sight of the finishing line. Yet, in reality, his new journey was only beginning.

"You are most kind, Lady Nylander, and we are sorry to intrude on your grief."

She stared at the floor as she said, "My husband died, over a year ago now, after many years of ill health. I'm sure you don't need me to tell you that the business of running the estate has overwhelmed me. I had no option but to sell the landscapes; there were debts." She waved her arm in the direction of the remaining paintings. "Though I have retained the portraits of his ancestors to fulfil a promise I made to him. I have only Mrs Tottlebury to attend me now and I have the services of a gardener occasionally and he will chop the wood and attend to..." A tear ran down her cheek. "The farm has gone to rack and ruin. Forgive me. I feel the need to explain."

"You owe us no explanation. I am devastated that I am too late to see my brother, however, we are delighted to be able to meet you, his wife."

Lady Nylander closed her eyes for a moment then recovered and peered at Nick. "He was older than you, I think. To my great regret, my son also passed to another place within days of his father's passing." She wiped away a tear slowly rolling down her cheek. "If you really are my husband's brother, tell me about him." Her face flushed and she could not meet Nick's eyes.

"Myself I remember nothing. I learnt, not so long ago, that I'd been declared dead at birth. However, you can see it isn't true."

Liberty was fascinated. How could Nick invent such far-fetched lies? Yet their future depended on them. The truth of being time travellers would seem even more unbelievable, she was finding it hard to believe herself. They'd probably be locked in an asylum for the rest of their short lives.

"I was sold to a wealthy family with no children and my first memories are of living in a white, clapboard house, with many rooms." He paused before saying quietly, "I can tell you more, if you wish, but the pertinent point is that after receiving years of good care and education, I discovered I was not their natural son when my mother called me to her bedside before her death, nearly a year ago now. She confessed the truth, told me I had been born near London in England and my birth mother was a titled lady, Lady Adelaide Nylander."

Lady Nylander clamped her hand over her mouth as her pupils grew larger. Liberty's eyes were also growing wider in awe of Nick's story. He should be a romantic novelist. Well maybe not romantic.

"My American mother explained to me that Sir Horatio Nylander, my true father, had been advised that I died at birth, badly deformed and it was not advisable to see my body. 'Too harrowing', she said he'd been told."

"Did he not ask to bury the body here so that they could grieve appropriately?"

Nick crossed his legs and scratched his chin. "I don't know. My mother said that those who had arranged my transport to America said Sir Horatio had been told my body would distress him. My body would therefore be used for medical research and it was an honourable fate. Apparently, these lies upset my American mother and that is why she begged me to find my real family. She told me that the guilt she'd had to live with had become crushing."

Lady Nylander clamped her hands to her cheeks and shook her head. "Such lies, such lies!"

Liberty tensed. Did she suspect?

"Lies to a knight of the realm too, while all the time you were growing to manhood in a foreign land."

Liberty breathed out.

"An island off the coast of the United States of America, to be precise."

Then Lady Nylander blurted, her eyes narrowing, "There is no mention of the death of a child in the Nylander history book."

Nick sat in abject silence.

Lady Nylander clutched her fists to her mouth. "I do apologize. I hadn't meant to add to your sorrow."

Nick, looking decidedly humble, wretched even, continued. "My suspicion is that I was sold – not to my American parents directly, I hasten to add. I believe unscrupulous midwives must have spirited me away from my true mother." Nick allowed a few moments before continuing, "Before dying, my American mother told me I had an elder brother and as her husband, had recently died, I had no kith nor kin to care for in the United States. She begged to be forgiven for taking me from..." he faltered, "my English birth family and handed me her Last Will and Testament. Everything was left to me."

Ooh, sneaky. That's how he's going to explain the wealth the jewellery should provide. Liberty decided to incline her head and look sad.

"I'd met Liberty, my wife, before my father died. She has been such a comfort to me. It is through her that I have become a worthier person, fit to give back to this world all it has given me, and more."

Was he still acting? Or did he really mean this? She tried to rake through her memories but none was accessible, yet she instinctively knew he had changed.

Lady Nylander's eyes transformed from pitying to hopeful as Nick said, "I hope you will not find me presumptive if I say we shall be delighted to assist in rebuilding the prosperity of Bleakheath Hall. I feel sure it can be returned to its former glory if you will give your permission."

Of course she would: he'd just claimed to be the wealthy heir.

Chapter Forty-Two
The route to deep joy

That evening, in the privacy of their own room, they began unpacking their cases. Jewellery and the gold bars were stored in the red silk ottoman at the end of the bed which Liberty christened 'the bank', and costumes were hung in the wardrobe.

"Someone called Laura Ashley has made this." She held up a white cotton, embroidered blouse and smiled with glee as she imagined wearing it. A pamphlet fluttered to the carpet. She picked it up and put it on a side table, she'd read it later, but a few words caught her eye, inspiring, underlined words she'd obviously wanted to remember. She paused to read just a sentence: "While little children go hungry, I'll fight." She would too – she'd make that her motto. Fluttering through her mind was the thought 'how large an income is thrift'. How odd. Was it a life lesson she had learned somewhere? Life lesson, what...? She frowned in concentration but to no avail. Anyway, it might be useful in these times.

Meanwhile, Nick unpacked medical equipment. "I haven't a clue what some of these things are. I've labelled this as a 'stethoscope'. Apparently, it's for listening to heartbeats. Could be useful." Instinctively, he hung it around his neck, seized the surprised Liberty and began listening to her heart. "It's beating faster, yes, faster by the second."

Liberty laughed. "I love you so much, Nick, so very, very much."

"Nicholas. You must call me Nicholas now. I am a new man." He pulled the stethoscope away from his ears, flung it on top of an armchair and said, "Let's unpack the rest tomorrow. Let's put the cases on the floor and get on the bed – together."

Liberty needed no persuasion.

Mrs Tottlebury knocked on the door and called out, "May I enter?"

Liberty leapt off the bed, nonchalantly calling "Enter."

The housekeeper brought a tray of tea and placed it on a small table by Liberty's side of the bed. "Lady Nylander asks if you require anything more tonight?"

After enquiring of Nick, Liberty replied, "No, this is sufficient, thank you."

The housekeeper closed the door quietly behind her.

"I can't find a nightgown."

"Neither can I," grinned Nick.

The tea remained in the teapot.

~

They woke to the sound of birdsong. Nestling together under the well-worn counterpane, they listened to the daybreak song of the blackbird, mesmerized by the sheer clarity and beauty of its melody.

Nick twirled her long, dark hair. "Love you, beyond any words I can find," he whispered.

Something was playing on his mind. Liberty raised her head. "What is it, Nicholas? Is something wrong?"

"I want to assure you that I intend never to lie again."

Liberty responded. "Oh Nicholas, I am sure you can be forgiven for concocting such an inventive story. You had no option. What would have been the consequences if we had not assumed the role within the Nylander family in the nineteenth century?"

Nick also kept his voice low as he thanked her for her understanding and reassured her that he would only do so if it was necessary for the good of themselves, the family or the local community. "To maintain our position here, we actually live a lie, but these circumstances apart, I intend to be worthy of the woman I know you to be."

Liberty reached out for his hand. *Her* intention was to be worthy of him. No, more than that; worthy of being part of a couple who would uphold standards and improve the little part of the country which was now theirs. Energy pumped through her at the thought of what lay ahead.

Nick squeezed her hand. "There is more. I haven't told you this before, yet I know I must." He reached for his brown leather notebook and turned a few pages before stroking one of them. "I woke earlier this morning and spent an hour or so familiarizing myself with my all-important memory prompts. I want to read you this."

Liberty snuffled against him, breathing in the scent of the man she adored.

"I made this note, dated 2020, to remind myself that it was destiny which brought me here."

Nick was not the sort of man to believe in destiny, was he? Yet there was something about his family... what? Yes, they all believed in something beyond this Earth. She too believed in something beyond Earth and it all seemed new, invigorating and astonishing. Nick believed destiny brought them here: she felt certain it was the all-powerful God she knew so little about. A melody floated through her mind and snatches of words, annoyingly she couldn't hold them in her mind. Something in her past, what could it be? An influence... she almost caught it, but it faded again. She would be that good, kind influence now and possibly, just possibly this was where it was needed most.

"I can see you are puzzled; I would be too if I hadn't written my feelings down. Yes, Liberty, your Nicholas has feelings, well-hidden to enable me to power through a multitude of tasks unhindered, but let me read this to you.

"'In the early part of the twenty-first century, which is when we first met. I, Nicolo Nylander, as a teenager, would visit my paternal grandparents. Grandpapa regularly alluded to time travel. He was utterly convinced he had met two time-travellers in the twentieth century, he kept talking about the sixties. He told me it was my destiny. Naturally, I thought he was beginning to suffer from dementia. He was also convinced I would travel further back in time, he kept harping on about 1814 and the family history book he had locked away somewhere. I told my father and my father said to ignore him. My father said, wisely, that if it were meant to be, then it would happen, but I should make no attempts to discover the truth about time travel, not if I wanted to become a doctor. Grandpapa, strangely, agreed and said doors would close, one by one, until no other option would be open except to go through the door which led to travelling in time.'

"That's all I wrote about it but it's enough, together with other notes in this book, for me to know that both you and I are meant to be here. It was you, Liberty, who led me here via the Swinging Sixties. I've made notes about those times further along." He turned over more pages, stared, then closed the book and put it on the bedside table. "You... you are my destiny. I have known it since the day I first saw you which has, unfortunately, been wiped from my memory."

"And mine," Liberty sighed.

"I have hardly dared to open my heart to you in case you didn't feel the same yet here we are together, married, yes as married as any other couple in the sight of God. We have no certificate to prove it and we have no birth certificates either. In order to continue living here in Bleakheath Hall, I shall lay no claim to the title, even if our servants declare us to be the rightful heirs and address us as a knight and his lady." He stopped to grin broadly and rearranged the many pillows and propped himself up comfortably. Looking around, he said, "I seem to have brought a library of medical and health related books, no wonder the cases were heavy. Later, once we have rescued this much neglected house, I might be able to make myself useful to the surrounding community. The rich can pay, the poor will be treated without payment."

Liberty hugged him, then propped herself upright too. "We can sell some jewellery and take on staff to help us which would also help the villagers to have the chance of an income, however small."

"Lady Nylander will, I am sure, be delighted to hand over the reins to us." He glanced at Liberty for her agreement which came in the form of energetic nodding.

She glowed with joy at the thought of organizing the household. "Also, I'd like to ensure that the most deserving of those in the village are taken care of. I shall seek them out. I shall make this world a better place." Where had she heard those words before? Someone she loved... someone... her father, it was her father, before he died he gave her a commission to make the world... if only she could grasp the memory but it had already slipped away, like all her other memories.

Nick watched her puzzling face, took hold of her hand and said, "And I shall rescue the farm. I saw packets of seeds in one of our cases, dozens of them. They will bring us a small return and with the right farm manager..." He grinned and raised his eyebrows. "And we must ensure the many cottages we can see from our window are renovated and fairly rented out." He raised her hand and kissed it. "And my darling, you must let me fend off the naysayers, the worrywarts and the cynics. There will be those who sling arrows because we are different, unique, they will be keen to mock us. Fear not, I have in my armoury the language of Shakespeare." He chuckled then added as if it were a secret, "He was exceptionally good with insults." Gently, he kissed her hand again. "You, my love, can feed my soul with what I need to become a better person." He grinned. "You'll find this hard to believe but I think I have begun. I now have a greater respect for God."

Liberty's eyes betrayed her surprise.

"Have you ever wondered why God made flies?"

She was able to respond quickly. "Yes, I have! Or at least I think so. They appear to have no use at all except to serve as food for spiders and birds."

Nick raised one eyebrow. "More than that, their maggots eat rotting flesh and can be used as an antibiotic."

"You are joking!"

"I am not. I read it in 'The History of Medicine' while you slept. At some point in the not too distant future, I shall appropriate a few unused rooms and set up a surgery. I cannot remember a thing about being a doctor, but I know I was one – it's here in my notebook. Maybe instinct will kick in, and my medical books will help."

Liberty hung onto his hand and, inhaling deeply, she said, "We can do this."

"Not a life of ease, but one of high endeavour – a well-trodden road to fulfilment and happiness."

She allowed herself to dwell on his words. Hadn't Lady Nylander written in the history book that the strangers brought with them the wisdom of the stars? How true his words were. And how true it is that laziness gets you nowhere. To have high endeavour, to strive for a worthy goal, that's the route to deep joy. She smiled – she could feel it in her bones, energy surging through her, empowering her. She longed to begin. Today, she would begin today.

Nick gently squeezed her hand. "Do you see what's hanging on the wall ahead of us?"

Liberty realized she had been staring for some time at a cross-stitch embroidery, framed and hung by a deep red ribbon. Colourful flowers surrounded the words:

In the tradition of Christ, the reward of work well done is more work to do.

"Are you ready?"

"You bet!"

THE END

If you enjoyed 'Mistake in Time', I should be so pleased if you would leave a review on Amazon.

If you 'Follow' Anna Faversham on Amazon, you will be kept up-to-date with new releases. The 'Follow' button is near the author biography/picture.

Other Books by Anna Faversham:

Hide in Time

Amazon #1 Best Seller in Books>Romance>Time Travel. A time travel romance about a love that never died

The Dark Moon Trilogy – Romance, thrills and mystery:

Book One:

One Dark Night

The choices we make determine our futures and Lucy is torn between two determined men as the secrets and lies undermining her life are exposed. A romantic thriller mystery. Award winning.

Book Two:

Under a Dark Star

Award winning. Reformed smuggler, Daniel Tynton, and his old enemy Lieutenant Karl Thorsen, join forces to defeat the evil that brings poverty and fear to 'the diamond isle'. The man known as the Dark Star takes his revenge.

Book Three:

One Dark Soul

Knowing Lieutenant Karl Thorsen still feel a hopeless passion for her, Lucy tries help him find happiness with a feisty young American. Then a charming and talented artist intrigues her. Journey into one very dark wounded heart.

Immortality: This is Probably a Novel

Are we alone in the universe? If a stranger said to you, "Let me take you to the world's best kept secret," would you go? You are invited into this mystery: intriguing, exciting and deadly. "The two most important days in your life are the day you are born and the day you find out why." —Mark Twain

One Stolen Kiss - ebook only

A little book of short stories and drabbles

Seventeen Questions for Book Clubs

1. What did you like best about this book?

2. Which characters did you like best?

3. If you were making a movie of this book who would you cast?

4. Share a favourite quote from this book and why did it stand out?

5. What other books have you read by this author? How did they compare to this book?

6. Would you read more of the author's books?

7. What feelings did this book evoke for you?

8. Which songs does this book make you think of?

9. Which character in the book would you most like to meet?

10. Which places in the book would you most like to visit?

11. What do you think of the title? How does it relate to the book's contents? What other title might you choose?

12. What do you think of the book's cover?

13. How original was this book?

14. Did any of the characters remind you of anyone?

15. Was the pace too fast/too slow/just right?

16. What message will you take away with you from this book?

17. If you had the chance to ask the author one question, what would it be?

'Someone Cares' ©

Words by John Gowans

Used by kind permission of The General of The Salvation Army

~

The Shell Grotto – www.shellgrotto.co.uk

~

'Merrygate' caves – www.margatecaves.co.uk

Mistake in Time

My grateful thanks to my writing friends
for their patience and advice

Lexi Revellian

lexirevellian.com

Julia Bell

juliabellromanticfiction.co.uk

cover photo

Evgeniy Lookyanov

Printed in Great Britain
by Amazon